TITLES BY PENELOPE DOUGLAS

The Fall Away Series

BULLY

UNTIL YOU

RIVAL

FALLING AWAY

THE NEXT FLAME
(includes novellas *Aflame* and *Next to Never*)

Stand-Alones

MISCONDUCT

BIRTHDAY GIRL

PUNK 57

CREDENCE

TRYST SIX VENOM

The Devil's Night Series

CORRUPT

HIDEAWAY

KILL SWITCH

CONCLAVE
(novella)

NIGHTFALL

FIRE NIGHT
(novella)

PRAISE FOR THE FALL AWAY SERIES

"Douglas follows *Bully* with a gritty, racy new adult tale peppered with raw emotions. This smoking-hot, action-packed story is a powerful addition to the edgy side of the genre, and readers will eagerly anticipate the next installment." —*Publishers Weekly*

"*Bully*, the first book in Douglas's new adult romance Fall Away series, was a self-published sensation, and *Rival*, the latest installment, is bound to capture even more readers with its intensely emotional writing, angst-driven plot, and abundance of steamy sex scenes." —*Booklist*

"*Bully* was a wonderfully addictive read that kept my heart racing from start to finish. I could not put it down! 5 stars!!" —Aestas Book Blog

"A heated and passionate novel, full of feeling and intensity that will appeal to the reader seeking an emotional rush." —IndieReader

"I love, love, love, love, love, love, love this book! What a wonderful debut novel by Penelope Douglas! This book had me hooked! So addictive! So witty! So devastating! So amazing!" —Komal Kant, author of *The Jerk Next Door*

"Jaxon Trent was so worth the wait! Penelope has masterfully combined the best of new adult with all of the scorching intensity of erotica to make *Falling Away* the best installment in [the] series." —Autumn Grey, Agents of Romance

CORRUPT

DEVIL'S NIGHT

PENELOPE DOUGLAS

BERKLEY ROMANCE

New York

BERKLEY ROMANCE
Published by Berkley
An imprint of Penguin Random House LLC
penguinrandomhouse.com

Copyright © 2015 by Penelope Douglas LLC
"*Corrupt* Valentine's Day Scene" copyright © 2016 by Penelope Douglas LLC
"Behind Devil's Night" copyright © 2023 by Penelope Douglas LLC

Library of Congress Cataloging-in-Publication Data

Names: Douglas, Penelope, 1977- author.
Title: Corrupt / Penelope Douglas.
Description: New York : Berkley Romance, 2023. | Series: Devil's Night ; book 1
Identifiers: LCCN 2023022543 | ISBN 9780593642009 (trade paperback)
Subjects: LCGFT: Novels.
Classification: LCC PS3604.O93236 C67 2023 | DDC 813/.6—dc23/eng/20230515
LC record available at https://lccn.loc.gov/2023022543

Corrupt was originally self-published, in different form, in 2015.

First Berkley Romance Edition: November 2023

Printed in the United States of America
5th Printing

Book design by George Towne

For Z. King

You are my creator, but I am your master.

—Mary Shelley, *Frankenstein*

DEAR READER,

This book deals with emotionally difficult topics, including revenge fantasy, abusive/violent and misogynistic behavior, toxic relationships, physical and sexual assault, date-rape drugs, dubious consent, bondage, kidnapping, group sex, and reference to incest. Anyone who believes such content may upset them are encouraged to consider their well-being when choosing whether to continue reading.

BEHIND DEVIL'S NIGHT

It all started with Michael Myers.

From the moment I saw *Halloween* as a child, I was hooked. Michael isn't like the other fictional slashers. He's not relatable, like Jason Voorhees, Jigsaw, or Pinhead. He's not flamboyant in his style like Ghostface or Freddy Krueger. And he's not funny, like Chucky. He's smooth and methodical.

There's no background story. No reason why he is the way he is. He's strong, quiet, and unsettling in his stalking skill. He's simple in his technique, and he never explains himself. He doesn't like to talk.

And neither do I. Lol.

The similarities don't end there, either! He's from the Midwest. I'm from the Midwest. He loves masks. I love masks.

He lives for Halloween, and my goodness, so do I. You'll often find me doing a marathon of *Halloween* movies on release days, because I find him much less stressful than putting a book out into the world.

So given all of this, is it any wonder why I named my hero in *Corrupt* Michael? I had to do a shout-out to my favorite slasher villain, especially since the story had a similar vibe.

When I decided to write *Corrupt*, it started out with the idea of a young woman who's blamed for sending some young men from her town to prison, and the storyline spun from there. I went crazy. I added in everything I loved—my entire dark heart and all the aesthetic I've been drawn to since I was a kid. Halloween, autumn, abandoned places, catacombs, cathedrals, cemeteries, suspense, murder, mystery, danger . . . I decided to show people the kind of world I really loved and wished I could live in sometimes. A whole theme park of adventure, chases, and dark spaces, and I can honestly say writing this book was when I realized how much I love worldbuilding. I loved that it had a plot outside of the romance, and it's one of the stories I consider my best work so far.

Of course, as with everything I write, there are things I hope to say to the world. *Corrupt* is all about owning who you are and not apologizing for what you like as long as it doesn't hurt anyone. But more than that, I wanted *Corrupt* and the Devil's Night series to be an escape into another world. I wanted readers to be immersed in a different reality where not only can we enjoy danger and fear in the safety of a book, but to have the opportunity to know these characters like we know ourselves. Every book gets bigger. Every installment more detailed. You don't say goodbye to any of them at the end of their individual story. You'll stay with them the whole way.

Thank you to everyone who supports this series, and I hope it's one you feel like revisiting often, because those are the best books!

L'appel du vide!
Pen

PLAYLIST

"Bodies" by Drowning Pool

"Breath of Life" by Florence + the Machine

"Bullet With a Name" by Nonpoint

"Corrupt" by Depeche Mode

"Deathbeds" by Bring Me the Horizon

"The Devil in I" by Slipknot

"Devil's Night" by Motionless in White

"Dirty Diana" by Shaman's Harvest

"Feed the Fire" by Combichrist

"Fire Breather" by Laurel

"Getting Away with Murder" by Papa Roach

"Goodbye Agony" by Black Veil Brides

"Inside Yourself" by Godsmack

"Jekyll and Hyde" by Five Finger Death Punch

"Let the Sparks Fly" by Thousand Foot Krutch

"Love the Way You Hate Me" by Like a Storm

"Monster" by Skillet

"Only Happy When It Rains" by Garbage

"Pray to God (feat. HAIM)" by Calvin Harris

"Silence (feat. Sarah McLachlan)" by Delerium

"37 Stitches" by Drowning Pool

"The Vengeful One" by Disturbed

"You're Going Down" by Sick Puppies

CORRUPT

CHAPTER I

ERIKA

He won't be here.

There'd be no reason for him to show up at his brother's farewell party, since they couldn't stand each other, so . . .

No, he won't be here.

Pushing up the sleeves of my lightweight sweater, I hurried through the front door of the Crist house and speed-walked across the foyer, heading straight for the stairs.

Out of the corner of my eye, I spied the butler rounding the corner, but I didn't stop.

"Miss Fane!" he shouted after me. "You're very late."

"Yes, I know."

"Mrs. Crist has been looking for you," he pointed out.

I shot up my eyebrows and immediately stopped, turning around to peer at him over the railing.

"Has she really?" I eyed him with mock astonishment.

He thinned his lips, annoyed. "Well, she sent *me* to look for you."

I broke out in a smile and leaned over the banister, planting a quick kiss on his forehead.

"Well, I'm here," I assured him. "You can get back to your important duties now."

I turned and continued up the stairs, hearing the soft music coming from the party out on the terrace.

Yeah, I highly doubted Delia Crist, my mother's best friend and the matriarch of Thunder Bay, our small East Coast community, was spending her precious time looking for me herself.

"Your dress is on your bed!" he called after me as I walked around the corner.

I exhaled an aggravated sigh and powered down the dimly lit hallway, grumbling under my breath, "Thank you, Edward."

I didn't need a new dress. I already had several I'd worn only once, and at nineteen, I could definitely pick out my own clothes. Not that he would be here to see it anyway, and if he was, he wouldn't look at me.

No. I should be grateful. Mrs. Crist thought of me, and it was nice of her to make sure I'd have a dress to wear.

A light spatter of sand covered my legs and feet, and I reached down to grip the ends of my loose jean shorts, inventorying exactly how wet I'd gotten down at the beach. Would I need a shower?

No, I was already late. Screw it.

Diving into my room—the one the Crists' let me have for when I stayed the night—I spotted a sexy white cocktail dress lying on the bed, and I immediately began stripping.

The thin spaghetti straps did almost nothing to hold up my breasts, but it fit perfectly, molding to my body, and it made my skin look darker than it was. Mrs. Crist had awesome taste, and it was probably a good thing that she'd gotten me the dress, after all. I'd been too busy preparing to leave for school tomorrow to bother with what to wear tonight.

Dashing into the bathroom, I rinsed my calves and feet of the sand I'd picked up on my walk, and I quickly brushed out my long blond hair and applied a little lip gloss. I scurried back into the bedroom, grabbed the tan strappy heels she'd left by the dress, and ran back into the hallway and down the stairs.

Twelve hours to go.

My heart pumped harder and harder as I jogged through the foyer and toward the back of the house. This time tomorrow I'd be completely on my own—no mother, no Crists, no memories . . .

And most of all, I wouldn't have to wonder, hope, or dread that I'd see him. Or teeter on the edges of elation and agony when I did. *Nope.* I'd be able to hold out my arms and spin in a circle and not touch a single person I knew. Heat flowed through my chest, and I didn't know if it was fear or excitement, but I was ready.

Ready to leave it all behind. At least for a little while.

Veering to the right, I bypassed the kitchens—one for everyday use and another adjacent to it for caterers—as I headed for the solarium at the side of the large house. Opening the double doors, I stepped into the massive ceramic-tiled garden room, the walls and ceiling made entirely of glass, and instantly felt the rise in temperature. The thick, wet heat soaked through the fabric of my dress, making it melt to my body.

Trees rose above and all around me in the quiet, dark room, lit only by the moonlight pouring in through the windows overhead. I inhaled the sweet smell of the palms, orchids, lilies, violets, and hibiscus, reminding me of my mother's closet and all the perfumes from her coats and scarves blending together in one space.

I turned left, stopping at the glass doors leading to the terrace, and slipped into my heels as I gazed out at the crowd.

Twelve hours.

And then I straightened, reaching up, grabbing a handful of hair, and bringing it over my shoulder to cover the left side of my neck. Unlike his brother, Trevor would definitely be here tonight, and he didn't like to see my scar.

"Miss?" a waiter said as he stepped up with a tray.

I smiled, taking one of the highball glasses that I knew was a Tom Collins. "Thank you."

The lemon-colored drink was Mr. and Mrs. Crist's favorite, so they insisted that the servers circulate it.

The waiter disappeared, moving on to the many other guests, but I stayed rooted, letting my eyes drift around the party.

Leaves fluttered on their branches, the calm breeze still holding remnants of the day's heat, and I surveyed the crowd, all dressed in their casual cocktail dresses and suit jackets.

So perfect. So clean.

The lights in the trees and the servers in their white waistcoats. The crystal-blue pool adorned with floating candles. The glittering jewels of the ladies' rings and necklaces that caught the light.

Everything was so polished, and when I looked around at all the adults and families I grew up with, their money and designer clothes, I often saw a coat of paint that you apply when you're trying to cover up rotting wood. There were dark deeds and bad seeds, but who cared if the house was falling apart as long as it was pretty, right?

The scent of the food lingered in the air, accompanied by the soft music of the string quartet, and I wondered if I should find Mrs. Crist and let her know I'd arrived or find Trevor, since the party was in his honor, after all.

But instead I tightened my fingers around my glass, my pulse quickening as I tried to resist the urge to do what I really wanted to do. What I always wanted to do.

To look for *him*.

But no, he wouldn't be here. He probably wouldn't be here.

He might be here.

My heart started thumping, and my neck heated. And, against my own will, my eyes started to drift. Around the party and over the faces, searching . . .

Michael.

I hadn't seen him in months, but the pull was everywhere, especially in Thunder Bay. In the pictures his mother kept around this house, in his scent, which drifted into the hallway from his old bedroom . . .

He might be here.

"Rika."

I blinked, jerking my head to the left, hearing Trevor call my name.

He walked out of the crowd, his blond hair freshly cut close to the scalp, his dark blue eyes looking impatient, and his stride determined. "Hey, baby. I was starting to think you weren't coming."

I hesitated, feeling my stomach tighten. But then I forced a smile as he stepped up to me in the doorway of the solarium.

Twelve hours.

He slipped a hand around the right side of my neck—never the left side—and rubbed his thumb across my cheek, his body flush with mine.

I turned my head, shifting uncomfortably. "Trevor—"

"I didn't know what I was going to do if you didn't show up tonight," he cut in. "Throw rocks at your window, serenade you, maybe bring you flowers, candy, a new car . . ."

"I have a new car."

"I mean a *real* car." He finally grinned.

I rolled my eyes and pulled out of his hold. At least he was joking with me again, even if it was just to dis my brand-new Tesla. Apparently electric cars weren't *real* cars, but hey, I could take the dig if it meant he was finally over making me feel like shit about everything else.

Trevor Crist and I had been friends since birth, gone to school with each other our entire lives, and were always thrown together by our parents as if a relationship were inevitable. And last year, I finally gave in to it.

We dated almost our entire first year in college, attending Brown together—or actually, I applied to Brown, and he followed—but it ended in May.

Or *I* ended it in May.

It was my fault I didn't love him. It was my fault I didn't want to give it more time. It was my fault I decided to transfer schools to a city where he wouldn't follow.

It was also my fault he gave in to his father's demand to transfer, as well, and finally attend Annapolis, and it was my fault I was disrupting our families.

It was my fault I needed space.

I let out a breath, forcing my muscles to relax. *Twelve hours.*

Trevor smiled at me, his eyes heating as he took my hand and led me back into the solarium. He pulled me behind the glass, holding me close by the hips and whispering in my ear, "You look gorgeous."

But I pulled away again, giving us a few inches of space. "You look good, too."

He looked like his father, with his sandy-blond hair, narrow jaw, and that smile that could make almost anyone putty in his hands. He also dressed like Mr. Crist, looking polished in his midnight-blue suit, white shirt, and silver tie. So clean. So perfect. Trevor did everything within the lines.

"I don't want you going to Meridian City," he said, narrowing his eyes on me. "You won't have anyone there, Rika. At least I was at Brown with you, and Noah was less than an hour away in Boston. You had friends close by."

Yeah. Close.

Which is exactly why I needed something different. I'd never had to leave the security of the people around me. There was always someone—parents, Trevor, my friend Noah—to pick me up when I fell. Even when I went off to college and gave up the comfort of having my mother and the Crists close by, Trevor had still followed me. And then I had friends from high school going to universities close by. It was like nothing had changed.

I wanted to get into a little trouble. I wanted to catch some rain, find something that made my heart pump again, and I wanted to know what it was like to not have anyone to grab onto.

I'd tried to explain it to him, but every time I opened my mouth, I couldn't find the right words. Out loud it sounded selfish and ungrateful, but inside . . .

I needed to know what I was made of. I needed to know if I had a leg to stand on without the umbrella of my family name, the support of others having my back, or Trevor's constant hovering. If I went to a new city, with new people who didn't know my family, would they even give me the time of day? Would they even like me?

I wasn't happy at Brown or with Trevor, and even though the decision to move on was hard and disappointing to those around me, it was what I wanted.

Own who you are.

My heart fluttered, remembering Trevor's brother's words. I could barely wait. Twelve more hours . . .

"But then again, I guess that's not really true, is it?" he asked, an accusing tone in his voice. "Michael plays for the Storm, so he'll be close to you now."

I hooded my eyes, taking in a deep breath as I set down my drink. "With a population of over two million people, I doubt I'll run into him often."

"Unless you look for him."

I crossed my arms over my chest, holding Trevor's eyes and refusing to let him engage me in this conversation.

Michael Crist was Trevor's brother. A little older, a little taller, and a lot more intimidating. They were almost nothing alike, and they hated each other. Trevor's jealousy of him had been there ever since I could remember.

Michael had just graduated from Westgate University, being snatched up by the NBA almost immediately afterward. He played for the Meridian City Storm, one of the top teams in the NBA, so yes, I would know one person in the city.

Lot of good it would do me, though. Michael barely ever looked at me, and when he spoke to me his tone was no better than if he were speaking to a dog. I wasn't planning on putting myself in his path.

No, I'd learned my lesson a long time ago.

Being in Meridian City had nothing to do with Michael anyway. It was closer to home, so I could visit my mother more often, but it was also the one place Trevor wouldn't go. He hated large cities, and he loathed his brother even more.

"I'm sorry," Trevor said more gently. He took my hand and pulled me in, sliding a hand around the back of my neck again. "I just love you, and I hate this. We belong together, Rika. It's always been us."

Us? No.

Trevor didn't make my heart pump so hard that I felt like I was on a damn roller coaster. He wasn't in my dreams, and he wasn't the first person I thought about when I woke up.

He didn't haunt me.

I tucked my hair behind my ear, noticing his gaze briefly flash to my neck. He quickly averted his eyes as if he didn't see it. The scar made me less than perfect, I guess.

"Come on," he urged, dipping his forehead to mine and gripping my waist. "I'm good to you, aren't I? I'm nice, and I'm always here for you."

"Trevor," I argued, trying to twist out of his hold.

But then his mouth came down on mine, the scent of his cologne burning my nostrils as his arms wrapped around my waist.

I pressed my fists into his chest, pushing at him and tearing my mouth away.

"Trevor," I growled low. "Stop it."

"I give you everything you need," he fought, his voice turning angry as he dived into my neck. "You know it's going to be us."

"Trevor!" I tensed every muscle in my arms and pressed against his body, finally pushing him off. He dropped his hands and stumbled away a step.

I immediately backed away, my hands shaking.

"Rika." He reached for me, but I steeled my spine, backing away again.

He dropped his hand, shaking his head. "Fine," he bit out, sneering. "Go to school, then. Make new friends and leave everything here behind all you want, but your demons will still follow you. There's no escaping them."

He ran his fingers through his hair, glaring at me as he straightened his tie and walked around me out the doorway.

I stared out the windows after him, anger building in my chest. What the hell did that mean? There was nothing holding me down and nothing I was trying to escape. I just wanted freedom.

I moved away from the door, unable to go back outside. I didn't want to disappoint Mrs. Crist by sneaking out on her son's party, but I no longer wanted to spend my last hours here. I wanted to be with my mom.

I twisted around, ready to leave, but then I looked up and instantly stopped.

My stomach flipped, and I couldn't breathe.

Shit.

Michael sat in one of the cushioned chairs all the way at the back of the solarium, his eyes locked on mine, looking eerily calm.

Michael. The one who wasn't nice. The one who wasn't good to me.

My throat thickened, and I wanted to swallow, but I couldn't move. I just stared, paralyzed. Had he been there since I first walked down? The whole time?

He reclined in his heavy armchair, nearly shrouded by the darkness and the shadows of the trees overhead. One hand rested on a basketball that sat on top of his thigh, and the other hand lay on the armrest, the neck of a beer bottle hanging from his fingers.

My heart started to pound so hard it hurt. What was he doing?

He raised the bottle to his lips, still watching me, and I dropped my eyes for a split second, embarrassment heating my cheeks.

He'd seen the whole episode with Trevor. *Dammit.*

I looked up again, seeing his light brown hair, which was styled to look like he should be on the cover of a magazine, and his hazel eyes, which always looked like cider with flecks of spice. They seemed darker than they actually were, hidden in the shadows, but they pierced me under straight brows that slanted inward, making him look just as formidable as he was. His full lips held no hint of a smile, and his tall frame nearly consumed his chair.

He wore black pants with a black suit jacket, and his white shirt was open at the collar. No tie, because, as usual, he did what he wanted.

And that's all anyone could ever go on with Michael. How he *appeared.* How he looked. I didn't think his parents even knew what was happening behind those eyes.

I watched him rise out of his chair and drop the basketball into the seat, keeping his eyes on me as he walked over.

The closer he got, the taller his six feet four inches looked. Michael was lean but muscular, and he made me feel small. In many ways. He looked like he was walking straight for me, and my heart hammered in my chest as I narrowed my eyes, bracing myself.

But he didn't stop.

The faint hint of his body wash hit me as he passed by, and I turned my head, my chest aching as he walked out the solarium doors without a word.

I folded my lips between my teeth, fighting the burn in my eyes.

One night, he'd noticed me. One night, three years ago, Michael saw something in me and liked it. And just when the fire was starting to kindle, ready to flare and burst apart in a flood of flames, it folded. It tucked its rage and heat away and contained itself.

I shot off, heading back into the house, through the foyer, and out the front door, anger and frustration chewing at every nerve in my body as I headed to my car.

Other than that one night, he'd ignored me most of my life, and when he did speak to me, it was clipped.

I swallowed the lump in my throat and climbed into my car. I hoped I wouldn't see him in Meridian City. I hoped we never crossed paths and I never had to hear about him.

I wondered if he even knew I was moving there. It didn't matter, though. Even in the same house, I might as well be on a different planet from him.

As I started the car, "37 Stitches" by Drowning Pool poured through the speakers, and I accelerated down the long driveway, pushing the clicker to open the gate. I sped out onto the road. My house was only a few minutes away and an easy walk I'd made many times in my life.

I forced deep breaths, trying to calm down. *Twelve hours.* Tomorrow I'd leave everything behind.

The high stone walls of the Crist estate ended, giving way to trees lining the road. And within less than a minute, the gas lamp-posts of my home appeared, lighting the night. Veering left, I clicked another button on my visor and inched my Tesla through the gate, seeing the outside lamps cast a soft glow around the circular driveway with a large marble fountain sitting in the center.

Parking my car in front of the house, I hurried to my front door, just wanting to crawl in bed until it was tomorrow.

But then I glanced up, doing a double take at seeing a candle burning in my bedroom window.

What?

I hadn't been home since late this morning. And I certainly hadn't left a candle burning. It was ivory colored and sitting in a glass hurricane candleholder.

Walking to the front door, I unlocked it and stepped inside.

"Mom?" I called out.

She had texted earlier, saying she was going to bed, but it wasn't unusual for her to have trouble sleeping. She might still be up.

The familiar scent of lilacs drifted through my nose from the fresh flowers she kept in the house, and I looked around the large foyer, the white marble floor appearing gray in the darkness.

I leaned against the stairs, looking up the flights into the three stories of eerie silence above. "Mom?" I called out again.

Rounding the white banister, I jogged up the stairs to the second floor and turned left, my footsteps going silent as they fell on the ivory-and-blue rugs covering the hardwood floors.

Opening my mother's door slowly, I crept in, seeing the room in near darkness except for the bathroom light she always left on. Walking over to her bed, I craned my neck, trying to see her face, which was turned toward the windows.

Her blond hair lay across her pillow, and I reached out my hand, smoothing it away from her face.

The rise and fall of her body told me she was asleep, and I glanced to her nightstand, seeing the half dozen pill bottles and wondering what she'd taken and how much.

I looked back down at her and frowned.

Doctors, in-home rehab, therapy . . . Over the years since my father's death, nothing had worked. My mother just wanted to self-destruct with sorrow and depression.

Thankfully the Crists helped a lot, which was why I had my own room at their house. Not only was Mr. Crist the trustee for my father's estate, handling everything until I graduated from college, but Mrs. Crist had stepped in to be a second mother.

I was immensely grateful for all their help and care over the years, but now . . . I was ready to take over. I was ready to stop having people take care of me.

Turning around, I left her room and quietly closed the door, heading for my own room two doors down.

Stepping in, I immediately spotted the candle burning by the window.

With my heart skipping a beat, I quickly glanced around the room, thankfully seeing no one else.

Had my mother lit it? She must have. Our housekeeper was off duty today, so no one else had been here.

Narrowing my eyes, I inched toward the window, and then my gaze fell, seeing a thin wooden crate sitting on the small round table next to the candle.

Unease set in. Had Trevor left me a present?

But it could've been my mother or Mrs. Crist, too, I guessed.

I removed the lid and set it aside, peeling away the straw and catching sight of slate-gray metal with ornate carvings.

My eyes rounded, and I immediately dived for the top of the crate, knowing what I was going to find. I curled my fingers around the handle and smiled, pulling out a heavy steel Damascus blade.

"Wow."

I shook my head, unable to believe it. The dagger had a black grip with a bronze cross guard, and I tightened my hand around it, holding up the blade and looking at the lines and carvings.

Where the hell had this come from?

I'd loved daggers and swords ever since I started fencing at age eight. My father preached that the arts of a gentleman were not only timeless but necessary. Chess would teach me strategy, fencing would teach me human nature and self-preservation, and dancing would teach me my body. All necessary for a well-rounded person.

I gripped the hilt, remembering the first time he'd put a fencing foil in my hand. It was the most beautiful thing I'd ever seen, and I reached up, running a finger along the scar on my neck, suddenly feeling closer to him again.

Who had left it here?

Peering back into the box, I pulled out a small piece of paper with black writing. Licking my lips, I read the words silently. *Beware the fury of a patient man.*

"What?" I said to myself, pinching my eyebrows together in confusion.

What did that mean?

But then I glanced up, gasping as I dropped the blade and the note to the floor.

I stopped breathing, my heart trying to break through my chest.

Three men stood outside my house, side by side, staring up at me through the window.

"What the hell?" I exhaled, trying to figure out what was going on.

Was this a joke?

They stood completely motionless, and I felt a chill spread up my arms at how they just stared at me.

What were they doing?

All three wore jeans and black combat boots, but as I stared into the black void of their eyes, I clenched my teeth together to keep my body from shaking.

The masks. The black hoodies and the masks.

I shook my head. *No.* It couldn't be them. This was a joke.

The tallest stood on the left, wearing a slate-gray metallic-looking mask with claw marks deforming the right side of its face.

The one in the middle was shorter, looking up at me through his white-and-black mask with a red stripe running down the left side of his face, which was also ripped and gouged.

And the one on my right, whose completely black mask blended with his black hoodie, so that you couldn't tell exactly where his eyes were, was the one who finally made my chest shake.

I backed up, away from the window, and tried to catch my breath as I dashed for my phone. Pressing 1 on the landline, I waited for the security office, which sat only minutes down the road, to pick up.

"Mrs. Fane?" a man answered.

"Mr. Ferguson?" I breathed out, inching back over to my windows. "It's Rika. Could you send a car up to—?"

But then I stopped, seeing that the driveway was now empty. They were gone.

What?

I darted my eyes left and then right, getting close to the table and leaning over to see if they were near the house. Where the hell did they go?

I remained silent, listening for any sign of anyone around the house, but everything was still and quiet.

"Miss Fane?" Mr. Ferguson called. "Are you still there?"

I opened my mouth, stammering, "I . . . I thought I saw something . . . outside my window."

"We're sending a car up now."

I nodded. "Thank you." And I hung up the phone, still staring out the window.

It couldn't be them.

But those masks. They were the only ones who wore those masks.

Why would they come here? After three years, why would they come here?

CHAPTER 2

ERIKA

Three Years Ago

Noah?" I fell back, leaning against the wall next to my best friend's locker as he retrieved a book between classes. "Do you have a date for Winterfest?"

He scrunched up his face. "That's like two months away, Rika."

"I know. I'm getting in while the getting's good."

He smiled, slamming his locker shut and leading the way down the hall. "So you're asking me on a date, then?" he teased in his cocky voice. "I knew you always wanted me."

I rolled my eyes, following him, since my classroom was in the same direction. "Could you make this easier, please?"

But all I heard was his snort.

Winterfest was a dance like Sadie Hawkins. Girls ask guys, and I wanted to take the safe route by asking a friend.

Students scurried around us, rushing to their classes, and I held the strap of my bag on my shoulder as I grabbed his arm, stopping him.

"Please?" I pleaded.

But he narrowed his eyes, looking worried. "Are you sure Trevor's not going to kick my ass? Judging from the way he's on you all the time, I'm surprised he hasn't GPS'd you."

That was a good point. Trevor would be mad I wasn't asking him, but I only wanted friendship, and he wanted more. I didn't want to lead him on.

I guessed I could chalk up my disinterest in Trevor to knowing him my entire life—he was too familiar, kind of like family—but I'd also known his older brother my entire life, and my feelings for him weren't at all familial.

"Come on. Be a buddy," I urged, nudging his shoulder. "I need you."

"No, you don't."

He stopped at my next class, which was on the way to his, and spun around, pinning me with a hard look. "Rika, if you don't want to ask Trevor, then ask someone else."

I let out a sigh and averted my eyes, sick of this conversation.

"You're asking me because it's safe," he argued. "You're beautiful, and any guy would be thrilled to go out with you."

"Of course they would be." I smiled sarcastically. "So say yes, then."

He rolled his eyes, shaking his head at me.

Noah liked to draw conclusions about me. About why I never dated or why he thought I shied away from this or that, and as good a friend as he was, I wished he'd stop already. I just didn't feel comfortable.

I reached up, rubbing a nervous hand over my neck—over the pale, thin scar I got when I was thirteen.

In the car accident that killed my father.

I saw him watching me, and I dropped my hand, knowing what he was thinking.

The scar ran diagonally, about two inches long, on the left side of my neck, and although it had faded with time, I still felt like it was the first thing people noticed about me. There were always questions and pitying expressions from family and friends, not to mention the jerk comments I got in junior high from girls laughing at me. After a while, it started to feel like an appendage, big and something I was always aware of.

"Rika," he lowered his voice, his brown eyes gentle, "baby, you're beautiful. Long blond hair, legs that no guy in this school can ignore, and the prettiest blue eyes in town. You're gorgeous."

The one-minute bell rang, and I shifted in my flats, gripping the strap of my bag tighter.

"And you're my favorite person," I retorted. "I want to go with you. Okay?"

He sighed, a defeated look crossing his face. I'd won, and I fought not to smile.

"Fine," he grumbled. "It's a date." And then he spun around, heading for English 3.

I grinned, my nerves immediately relaxing. I was no doubt taking Noah away from a promising night with another girl, so I'd have to do something to make it up to him.

Walking into precalculus, I hooked my bag on the back of my chair in the front row and pulled out my book, setting it on the desk. My friend Claudia planted herself in the seat next to me, meeting my eyes and smiling, and I immediately sat down and started writing my name on the blank piece of paper that Mr. Fitzpatrick had set down on everyone's desk. Friday classes always started with a pop quiz, so we knew the drill.

Students hurried into the room, the girls' green-and-blue-plaid skirts swaying and most of the boys' ties already loosened. It was nearly the end of the day.

"Did you hear the news?" someone said behind us, and I jerked my head around to see Gabrielle Owens leaning over her desktop.

"What news?" Claudia asked.

She lowered her voice to a whisper, excitement crossing her face. "They're here," she told us.

I glanced at Claudia and then back at Gabrielle, confused. "Who's here?"

But then Mr. Fitzpatrick came in, booming in his large voice, "Take a seat everyone!" and Claudia, Gabrielle, and I immediately faced the front of the room and straightened, ending our conversation.

"Please sit down, Mr. Dawson," the teacher instructed a student in the back as he came to stand behind his desk.

They're here? I leaned back in my chair, trying to figure out what Gabrielle meant. But then I looked up, spotting a girl jogging to the front of the room and handing Mr. Fitzpatrick a note.

"Thank you," he responded, opening it up.

I watched him read it and saw his expression turn from relaxed to agitated, his lips pressing together and his eyebrows narrowing.

What was going on?

They're here. What did that . . . ?

But then my eyes widened and flutters hit my stomach.

THEY'RE HERE. I opened my mouth, sucking in a quick breath, fire and fever making my skin tingle. Butterflies filled my stomach, and I clenched my teeth, holding back the smile that wanted loose.

He's here.

I raised my eyes slowly, looking at the clock and seeing that it was nearly two in the afternoon.

And it was October 30, the night before Halloween.

Devil's Night.

They were back. *But why?* They'd already graduated—more than a year ago, so why now?

"Please make sure you have your name on your paper," Mr. Fitzpatrick instructed, an edge to his voice, "and solve the three problems on the board." He switched on the projector, not wasting any time as the problems flashed on the smart board ahead of us.

"Turn it facedown when you're finished," he called out. "You have ten minutes."

I gripped the pencil, my entire body buzzing with nerves and anticipation as I tried to concentrate on the first problem dealing with quadratic functions.

But it was fucking hard. I glanced at the clock again. *Any minute . . .*

I bowed my head and forced myself to focus, my pencil digging into the wooden desk underneath as I blinked my eyes, bringing them into focus on my task. "Find the vertex of the parabola," I whispered to myself.

I quickly worked through the problem, moving from one thing to the next, knowing that if I stopped for a second, I'd be distracted.

If the vertex of the parabola has coordinates . . . I kept going.

The graph of a quadratic function is a parabola, which opens up if . . .

And I kept working, finishing one, two, and moving through number three.

But then I heard soft music, and I instantly froze.

My pencil hovered over my work as the sound of a faint guitar riff drifted through the loudspeakers. It got louder and louder, and I stared at my paper, heat stirring inside my chest.

Whispers sounded around the room, followed by a few excited giggles, and then the soft beginning of the song over the speakers gave way to a violent onslaught of drums, guitars, and a fast, sharp, heart-pounding mania. I tightened my fingers around my pencil.

Slipknot's "The Devil in I" blared through the classroom—and, I assumed, the rest of the school, as well.

"I told you!" Gabrielle burst out.

I popped my head up, watching as students raced out of their seats for the door.

"Are they really here?" someone damn near squealed.

Everyone crowded around the classroom door, peering out the small window at the top, trying to catch a glimpse of them coming down the hallway. But I stayed in my seat, adrenaline rippling through my body.

Mr. Fitzpatrick's chest heaved with a sigh as he folded his arms over his chest and turned away, no doubt waiting for it to be over.

The music pounded, and the thrilled chatter from the other students filled the room.

"Where— Oh, there they are!" a girl shouted, and I heard pounding coming from the hallway, sounding like fists beating on lockers, getting closer and closer.

"Let me see!" another student argued, pushing others aside.

A girl popped up on her tiptoes. "Move!" she ordered someone else.

But then everyone suddenly backed up. The door swung open, and the students fanned out like a ripple in a lake.

"Oh, shit," I heard a boy whisper.

Slowly, everyone spread out, some falling back into their seats while others remained standing. I gripped my pencil with both hands, my stomach flipping like a roller coaster as I watched them slowly step into the classroom, eerily calm and in no hurry.

They were here. The Four Horsemen.

They were Thunder Bay's favorite sons, and they'd gone to high school here, graduating when I was a freshman. All four went on to separate universities afterward. They were a few years older, and while not one of them knew I existed, I knew almost everything about them. All four of them stalked slowly into the room, filling the space to where the sun's rays turned black across the floor.

Damon Torrance, Kai Mori, Will Grayson III, and—I locked my gaze on the black hoodie and trailed it up to the bloodred mask covering the face of the one always in the lead a little more than the others—Michael Crist, Trevor's older brother.

He twisted his head left and jerked his chin toward the back of the room. Students turned, watching one of the male students step forward, a smile pulling at his jaw even though he tried to hold it back.

"Kian," a guy called out, his voice filled with humor as he slapped Kian on the back as he walked past him on his way to the Horsemen. "Have fun. Wear a condom."

Some students laughed, while a few girls fidgeted nervously, whispering and smiling to each other.

Kian Mathers, a junior like me and one of our school's best basketball players, stepped up to the guys, the one in the white mask with the red stripe hooking him around the neck and pulling him out the door.

They grabbed another student, Malik Cramer, and the one in the full-black mask pulled him out into the hallway, following the other two and probably off to collect more players from other class-rooms.

I watched Michael, the way his size had nothing to do with how he filled a room, and I blinked long and hard, feeling the heat flow under my skin.

Everything about the Horsemen made me feel like I was walk-ing a high wire. Cast your balance a hair in the wrong direction or tread too hard—or too softly—and you'd plummet so far off their radar, you'd never reappear.

Their power came from two things: They had followers and they didn't care. Everyone idolized them, including me.

But as opposed to the other students who looked up to them, followed them, or fantasized about them, I simply wondered what it would be like to be them. They were untouchable, fascinating, and nothing they ever did was wrong. I wanted that.

I wanted to look down at the sky.

"Mr. Fitzpatrick?" Gabrielle Owens sauntered up, followed by her friend, both of them carrying their books. "We have to go to the nurse. See you Monday!" And then they squeezed between the Horsemen, disappearing out the door.

I shot my eyes over to the teacher, wondering why he was just letting them leave. They were clearly not going to the nurse. They were leaving with the guys.

But no one—not even Mr. Fitzpatrick—tried challenging them.

The Four Horsemen not only ruled the student body and the town when they attended school here, but also commanded the court and hardly ever lost in the four years they played.

Since their departure, though, the team had suffered, and last year was a humiliating disaster for Thunder Bay. Twelve losses out of twenty games, and everyone had had enough. Something was missing.

I assumed that's why the Horsemen were here now, called back from college for the weekend to inspire the team or do whatever they had to do to pump them up and get them on track before the season started.

And as much as teachers like Fitzpatrick frowned on their hazing, it had certainly helped make the team a unit in their time here. Why not see if it would work again?

"Everyone sit down! You boys move on," he told the Horsemen.

I dropped my head, and elation filled my body as my stomach floated up to my chest. I let my eyes fall closed, my head feeling light and high.

Yeah, this was what had been missing.

Opening my eyes again, I saw a pair of long legs in dark-wash jeans walk past my desk, next to the window, and stop.

I kept my eyes down, afraid my face would give away what was happening in my chest. He was probably just scanning the room anyway, seeing if we had any other players in here.

"Anyone else?" one of the other guys asked.

But he didn't answer his friend. He just kept standing over me. What was he doing?

Keeping my chin down, I tipped my eyes up, seeing his fingers, slightly curled, at his sides. I made out the vein over the top of his strong hand, and the whole room seemed to suddenly grow so quiet that dread filled my stomach and my breathing stopped.

What was he doing just standing there?

I slowly raised my eyes and instantly tensed, seeing golden hazel ones staring straight down at me.

I shifted my gaze from side to side, wondering if I'd missed something. Why was he looking at me?

Michael looked down, his vicious red mask—a replica of one of the deformed and scarred *Army of Two* masks from the video game—making my knees weak.

I'd always been scared of him. The thrilling kind of scared that got me turned on.

I tightened the muscles in my thighs, feeling the throb between my legs, in the space that only felt empty when he was close but not close enough.

I liked it. I liked being scared.

Everyone sat silently behind me, and I watched him cock his head just a little as he regarded me. What was he thinking?

"She's only sixteen," Mr. Fitzpatrick spoke up.

Michael held my eyes for another second and then turned his head, looking at Mr. Fitzpatrick.

I was only sixteen—until next month, anyway—which meant they couldn't take me with them. The basketball players' ages didn't matter, but any girls who joined them had to be eighteen, leaving school grounds of their own free will.

Not that they were going to take me anyway. Mr. Fitzpatrick was mistaken.

The teacher glared, and even though I couldn't see Michael's eyes, turned away from me as he was, I deduced that it unnerved

Mr. Fitzpatrick, because his stare faltered. He dropped his eyes, blinking and backing down.

Michael turned his head, looking at me once more as a drop of sweat glided down my back.

And then he walked out of the room, followed by Kai, who I knew wore the silver mask, the door swinging closed behind them.

What the hell was that about?

Whispers broke out across the room, and I could see Claudia's head turned toward me out of the corner of my eye. I glanced at her, seeing her eyebrows raised in question, but I just ignored her, turning back to my paper. I had no idea why he was looking at me. I hadn't seen him since he'd been home from college briefly in the summertime, and he'd ignored me then, as usual.

"All right, everyone!" Mr. Fitzpatrick barked. "Back to work. Now!"

The excited chatter lowered to whispering, and everyone slowly got back to work. The music, which had faded into a distant hum, cut off, and for the first time since I entered the room, I let go of the smile I'd been holding in.

Tonight would be chaos. Devil's Night wasn't just hazing. It was special. Not only would they grab players from all of the rooms, take them to an undisclosed location, rough them up a bit, and get them drunk, but later . . . the Horsemen would wreak havoc and turn the whole town into their playground.

Last year, with them gone, it had been boring, but everyone knew that it was on tonight. Starting right now in the parking lot as all the guys and a few girls loaded up in the cars, no doubt.

I picked up my pencil, my breathing turning shallow as I bobbed my right knee up and down.

I wanted to go.

The heat in my chest was already starting to dissipate, and my head, which had just felt like it was higher than the trees a minute ago, was slowly descending and returning to the ground.

In another minute I'd feel the same way I had before he walked in the room: base, cold, and trivial.

After class, I'd go home, check on my mom, change clothes, and then head over to the Crists' to hang out, a routine that had started shortly after my father passed away. Sometimes I'd stay for dinner, and sometimes I'd go back home to eat with my mom if she was up for it.

Then I'd go to bed, trying not to worry about how one brother tried to wear me down more every day while denying what woke up inside of me whenever the other one was close.

Laughter and howls drifted in from outside the windows, and I faltered, stopping my knee from bobbing.

Fuck it.

I reached into my bag, grabbing my precalc textbook, and leaned over, handing it to Claudia with my bag and whispering, "Take this home with you. I'll pick it up this weekend."

She pinched her eyebrows together, looking confused. "Wha—"

But I didn't let her finish, already slipping out of my desk and walking toward the teacher.

"Mr. Fitzpatrick?" I approached his desk, my hands clasped behind my back. "May I use the restroom, please? I finished the assignment," I lied in a quiet voice.

He barely looked up, nodding and waving me off. Yeah, I was that kind of student. *Oh, Erika Fane? The demure one who's always in dress code and volunteers to work concession at the athletic events for free? Good kid.*

I headed straight for the door, not even hesitating as I left the room.

By the time he realized I wasn't coming back, I'd be gone. I might still get in trouble, but it would already be too late to stop me. Deed done. Suffer the consequences on Monday.

Racing out of the school, I spotted a group of cars, trucks, and SUVs way off to the left, trailing around the corner of the building.

I wasn't planning on asking them if I could come or letting anyone know I was there. I'd either get laughed at or get patted on the head and sent back to class.

Nope. I wouldn't even be seen.

Jogging toward the group of cars, I spotted Michael's black Mercedes G-Class and dived behind it, hiding as I peered around the corner.

"Get 'em in the cars!" someone shouted.

I spotted Damon Torrance right away. He had his black mask sitting on top of his head as he walked through the cluster of cars and tossed a beer to a guy in the bed of a pickup truck. His black hair was pushed back, hidden under the mask, and I noticed his high cheekbones and still-striking black eyes. Damon was good-looking.

But I didn't like anything else about him. Since I was a fresh-man when they were all seniors, I didn't have much firsthand knowledge of their demeanors at school, but I'd seen plenty of him at the Crist house to know that something was wrong with him. Michael gave him a long leash, but it was still a leash and for a good reason. He scared me.

And not in the way Michael did that I liked.

There were about twenty-five people so far, counting the bas-ketball team and some girls, but school would be out in less than an hour, which meant carloads more would be searching them out to join the party.

"Where are we going?" one of the guys asked, looking at Damon.

But it was Will Grayson who stepped up, slapping Damon on the shoulder as he passed. "Where no one can hear you scream," he answered.

Smirking, he opened the door to his black Ford Raptor, climb-ing up and standing between the open door and the truck, looking over the hood.

Will held his white mask with a red stripe in his hand, his brown hair styled in a fauxhawk and his seductive green eyes laughing. "Hey, did you see Kylie Halpern?" he asked, looking over Damon's head to someone else.

I peered around the car, seeing Kai with his silver mask on top of his head, and Michael, his face still hidden behind his.

"Holy shit, those legs!" Will went on. "A year did her a lot of good."

"Yeah, I'm missing high school girls," Damon said, opening the passenger door to the Raptor. "They don't give any lip."

I watched Michael, less than five feet away, open the rear driver's-side door of his G-Class and toss a duffel in, slamming the door closed when he was done.

I tightened my fists, my arms suddenly feeling weak. *What the hell was I doing?* I shouldn't be doing this. I'd either get in trouble or be embarrassed.

"Michael?" I heard Will's voice call. "It'll be a long night. Did you see anyone you liked?"

"Maybe," I heard him respond in a deep voice.

And then I heard another voice laugh softly. I thought it was Kai. "Dude," he challenged like he knew something. "She's beautiful, but wait until she's legal."

"A year did her a lot of good, too," I heard Michael say. "She's getting harder not to notice."

"Who are you guys talking about?" Damon cut in.

"No one," Michael snapped, sounding suddenly short.

I shook my head, brushing off their words. I needed to get out of sight before anyone saw me.

"Get everyone in the cars," Michael ordered.

My chest rose and fell faster, and I sucked in a deep breath and squeezed the handle on the truck, hearing it click open as I pulled on it.

With a quick glance to the guys again and my ears on alert, I opened the door and quickly dived inside, pulling the door closed and hoping they didn't notice in the madness of everyone loading into other cars.

I shouldn't be doing this.

Sure, I'd paid attention to them over the years. Absorbed their conversations and mannerisms, noticing things that others didn't, but I'd never followed them.

Was this stage one or stage two of stalking? *Oh, Jesus.* I rolled my eyes, not even wanting to think about it.

"Let's go!" Kai shouted, and car doors started slamming shut.

"See you there!" I heard Will call out.

The car under me shook, and I widened my eyes as people climbed into Michael's car.

And then, one by one, all four doors slammed shut, the silent cabin now filled with the laughter and banter of several male voices.

The SUV roared to life, vibrating under me, and I rolled onto my back, letting my head rest on the floor, not sure if I should feel good that I hadn't gotten caught or sick that I had no idea what I'd gotten myself into.

CHAPTER 3

ERIKA

Present

This way, Miss Fane." The man smiled and took a set of keys, leading me toward some elevators. "I'm Ford Patterson, one of the managers."

He held out his hand, and I shook it.

"Nice to meet you," I replied.

I looked around the lobby of my new apartment building, Delcour, as we walked. It was a twenty-two-story skyscraper in Meridian City, built to house apartments and penthouses, and even though it wasn't nearly as tall as some of the buildings surrounding it, it still stood out. Entirely black, with gold fixtures on the outside, it was a work of art, and the interior was just as lavish. I couldn't believe I was living here.

"You're all the way up on the twenty-first floor," he explained, stopping us at the elevator and pushing the button, "which has an amazing view. You'll be pleased."

I gripped the strap of my bag over my chest, barely able to wait. Nothing sounded so good as to wake up in the morning and gaze over the vast city, a horizon of buildings that touched the sky and millions of people working and living.

While some felt lost in large cities—the lights, noise, and action too much—I couldn't contain the thrill of being part of something bigger. The energy excited me.

I checked my phone again, making sure I hadn't missed a call from my mother. I was still worried about her. And kind of worried about me, too, even though I didn't let it stop me from leaving Thunder Bay this morning.

After Mr. Ferguson had left my house last night, having found nothing inside or around the premises, I'd crawled into bed with my mom and stared at the note that had been left in the box with the dagger.

Beware the fury of a patient man.

I'd Googled it to find that it was a John Dryden quote, and I knew what it meant. Those who are patient plan. And beware the man with a plan.

But a plan for what? And who was that at my house last night in masks? Could it have been the Horsemen? Would they have sent me the dagger?

I woke up this morning, ignored a curt message from Trevor, who was angry with me for leaving the party early, and questioned my mom and Irina, our housekeeper, both of whom knew nothing about the mysterious gift or who'd left it.

The note wasn't signed, and no one knew how the box got there.

I'd caught the momentary flash of worry that crossed my mother's face, so I'd hidden the note and brushed off the dagger as something Trevor had probably left for me as a surprise. I didn't want her to be scared for me.

But I definitely was.

Someone had been in my home, right under my mother's nose.

In the rush to get on the road this morning, I'd slid the slender box, with the dagger, into the car and drove off not knowing why I'd brought it. I should've just left it at home.

The soft bell dinged, and I followed Mr. Patterson into the

elevator, seeing him press twenty-one. But I narrowed my eyes, noticing that there were no floors higher than that.

"I thought there were twenty-two floors," I inquired, standing next to him.

"There are." He nodded assuredly. "But that floor houses only one residence, and he has his own private elevator across the lobby."

I turned my head forward again, understanding. "I see."

"Your floor only has two apartments," he explained, "since the apartments are quite a bit larger. And the other apartment on your floor is currently vacant, so you'll enjoy lots of privacy."

The apartments were quite a bit larger on my floor? I didn't remember anyone saying anything about that when I'd emailed the management to set up the lease.

"And here we are," he chirped, stepping forward with a smile as the doors opened. He held out an arm, inviting me to go first.

Stepping out of the elevator, I looked left and then right, seeing a narrow, well-lit hallway with black marble floors and walls the color of a sunset. He veered left, leading me to an apartment door, but I cast a quick look over my shoulder, seeing a massive black door with the gold numbers 2104 on it.

That must be the empty one.

We reached the other apartment door—mine, apparently—and the manager immediately slid the key in and swung the door open, walking right inside.

I watched him saunter off into the apartment, while I remained standing in the doorway, frozen.

"Um . . ." *Okay.*

This didn't make sense. This apartment was huge.

I slowly stepped inside, my arms hanging limply at my sides as I took in the high ceilings, spacious living room, and a full wall of windows, giving away the beautiful patio courtyard, complete with a fountain and actual grass outside. The same black marble floors carried in here from the hallway, but the apartment walls were cream-colored.

"As you can see," Mr. Patterson began as he went to the window wall and unlocked the glass, "you have a full gourmet kitchen with top-of-the-line appliances, and you'll love how the open floor plan preserves your view of the city."

I glanced at the kitchen, the granite island shining in the sunlight spilling in through the windows. The chrome appliances were just as impressive as the ones in my own home, and the wrought-iron kitchen chandelier—simple, sophisticated, and pretty—matched the one hanging above me in the living room.

He went on talking about three bedrooms, heated floors, and a rainfall shower, and I started shaking my head, overwhelmed. "Wait—"

But he cut me off. "There's a community gym on the second floor as well as an indoor pool. Both are open twenty-four seven, and since you're in one of the penthouses, you also enjoy a private courtyard."

My eyebrows narrowed in confusion. *I was in a penthouse? What?*

"Wait." I laughed, a little freaked out.

But he just kept going. "There are two doors to your apartment," he told me, his tone turning serious. "The other one leads to a stairwell in case of a fire, but be sure it's locked at all times." He pointed to the end of the hall, and I jutted out my head to see the metal door down the dark hallway. "We are very tight on security here, but I wanted to make you aware of the alternate entrance."

I brought my hand to my forehead, wiping away the light layer of sweat. What the hell was going on? The apartment was already completely furnished with expensive-looking sofas, tables, and electronics, and I watched him pick up a tablet and start to work the privacy glass on the wall of windows facing the city.

"Now let me show you—"

"Wait," I blurted out, cutting him off. "I'm sorry. I think there's been a mistake. I'm Erika Fane. I leased a one-bedroom with one bath—not a penthouse. I have no idea whose apartment this is, but I'm paying rent for something much, much smaller."

He looked confused, and then he picked up his file folder, probably checking his information.

Not that I didn't love the penthouse, but I wasn't forking over thousands of dollars every month for something I didn't need.

He breathed out a laugh, studying the paperwork. "Ah, yes. I forgot." He looked up at me. "That apartment was rented out, unfortunately."

My shoulders dropped, disappointment hitting me. "What?"

"It was a mix-up, and we're very sorry. I was advised by the owners to honor the contract you had signed as an apology. There were two penthouses, both vacant, so we saw no reason why you shouldn't have one of them. Your lease is still for a year, and your rent will remain the same during that time." He held out the keys to me. "No one called you?"

I stared off, reaching out and taking them.

"No," I answered. "And I'm still a little confused. Why would you give me twice the amount of apartment for the same price?"

He offered a smile, straightening his shoulders. It was how my mother looked as I was growing up when she was done answering questions.

"As I said," he placated, "we're very sorry about the mix-up. Please accept our deepest apologies, and I hope this penthouse meets your expectations as you continue your studies this year." He bowed his head. "Please let me know if you need anything, Miss Fane. I am at your service."

And then he brushed past me, out of the apartment, and closed the door behind him.

I stood there, feeling my stomach churn like the wind had been knocked out of me. I couldn't believe it. How had this happened?

I turned in a slow circle, taking in the room, the reality, and, most of all, the silence. I was completely alone up here.

And although it was beautiful, I'd been excited about sleeping on an air mattress tonight before I went out to buy my own furniture tomorrow. I'd been excited about a small, cozy apartment and neighbors.

But school started in two days. I didn't have time to find another place. "Dammit," I growled under my breath.

Trailing slowly down the hallway, I wandered in and out of all the rooms, finding the spacious bathroom with a double vanity and a slate-tiled shower. Swinging open cabinets next to the sink, I noticed towels and washcloths stocked and ready, as well as a loofah.

And then, trailing into the master bedroom, I noticed that it was already set up with a king-size bed and furniture that matched the white bedding and drapes. The damn clock on the nightstand was already set, too.

Unbelievable. Everything was done for me. Just like at home.

The décor might be slightly different, and the scenery had certainly changed, but my life hadn't. Everything was taken care of already. I'd even bet that if I opened the refrigerator, I'd find that stocked, as well.

Got to hand it to those Thunder Bay mothers making sure one of their princesses was tucked in all tight. There's no way this was a welcome committee just leaving a basket of fruit.

I shook my head, feeling the walls close in.

The women in Thunder Bay were busy ladies. They were powerful, influential, and thorough, and as their children, we sat comfortably under that umbrella. I even more so, because my father was deceased, and my mother was . . . weak.

As a kid, I'd appreciated the safety of the shelter they provided, but I wanted to do things for myself now. Space, distance, and maybe a little trouble. That's what I was looking for.

I let out a sigh and slipped the keys into the pocket of my white jean shorts. Grabbing the hem of my black sweater, I pulled it up and over my head, leaving me in my short-sleeved gray T-shirt.

Walking back through the apartment, I stepped across the open threshold from the living room and into the courtyard, my toes in my black flip-flops touching the grass. Gazing around the expansive area, I noticed that it was designed in the shape of a rectangle, with one long side open to offer a view of the city.

To my left, I saw more windows, probably belonging to the vacant apartment I shared the floor with. And then, as I turned right, my gaze drifted up, up, up, and I craned my neck to see the floor above me, whose residence curved around the side of the building, making the windows partly visible from here.

It also appeared to have more than one balcony and a perfect view into the courtyard. I wondered if a family lived there, to need so much space, but then I remembered Mr. Patterson saying "he."

I let my gaze linger on his windows, realizing I wasn't alone up here, after all.

I blinked awake, the blanket of sleep weighing heavy as I lay on my stomach hugging my pillow.

My ears perked, hearing a tapping sound coming from somewhere far away.

Tap, tap, tap . . . tap . . . tap.

I leaned up on my arms, trying to bring my eyes into focus.

Was that knocking? But who would be knocking? I didn't know anyone here—not yet anyway. I'd just arrived today, and I didn't have any neighbors . . .

And—I glanced at the alarm clock on my nightstand—it was after one in the morning.

Turning over, I sat up and rubbed the sleep from my eyes, slowly feeling the fogginess dissipate.

I thought for sure that I'd heard knocking. Like a steady thumping.

I looked around me, the moonlight streaming in from the window and falling across the white sheets as I listened for any sound in the silence of the still and dark apartment.

But then a loud *thud* hit, and I jumped, sucking in a breath. Throwing off the sheets, I grabbed my phone from the nightstand.

That wasn't a knock.

Clutching the phone in my hand, I slowly tiptoed across my bedroom floor, listening for another sound and searching my brain, trying to remember if I'd locked all the doors. The front, the glass partition to the courtyard, and . . .

Had I locked the rear entrance? *Yeah.* Yeah, of course I had.

But then the *thud* hit again, and I halted. *What the hell?*

It was dull and heavy, like deadweight falling, and I had no idea if it was above me, below me, or next to me.

I crept down the hallway, into the living room, and past the load of paint supplies I'd bought earlier today. I might not have gotten the tiny apartment I wanted or been able to buy my own pots and pans, but I could sure as hell make this place mine with a little color.

Jogging silently into the kitchen, I grabbed a knife out of the block and fisted the handle, the blade facing behind me as I approached the front door. I still wasn't sure where the sound had come from, but common sense told me to check the entrances.

I peered through the peephole, every hair on my arms standing on end. As much as I'd wanted to be on my own, I was a little freaked out about that now.

Arching up on my tiptoes, I peered through the hole, spotting the elevator a few feet down the hall and the soft flicker of the sconces.

But there was nothing and no one visible. The hallway appeared empty.

I jerked my head behind me as the booming *thuds* sounded again.

I fell back to my feet and crept through my apartment as I listened to the pounding, which had now become a steady attack. My feet followed the sound, stepping absently closer to it, and I finally pressed my ear against the wall, my heart racing as the vibrations touched my skin.

Resting my cheek against the surface, I swallowed the tight lump in my throat as the thumping against the wall grew faster and faster.

There was someone over there. In the empty apartment.

Holding up my phone, I dialed the office downstairs but got no answer. I knew there was a night manager named Simon Something-or-Other, but I didn't think many people were on duty at night. He must be away from his desk.

I continued listening, wondering if I could ignore it and just wait until morning to ask the manager about it, but the farther down the hall I traveled, the louder it got, until I was standing next to the rear entrance.

Opening up the door, I peeked my head into the stairwell, holding the heavy steel exit open just enough to inspect.

Glancing to my right, I saw a door just like mine. And then I heard a woman's high-pitched cry ring out around me, and I started breathing harder.

And then there was another cry. And another, and another, and . . .

Was she having sex? My mouth fell open as I tried not to laugh. *Oh, my God.*

But I thought the place was supposed to be empty.

I stepped out, knife in hand—just in case—and walked quietly down to the other door, glancing up and seeing small security cameras along the wall, probably installed when the apartments were built.

Pressing my ear to the door, I listened, still hearing the *thump, thump, thump* of something hitting the wall, and the girl's breathy cries over and over again.

I folded my lips between my teeth, covering my smile with my free hand.

But then the woman cried out. "Ah, oh, God! Please!"

And my face fell, hearing the fear in her voice. The short, shrill screams were now different. Panicked and scared, and her cries sounded struggled. My mouth suddenly went dry as I stood there listening.

"Ah!" she cried out again. "No, please stop!"

I backed away from the door, not finding it funny anymore.

But then something hit the door from the other side, making a loud *thud*, and I scurried backward. "Oh, shit," I gritted out under my breath.

I shot my head up to the cameras, now wondering if they fed to Security downstairs or to whoever was inside the apartment. Did they know I was out here?

I spun around and dashed for my door, grabbing the handle and trying to twist it.

But it was locked. "Dammit!" I mouthed. Fucking thing must lock automatically.

Another *thud* hit the door, mere feet away from me—so close— and I darted my eyes over to it, my breathing turning fast and painful.

I pulled on the door handle again, twisting and yanking, but it didn't budge.

Another *thud* hit the door, and I jerked upright, dropping the knife.

"Shit."

I dived down to pick it up, but just then I heard the other door swing open, so I bolted down the stairwell, hiding behind the wall and forgetting about the knife.

Fuck!

Screw this. Whoever was coming out of the vacant apartment was definitely someone I didn't want to meet. I dashed down flight after flight, a cry lodged in my throat as fear gripped my chest.

A pounding echoed above me, and I spared a quick glance upward, seeing a hand sliding down the railings as whoever it was jumped flights of stairs.

Oh, my God. I raced down, one flight after another, a drop of sweat gliding down my neck. The pounding was getting closer and closer, my legs about to give out as my exhausted muscles worked as fast as they could. I gasped, seeing the door labeled LOBBY. I yanked it open and burst through, looking behind me once again to see if he—or she—was behind me.

But then I slammed into a wall, and I let out a small cry as hands gripped my upper arms.

I looked up and exhaled a breath, seeing Michael Crist towering over me, his eyes narrowed.

"Michael?" I breathed out, frozen in confusion.

"What the hell are you doing?" He arched a brow and set me back, away from him, and let go of my arms. "It's after one a.m."

I opened my mouth, but nothing came out. Why was he here?

He stood in front of an elevator, a different one than I had taken this morning, dressed in a black suit, looking like he'd just been at a club or something. A young brunette stood next to him, beautiful in a tight navy-blue cocktail dress that fell to mid-thigh.

I suddenly felt exposed, dressed in my silk sleep shorts and black tank top, my hair hanging about, probably in tangles.

"I . . ." I looked over my shoulder again, noticing that whoever had followed me down the stairs hadn't come out the door yet.

I twisted my head back, looking up at Michael. "I heard something up on my floor," I told him.

And then I shook my head, still confused. "What are you doing here?"

"I live here," he shot back, and I immediately recognized that ever-present intolerant tone that he always used with me.

"Live here?" I questioned. "I thought you lived in your family's building."

He slid a hand into his pocket and cocked his head, looking at me point-blank like I was stupid.

I closed my eyes, expelling a sigh. "Of course," I breathed out, realization hitting. "Of course. You're the one who lives on the twenty-second floor."

I started connecting all the pieces: the separate elevator he and the girl stood by, the lone gentleman living above me, Mrs. Crist sending me the link for Delcour as a suggestion and not telling me their family owned the building . . .

And the luxury apartment all to myself, ready to go and just waiting for me.

Mrs. Crist—and most likely her husband, as well—made sure I ended up here. Keeping me close and under their thumb.

"And who's this?"

I glanced over, seeing the young woman with chocolate hair and piercing eyes, polished like a movie star on premiere night.

Michael looked ahead, his lips twisting slightly. "My little brother's girlfriend."

"Aw . . ." she responded.

I averted my eyes, aggravated.

His little brother's girlfriend. He couldn't even say my name.

And I wasn't Trevor's girlfriend anymore. I wasn't sure if he knew that, but it had been months. It had to have come up in conversation in his house.

"What did you hear?" he demanded, and I looked up to see him staring down at me.

I hesitated, not sure if I should tell him about the noises or the

woman's cries. I didn't feel safe up there now, and I wanted a manager, but Michael barely gave me the time of day. He probably
wouldn't hear anything I had to say.

"Nothing," I finally said, letting out a sigh. "Forget it."

He studied me for a moment and then reached out and swiped
a white card in front of a sensor on the wall, his private elevator
doors immediately opening. He turned to the girl. "Don't get too
comfortable. I'll be up in a minute."

She nodded, a slight smile playing on her lips as she walked into
the elevator and pushed the button, the doors quickly closing before her.

Michael ignored me and walked over to the front desk, talking
to the person on security. The man nodded and handed him what
appeared to be keys, and then Michael sauntered back over to me,
his height and athletic frame making my mouth go dry again.

God, he was beautiful.

After all these years, my entire life following him with my eyes,
my body still warmed whenever he was close.

I crossed my arms over my chest, trying to dull the thud of my
thrilled heart. I shouldn't want to be close to him. Not after how
he'd pushed me away nearly my entire life and how he'd treated me
all those years ago.

I brought my hand up to my neck, absently running a finger
over the jagged line.

"Simon is going to do a walk-through of the stairwell and your
floor," he told me. "Come on. I'll take you up."

"I said forget it," I insisted, not budging. "I don't need help."

But he walked to the other elevator anyway, and I spotted the
security guard opening the door to the stairwell and disappearing.

Reluctantly, I followed Michael, stepping into the elevator in
my bare feet and watching him push twenty-one.

"You know what floor I live on?" I asked.

But he didn't answer.

The elevator began ascending, and I stood there next to him, trying to remain still. I didn't want to breathe too hard or fidget too much. I'd always been hyperaware of Michael, and I was afraid he could tell. Maybe if I thought he saw me as anything other than trivial, I wouldn't worry what he thought so much.

But as I dropped my arms and stared ahead, the slight flow of air coming through the vent making my hair dance across the skin of my chest and the tops of my breasts, I licked my lips, feeling the pull of him right there, only inches away. My chest rose and fell, heat cascading down my neck, and I felt my nipples tighten as the fire over my skin moved across my belly and pooled between my thighs.

My sleep shorts felt too tight all of a sudden, and my stomach felt hollow, aching like I hadn't eaten in days.

Jesus.

I reached up, brushing my hair behind my ear and feeling like he was looking at me.

But I wouldn't dare a glance. After seeing the cover model he'd brought home for the night, all I could do was straighten my back, square my shoulders, and deal.

Like I had for years.

The elevator stopped, and the doors opened, Michael stepping out first, clearly not the gentleman Mr. Patterson was. He walked directly for my apartment, and I followed, speaking to his back.

"When Mr. Patterson showed me around today, he told me that apartment was empty." I glanced behind me at the door of the supposedly vacant apartment. "But I heard noises just a little while ago."

He turned around, eyeing the door behind me. "What kinds of noises?"

Headboards banging the walls, cries, screams, pants, people going at it . . .

I shrugged, deciding to be vague. "Just noises."

He exhaled a sigh through his nose, sounding annoyed. Walking around me, he made for the other apartment and jiggled the door handle, knocking several times when it didn't work.

The door opened, and I widened my eyes in surprise, but then the same security guard from downstairs emerged.

"Nothing here, sir. I checked the stairwell, and there's no sign of a disturbance."

"Thank you," Michael offered. "Make sure the apartment is locked, and head back downstairs."

"Yes, sir."

I watched the guard lock the front door and then wait at the elevator as Michael walked back over to me, keys out and his hazel eyes looking even more impatient.

He brushed past me and unlocked my front door.

"How did you know I locked myself out?" I followed him into the apartment.

"I didn't." He slid the keys into his pants pocket. "But I figured it was a safe bet. You didn't have keys on you, and the rear apartment entrances leading to the stairwell always auto-lock. Remember that."

I rolled my eyes, watching him charge through my apartment. Three years ago—hell, five days ago—I would've loved to have him in my space. Talking to me, watching out for me . . .

But that's not what he was doing now. I was still as invisible to him as the air he breathed. And far less important.

One night. It still lived in my memory, vivid and wild, and I wished he'd remember it. But it had turned to shit, anyway, just like the way he treated me.

Crossing my arms over my chest and steeling myself, I stared off, just waiting for him to leave.

He checked the rooms, the rear entrance, and came back out, pushing on the glass doors to make sure they were secure.

"It's not unusual for the staff to take breaks in one of the empty apartments," he explained in a flat tone. "In any event, it's quiet now."

I nodded, forcing a defiant look. "Like I said, I don't need help."

I heard him breathe out a quiet laugh, and I looked up, seeing a condescending smile in his eyes.

"You don't, huh?" he replied, sounding snide. "You got everything covered? You're in control?"

I lifted my chin slightly, not answering him.

He strode back over, eyeing me with arrogant amusement. "It's a nice apartment," he commented, gazing around him. "You must've worked hard to earn the money to pay for it. As well as the bills to those credit cards in your wallet, and that nice new car you just got."

I ground my teeth together, a flood of emotions I wasn't sure what to do with hitting me. I hated what he was saying. It wasn't that simple, and it wasn't fair.

He stepped up to me, narrowing his eyes. "You ran away from my brother, my family, your mother, and even your own friends," he pointed out, "but what if one day you found that all of those securities you took for granted—your house, your money, and the people who love you—weren't there anymore? Would you need help then? Would you finally realize how very brittle you are without those comforts you seem to think you don't need?"

I stared up at him, hardening every muscle, so I wouldn't give myself away.

Yeah, sure. I enjoyed the money. And maybe if I were really serious about being on my own, I'd have chucked it all. The credit cards, the car, and the tuition money.

So was I what he implied? A coward who talked a good talk but would never really know pain or the struggle of having to fight for anything?

"No, I think you'd be fine," he said in a low, sultry voice as he took a lock of my hair, grinding it between his fingers. "Pretty girls always have something to trade in, right?"

I shot my eyes up, locking gazes with him as I knocked his hand away. What the fuck was the matter with him?

The corner of his mouth tilted in a smile, and he walked around me toward the door. "Night, Little Monster."

And I whipped around, just seeing him slip through the door and close it behind him.

Little Monster. Why had he called me that? I hadn't heard that name in three years.

Not since that night.

CHAPTER 4

MICHAEL

Present

*D*on't be alone with her.

My one rule. The one thing I'd kept to myself and promised to heed, and now I'd broken it.

I breathed hard, my arms folded across my chest as I glared ahead at the rising numbers on the elevator wall. *No one else knew her.*

Not the way I did. I knew better. I knew how good she was.

Erika Fane played her parts well. The dutiful, self-sacrificing daughter for her mother, the pleasant, agreeable girlfriend for my brother, and a shining student and beauty in our seaside community growing up. Everyone loved her.

She thought she was nothing to me, insignificant and invisible. She wanted me to open my eyes and see her again so fucking badly, but she didn't realize that I already did. I knew the deceiving cunt that stewed underneath that perfect little sheen of hers, and I couldn't forget.

Why the fuck did I take her to her apartment? Why did I have to make sure she was safe? Being near her made me falter. It made me forget.

She'd burst through the stairwell doors, frightened and flushed, looking small and fragile, and instinct immediately kicked in.

Yeah, she played her parts well.

Don't be alone with her. Don't ever be alone with her.

The elevator doors opened, and I stepped directly into my foyer, rounding the corner into my darkened living room, but then I slowed, noticing the girl I had sent up and nearly forgotten about. She sat in the middle of the floor, straddling a wooden chair.

Completely naked.

I held back a smile, surprised at her ingenuity. Most women waited for direction.

I narrowed my eyes, approaching the chair as her lips quirked in a small smile. Her forearms rested on the top of the chair back, while her legs were spread wide and her high-heeled feet were planted on the floor on either side of the chair.

Stopping a foot in front of her, I let my eyes fall to her exposed body: supple, open, and ready for me. Her breasts were perfect and round, and I gazed down at her tan stomach, letting my eyes drop to her bare pussy and wondering if she was already wet.

I reached up, running the back of my hand over her cheek, and she leaned into it, eyeing me playfully as her long, silky hair draped over her breasts. And then she darted out, catching my thumb between her teeth and biting it gently.

I stared down at her, waiting to see what she would do next. Suck on it? Lick it? Maybe bite it harder? I liked it when I got as good as I gave. When a woman showed the fire in her instead of sitting idle.

But then she just let it go, offering me a shy look and leaving the ball in my court. It was my job to attack and hers to be the willing piece of meat, I guess. God, I was so fucking bored.

I tipped her chin up, ordering in a gentle voice, "Stay here."

I needed a breather to get in the mood for what I no longer wanted.

I walked past her, up the stairs, slipping off my jacket as I climbed. Entering my bedroom, a large space with a king-size bed and plenty of room to relax, I walked toward the shower, which sat between the bedroom and the master bathroom. It was out in the open and completely visible from the bed. Sometimes it came in handy when I had a girl or two over and wanted to watch them play.

I stripped out of my clothes, tossing them on the ground and stepping into the shower, in no hurry to return downstairs.

The rainfall overhead poured down, immediately drenching my hair and spilling its heat over my shoulders and back. I wished I could say it was all the hours logged in at the gym, the personal trainer making sure I was ready for the season, or the constant practices we'd been attending since they increased our workout schedule, that caused the tension in my head and body, but I knew that wasn't it. I was twenty-three, in the best shape of my life, and contending with demands I'd lived with for nearly my entire life.

It wasn't basketball. It was her.

After three long years, she was here, they were here, and I could hardly think of anything else.

I wondered if she'd still want me when all was said and done. After all the years of watching me, probably wishing I'd touch her, wouldn't it be fucking ironic if when I finally did take her in my hands and pressed my body to hers, she despised me?

Yeah, you're going to be in my bed, baby, but not until you wish you hated me.

I let out a breath, bowing my head and closing my eyes.

Jesus. I wrapped my hand around my cock, feeling it throb and pulse as it grew thick and hard at the thought of her.

I ran my thumb over the fat tip, wiping away the cum that was only a small measure of what was begging to get out.

Goddamn.

All it took was the thought of her, and how I'd almost given myself away in the elevator with her earlier.

She'd been amusing. The way she tried so hard to not look like she was losing her fucking mind with me around. How her shallow breathing made her tits rise and fall, and how those nipples poked through that tight little tank top of hers, making me want to take one between my teeth and teach her how to scream my name so well she'd say it in her sleep.

That golden skin, tan from her summer in Thunder Bay, looked like a feast, and that hair, blond and straight and brushing across her face and neck as it spilled down her back. It looked so soft, I couldn't resist touching the bright strands.

I'd done very well at ignoring her during my life, at first because she was too young for me to care and then because I needed to be patient.

Now the timing was perfect, she was here, and so was I.

Only I wasn't alone.

And the best part? She didn't know that we knew. She didn't know that we were coming for her.

Turning off the water, I breathed in and out, my cock aching and damn near sticking straight out, needing release. I wrapped a towel around my waist and combed my fingers through my hair, walking out of the bedroom and down the stairs.

Alex, the young woman I'd taken to the team party tonight, still sat dutifully in the chair, her heart-shaped ass somewhat more appealing now that I was rock hard.

But I still wasn't quite ready. Pouring myself a drink, I walked to the windows overlooking the city. The lights and the energy lit up the night, making it look like a sea of stars floating ahead of me, and it was one of the first things I learned when I'd visited this place as a kid. Meridian City was certainly more inspiring from a distance. Most things were, I'd come to realize.

The closer you got to anything beautiful, the less beautiful it became. Allure was in the mystery, not the appearance.

Letting my gaze fall, I spotted Rika through her windows. Her apartment sat on the level below but not directly beneath mine, so my windows offered an excellent view into the courtyard, as well as into her apartment. I narrowed my eyes, watching her flit about and wondering what she was doing.

She had splayed out a drop cloth below a wall, and there were cans of paint sitting on the living room floor. She stepped up on a ladder and arched up on her tiptoes, reaching for where the wall met the ceiling, smoothing something over with her hands.

She must've been putting up painter's tape. It was nearly two in the morning. Why was she painting?

Her nice little ass jutted out, and the black lace trim around the bottom of her tank top rode up, revealing the skin of her stomach.

Heat spread over my chest and down to my groin, my heart beating harder. Rika had a hell of a body, even though she didn't have a clue how to use it.

Soft, cool hands ran over my shoulders as the girl came up behind me, standing naked at my side. The privacy glass wasn't on, but neither were the lights, so Rika wouldn't be able to see anything up here if she looked.

Alex gazed out the window, probably seeing what I was looking at, and then turned back to me, slipping her hand under my towel.

"Mmm . . ." she moaned, feeling how hard I was. "You like her."

I stayed still, watching Rika as the girl stroked me. "No."

One time I thought I might. For a few hours, long ago, we looked through the same eyes, and I felt like I could trust her.

It had been a mistake that cost my friends their freedom.

"But you want her," she pushed, rubbing me faster and knowing exactly where my hard-on came from.

I let her handle me, but unfortunately I had no desire to reach out and touch her. I stared down, seeing Rika step off the ladder and drop to her hands and knees, running tape along the crown molding as she arched her back, taunting me.

I grunted, feeling the girl's strokes get faster.

"Yeah," she taunted. "So sweet and innocent, isn't she?"

I swallowed through the dryness in my mouth and glared down at Rika. "She's neither," I gritted out under my breath.

"Maybe not," the girl teased. "The shy ones tend to be the baddest after all."

And then she leaned in, burying her lips in my neck and whispering, "I'll bet your brother can tell you what a bad girl she is."

Jesus.

I planted my hand against the window, leaning in as Rika sat back on her knees and looked up at the wall that she appeared to be getting ready to paint.

I hoped that wasn't true. I only wanted two things . . . that my brother hadn't done as much as he bragged and that Rika had as much fight in her as I hoped.

"Yeah," the girl breathed, kissing a trail down my jaw. "I'll bet he knows exactly how she likes it."

I instantly straightened, turning my head and placing a hand under her jaw, holding it tight. "My brother is the last person that knows anything about her," I bit out, glaring down at her. "Now, go home. I'm not in the mood."

I pushed her away, and a shocked breath escaped her as she pinched her eyebrows together, looking confused.

"But you're . . ." she protested, gesturing to my cock tenting the black towel.

"That's not for you, and you know it."

Facing the window again, I tightened the towel around my waist and watched Rika pull her hair up in a ponytail and then bend over to pick up a can of paint.

But then I heard the *ding* of the elevator behind me, signaling that it was descending to pick up whoever had called it, and I quickly glanced over my shoulder to see the girl still standing there naked.

"You'd better hurry," I warned. "I've got company coming up, and they'd love nothing more than to find you like that." I let my eyes fall down, indicating her naked form.

Her eyes shifted from side to side as she hesitated, looking displeased. I didn't know if she was really disappointed or just offended.

I really didn't care. I'd already paid her, after all.

She finally turned, hurrying for wherever she'd dropped her clothes, and I heard rustling as she got dressed.

Looking back down, I saw Rika pour paint into a tray and then dip in a roller, soaking it in red.

My favorite color.

It was brave and confident but also aggressive and violent. Not sure why I favored it, but I always had.

The elevator bell dinged again, and I stood up straight, steeling my back as I heard deep voices enter the penthouse.

Turning around, I saw the girl, Alex, slip on her last shoe and grab her clutch purse before hustling in the direction of the elevators.

But regardless of whether or not she was dressed, she wouldn't go unnoticed.

Damon, Will, and Kai emerged from around the corner, dressed in similar black suits, having just been out themselves, smiling over a shared joke.

Alex stepped quickly, trying to scurry past, but Damon caught her, wrapping his arms around her waist.

"Whoa, where do you think you're going?" he teased, tightening his hold against her fake struggles. "Did Michael use his full hour already?"

Will laughed, shaking his head as he and Kai kept walking, making their way into the apartment.

Damon walked her backward, into the living room again, one of his hands squeezing her ass.

I leaned over to the chair, picking up the lounge pants I'd thrown there this morning. Slipping my legs in, I pulled them up and then whipped off the towel, tossing it on the floor.

"Just leave her alone," I told him.

But his dark eyes, nearly black, drifted up to me, a challenge lurking there that I was getting fucking tired of seeing.

His lips curled in a smile as he reached into his pocket, taking out a roll of bills.

"I'll be gentle," he whispered against her cheek, holding up the money.

She turned her head, eyeing me, probably wondering what the protocol was. Was she supposed to indulge an opportunity while another was still in the room?

I didn't care what she did. She was available, and when it came right down to it, it was her business, not her pleasure. I'd simply needed someone on my arm tonight for a private party, and Will knew her well enough to know she was discreet and hassle-free.

I was just sick of Damon's antics.

But she turned back to him and slowly took the money.

And he didn't hesitate. Yanking the top of her dress down to her waist, he picked her up and guided her legs around his waist.

"I lied," he said, baring his teeth next to her ear. "I'm never gentle."

He dived for her, covering her mouth with his as he carried her down the hall, disappearing into a spare bedroom.

I exhaled a hard breath through my nose, aggravated with the constant tug-of-war with him. It never used to be like that.

My friends and I all butted heads over the course of our friendship. Of course. We had our own temperaments, vices, and senses of right and wrong.

But those differences strengthened us back then. As individuals we had weaknesses, but as the Horsemen we were invincible. We each brought something different to the table, and where one lacked, the others stepped in. We were a unit, on and off the court.

I wasn't so sure that was true anymore. Things had changed.

Kai sat down on the couch while Will walked to the refrigerator, grabbing a sandwich off the plate of leftovers and a bottle of water.

I twisted around and grabbed the game ball I'd been awarded after we'd won the state championships in high school and shot it over at Will, slamming him in the upper arm.

He jerked, dropping the bottle of water and glaring at me with a mouthful of sandwich.

"Ow!" he barked, holding out his hands. "What's your problem?"

"Were you in 2104?" I shot out, already knowing the answer.

There was a reason we'd moved Rika to the twenty-first floor. It isolated her from neighbors. But I was also well aware that my friends probably wouldn't let the vacant apartment next door to her—or the opportunity to fuck with her—go to waste.

They didn't live in the building, but they'd somehow gotten a key to the apartment.

Will averted his eyes, but I caught the grin on his face. He swallowed his food and faced me, shrugging. "We may have brought a couple of girls back from the club," he admitted. "You know Damon. He put on a show for Rika. It got loud."

I shot Kai a look, knowing he wasn't in on it but pissed that he hadn't stopped them.

I combed my fingers through my damp hair and pinned Will with a stare. "Erika Fane may be inexperienced, but she's not stupid," I pointed out, looking between him and Kai. "You're going to have fun with her. I promise. But not if you get her running before we have her where we want her."

Will bent down to retrieve the basketball. At six feet tall, he was shorter than the rest of us, but his build was just as strong.

"Kai and I have been out for months," he charged, pressing the ball between his hands in front of his chest and looking at me as he approached. "I agreed to wait so Damon could have his part in this, but I am done fucking waiting, Michael."

His patience was wearing thin, and I'd known that for some time. He and Kai had received lesser sentences based on the charges, but to be fair to Damon, we'd held back on doing anything until he got out as well.

"Like that stunt last night?" I threw back. "Showing up at her house in masks?"

He laughed to himself, all too pleased. "It was for old time's sake. Give us a break."

But I shook my head. "We've been patient this long."

"No," he retorted. "*We've* been patient. You've been in college."

I stepped up to him, a good four inches taller, and grabbed the ball out of his hands. I kept my eyes on him as I shot it out to my side and let it roll off my fingers, seeing Kai catch it in one fluid movement.

"We wanted her in Meridian City," I told Will, "and she's here. With no friends and no roommates. We wanted her in this building with all of us, and there she is." I tilted my head to the window behind me, gesturing. "All that separates her from us is a door. She's a sitting duck, and she doesn't even know it."

His green eyes narrowed on me; he was still listening.

"We know exactly what we're going to take from her," I reminded him, "so don't fuck this up. Everything's going according to plan, but it won't if she feels she's in danger before it's time."

He hooded his eyes and looked away, still pissed but obviously letting it go. Taking a deep breath, he slid off his black jacket, tossed it on the sofa, and left the room, heading down the stairs into the private basketball court off the living area.

Within seconds, I heard the echo of a basketball pounding against the hardwood court.

Kai rose from the sofa and walked to the windows, crossing his arms over his chest and staring silently outside.

I stepped up next to him. Planting my hand on the window, I

followed his gaze, watching Rika run the roller up and down, her once-white wall now turning bloodred.

"She's alone." I spoke low. "Completely alone now. And soon she'll have nothing to eat but our goodwill."

I shifted my eyes to Kai, seeing his narrowed ones studying her. His jaw flexed; at times he could be more formidable than Damon. At least Damon was an open book.

But with Kai and his stern dark eyes and hardened expression, it was always a guess what he was thinking. He rarely spoke about himself.

"Are you having second thoughts?" I asked.

"Are you?"

I continued staring out the windows, ignoring the question. Whether or not I wanted this or liked any of it, it was never a question.

Three years ago, curious little Erika Fane wanted to play with the boys, so we indulged her, and she betrayed us. There was no way we'd forget. Once restitution was paid, my friends could have peace.

Kai kept his eyes on her as he spoke. "Damon and Will are blind action, Michael. Over three years, that hasn't changed. They act and react from the gut, but for two men that once believed money and power could get them out of anything, they now know that's not true."

He turned his head, locking eyes with me. "There were no games in there. No real friends. No hesitation. Act and commit. That's what they learned."

I turned my gaze back out the windows. *In there.* That was as much as Kai had talked about prison since he'd gotten out.

I hadn't asked, either. Maybe I knew he'd talk when he was ready, or maybe I felt guilty, knowing that it was all my fault. I'd brought her with us that night, after all. I'd trusted her. This was on me.

Or maybe, just maybe, it was because I never wanted to know what the last three years had been like for my friends. What they'd lost. How they'd waited.

How they'd changed.

I shook my head, trying to brush off his warning. "They were always like that," I argued.

"But they were always controllable," he challenged. "They were appeasable. Now they don't have limits, and the only thing they truly understand is that they are the only person they can trust."

So what was he saying? That they might have their own agendas?

I let my eyes fall to her, working vigorously as she rolled on the red paint.

And something coiled inside of me, twisting and tightening until my chest ached.

What would I do if they jumped ship? Took their own course of action? I didn't like that idea.

But for three years, I'd been forced to look at her in my house, hear about her, and bide my time, when all I wanted was to be her nightmare. She was here, and we were ready.

"We can't stop," I nearly whispered. We could control Will and Damon. We always had.

"I don't want to stop," he retorted, his dark eyes pinned on her. "She deserves everything that's coming to her. But I am saying that things never go according to plan. Remember that."

I picked up the glass of bourbon I'd poured earlier and tossed it back, swallowing the remainder of the liquid in one gulp. The burn sat at the back of my tongue, my throat tightening as I set the glass down.

I'd remember it, but I wasn't going to worry about it. It was finally time to have some fun.

"Why is she painting at two a.m.?" he asked, as if just finally realizing what she was doing.

I just shook my head, looking down at her and having no idea. Maybe she couldn't sleep after Damon and Will's escapade next door.

Kai exhaled, gazing down at her with a slight smile, curling his lips. "She grew up nice, didn't she? Beautiful skin, hypnotic eyes and lips, tight body . . ."

Yeah.

Rika's Dutch South African mother married into money and power, using a face and body that were still only half as beautiful as her daughter's. Rika may have inherited her mother's blond hair and blue eyes, her full lips and mesmerizing smile, but the rest was all Rika.

The sun-kissed, glowing skin; the strong, toned legs from years of fencing; and the way she looked so alluring and sweet but with a hint of mischief in her eyes.

Like a baby vampire.

"Yo!" Will bellowed from below. "What the fuck are you guys doing? Let's play!"

Kai smiled, turning for the court.

But I hesitated, still thinking about his warning.

He was right. Damon and Will leered, waiting to dive in for the kill. But what about Kai? How far would he go?

We had rules, a way that this was supposed to work. We weren't going to hurt her. We were going to ruin her. I knew Damon and Will would try to break those rules, but what about Kai? Would he step in and reel them back in as he'd always done?

Or would he follow this time?

"What about you?" I finally asked, making him stop. "Did prison change you?"

He turned, looking at me with eerie calmness. "I guess we'll see."

CHAPTER 5

ERIKA

Three Years Ago

The SUV turned, and I rocked back and forth on the floor of the G-Class, the drive turning from smooth to bumpy. The ground underneath the tires suddenly sounded like a grinder, and I knew that we'd hit gravel.

Car stereos blasted outside, and I heard honking, telling me that the whole parade was in tow. We stopped, and before I knew what was happening, doors opened, the engine died, and howls filled the air as all the passengers joined each other outside.

I stayed put, resisting the urge to peek out the windows and hoping Michael didn't need to open the back door to get anything. Within a few minutes, though, the chatter and laughter began to fade, and then it disappeared altogether.

I slowly pushed myself up, keeping my head low as I peered out the window.

I scanned the area; tall trees dotted the clearing where everyone had parked. Cars, trucks, and SUVs cluttered the space, and I narrowed my eyes, noticing we were in the forest.

Why the hell were we out here?

But then I turned around and immediately spotted a massive stone structure ahead of me.

I tilted my head back, following the spires of the old abandoned church peeking out through the bare autumn tree branches as it sat broken, dead, and silent in the woods.

St. Killian's. I'd never been here, but I knew it from the pictures I'd seen in the newspaper over the years. It was an old landmark, dating back to the 1700s, when Thunder Bay was first settled.

In 1938, however, it suffered structural damage due to a hurricane, and it closed, never reopening.

Everyone must've gone inside.

I ventured one more glance around the area, making sure no one was near, and quickly climbed over the back seat, opening one of the back doors and hopping out.

The brisk October air hit my legs, and I felt the brittle fallen leaves brush against my bare ankles. I was in my school skirt and flats, my legs completely bare, and chills broke out all over my body.

I jogged across the clearing, seeing the massive wooden doors of the cathedral boarded shut, and rounded the corner, heading to the side. The grass was overgrown with weeds, and stones from the foundation were dislodged and broken, lying along the cathedral walls.

Music poured out of the broken stained-glass windows, and I reached up, grabbing the bottom of the windowsill and stepping up on one of the three-foot-high arches carved into the bottom of the church wall. Pulling myself up, I peered into the church and let out a small smile.

Damn.

Speakers were set up around the room, blasting music, while two guys—one of them Kai, shirtless and without his mask— battled barefisted in the center of the wide-open floor, surrounded by male and female students cheering him and the other guy on.

Judging by the relaxed crowd and the grin on Kai's face as he jabbed at his opponent, I guessed it wasn't a *fight* fight.

More like sport.

While the music blared and small groups of students wandered about, talking, laughing, and drinking from their beer bottles, I saw a few people disappearing behind the sanctuary and down some stairs.

Did old buildings like this have basements? Or—*no*—I thought to myself, St. Killian's had catacombs. I'd heard about that.

Shifting my eyes up, I noticed the vast space above, the balcony section of the old church forming a semicircle that looked down over where the altar would've once sat. Most of the hardwood pews had been torn out and sat in piles around the room, while the old cast-iron chandelier, reminiscent of medieval times with its candle-holders and ornate design, still hung above the unholy debauchery of fighting and drinking going on below.

I spotted Miles Anderson making out with his girlfriend on a pew, and I immediately dipped my head down. I didn't like him or her, and I didn't want them to see me.

"You're not supposed to be here."

I widened my eyes, my stomach instantly knotting as I turned my head to the right.

Michael stood a few feet away, his chin tipped up, staring at me through his mask.

Gripping the sill, I felt my heart pick up pace. "I . . ." I started to speak but felt too stupid to say anything. I knew I shouldn't have come. "I wanted to see."

He cocked his head, but I had no idea what he was thinking. I wished he'd take off that damn mask.

I held my breath, watching as he climbed up behind me, gripping the windowsill at my sides and planting his black boots on the two arches to my left and right.

What was he doing?

The heat of his body covered my back, and I braved a glance up, watching him gaze through the broken cathedral window, seeing what I saw.

Swallowing the lump in my throat, I finally spoke up. "If you want me to leave—"

"Did I say that?"

I snapped my mouth shut, watching his fingers tighten around the bottle of Kirin in his hand. Michael had big hands, like most basketball players, but they were nothing compared to his height. He was nearly a foot taller than me, and I hoped he was done growing. I already had to look up at him.

I closed my eyes for a moment, desperate to just lean back and relax into him, but I held back. Instead, I dug my nails into the stone, forcing my eyes forward and watching Kai take the other guy to the ground, both of them wrestling, like an MMA fight on the concrete floor.

Michael brought the beer up to his lips, and he must've lifted his mask, because I heard him take a drink. But then my eyebrows shot up as I saw the bottle appear in front of my chest.

Befuddled, I hesitated only a moment before I took it, keeping my smile to myself as I tipped it up and drank. I held it between my lips, letting the bitter taste sit on my tongue and then swallowing.

When I tried handing back the bottle, he waved me off. I relaxed, taking a few more sips, content that he wasn't kicking me out. Yet.

"That door leads to the catacombs, right?" I asked, gesturing to the students inside who were heading through the darkened doorway behind the sanctuary.

I held the bottle to my chest, turning my head up to Michael. He nodded.

I turned back, watching the two guys and girls disappear. "What are they doing down there?"

"Having other kinds of fun."

I tightened my jaw, frustrated with his brief, cryptic response. I wanted to go inside.

But then I heard him breathe out a small, quiet laugh and felt his mask brush against my ear, his low voice whispering in my ear, "No one knows about you, do they?"

I pinched my eyebrows together, wondering what he meant. He took the bottle out of my hands and set it down on the sill.

"You're such a good little girl, aren't you, Rika? Good girl for mommy, good girl for teachers . . ." He trailed off before continuing. "You're a good girl on the outside, but no one knows who the hell you are on the inside, do they?"

I clenched my teeth, staring ahead at nothing.

His hot breath fell on my neck as he spoke. "I know what you want to watch, Rika," he gritted out. "I know you like to watch me. Schoolgirls shouldn't be so naughty."

My eyes rounded, and I sucked in a breath, pushing out from between his arms and jumping to the ground.

Embarrassment warmed my face as I dashed for the parking lot, but a hand suddenly caught mine, and I was pulled back in the opposite direction.

"Michael," I gasped, my throat thick with fear. "Let me go."

He stepped closer. "How do you know I'm Michael?"

I blinked, dropping my head, unable to look at him. My eyes fell on his hand holding mine. My skin burned so hot, I wasn't sure if I was on fire or freezing.

I swallowed the tightness in my throat. "It feels like you."

But he leaned in, making my violent heart pound even harder, and whispered, "You don't know what I feel like."

Then he reached up and grabbed my school necktie, yanking my body in as he pulled the tie roughly, loosening it and slipping it over my head.

"What are you doing?" I breathed out.

But he didn't answer.

I narrowed my eyes, watching him as he pulled the tie apart and walked around behind me, holding it over my eyes.

But I pushed it down, turning to look at him. "Why?"

Why did I need a blindfold?

"Because you'll see more with your eyes closed," he answered.

And I stood still as he fastened my tie around my eyes, his fingers touching my hair.

He let go of the tie, but I still felt his chest at my back, and I swayed an inch, feeling my equilibrium shift. I almost wanted to smile, feeling the butterflies in my stomach.

"Michael?" I said softly.

But he remained silent.

I breathed faster, feeling overwhelmed with the sensations. The scent of the hemlocks and red maples mixed with the cool sea air and dying leaves rushed me along with the light breeze that chilled my cheeks.

My nipples hardened, and every hair on the back of my neck stood up. What was he doing?

"Michael?" I said more quietly. I was starting to feel dumb.

But he still didn't say anything.

My heart started pounding, and I clutched the hem of my skirt, fighting the heat between my thighs.

I swallowed, slowly turning around and holding up my hands, finding his chest and placing my palms on him.

"You can't scare me," I told him.

I felt his hands take mine and pull them off his chest. "I already do."

And he walked around me, pulling me after him. I jogged a few steps, coming up to his side and holding on to his arm, trying not to stumble as we waded through the weeds, rocks, and uneven ground.

I tightened my fingers around his hand, the coarse skin of his palms feeling so good. What would his hands feel like on the rest of me?

"There's stairs," he warned, cutting off my thoughts. I slowed, stepping up and finding my footing.

"Come on," he urged, leading me up. After several steps, the sunlight coming through the blindfold faded, and I knew we were inside.

The dank smell of rain and rot from years of neglect surrounded me, and I turned my head, trying to locate the echoes of voices all around. I followed Michael, walking slowly, as I figured the floors were filled with debris.

Male shouts and cheers came at me from the left, and I listened, hearing them laughing and howling. Grunts and groans followed, and I gauged that the fight was still going on.

I followed Michael, still holding on to him, but I raised my other hand, touching the blindfold. I didn't like not being able to see, not knowing whether or not someone was coming at me. I felt like everyone was staring at me.

"Why won't you let me see?" I asked, coming to a stop next to him.

"Would that be more exciting for you?"

I twisted my head to him, even though I couldn't see him. "Is having me blindfolded more exciting for you?"

But then I turned my head forward again, stunned at how flippant I'd sounded. I'd always been nervous around Michael, and I was shocked—and maybe a little proud—that it had come out so easily.

I heard a couple of quick breaths come out of him, and I thought that he had laughed, although I couldn't tell for sure.

"I want you to do something for me." He let go of my hand, and I felt him brush against my shoulder as he came to stand behind me. "I want you to keep the blindfold on and don't take it off. I'll be back."

"Be back? What?" I pinched my eyebrows together, feeling chills sweep up my legs and worry knotting my stomach.

I felt him touch the middle of my back, and his breath fell across my temple. "Show me what you're made of."

And then he pushed me.

I gasped, stumbling forward, my flats grinding against the dirt- and dust-ridden stone floor as my arms shot out, trying to keep me from falling as I breathed quickly.

"Wha—" I choked out. "Michael?" I called, turning my head from side to side.

Where the hell was he? I reached up and grabbed the blindfold. Screw this.

But then I stilled, his words playing back at me in my head. *Show me what you're made of.*

He was testing me. Or playing with me. I inhaled a deep breath, steeling myself.

I could wait a little longer. *You're okay. You can do this.* I wasn't tapping out yet.

The grunts and growls of the fight were only a few feet away, and I could hear people talking and laughing. I wasn't sure if it was because of me or the fight, but my face burned anyway, embarrassment making me want to hide. It felt like I had a thousand eyes on me, watching my every move.

My bottom lip trembled, and I held out my arms, my chest rising and falling a mile a minute as I tried to see if anyone was near me. I felt exposed, and I didn't like it.

I took small steps, touching nothing but air as I felt my way.

"Michael?" I called again, a small cry stretching my throat that I refused to let out.

"Ah, fuck!" someone shouted, and I listened, gauging that it was coming from the fight.

I heard scuffling and a punch landing, and then cheers rang out, echoing in the vast space above.

"Woo!" a male voice shouted while others laughed.

I heard a couple of girls giggle not far off, and I sucked in a breath, hearing footsteps near me.

"Not sure what they have planned for you, honey," a female voice teased, "but I'm jealous."

Another girl laughed, and I scowled under the blindfold, anger warming my skin.

I straightened my back and touched the blindfold again, just wanting to peel it away.

But I curled my fists around the fabric, resisting. If I took it off, he would win. Michael would've kept it on, because he didn't care. Who's looking at me? Are they whispering about me? Are they laughing at me? Michael wouldn't care.

I could do this.

I dropped my hands and squared my shoulders, my pulse still throbbing in my neck.

Nothing was wrong. I was embarrassed, insecure, and uncomfortable, but it was in my head.

Until someone brushed my shoulder, and I stilled, feeling a hand graze my ass.

"Mmm, I know you," the male voice said. "Rika Fane, Trevor's girlfriend, right?"

No. Not right, I immediately thought.

But then I froze, recognizing the menacing tone that always seemed to carry a double meaning no matter what he said.

Damon.

"What are you doing here without your man?" he taunted. "And who got you all trussed up like this?"

The skin on my arms hummed, and I wanted to rip the blindfold off. I didn't like him looking at me when I couldn't see.

Damon wasn't safe.

I swallowed the lump in my throat, holding my ground. "Trevor's not my boyfriend."

"Too bad. I like playing with shit that's not mine."

And then his finger grazed my bottom lip, and I twisted my head away. "Stop," I demanded.

But then he wrapped a hand around the back of my neck and pulled me in. "You sleep over at the Crists' sometimes, huh?" he growled low, his breath falling on my lips. "You've got your own room there?"

I planted my hands on his chest, trying to push away, but he gripped my hip with the other hand, holding me in place.

"Damon!" I heard a bark come from behind him. "Fuck off and leave her alone!"

It wasn't Michael's voice.

Damon sighed and challenged in a bored tone, "I take what I want when I want it, Kai. We're not in high school anymore."

I ground my teeth together, struggling against him, but he wrapped both arms around my waist like a steel band, and I felt his whisper above my ear.

"How about I visit your room tonight, huh?" His hands dropped to my ass, and I squirmed, pushing against him, but he was too strong.

"Will you open the door for me?" he whispered against my lips. "Will you open other things for me?"

And then his hand dropped between us, sliding between my legs and rubbing me over my skirt. I let out a scream, but he cut me off, covering my mouth with his. I couldn't breathe as I squirmed and cried out, the sound muffled under his lips.

Michael, where the fuck are you?

I balled my fists against his chest and grabbed his bottom lip between my teeth, biting down hard until he released me and shot backward.

"Fuck!" he yelled, and I drew in ragged breaths, holding out my hands, because I didn't know where he was or if he was coming back at me.

I felt a small breeze, sensing someone else coming up.

"I said back off!" Kai yelled, sounding as if he was in front of me.

"She bit me!" Damon raged.

"Then you got less than you deserved!" Kai shot back. "Go downstairs and blow off some steam. It's going to be a long fucking night."

I reached up, grabbing the blindfold and wanting to see, but instead, I dropped my hands, curling my fists in anger.

"You okay, Rika?" Kai asked.

I heaved breath after breath, my body swaying as my head swam.

I bit him. I suddenly wanted to laugh. My hands tingled, and I straightened, feeling a little stronger.

"I wish I could say he was all bark and no bite, but . . ." Kai trailed off, letting the thought sit.

Yeah. We both knew that wasn't true.

I inhaled, his heady body wash with only a hint of sweat hitting me. "I'm fine," I answered. "Thanks."

I pulled away and turned to my right, fed up with standing there like a target.

"Where are you going?"

"To the catacombs," I replied.

"You can't."

I pursed my lips, twisting my head to face him. "I'm not a kid. You got that?"

"Yeah, I got it." His deep voice held a hint of humor. "But you're facing the wrong direction."

I sucked in a quick breath, feeling him take my shoulders and spin me farther to the right.

"Oh," I mumbled, embarrassment heating my face. "Okay. Thanks."

"No problem, kid," he said, his voice thick with a laugh I could tell he was trying to hold back.

I held out my hands just a bit, still refusing to let Michael win by taking off the blindfold as I took a hesitant step forward. But then I stopped and turned my head again.

"You knew my name," I stated, remembering that he'd called me Rika. In fact, Damon had said my name, too.

"Yeah." Kai approached my back. "Why wouldn't I?"

Why wouldn't he?

Why would he? I'd never spoken to these guys. It at least made sense that Michael knew *of* me, since I spent so much time at his house, but I was sure the others had never even noticed me.

"You study fencing," Kai started, "you're heir to a fortune in diamonds, and you've been on honor roll since birth."

I smiled to myself, finding his sarcasm a hell of a lot easier to deal with than Damon's hands.

"And," he continued behind me, his voice lowering, "you wore an amazing black bikini at the Fourth of July cookout at the beach this past summer. I looked longer than I should have."

My cheeks instantly warmed. What did he just say?

Kai Mori was as handsome as Michael and equally sought after by women. He could have anyone. Why would he even have given me a second glance?

Not that I ever held out hope he would. He wasn't Michael, of course.

"Michael shouldn't have let you come in here," Kai warned. "And I don't think you should go down there."

I felt a smile pull at my lips. "I know. That's the same thing everyone else would tell me."

I turned around, adding under my breath, "Except Michael."

I held my hands out a few inches in front of me, spreading out my fingers and stepping slowly forward, moving toward the dull hum of the music and howls coming from deep below.

I shouldn't go down by myself.

Kai had sent Damon down there, and even though I wasn't sure he would try anything again, I did know I wasn't safe with him.

Michael had told me to wait—he'd take me down—but . . .

But something inside of me hated being at anyone's mercy. I didn't want to follow, I didn't want to wait, and I didn't want to wonder. All of those things made me feel uncomfortable, like someone else was leading me around by the nose, and I didn't like being controlled.

That's what I admired about the Four Horsemen. They were always in control and always visible. Why wait for Michael when I could do it myself?

Cool wind blew across my bare legs, and I inhaled the smell of earth, water, and old wood drifting up through the door from the catacombs. I was close.

But then someone grabbed one of my outstretched hands, and I sucked in a quick breath, planting both of my palms on his chest and clutching the soft cotton of his sweatshirt.

"Michael?" I moved my hands up, noticing that his shoulders were nearly level with the top of my head. "Have you been here the whole time?"

But he remained silent.

I breathed in and out, trying to calm my heartbeat. The full length of his legs and torso was flush with nearly every inch of mine, and my skin warmed.

I stepped back.

"Why did you do that?" I asked. "If you've been here the whole time, why would you let Damon handle me like that?"

"Why didn't you just take off the blindfold and run away?"

I straightened my back, steeling my spine. Was that what he had wanted? For me to tap out and run away? Why was he testing me?

It didn't matter. How could he just stand there—see what was going on—and not step in? Kai had put a stop to it, and I thought Michael . . .

I dropped my head, afraid he could see my face heating. I guess I thought more of Michael than I should.

I tipped my chin back up, trying to keep emotion out of my voice. "You shouldn't have been okay with it."

"Why?" he retorted. "Who are you to me?"

I clenched my hand into a fist at my side.

"Toughen up," he bit out in a whisper as his breath fell across my cheeks. "You're not a victim, and I'm not your savior. You handled it. End of story."

What the hell was the matter with him? What did he want from me? I would've thought he'd show concern. *Jesus.*

All of the men in my life—my father, Noah, Mr. Crist, and even Trevor—hovered over me like I was a baby learning how to walk. I never cared so much for their concern, and even found it stifling at times, but from Michael . . . I might've liked it. Even just once.

He placed a finger under my chin, tipping my head up as his voice softened. "You did well. Did it feel good? To fight back?"

I caught the hint of amusement in his tone, and my stomach fluttered.

Michael had been right. I wasn't a victim, and even though the thought of him showing up to save the day would've given me some kind of hint as to what he felt about me—if anything—the fact remained that I never wanted to be someone who couldn't fight their own battles.

Hell yes, it felt good.

I felt him move away, but his fingers slid between mine.

"So you want to go downstairs?" he asked in a low voice.

My lips quirked despite my agitation.

I let him lead the way as we continued in the direction Kai had set. Howls echoed up from deep below, and my chest shook with anticipation.

Any bit of light from the other side of the blindfold disappeared and everything turned black as the air around me became cooler, thicker, and filled with the scent of earth and water, like a cave.

"There are stairs," he warned.

I immediately slowed my step. "Can I take off the blindfold, then?"

"No."

I pushed down the anger boiling up and stuck out my other hand, finding the rough and bumpy rocks of the stone wall to my right. Michael slowed down, letting me cautiously feel my way down the stairs as we traveled in a spiral.

The grains of dirt ground under my flats, and chills spread up my thighs, reminding me that it was getting colder and darker . . .

And that I was too unaware of my surroundings.

I didn't know who was down here, what they were doing, and depending on how deep we traveled into the maze, I might not be able to find my way out, either.

Michael had made it very clear that, while he might have my hand right now, he didn't have my back. So why didn't any of that make me want to stop?

I slid cautious steps down the stairs, traveling deeper and deeper and feeling like the walls were getting closer to me. I inhaled a hard breath, the thin air under the earth weighing on my skin like a heavy blanket.

Michael took another step, and I followed, coming up to his side where he'd stopped.

Like a Storm's "Love the Way You Hate Me" played all around me, and I gathered that all the tunnels were wired with speakers, the music probably filling every room.

But then a cry rang out, and I jerked my head to the right, hearing the high-pitched moan traveling toward me.

Hushed whispers seemed to spill out of the walls, groans and breaths floated around me, and I twisted my head to my other side, hearing bellows and cheers ring out from my left.

I slid my foot forward along the ground, feeling dirt instead of stone now, and listening for any sound I could grasp.

A woman's moans carried down the tunnel, vibrating off the walls, and I licked my lips, my chest rising and falling faster.

Other kinds of fun.

Michael's hand slid into mine again, making my skin tingle. "So how far you want to go?" he asked, his voice thick and husky.

The girl cried out again, sounding high and euphoric, and laughter and groans followed.

I rubbed my palm up and down my thigh, trying to distract from the heat building between my legs. God, what was happening to her?

I pulled my hand out of Michael's. *How far would I go?*

I held out my hands, stepped toward the noises, and shook my head, wondering instead if I'd ever stop.

I knew from pictures that the catacombs were a small collection of tunnels and vaults, or rooms, underneath the church, and I wasn't waiting for an invitation from him or his permission. He brought me down here, he wanted to play with my head, but I wasn't playing anymore. I'd do it myself.

And he seemed to finally realize that. He hooked the inside of my elbow and jerked me back. I let out a small gasp as I stumbled.

"You stay with me down here, you understand?"

I stood still and remained silent as I swallowed the lump in my throat. He'd suddenly become more protective than he had been upstairs. Why?

He took my hand, pulling me gently along down the tunnel. My legs broke out in chills, but my neck and face heated up as the moaning and deep male voices got closer and louder.

Michael made a turn, taking me with him as we rounded a

corner—or a doorway, I couldn't be sure—and slowed our walk as the air suddenly changed, smelling of sweat, hunger, and men. My heart pumped in my chest so hard it hurt, and I couldn't slow my breathing.

A woman's moans and pleasure-filled panting filled the air, and I instantly touched my blindfold, the urge to take it off strong.

But I held back. I didn't want to give him an excuse to send me back upstairs.

I dropped my hand and let Michael take me farther into the room. At least I thought it was a room. He stopped, both of us facing the sounds, and my whole face warmed with embarrassment. I turned my head, my nose touching the sleeve of his sweatshirt.

"Ah, Christ," a guy groaned. "Fuck, she feels good. You like that, don't you, baby?"

I heard her sexy, lustful laugh as she breathed hard, and my stomach flipped, hearing the sounds of approval and laughter around the room.

From all the men. *Oh, God.*

I opened my mouth in shock, speaking quietly to Michael. "Are they hurting her?" I asked, knowing he could see everything.

"No."

I licked my lips, listening to the grunting and kissing, the gasping and growls. Was she the only girl in here?

I faced the noises again. "Are they . . . ?" I trailed off, not sure how to ask what I wanted to know.

"Are they what?" Michael's low voice taunted.

I opened and closed my mouth, hating the amusement I caught in his tone. He was laughing at me.

I cleared my throat. "Are they . . ." I inched out. "Are they fucking?"

I rarely ever used that word, but it felt appropriate.

The sound of skin hitting skin, hard and fast, filled the room, with the moans matching the rhythm, and I gritted my teeth to stifle the groan in my own throat, feeling the heat grow between my thighs.

"Michael?" I called when he didn't answer me.

But he still said nothing. A white-hot heat fell on my left cheek, and I turned my head to face him.

"Are you staring at me?" I whispered.

"Yes."

My breathing got shallower, and I adjusted my hand in his, not sure if it was his sweat or mine I was feeling.

"Why?" I asked.

He hesitated a moment before answering. "You surprised me," he said quietly. "Do you use the word 'fucking' a lot?"

My shoulders started to drop. Was I too crude?

"No," I admitted, looking away. "I—"

"It sounds good on you, Rika," he cut me off, putting me at ease. "Use it more often."

Excitement rushed under my skin, and I wasn't sure I would heed his request, but I smirked anyway. I didn't care if he saw it.

The men in the room started to roar, and I wasn't sure what was happening, but they were getting more excited.

"They are, aren't they?" I asked again, but I really didn't need Michael to confirm.

If the panting and the dirty words weren't enough to give it away, I couldn't mistake the pleasure in her hot, sweet whimpers, which picked up rhythm, going faster and louder as the heated vibes of the onlookers surrounded me. I could only picture what was happening to her.

"Why are people watching them?" I asked.

"For the same reason you want to," he shot back. "It gets us excited."

I paused, thinking about that one. Did I want to watch?

No.

No, I didn't want to see her on display for anyone who cared to look. I didn't want to see all these guys—and a few girls, from the voices I heard—watching her do something that should be private. And no, I didn't want to know who she was or the guy she was fucking, so I wouldn't have to think about what I'd seen every time I ran into them in town.

But . . .

"Fuck," she whispered, sounding so desperate and high. "Oh, God. Harder."

But maybe Michael was a little right. Maybe I wanted to see what she looked like and what she was feeling written all over her face. Maybe I did want to see the guys watching her, because I wanted to know what turned them on, see the lust in their eyes, and feel a measure of it when I looked at them.

And maybe I wanted to see Michael watching her. To see if there was need and hunger there, and how hot it would feel to be her and have his eyes on me like that.

Did I want to be screwed in front of a room full of people? No. Not ever.

But I wanted to lose the blindfold and see some of what I had yet to experience. To live through her and imagine what she was feeling.

And imagine that it was Michael's hands on me.

The pulse in my clit started to throb, and I bit my bottom lip, trying to resist the urge to lean into him.

"Sex is an unnecessary need, Rika." Michael spoke low next to me. "Do you know what that means?"

I shook my head, too weary to do anything more.

"We don't need sex to survive, but we need it to live," he explained. "It's a high, and one of the few things in life where all five senses are at their absolute peak."

I felt him brush my arm and knew he'd moved behind me, the warmth of his chest blanketing my back.

"They see her," he whispered in my ear, still not touching me, "that beautiful body moving and panting underneath him as he fucks her."

I breathed harder, closing my fists around the hem of my skirt.

"They hear her moans," he went on, "and it's like music, because it shows that she's loving everything that's happening to her right now. He can smell her skin, feel her sweat, and taste her mouth."

He leaned into my back, pushing his chest into me, but I still couldn't feel his hands. I squeezed my eyes shut behind my blindfold. *Touch me.*

"It's a feast for his body," Michael's sultry voice breathed out above my ear, "and that's exactly why, next to money, sex is the one thing that drives the world, Rika. That's why they're watching. That's why you want to watch. Nothing compares to having someone own you like that, even if it's just for an hour."

I slowly twisted my head, speaking to him. "And what about love?" I challenged. "Isn't that better than sex?"

"Have you ever had sex?"

"Have you ever been in love?" I threw back.

He remained silent, and I wondered if he was playing with my head again or if he didn't want to tell me yes. I ignored the latter, choosing to believe the former. Please tell me he hadn't been in love with anyone. Or worse, loved someone now.

I felt him move back to my side, and chills spread over my body at the loss of his heat.

"Isn't she afraid people will find out?" I asked quietly. "Like at school?"

"Do you think she should be?"

Well, I would be. I might be inexperienced, but that didn't mean I was innocent. Things done in the dark hours of night, behind closed doors, or in the heat of the moment looked a lot different in the morning, out in the open, and with a clear head. Yeah, there were things we wanted, impulses we felt, but acting on those desires brought consequences we weren't always willing to accept, either. And maybe they were consequences we shouldn't have to accept, but they existed nonetheless.

The girl, whoever she was, was acting on her own rules, but she'd suffer according to everyone else's.

Which sucked.

Maybe that's what Michael wanted me to *see*. Down here, in the dark, in an underground tomb with him, I got a taste of a different reality. One where the only things taboo were the rules, and to see all the things people dared to do in an environment where they had freedom.

Reaching up, I slid my fingers under the necktie secured around my eyes, ready to slip it off, but he took my hand, pulling it away from my face.

I turned my head, speaking to him at my side. "I want to see."

"No."

I exhaled a sigh and turned forward again, hearing the girl's panting getting faster and louder. "You think I'm too young," I stated. "But I'm not."

"Did I say that?" he snapped, his tone suddenly gone hard. "You keep putting words into my mouth."

"Then why did you let me come down here?"

He paused and then answered in a flat tone, "Who am I to deny you anything?"

I drew in a sharp breath, anger seeping into every muscle in my body. "I'm sick of your vague responses," I bit out. "Why did you let me come down here?"

What did he want with me? Why press that I could do what I wanted and handle myself, and then keep me restrained, still tethered on a leash?

Did *he* even know what he was doing?

Screw this. I didn't need his permission.

I reached up and whipped off the blindfold. But instead of

checking out the room and the display being put on like I'd originally wanted, I immediately spun around and came to stand directly in front of him, looking up.

His hazel eyes, all that was visible behind his crimson mask, which made my heart pump with fear, locked on mine, not blinking or reacting.

"Why did you bring me down here?" I pressed again, searching his eyes for any sign of emotion. "Did you think it would be funny? Get your kicks by seeing how far you could push me before I'd run away?"

But he just stood there. He didn't speak, didn't move, and it didn't even look like he was breathing. He was a machine.

I shook my head, an ache settling behind my eyes. After years of fucking waiting for him to look at me and finally see me, he'd given me something—just one part of a single day—and now he'd taken it away as if I were a void standing in front of him. I was transparent and of no consequence. I didn't know what was going on in his head, and I finally realized I never would.

"I'll find my own way out," I told him, turning away and heading for the door before he could see my lips tremble.

But then he caught the inside of my elbow and yanked me backward, and I gasped as my back crashed into his chest.

"Don't go." His voice shook.

Tears pooled in my eyes, and he wrapped an arm around my waist, keeping me glued to his chest as he walked us to the right, rushing into another dark room, this one empty.

My eyes darted around me, but I could barely see anything, the only light coming from the candles in the other room.

"Michael, stop," I breathed out. Everything was happening too fast. What the hell was he doing?

He walked us across the room, and I dug in my heels to stop him from pushing me, but it was too late. I was pressed into the wall, my chest meeting the stone, and I immediately felt something hit my foot. I looked down to see his red mask lying on the ground as he hovered over my back.

I opened my mouth to protest, but then I froze, feeling his arm tighten around my waist and his breath fall on my neck, over my scar. I stopped breathing, letting my eyes fall closed as my skin burned and my head swam with pleasure. His face and lips nestled into my skin as he held me caged between him and the wall, but he didn't move further. No kissing, no caressing, just holding as he breathed in and out against my skin.

"You want to know why you're here?" he asked me, sounding strained in my ear. "You're here because you're like me, Rika. You're here because there are enough people who try to tell us what to do and try to keep us in a box."

He grazed his lips up my neck as he spoke. "They tell us that what we want is wrong and that freedom is dirty. They see chaos, madness, and fucking as ugly, and the older you get, the smaller that box gets. You feel it closing in already, don't you?"

My lungs tightened, and I finally sucked in a breath, forcing myself to breathe. His hand dropped from the wall and gripped the front of my neck, bending it back to him.

"I'm hungry, Rika," he said, pressing his hard body into my back, his lips hovering over mine. "I want everything they tell me I can't have, and I see that hunger in you, too."

I blinked up, trying to make out the outline of his face in the near darkness. All I could see, though, was the straight ridge of his nose and the angle of his strong jaw.

"There are too many people that try to change us," he went on, "and not enough people who want us to be who we really are. Someone once made me see that, and I wanted to give that to you."

I stared up at him, my heart racing but so happy I wanted to cry. He knew. He understood what I wanted more than anything.

Freedom.

"Own who you are," he commanded. "And don't apologize. Do you understand? Own it or it will own you."

Relief flooded me. For the first time in my entire life, someone told me it was okay to want what I wanted. To get into messes and to dive in headfirst.

To have a little fucking fun before I died.

I dropped my hands from the wall and slowly turned around, feeling his arm around my waist loosen to let me move.

"Is that all you wanted to give me?" I asked quietly.

He dipped his head down, his heat and scent only inches away.

"I'm not sure you're ready for more," he said in a low voice.

And my breath shook, feeling his fingertips trail up my thigh, dragging my skirt up with them. His fingers grazed over the intimate curve where my leg met my hip, and I whimpered, clutching his sweatshirt.

Give me everything you have.

"Rika!"

I sucked in a breath and straightened, hearing my name.

Who . . . I tried to peer around Michael, but he was too tall, and he had me locked in.

And he made no effort to move, staying in front of me and letting his fingers linger on the skin of my hip bone.

But after a moment, he dropped his hand and stood up, turning around and giving me room to see who was behind him.

Trevor stood in the light of the doorway between the two rooms, having probably witnessed the public display over there before making it into here.

He still wore his school uniform, khaki pants with a light blue oxford and a navy-and-green necktie.

"Rika, what the hell were you thinking?" He barged over and grabbed my hand, making me stumble as he hauled me over to his side. "Your mother is worried sick. I'll take you home."

But before I got a chance to say anything, he stepped up to Michael. "And you stay the fuck away from her," he ordered. "There are a dozen other chicks here. She's not your toy."

And without waiting for Michael to respond, Trevor squeezed my hand and pulled me toward the door. I looked back, catching one last glimpse of Michael's eyes as he watched me leave.

CHAPTER 6

ERIKA

Present

My phone vibrated and I let out a low groan as I opened my eyes and reached behind my head, fumbling for it on the end table. Grabbing it, I yanked it off the cord, my mouth stretching in a yawn as I swiped the screen and saw that I'd missed the call.

Three missed calls, actually. Trevor, Noah, and Mrs. Crist.

Jesus. Why so early? But then I blinked again, widening my eyes as I saw the time in the top right-hand corner.

Ten o'clock!

"Shit!" I gasped, popping my head up off the sofa. "Dammit!"

I jumped to my feet, knowing I wouldn't have time for a shower. I was supposed to be meeting with my advisor right now.

Son of a bitch! I hated being late.

I dashed into the hallway, but then I caught myself, halting as I spotted the massive splash of red in front of me and remembering what I'd done last night.

That was why I'd been up so late. I straightened, gazing at the wall I'd painted and decorated.

After Michael had sauntered out of here, I'd been so angry I had a fit. But unlike a kid who cries, screams, and hits, I'd painted, pounded, and wore myself out instead. I wasn't even sure if I was allowed to change the wall color, but I hadn't cared.

Michael's smug assumption that I was at the mercy of everyone else in my life—and how fragile I was—had gotten under my skin, and I'd needed to change something. Maybe he thought I was still a schoolgirl, naïve and inexperienced, but he didn't have me pegged as well as he thought he did.

I hoped I wouldn't see him today. Or regularly for that matter.

I gazed at the color that reminded me of Christmas and apples, roses, and rows of Autumn Blaze maples I'd seen as a kid. Of fire and hair ribbons and my mother's evening dresses.

I'd also hung some photographs I'd brought with me, as well as the Damascus blade, on the wall. I couldn't shake the suspicion that it was from one of the Horsemen. Or all of them. The mysterious gift along with their sudden appearance in Thunder Bay was too coincidental.

But why would they leave it for me? And did Michael have anything to do with it?

My phone beeped with a voicemail, and I blinked, remembering the time.

Shit.

I raced into my room and threw on some clothes and tied my hair up in a ponytail. Grabbing my brown leather school bag, wallet, and phone, I ran out of the apartment and hurried into the elevator, casting a quick glance to the other penthouse door down the hall.

I hadn't heard any other noises after Michael left last night, but someone was in that apartment. I'd have to try to catch the manager today. I didn't feel safe, especially after being chased in the stairwell.

"Good morning, Miss Fane," Mr. Patterson greeted as I walked off the elevator.

"Morning," I called, giving him a quick smile as I dashed past the reception desk and out the revolving doors.

I stepped right onto the sidewalk, immediately caught in the bustle and noise of the city. People walked to and from work or carried on with their daily errands, moving quickly around slower pedestrians and veering across the street through the blares of taxi horns and whistles.

The clouds overhead hung low and looked smoky with a tinge of deep purple, and the breeze blew cool, although it was late August. I inhaled the smell of earth, even though everything around me was brick and concrete. I turned right, hurrying in the direction of Trinity College.

After apologizing like crazy, I got my advisor to squeeze me in between appointments, and we were able to finalize my schedule, as well as my long-term plan. Classes started in a couple of days, so it was a relief to touch base with her and start the year off right.

Afterward, I hit the bookstore for a few paperbacks that had been added to my reading list, picked up a coffee, and strolled the surrounding area, taking in the shops, the unusually cool day, and the beauty of the dark city.

I loved it here.

This bustling metropolis was second to none with its arts culture, libraries, and museums. The variety of fare offered at the restaurants kept even the pickiest diners entertained, and you couldn't help but appreciate the trees lining the sidewalks and the plants and hedges that sat in flower beds outside of buildings. It was truly stunning and unique.

But there was a dark allure about it, as well.

How the tall skyscrapers blocked out the light. How the cover of trees in the park surrounded you in a cave-like canopy, turning the green grass nearly black. How the silent alleys were lost in the fog in the early mornings, leaving you to wonder what was in there, because you knew you'd never be so brave as to see for yourself. I think the dark side of Meridian City was what I loved most when I'd visited as a kid.

My phone buzzed against my leg, and I reached into my satchel as I strolled down the sidewalk, picking out my cell phone.

I inhaled deeply, seeing Trevor's name on the screen.

"Is that you, Midshipman?" I answered, trying to tease. I'd probably see Trevor here and there for the rest of my life—our families being so close—and I wanted to be on good terms with him.

"How's your first day in the big city?" he asked, sounding a lot more relaxed than he was at the party.

"Great." I tossed my coffee in the garbage can I passed and kept walking. "I was just at the bookstore getting the rest of my texts."

"Good, and how's your apartment?"

I breathed out a quiet laugh, shaking my head. "Big. As I'm sure you know. I love your mom, Trevor, but she could've left this one alone, you know?"

"What are you talking about?"

"The apartment in your family's building . . ." I hinted.

He must've known about it, since he assumed I would see Michael.

"What do you mean, my family's building?" His voice turned sharp.

"Delcour," I told him. "I didn't know it was a Crist building."

"Fuck," he growled. "You're living at Delcour? Why didn't you tell me that?"

I didn't answer, confused as to why that was important to him in the first place. During the summer, I'd only mentioned finding an apartment but no details. And he hadn't asked.

Was there something wrong with Delcour? Other than I'd gotten a little played in order to live there?

"Rika," Trevor started, sounding rigid. "Find something else."

"Why?"

"Because I don't want you there."

"Why?" I pressed again.

His parents had tricked me into leasing the apartment, not

telling me it was their building, and now Trevor was ordering me out. I'd had enough of people telling me what to do.

"You really have to ask that?" he snapped. "Get your stuff and go to a hotel until you find another place. I mean it. You're not living at Delcour."

I stood there with my mouth slightly open, not understanding what the hell his problem was. Delcour belonged to his family. If anything, why *wouldn't* he want me to stay there? And what did he think, ordering me around? He knew better.

"Look," I said, keeping my voice calm, "I have no idea what's going on, but it's got great security, and even though it's not what I had planned, school starts in two days. I don't want to move while I'm in the middle of classes."

Not if I didn't have to, anyway.

"I don't want you there," he reiterated, barking his order. "Do you understand?"

I clenched my teeth. "No," I gritted out. "I don't understand, because you're not explaining it to me. And the last time I checked, you're not my father."

I heard his bitter laugh on the other end. "You probably planned this, didn't you? You knew exactly what you were doing."

I shook my head, closing my eyes. I had no idea what he was talking about, but I no longer cared. "I'm not moving. I don't want to."

"No. I don't suppose you do."

"What is that supposed to mean?" I shot out.

But then my phone beeped again, and I pulled it away from my ear, seeing *Call Ended*. I dropped my head back, exasperated. What the hell?

Why wouldn't Trevor want me at Delcour? He hated Meridian City, but what did Delcour have to do with that?

And then I lifted my head, closing my eyes as the realization hit.

Michael. Trevor hated Michael, and Michael was at Delcour. He didn't want him around me.

But if Michael didn't give me the time of day at home, nothing would be any different here. Hell, I probably wouldn't even know he lived at Delcour if I hadn't run into him last night. I had no reason to think I'd see him on a regular basis.

I let out a sigh and ran my fingers across my forehead, wiping away the light layer of sweat. The argument had me heated now.

And with energy to spare.

I gripped the phone, feeling the hilt of a blade in my fist and the fire in my legs to move.

Bringing up my phone, I typed in a search for "fencing clubs."

H ello." I approached the front desk of Hunter-Bailey, seeing the attendant's head pop up. "I saw online that you have a fencing club, and I was wondering if you have open-bouting nights."

He pinched his eyebrows together, looking confused. "Excuse me?"

I shifted uncomfortably. Hunter-Bailey was reputed to have one of the most active fencing clubs in the state, with private lessons and a large area for group workouts. It was also the only location in the city to offer fencing.

The facility was a little more intense than the Thunder Bay Rec Center that I was used to, though. Massive area rugs adorned the hardwood floors, while dark wood made up the stairs and all of the furniture. The upholstery was kept to dark tones like forest green, black, and midnight blue, and the place was old, dark, and very male. I'd also noticed the fancy marble dome ceiling and stained-glass windows when I'd walked in.

"Fencing," I clarified, looking at the young man dressed in a suit. "I'm looking for a club. I'll purchase a membership if I need to."

I really didn't need classes. I'd been studying nearly my entire life. But I would love a chance to connect with other fencers, pair up for practice bouts, and make some friends.

But the guy was looking at me like I was speaking in Japanese.

"Rika," a deep voice called, and I twisted my head, seeing Michael walk across the foyer from the front doors.

What was he doing here?

He approached me, wearing loose jeans and a navy blue T-shirt, everything he wore always accentuating his chest, arms, and height. A gym bag hung off his shoulder with a black sweater draped over it.

"What do you want?" His sharp tone bit.

I opened my mouth. "I . . . um—"

"You know this young woman, Mr. Crist?" the clerk asked, chiming in.

Michael stared at me, looking none too pleased with running into me, either. "Yes."

The clerk cleared his throat. "Well, she's interested in joining our fencing club, sir."

The corner of Michael's mouth quirked in a grin, and he nodded at the clerk. "I'll take care of it."

I watched the clerk disappear into the back, leaving us alone in the quiet area, distant voices from the closed doors behind me drifting through.

I gripped the strap of my satchel lying across my chest. "I didn't know you fenced."

"What makes you think I fence?"

I looked around, indicating where we were. "Well, you're in a fencing club."

"No," he drawled out, looking amused. "I'm in a gentlemen's club."

A gentlemen's club. Like a strip club?

But looking around, I didn't see anything that gave the indication that there were pole dancers, private rooms, or lap dances being performed here.

Hunter-Bailey was pristine, elegant, and old, like a museum where you were told to be quiet and not touch anything.

I shook my head, befuddled. "I'm lost. What do you mean?"

He let out a sigh, tipping his chin down and looking at me like his patience was wearing thin. "This is Hunter-Bailey, an exclusive men's club, Rika," he explained. "A place where guys go to work out, swim, steam, drink, and bullshit away from all the people that bug the shit out of them."

Bug the shit out of them?

"Like women?" I guessed.

He just stared at me, holding the strap of his bag with his head slightly cocked.

"So . . ." I looked around and then back to him. "Women aren't actually allowed in here, then?"

"Nope."

I rolled my eyes. "That's completely ridiculous."

No wonder the clerk had looked at me so funny. Why didn't they post a sign outside saying *No Women Allowed*, then?

But . . . I guessed that would probably just make women want to come in more.

Michael stepped up to me. "When women get to enjoy 'Ladies' Night Out' specials or their own private workout area at a gym, it's okay, but when a guy wants their own space, it's archaic?"

I held his hazel eyes, the golden amber in them taunting and playing with me like a cat with a mouse. He had a point, and he knew it. It was okay for men to want their own space. No harm. No foul.

But it aggravated me that they offered something I enjoyed and I was shut out.

I shrugged. "I just wanted to fence, and this town is limited as far as facilities go, so . . ."

"So I'm sorry more women don't take an interest for you to have your own club," he replied flatly, sounding not the least bit sorry. "Now, it's raining outside. Do you need a ride back to Delcour?"

I dropped my gaze, noticing the small dark splotches on his shoulders. The rain must've started right after I'd stepped inside.

I shook my head, seeing very clearly that he was trying to get rid of me.

"Fine." He veered around me to the wooden double doors, and I took a step, ready to leave. But then I spotted a tweed flat cap sitting on a stack of antique books on top of a curio cabinet.

I smiled, biting my bottom lip, because I couldn't stop myself. Without hesitating, I dropped my bag on the floor, ran over, and snatched up the cap, and then darted up the stairs, taking two at a time as I stuck the hat on my head. I stuffed my ponytail inside, hiding my hair underneath the hat.

"Erika!" Michael's voice boomed behind me.

But I didn't stop. My heart raced, and I squeezed my fists, the adrenaline making them tingle. Reaching the second floor, I darted around the corner, quickly stuffing any stray hairs up underneath the cap and hurrying down the hall.

I heard the stairs creak behind me, and I glanced back, not seeing Michael but hearing his footfalls as he powered after me.

Shit. I almost laughed, remembering all those years ago when he'd found me at the catacombs. He'd liked my curiosity then, I think, and even had fun indulging me. And then immediately after that night he'd pulled back as if nothing had happened.

Maybe he'd remember.

I speed-walked down the hall, hearing banter and laughter around me as I passed several open doors. But I didn't stop to look.

Two men in suits, one of them holding a cigar, came in my

direction down the hall, laughing with each other. I dipped my head, knowing that my figure did nothing to disguise that I was a woman.

Passing them by, I saw one do a double take out of the corner of my eye, but he didn't stop me.

Reaching the end of the hall, I opened the door and entered, quickly closing it behind me. I let out a breath, not knowing if Michael saw where I went, but I didn't mind him finding me, anyway. That was the point, after all.

Turning around, I noticed a boxing ring sitting in the center of the room. It was surrounded by a variety of equipment and punching bags, as well as fifteen or so men, working out, sparring, and chatting. I quickly stepped behind one of the many columns spread throughout the room, looking around the corner to make sure no one had seen me.

The door behind me opened, and I jerked my head, seeing Michael step through, hell written all over his face.

He closed the door, straightened, and pinned me with his look that said my ass was grass.

Crooking his finger, he mouthed, "Come here," as he slowly approached me, probably trying to keep my antics quiet so I wouldn't embarrass him.

I tried to hold back my smile, but I knew he saw it.

Instead, I played. Spinning around, I walked around the perimeter of the room, careful to stay behind the columns. Then I slipped through another door, seeing him come after me, his lips tight, before I closed it on him.

But as soon as I looked down, saw the slate tile, and heard the running water, I knew I'd fucked up.

"Shit," I growled in a whisper.

I hesitated, thinking about going back, but I knew Michael was coming that way.

Putting my head down, I followed the short tunnel, passing a steam room, a sauna, and two large Jacuzzis, feeling eyes on me, and not so much as breathing as I passed a few guys lounging about on couches around the spa. Dashing into the adjoining locker room, I looked up and saw a young blond-haired man coming my way, so I veered to the left, down an empty aisle, and heard more voices. I stopped and hid myself at the end of a row of lockers.

Doors slammed on my left, two men chatted on my right, and Michael would be on my back any second.

I leaned against the cold steel, looking around and trying to figure out where the exit was. If there even was another one.

But then I jerked, a locker door slamming and its vibrations hitting my back.

"Mr. Torrance," a man called. "There's no smoking in here."

"Fuck off."

And chills immediately spread down my arms, making my heart skip a beat. I stilled, afraid to move.

I knew that voice. *Mr. Torrance.*

Slowly turning my head, I twisted my body around completely and inched toward the edge of the lockers. I peered around the side just enough, hoping not to see what I knew I would.

A lump stretched my throat. "Oh, shit," I whispered.

Damon Torrance.

He sat in a cushioned chair, leaning his head back with his eyes closed, droplets of water glistening down his neck, arms, and torso—bare since he only wore a towel around his waist.

He pinched a cigarette between his fingers and brought it to his lips, the ashen end burning orange as he inhaled. Then, just as I re- membered, he blew it out slowly, letting it drift up instead of out, looking more like fog than smoke as it dissipated in the air above him.

My stomach churned at the stench, bringing back memories of that night. I'd had to take two showers to get that smell off me.

I might have felt a little bad over the years about what happened to his friends, but to him . . . not so much.

Suddenly, a hand came down on my mouth, and I sucked in a quick breath, rearing back against a hard chest.

"I don't have time for this," Michael warned in my ear.

He released me, and I spun around, looking up at him. His eyes were hot with anger, and I guessed my plan hadn't worked. He wasn't amused.

"How come I didn't know that your friends were out?" I asked quietly.

"What interest is it of yours?"

What interest of mine? A lot, actually. I'd been with all of them the night before they were arrested. And more that happened later on that night that Michael probably wasn't aware of.

"I just thought it would've been a big deal," I said, keeping my voice down. "In Thunder Bay, anyway. I hadn't heard anything about their release, which seems strange."

"What's strange is that I'm still standing here wasting my time with you." He dipped his head down, hovering close. "Are you done yet?"

I stared ahead, his chest level with my gaze, and I furrowed my brows, trying to stay the ache behind my eyes.

I opened my mouth, speaking softly. "You don't have to . . ." I trailed off, unable to look at him.

"To what?"

I hardened my jaw to keep my chin from trembling as I looked up at him. "To speak to me like that. You don't have to be so mean."

He continued to stare down at me, his entire face hard and frozen.

"There was a time," I went on, softening my expression, "when you did like talking to me. Do you remember? When you noticed me and looked at me and—"

But I stopped, seeing his face inch closer as he planted his hands on the column behind my head.

"There are some places that aren't for you," he said slowly, filling each word with meaning as if talking to a child. "When you're wanted, you're invited. If you weren't invited, then you weren't wanted. Does that makes sense?"

He peered down at me, looking like he was explaining why I needed to eat my vegetables before dessert.

It's an easy enough concept, after all, Rika. Why can't you understand it? He was saying that I was in the way and a bother. He didn't want me around.

"You don't belong here, and you're not welcome. Do you understand?" he asked again.

I glued my teeth together, air pouring in and out of my nose as I tensed every goddamn muscle in my body, trying not to break. Lightning struck behind my eyes, making them ache and burn, and I couldn't remember ever feeling like this. He'd ignored me, condescended, and insulted on occasion, but the cruelty hurt beyond words.

"That was English, Rika," he barked, making me jump. "A dog listens better than you."

Tears immediately pooled, and my chin trembled. I swallowed the lump, feeling my stomach ache, and I felt like I wanted to sink into a hole, disappear, and forget.

Before he could enjoy the satisfaction of seeing me crumble, I shot out, pushing his arm away and breaking into tears as I ran back the way I'd come. Everything in my sight blurred as I passed the spas again and yanked open the locker room door, hurrying out as I fought against the sobs in my throat.

The hat spilled off my head, falling to the ground and freeing my ponytail. I ran through the boxing gym, not giving a shit who saw me, and pulled open the next door, wiping away the tears as I dashed into the hallway and down the stairs.

But then I crashed into another person halfway down, and I stopped, jerking my head up and my insides going cold.

"Kai?" I nearly whispered, stunned to see him.

And confused.

Damon was here. Kai was here. Was Will, as well? Were they all in Meridian City? I hadn't been certain if Michael even kept in touch with them while they were in jail, but it was obvious now that he had.

Kai cocked his head and took his hand out of his black pants, placing it on my arm to stabilize me. But I pulled my arm away.

He stared at me, his white shirt and black suit coat neatly pressed, making him just as good-looking as ever, although much more muscular than the last time I'd seen him.

I heard hard footsteps behind me and jerked my head around, seeing Michael come around the corner.

They were all together again?

I shot around Kai, continued down the stairs, and grabbed my bag off the floor before dashing out the door. Michael was one thing, but I didn't want to be near his friends.

"Rika!" I heard Michael yell behind me.

But the door closed, cutting him off, and I raced off the steps, the cool rain hitting my hair, face, and arms.

I hooked the bag over my head and ignored the valet attendant holding an umbrella out for me. "Need a cab, miss?"

I shook my head and turned right, heading down the sidewalk as light droplets covered my arms.

"Get my car!" I heard a bellow behind me and turned to see Michael barking at the attendant.

He then turned, locking eyes with me, and I spun back, hurrying away from him.

"Stop!" he ordered.

I pivoted on my heel, walking backward and crying out, "I'm gone! Okay? What more do you want?"

Turning around again, I hurried along the sidewalk.

But then Michael grabbed my bag strap and yanked it over my head, my neck twisting as he pulled it off.

I jerked around. "What the hell are you doing?"

He just walked away from me, though, carrying my bag as he stepped up to his car, the valet attendant handing him his keys.

Michael swung open one of the back doors and tossed my bag in, my phone and house keys with it, and stepped up to the front passenger-side door, pulling it open.

"Get in!" he demanded, anger written all over his face.

I breathed hard, shaking my head. What the fuck? I was half-tempted to beg the manager for a new set of keys and go buy a new fucking phone, just to show him.

But my books were in there, my class schedule, not to mention the birth certificate and immunization records that I'd had to let the admissions office make copies of after I'd left my advisor earlier.

I scowled, the tears gone and rage in its place.

Stepping up to the car, I jumped into the passenger seat and yanked the door out of his grasp, closing it on my own. As soon as I saw him round the front of the car, making his way for the driver's side, I twisted around, grabbed my bag out of the back seat, and pushed open the car door, darting out.

I didn't make it far.

Before my ass was even off the seat, Michael's hand crashed into my shoulder, grabbing my collar and hauling me back in.

I cried out, but he swiped the bag away and tossed it into the back seat once more.

"Mr. Crist, can I call for help?" The attendant appeared in my open door, sounding concerned.

Michael's hand was on my collarbone, holding me to the seat, and my face started to crack again as tears pooled.

"Sir." The attendant reached for me, concern on his face. "The young lady—"

"Don't touch her," Michael growled. "Close the door."

The attendant's mouth sat agape for a moment—it seemed like he wanted to argue—but he just looked at me and eventually backed away, shutting the door.

"I told you I didn't need a ride home," I gritted out. "You wanted me gone, so let me leave!"

He started up the car, the muscles in his neck flexing and his hair glistening with rain. "Last thing I need is my mother bitching because you went crying," he spat out.

My chest rose and fell, fury boiling under my skin as I turned around and planted my knees underneath me, leaning over to his side of the car.

"I've got more mettle than you give me credit for," I yelled, "so you can go fuck yourself!"

He darted his arm out, wrapping his hand around the back of my neck and yanking me in. I whimpered, feeling the burn in my scalp from his fingers fisting in my hair.

"What do you want from me? Huh?" he asked, breathing hard and glaring at me. "What do you see in me that's so fucking fascinating?"

I trembled, just holding his eyes. What *did* I see in him? The answer was so easy I didn't even have to think about it. It was the same thing he saw in me all those years ago down in the catacombs.

The hunger.

The need to break away, the desire to find the one person on the planet who would understand me, the temptation to go after all the things they tell us we can't have . . .

I saw me, and through all the times growing up that I felt alone or like I was searching for something I couldn't put into words, I didn't feel so lost when he was around.

It was the only time I didn't feel lost.

I shook my head, dropping my eyes as a silent tear spilled over. "Nothing," I nearly whispered, despair tightening my throat. "I'm just a stupid kid."

I inched away, feeling him slowly release his grasp in my hair. Shifting my feet out from under me, I sat down on my seat and swallowed the hard lump in my throat, pulling the collar of my plaid shirt tighter around my neck, covering my left side.

He didn't want to know me. He didn't like me.

And I wanted that fact to stop hurting. I was so sick of dreaming.

Sick of having forced a relationship with Trevor because I believed he would set me straight, and sick of wanting a nightmare that treated me like a dog.

Sick of both of them.

I straightened my back and stared at my lap, trying to force the weariness from my voice.

"I want to walk home," I told him, grabbing my bag from the back and taking hold of the door handle.

And then I paused, still not looking at him. "I'm sorry about sneaking off inside. It won't happen again."

Opening the door, I immediately stepped out into the downpour, thunder cracking overhead as I took the long way home.

CHAPTER 7

MICHAEL

Present

God, what was she doing to me?

Did she really think she was just a stupid kid? Did she really not see how every fucking person in Thunder Bay adored her?

I breathed hard, pulling my open collar away from the heat on my neck. Hell, I'd even caught my piece-of-shit father looking at her once or twice over the years. Everyone thought the world of Rika, so why did she act like mine was the only opinion that mattered to her?

I marched into Realm, a dark nightclub downtown, and glanced upward, seeing my teammates hanging around the balcony of the VIP lounge above. There was a press event tonight, but it was the last thing I could focus on even though I should. I needed my brain on something else.

Heading for the bar, I placed my hands on the marble counter, jerking my chin at the bartender. He nodded, knowing what to get. Damon, Will, and Kai were already here, Realm being a favorite of ours.

I bowed my head, closing my eyes and trying to calm down.

I was losing. When she was around, she made everything else small, and all I could see was her. All the years of misery she caused my friends suddenly didn't matter, my focus blurred, and I lost sight of what she'd done and how my friends had suffered.

And how she needed to pay.

I hated her.

I had to hate her.

I didn't have to force her in the car today. I didn't care about the tears in her eyes or the way she couldn't look at me before she climbed out.

I didn't want to wipe away the hurt, I didn't want to touch her, and I didn't want to get her to scream at me again, because I'd never been so turned on.

She got out of the car, left me behind, and, according to the doorman, hadn't left Delcour since getting home that afternoon.

Good. Let her get used to that cage.

The bartender stepped over, carrying a fresh bottle of Johnnie Walker Blue Label and a rocks glass, setting them down in front of me. I poured a double shot and tipped back the glass, taking down the whole damn thing.

"Where the hell have you been?"

I tensed, hearing Kai's voice at my side.

But I just poured another double, not answering him.

I'm just a stupid kid. My chest rose and fell faster, and I shot back the drink, taking all of it down again.

I set the glass down, blinking long and hard.

"Jesus. Are you okay?" he asked, sounding more worried than angry now.

"I'm fine."

He placed both hands on the bar, leaning in as he peered over at me. "What was she doing there today?"

I downed a third shot, starting to feel the burn in my stomach blanket my veins in a warm buzz. The edges were blurring, and the tips of my fingers hummed.

I shook my head, setting the glass down. Out of everyone in my life—my father, my brother, my friends—it ended up being her who drove me to drink. Her fucking eyes, going from defiant to mischievous to hurt to on fire, and then finally, to broken.

Don't be alone with her.

"Michael?" Kai prompted.

I let out a hard sigh, running my fingers over the top of my head. "Could you just . . ." I gritted out, "fucking shut up for five minutes and let me get my head straight?"

"Why isn't your head straight already?" he demanded. "Because, you know, we had a plan. Take everything and then take her, but all I see you doing is dicking around."

I immediately straightened and darted my hand out, grabbing his collar.

He shoved my arm to the side, shaking his head and sneering, "Don't go there. I want our little monster, with her big doe eyes, kneeling at my feet, and I'm not waiting anymore. I'd like you in on this, but I don't need you."

Not waiting anymore. She just got here! She was in Meridian City because of me. At Delcour because of me. Isolated because of me.

And there were only a couple more things to take from her. They hadn't waited that long.

But then I looked away. *Yeah, they had.* They'd waited far too long.

I pushed the bottle and glass away. "Where are they?" I asked him.

Kai stayed silent, still looking pissed, but turned around and led the way.

I followed, the hard bass of the music vibrating under my feet as we walked through the club toward the private areas in back.

Kai and I had never fought in the past. I shouldn't have taken that shot at him.

But for some reason, he kept challenging me, and I felt farther away from him now than when he was in prison. What the hell was going on? I expected Damon and Will in my face. Not Kai.

In many ways, he was the same as he'd always been. The thinker, the reasonable one, the brother who always looked out for the rest of us . . . But in many ways he had changed beyond recognition. He never smiled anymore, he took courses of action he wouldn't have in high school, even knowing the consequences, and not once did I see him do one thing for pleasure since he'd gotten out. Damon and Will partied, drank, smoked, and buried themselves in pussy the first two weeks they were free.

Kai, on the other hand, hadn't had a single drink or a woman in his bed. Not that I knew of anyway. Hell, I didn't even think he listened to music anymore.

He needed to lose control, because I was starting to get concerned about whatever he was bottling up.

Following him into a semiprivate area with an L-shaped sofa and a table, I spotted the back of Will's head, slouched against the couch, and Damon relaxing across the table from him with his hand resting between some girl's thighs.

Damon was the exact opposite of Kai. He rarely thought about anything he did, and if someone put a wall in his way—justified or not—he came in swinging without hesitation or regret. This had been a useful quality on our high school basketball team. His reputation spread, and just the sight of him by the opposite team had them pissing themselves.

He also more than made up for all the vices Kai wasn't indulging in.

I stopped next to the couch, jerking my chin at Damon to get rid of the girl. He shifted, taking his hand out from between her legs, and nudged her thigh, sending her off.

Kai took a seat and Will sat up, all of them turning their eyes on me. Impatience and agitation were clear in their expressions, and I crossed my arms over my chest, suddenly feeling like there was a wall between them and me.

Because, after three years, they now had a bond that didn't include me. Everything was fucked because of her.

I narrowed my eyes on Kai. "You okay to drive?"

"Why wouldn't I be?"

I nodded, reaching into my pocket and taking out my keys. "Let's do this, then," I told them. "You guys ready?"

Will perked up, looking at me, surprised. "The mother?"

I nodded again.

He shot Damon a look, smiling.

"How gone do we want her?" Kai inquired, suddenly back in the game.

"Buried," I replied. "I want no Fanes for Rika to run to. We'll go to Thunder Bay tonight."

"You guys go," Damon teased, leaning back and putting an arm behind his head. "I'll stay and keep an eye on Rika. She's more fun to look at."

"Have you seen her mother?" I raised my eyebrows, amusement lifting the corners of my mouth. Christiane Fane was still young and fairly fucking gorgeous. She wasn't Rika, but she was still beautiful. "You're coming with us."

There was no way I trusted him alone here with Rika.

Reaching into the breast pocket of my black suit jacket and pulling out a small baggie, I tossed it to Damon. He shot up his free hand and caught the bag, glancing around to see if anyone was looking.

He then held it up, examining the contents, as Kai and Will took interest, as well.

Suddenly, Damon's lips spread in a wide smile and he looked over at me like I'd just made his night.

Yeah, I suspected Damon would know what it was. Sick fuck.

Rohypnol was known as a date-rape drug, used to make its

victims pliable and weak in no more than fifteen minutes. Surprisingly, I had little trouble getting ahold of it, too. A few of my teammates were on something or other illegal, be it recreational or body enhancing, and all I'd needed was to get in contact with their dealer to get the pills.

If we didn't find Rika's mother drunk as usual, one of those pills would help make her very agreeable.

"Give it to me." Kai looked pointedly at Damon, holding out his hand for the baggie.

Damon arched an eyebrow, doing nothing.

"Now," Kai insisted, still holding out his hand.

Damon smirked and opened the bag, tapping out a pill into Kai's hand. "You only need one for the mom. These things are pretty effective."

Will breathed out a laugh, shaking his head but not sounding the least bit amused with the joke. Even he had limits.

Not that Damon didn't. We just didn't know for sure. If we'd ever seen him use anything like that, we would've killed him, but he also never gave us the impression that he wasn't just that fucked up.

For now, we'd adopted an "if we don't see it, it's not a problem" attitude.

Kai sat with the pill in his hand, staring at Damon, and then darted out, snatching the bag out of his hand.

Damon laughed, standing up and smoothing down his black jacket. "It was a joke," he grumbled. "You really think I need to rape women?"

Kai stood up, slipping the bag into his breast pocket. "Well, you were in jail."

"Oh, Jesus," I breathed out, running my hand through my hair. "What the fuck is the matter with you?" I stared hard at Kai as Damon stood and turned on him, as well, his jaw flexing and his black eyes ready to rip him apart.

But Kai didn't back down. They stood head to head, both of them the same height, as they glared at each other.

"I didn't rape her," Damon gritted out.

I shook my head. Why the hell would Kai take a shot like that?

"We know that," I answered for Kai, pushing Damon back.

The girl had been underage, and Damon had been nineteen. He shouldn't have done it, but he hadn't forced her, either.

Unfortunately, the law believed differently. Minors couldn't consent to anything, and Damon had simply fucked up. But it wasn't rape.

Kai stared at Damon and then faltered, dropping his eyes and taking shallow breaths. "Sorry," he said under his breath. "I'm just on edge."

I was glad he'd noticed.

"Good. Use it tonight," I said, hooking an arm around his neck and bringing him in. "Your nightmare is over. Hers is just starting."

The hot spray of the shower cascaded over my shoulders and back, and I closed my eyes, trying to drown out all the noise of the other players in the locker room.

The last few days had sucked. I'd done everything I could to stay away from Delcour, unless it was to sleep, but it had been hard. I didn't want to be anywhere else.

The mother was taken care of, and it wouldn't be long before Rika noticed, but the run-in with her at Hunter-Bailey had thrown me off. I knew I needed to keep my distance for now.

The one thing I'd learned about what it took to be strong was recognizing and acknowledging any weakness and then making adjustments. I couldn't be near her.

Not yet.

When I went off to college, it wasn't that hard. Out of sight, out of mind. Or, at least, out of the forefront of my mind.

But knowing I could run into her at any time now, look down and see her in her apartment, catch her eye as we passed in the lobby . . . I hadn't planned on what it would be like to see her every day. Having her close was entirely too tempting.

She wasn't sixteen anymore, and the fight I put up then to restrain myself was no longer necessary. She was a woman, no matter the nervous eyes, trembling lips, and tough little act she displayed. I could barely wait.

She was only a floor away, and I had the key to her apartment burning a hole in my pocket. I needed her on her hands and knees as I took whatever I wanted, whenever and however *hard* I wanted it. I was going crazy.

"Shit."

I could feel my dick hardening, and I dropped my eyes, seeing it standing straight out and ready.

Goddammit. I blew out a sigh and shut the shower off, thankful that I was in here alone.

There were several players loitering around the locker room, one of the assistant coaches having scheduled special drills with a few of us today, but I'd taken my time in the shower, in no hurry to get home.

Wrapping a towel around my waist, I grabbed a second one and dried off my chest and arms as I walked toward my locker. Seeing a few other players standing around and still feeling my dick hard, I placed the towel in front me, not wanting any sideways glances.

Digging into my shelves, I pulled out my phone, seeing a few texts from the guys. Since Rika's mother was gone, they were ready for stage two.

I tossed my towel down and slipped on my boxer briefs and jeans and then grabbed my watch, fastening it to my wrist.

My phone started ringing. I picked it up, seeing the name on the screen.

I steeled my jaw, annoyed. Talking to my brother always pissed me off. However, he rarely called, so curiosity nipped at me. I slid my finger over the screen, answering it.

"Trevor," I said, holding the phone to my ear.

"You know, Michael . . ." he started, not even saying hello. "I always thought this brotherly connection you and I were supposed to have would eventually form."

I narrowed my eyes, staring ahead at nothing as I listened.

"I thought, maybe when I grew up, we'd have more in common or we'd speak to each other in more than two-word sentences," he went on. "I used to try to blame it on you. You were cold and distant, and you never gave us a chance to be brothers."

I gripped the phone in my hand, standing frozen. The voices of the players around me faded.

"But then you know what?" he asked, a sharp edge to his voice. "When I was about sixteen I realized something. It wasn't your fault. I honestly hated you as much as you hated me. For the same . . . single . . . reason."

I clenched my teeth, lifting my chin.

"Her."

"Her?" I fished.

"You know who I'm talking about," he stated. "She always had her eyes on you, wanting you."

I sneered, shaking my head. "Trevor, your girlfriend is your issue."

Not that she was his girlfriend anymore—I'd heard about the breakup—but I liked thinking of her as his. It would make all of this so much sweeter.

"But that's not true, is it?" he replied. "Because when I was a teenager, I realized it wasn't just her. It was you, too."

I glared ahead.

"You wanted her," he insisted, "and you hated that I was always around, and you definitely hated that she was meant for me. You couldn't be my brother because I had the one thing you wanted."

He paused and then continued. "And I hated you because the one thing I had wanted you instead."

My heart started drumming harder.

"So when did it start?" he asked, his tone casual while my stomach knotted. "When we were kids? When her body filled out and you saw how fucking hot she was? Or maybe . . . it was when I told you last year how her cunt was the tightest thing I'd ever felt?"

I squeezed the phone in my hand.

"No matter what . . ." he taunted, "I'll always have that on you."

I curled my fist, every bone in my hand aching.

"So now that you got her to Delcour," he went on, "finally all to yourself, and you do to her whatever it is you have planned, remember that I will get her back, and it will be me who puts a ring on her finger and keeps her forever."

"You think that hurts me?" I bit out.

"It won't be you I'm trying to hurt," he threw back. "If that slut spreads her legs for you, I will make sure marrying me will be the nightmare of her life."

CHAPTER 8

ERIKA

Three Years Ago

Trevor hadn't spoken to me since he'd brought me home from the catacombs. He'd been an asshole in the car, too, and the only reason I'd left with him was because I was afraid he'd tell my mom.

Or worse. Tell Mrs. Crist and get Michael into trouble.

Michael. I still felt the heat on the hand he'd held today. I stood in the Crist kitchen, dishing spoonfuls of food onto a plate, playing over the afternoon in my head. Had he really meant all those things he'd said today? What would've happened if Trevor hadn't come in?

I blew out a long breath, heat stirring low in my belly. What was going to happen now? Would he finish what he'd started?

"The Vengeful One" by Disturbed echoed through the house, probably coming from the indoor basketball court, where I knew Will, Damon, Kai, and Michael were all goofing off, playing ball. It was already dark, and soon they'd be heading out for the night.

I heard my phone vibrate, and I glanced at it lying on the counter, seeing *Mom* on the screen.

"Hey," I answered, wrapping tinfoil around a plate of food Mrs. Crist insisted I take to my mother when I ate here.

"Hey, sweetie," she chirped, trying to sound energetic. I knew she was anything but; however, she tried to put up a good front for me. Between the tranquilizers that kept her numb and the fact that she almost never left the house, I knew the guilt that weighed on her was starting to exceed the depression.

"I'll be home soon," I told her, nodding a thanks to Mrs. Haynes, the Crists' cook, and setting the plate down on the counter as I left the kitchen. "Are you up for a movie tonight? We could rewatch *Thor* again. I know you like his hammer."

"Rika!"

I snorted, walking into the dining room and seeing the table already set for dinner. "Well, then, pick a new movie to download," I suggested. "We still haven't eaten over here yet, but as soon as we're done I'll change my clothes and head back home. I'm bringing you a plate."

Even though I knew she'd barely eat any of it. Her appetite hardly existed anymore.

Trevor had dropped me off at home earlier this afternoon, but after I'd checked on my mom, I'd trailed back down the road to the Crists' for dinner. My mother was always welcome, of course, but it was only me who ever joined them. No one wanted me eating alone, so my mom, out of guilt, allowed me to have meals here for some conversation and laughter. The Crists could give me what she couldn't.

Or what she refused to give me.

Over time, though, my need to be here became stronger. More than just for dinner or to play video games with Trevor when we were growing up.

It was for the distant sound of a basketball thumping against a floor somewhere in the house or the way my body would hum and every hair would stand on end when he walked into a room. I just liked being here if he was here, despite Trevor's growing possessiveness.

I heard my mother sigh as I walked up to the mirror hanging on the wall.

"I'm fine," she insisted. "You don't need to bring a plate tonight. Go out with your friends. Please."

I opened my mouth to speak, but then the dull beat of the music in the house suddenly died, and I jerked my head to the doorway of the dining room, hearing voices and laughter coming from somewhere in the house, getting closer.

I glanced in the mirror, fixing the collar of my school uniform, making sure my scar was mostly hidden.

"I don't want to go out," I said, heading to the table and sitting down.

"*I* want you to go out."

Leaning over the table, I grabbed a roll and put it on my plate before the boys took them all. "Mom—" I started to argue.

But she cut me off. "No," she said, sounding unusually stern. "It's Friday night. Go have some fun. I'll be fine."

"But . . ." I trailed off, shaking my head. Was this her overcompensating or something? She knew damn well I went out, just maybe not as much as she would like.

"Fine," I drawled. "I'll call Noah and see . . ." But then I stopped, hearing thunder roll down the hallway.

My heart picked up pace, and I turned my head toward the noise. Voices, laughter, and a couple of howls drifted in, and my feet soaked in the vibration off the floor.

I gripped the phone in my hand, speaking quickly, "Okay," I answered. "I'll see what Noah's up to tonight, but if I need bail money or I come home pregnant, you only have yourself to blame."

"I trust you," she replied, sounding amused. "And I love you."

"Love you, too." And I hung up, setting the phone on the table.

Trevor walked in the dining room first, having been in the media room, probably waiting for me to join him like I often did. He thought he had a right to be angry, but whatever he thought was between us, we were still just friends. He had no right to take me out of there today, and I was sick of him putting on a show to everyone like I belonged to him.

He took the seat next to me, as usual, pulling out the chair and plopping down. He immediately started grabbing food to load onto his plate.

Mrs. Crist walked in next, dressed in a tennis skirt and a white polo, probably having just come from the club. She smiled at me and touched my shoulder as she walked to her seat. "How's Christiane?" she asked.

I nodded, laying my napkin in my lap. "Fine. We're working our way through all of Chris Hemsworth's movies."

She laughed and began serving herself as loud voices started to fill the room.

"It's already dark out," I heard Will say, sounding out of breath.

I glanced up, seeing Michael and all of his friends charge into the dining room. My heart fluttered, and I tensed, the large dining room suddenly ten times smaller with their huge forms filling the space.

They were sweaty and breathing hard, having just come from the indoor court. It was an addition that was made to the house for Michael's fourteenth birthday, when his mother realized he wasn't kidding about basketball and his father relented. He loved the game, much to Mr. Crist's distaste.

"Don't be in such a damn rush." Damon pushed Will's head forward as he walked behind him. "I want to enjoy tonight."

They descended on the table, towering over us as they grabbed their plates—Michael dropping his basketball to the floor, where it slowly rolled to the wall near the fireplace—and loaded food like wolves, oblivious to the rest of us waiting to see what was left over.

"Rika, get your milk," Mrs. Crist whisper-yelled, and I looked at her, both of us grinning and sharing in the joke. She had the cook buy chocolate milk for me, but it always ended up disappearing before I barely got a glass out of it.

I reached over, quickly uncapping the container and pouring a glass before setting it back down again.

"Where's Dad?" Trevor asked.

"Still in the city, unfortunately," his mother answered.

"Yeah, right."

I looked up at the whisper, seeing Michael tower over me as he reached for the chocolate milk in front of me.

It was no secret that their father kept multiple women. Well, actually, it was a secret. One that everyone knew but no one talked about. Including Michael. His mother was the only person I was sure he would never hurt, which was why I was the only one to hear his snide remark.

"Hell yeah," Will gushed over some sweet potato dish Mrs. Haynes had set down as he piled the mushy concoction high on his plate.

"Hand me two." Damon held out his plate to Kai, who doled out deviled eggs.

They weren't sitting, which meant they were probably taking their food off to the media room for privacy. They had plans for tonight to talk about, no doubt.

But they didn't get far.

"Michael? All of you, sit down now," Mrs. Crist ordered, pointing her finger.

The guys stopped and smiled to themselves, indulging her as they turned back around and took seats.

Michael sat in his father's place at the head of the table, his friends on his right with Trevor between him and me on his left.

Everyone dug in.

"I'm going to trust that I don't have to worry about tonight," Mrs. Crist warned, picking up her fork and gazing around at the guys.

Michael shrugged, uncapping my chocolate milk and drinking from the container without answering her.

"We have no choice but to keep it low-key," Kai stepped in and answered, humor thick in his voice. "Michael would lose his spot on the team if we wound up on the news."

"Again," Will finished, pride evident in his green eyes, before sticking a forkful of potatoes into his mouth.

While other teens might spend Devil's Night toilet papering houses, nailing tires, and smashing pumpkins on the streets, the Horsemen were rumored to take their pranks a little further.

Fires, break-ins, vandalism, and destruction of property were all credited to them even though there was never any proof, their faces being covered by masks as they were.

But we always knew who it was. And even though the cops probably did, too, when you're born with the blessing of the right name, connections, and money, you'll use it.

Damon Torrance, son of a media mogul.

Kai Mori, son of an influential socialite and banker.

William Grayson III, grandson of Senator Grayson.

And Michael Crist, son of a real estate developer.

The boys may have shunned the rigidity and expectations of their parents, but they certainly enjoyed the umbrella of their protection.

"Is it good to be back?" Mrs. Crist asked as she cut a piece of lettuce. "I know it must be hard, being separated at college."

"It is hard," Will said mournfully. "But I just call one of the guys when my heart needs a hug."

I pursed my lips, trying to hide my smile, as Damon snorted across the table.

"Actually," Kai started, leaning back in his chair. "I'm considering transferring to Westgate. I'm bored at Braeburn, and Westgate has a much better swim team, so—"

"Great," Trevor cut in. "You and Michael can continue your bromance now."

"Aw," Will cooed, looking over the table at Trevor. "You feeling left out? Come here, pretty boy. I'll show you some attention." And then he leaned back in his chair, patting his thigh for Trevor to sit in his lap.

I snorted, bowing my head and feeling eyes on me. Probably Trevor's glare.

I picked up my fork to start eating, ignoring him. Trevor didn't tolerate Michael's friends any more than he tolerated his brother.

I looked up, seeing Mrs. Haynes through the doorway to the kitchen holding the house phone and mouthing something to Mrs. Crist.

"Excuse me for a moment." Mrs. Crist stood, pushed out her chair, and walked past the table, disappearing through the doorway.

As soon as she was gone, Trevor shot out of his chair, and I jerked my eyes up, seeing him scowling at his brother.

"Stay away from her," he ordered.

I let my eyes fall closed as I tipped my chin down. Embarrassment heated my cheeks, and I could feel everyone's eyes on me.

Jesus, Trevor.

No one said anything for a few moments, but judging from the silence and lack of movement as I stared at my plate, everyone was waiting for Michael.

"Who?" I finally heard him ask.

And I swallowed, hearing a couple of quiet laughs go off around the table.

"Rika," Trevor growled. "She's mine."

I heard Michael breathe out a laugh, and out of the corner of my eye I saw him push back his chair and stand up. He tossed down his napkin on his plate and grabbed the milk.

"Who?" he asked again.

Will bowed his head, laughing louder this time as his body shook. I looked up, seeing Damon, smiling wide and looking smug.

I wanted to fold into myself and disappear. That stung.

I must've been amusing today. A momentary distraction for

Michael, and now it was back to being nothing but something to sidestep as we passed each other in the house.

Trevor's anger radiated, and I stared ahead while they all got up from their chairs, laughing and gloating as they followed Michael out of the dining room.

I wasn't sure who I was most angry with: Trevor or them. At least I knew what Trevor wanted. He didn't mind-fuck me.

Trevor sat back down, hard breaths making his chest rise and fall fast.

I pushed my plate away, no longer hungry. "Trevor . . ." I started, feeling guilty, but I didn't know what else to do with him. "I'm not yours. I'm not anyone's."

"You'd fuck him in a heartbeat if he looked at you twice."

I scowled, hardening my jaw. I was sick of being pushed around. Shoving back my chair, I bolted up and stormed out of the dining room.

My eyes burned with anger, and I charged across the foyer, noticing the door leading to the garage was open. I glanced up, seeing Michael toss a black duffel to Kai, who stowed it in the G-Class.

He turned his hooded eyes on me but then immediately dropped them, carrying on with loading his car as if I wasn't there.

I jogged up the stairs and powered down the hallway to my room. Slamming the door closed behind me, I breathed hard, shaking and running my fingers over the top of my hair, trying not to cry.

I needed to get out of here.

The Crist house was becoming a cage. I constantly had to fend off one brother while putting up a front of indifference with the other, and I needed some fun.

Noah. He was no doubt hitting the warehouse tonight. I'd call him and see when he was leaving.

Slipping off my flats and tearing off my uniform, I opened a dresser drawer and dug out some clothes I kept here. I unhooked my bra, discarding it on the floor.

My skin crawled, and I yanked on a tank top and pair of jeans, wanting nothing more than to scream my fucking lungs off.

Assholes. All of them.

Slipping on some sneakers, I grabbed my black hoodie off the hook in the closet and hurried back down the stairs, hearing the shower running in the bathroom as I passed. The guys were probably getting ready to leave.

I grabbed my phone and keys from the entryway table and left through the front door, pulling on my hood and stuffing my hands into the front pocket of my sweatshirt.

Only October 30, and the chill in the air already had a bite. Nearly all the trees were bare, and all the brown, orange, yellow, and red leaves that had fallen now graced the lawn. Mrs. Crist never made the gardeners remove them, knowing it would be the last bit of color we'd enjoy before the snow started in a few weeks.

The cold washed over me, and I slowly started to calm as I walked down the driveway.

The towering branches above, like veins across the sky, melted together, creating a bare, dead canopy over the driveway that would be right at home in any Tim Burton film. I half expected to see some creepy fog floating across the ground at me.

Jack-o'-lanterns lined the driveway, glowing with their firelight, and I inhaled the smell of burning wood coming from somewhere. There were several bonfires going tonight, everyone either enjoying the mischief or taking part in it.

There were also some parties, and I hoped Noah was up for some fun tonight. I needed a distraction.

Reaching the big gate, I stuck my key into the adjoining door, which allowed anyone on foot to enter or exit without needing to disturb Edward, the butler, to open the larger gate. I used it often, since my home was close enough to walk back and forth, and Michael used it, since he took jogs off the property.

Closing the smaller gate—it automatically locked behind me—I turned left and kept to the side of the road as I made my way home.

My hair spilled out of the hoodie, hanging down my chest on both sides, as I hurried down the black pavement. It was already dark out, but the roads weren't completely without light. Lanterns from the Crist estate on the other side of the rock wall and—soon—lights from my family's property offered some comfort from the fear of being out here alone. Especially with the desolation of having nothing but a forest to my right on the other side of the road.

When you were scared, your senses grew sharper. Fireflies in the night might look like a pair of eyes or the wind in the trees might sound like whispers. I walked faster, feeling the chill seep through my jeans.

But looking ahead, I spotted lights falling across the dark road. I spun around, seeing a car slowing to a stop right behind me.

I pinched my eyebrows together, my heart thumping harder in my chest as I kept walking backward.

What were they doing? They were on the wrong side of the road.

I chewed my bottom lip, holding my hand over my eyes to shield them from the bright headlights. I continued to back away, ready to bolt if I needed, but I stopped, seeing the driver's-side door open and black boots hit the pavement.

Michael stepped in front of the headlights, wearing jeans and the same black hoodie from earlier today.

What was he doing?

"Get in the car," he ordered.

My stomach flipped at his command. *Get in his car?*

I turned my eyes on the windows, seeing the three dark forms of Kai, Will, and Damon inside.

But I steeled myself, having had enough whiplash from Michael today. He finally says more than two words to me and then turns around and acts like he doesn't even know my name at the dinner table?

"Don't bother," I told him, not even trying to hide my sneer. "I can make my own way home."

And I turned around, heading for my house.

"We're not taking you home," he said, his voice dark.

I stopped and turned my head, my heart thumping in my chest. His light brown hair, still wet from his shower, shined in the light, and I saw a dare in his eyes.

He turned around and walked to the passenger door right behind the driver's seat and opened it.

I pivoted my whole body back around, facing him.

His voice was soft and sultry. "Get in."

I dug my fingers into my thighs, trying to keep myself from fidgeting as the presence of four men, all more than six feet tall and well over 180 each, filled the pitch-black interior of Michael's SUV.

He sat in front of me, driving, while Kai sat next to him in the passenger's seat. Will sat to my right, and I could feel his eyes on me.

But it was Damon at my back who made the hair on my neck stand up. I tried to ignore the tension, but I couldn't resist. I inched my chin over my shoulder anyway and glanced at him sitting on the bench seat behind me.

I immediately wanted to hide.

His dead eyes were on me as smoke drifted out from between his lips, floating above him, and it scared the shit out of me how calm he was. Both of his arms hung around the back of the seat, and he tipped his chin down, just holding my gaze.

I quickly turned back around again, spotting Will next to me, chewing a piece of gum and grinning at me like a cocky little shit who knew I was about to piss myself.

I wondered if they knew why Michael had picked me up.

"Let the Sparks Fly" by Thousand Foot Krutch blared out of the speakers, cutting into my ears, and I forced myself to calm down, inhaling a slow, deep breath.

We drove through town, passing restaurants and local hangouts bustling with teenagers, and continued into the country. After twenty minutes of nothing but loud music, Michael turned down the radio and veered up a dark gravel road, his SUV slowly climbing the steep incline into the trees.

Where the hell were we going?

We weren't in Thunder Bay anymore, but we weren't that far outside of town, either. I'd never been up here or hung out in the smaller communities outside of ours.

Will reached down between his legs and dug into a black duffel, pulling out masks.

I watched as he tossed Damon's black one to him, tapped Kai on his shoulder, handing him his silver one, and set Michael's red one on the console between him and Kai.

Will smiled at me, flaring his eyes like a little devil before slipping his horrid white mask over his face.

Jesus, what were we doing?

I prayed that I wouldn't have to watch them jump some poor guy who'd mistakenly offended them or witness them robbing a jewelry store. Not that I'd ever heard of them doing things like that, but I really had no idea what I was in for.

I definitely knew we weren't merely toilet papering a car or spray-painting a street sign, though.

Or maybe it wasn't "we." Maybe they didn't want me to do anything with them at all. Who knew why I was here? Maybe I was the getaway driver. Maybe the lookout.

Maybe the bait.

"Hey, Michael?" I heard Will's muffled voice. "She doesn't have a mask."

I shot my eyes up to the rearview mirror, seeing Michael's gaze meet mine, a hint of a smile on his face.

"Uh-oh," he taunted, and Kai laughed at his side. I folded my arms over my chest, trying not to look nervous.

We pulled to a stop on what looked like an abandoned street. I peered out the windows and took in the small old houses—broken, dilapidated, and dark—with their busted windows and crumbling roofs.

"What is this place?" I asked as Michael shut off the car.

Damon's large body climbed up from the back, following Will out of the car, and before I knew it I was left alone.

Twisting my head, I saw them step onto a worn lawn in front of a house, Michael having put on his mask, as well.

Were there people up here? The tiny community appeared deserted, so why wear masks?

I hesitated a moment before letting out a sigh and opening the door. I'd kept my hood up, but I pulled it farther down over my eyes, just in case.

The light breeze blew my hair as I walked around the car, and I looked up, seeing Will carrying the duffel into a house, followed by Damon and Kai.

There was no door.

I stuffed my hands into my middle pocket, stopping next to Michael, who simply stared at the crumbling structure. His hood was drawn, covering his hair, and only the small amount of light coming from the moon showed the red profile of the mask. Inside the house, I saw flickers of light. The boys must have flashlights.

I clutched the small box in my pocket, hearing the wooden

matchsticks inside jiggle. I'd forgotten I slipped them in there the last time I wore the sweatshirt.

Michael turned his head and looked down at me, his eyes nearly black voids that I could barely make out. My heart caught in my throat, and I felt like I'd been flipped upside down.

That damn mask.

He reached into my sweatshirt pocket, and I pulled my hands out, wondering what he was doing. He took out the matchbox and held it in his palm.

"Why do you have these?" he asked. He must've heard them shake in my pocket, too.

I shrugged, taking the matchbox back. "My dad collected matchboxes from restaurants and hotels when he went on business trips," I told him, sliding open the box and bringing it up to my nose. "I took a liking to the smell. It's like . . ."

Without thinking, I closed my eyes and inhaled through my nose, the sulfur and phosphorous instantly making me smile.

"Like what?"

I closed the box and looked up, feeling lighter for some reason. "Like Christmas morning and sparklers rolled into one. I kept the collection close to me after . . ."

After he died.

I kept all of the little matchboxes in an old cigar box, but I started carrying one with me after he died.

I stuffed the box into my pocket again, realizing I'd never told anyone that before.

I peered up at him, narrowing my eyes. "Why did you bring me along tonight?"

He faced forward, staring at the house again. "Because I meant what I said in the catacombs today."

"That's not what it sounded like at the dinner table," I argued.

"I've known you my entire life, and you act like you barely know my name. What is it with you and Trevor, and why do I get the feeling that . . ."

He stared ahead, unmoving. "That what?"

I dropped my eyes, thinking. "That it has something to do with me."

Michael finally took notice of me today. He'd told me things that I'd only ever dreamed of hearing, and he put into words everything I was feeling.

And then at dinner, with Trevor, he'd shut down again. Just like the old Michael. I wasn't even in the room to him. Did I have something to do with why he and Trevor never got along?

But then I shook my head. *No.* That would be ridiculous. I wasn't that important to Michael. His and Trevor's issues stemmed from something else.

He remained silent, not answering, and my cheeks heated with embarrassment. I shouldn't have said that. God, I was a stupid kid.

I didn't wait for him to answer or continue to ignore me. Climbing the small incline into the yard, I stepped onto the porch, hearing it whine like a dying animal under our weight as Michael fell in behind me. Hurrying into the house, I spotted the boys flashing their lights around and exploring the various rooms.

A ripe, pungent scent hit my nose, and I winced as I looked around and took in the old house.

The place was uninhabitable.

Old furniture, stained and ripped, was strewn about, while piles of wooden debris, looking like it had once been chairs and other furniture, sat in corners. Probably waiting to be used as firewood.

All the windows I could see were broken, and I dropped my eyes, seeing garbage and puddles on the floor among small glass vials, pipes, and needles.

I twisted up my lips, hating this place already.

Why would Michael want to come here? I couldn't deny that dark and dangerous held a lot of allure, but old filthy mattresses on the floor, stained with fuck knows what, and dirty needles strewn about?

This place was ugly. I didn't want to be here.

I cocked my head, peering in front of me and seeing an open door ahead. When one of the guys' flashlights danced across the room, I vaguely made out spray paint on a white wall inside the door. It looked like the entry to a basement.

I definitely didn't want to go down there, either.

But then I lurched forward, a body passing mine, shoving my shoulder.

"You shouldn't be here," Will warned, walking past and looking over his shoulder at me. "This house isn't safe. A girl got violated here a few months ago."

"Raped," Damon taunted, whipping around to stand in front of me and getting in my face. I immediately reared back.

"She was drugged and taken downstairs." He jerked his head behind him, gesturing to the basement, with thrill in his eyes.

My breath shook as I swallowed the lump in my throat.

A girl got attacked here? I pinched my eyebrows together, fear speeding up my breathing.

"Yeah," I heard Kai's voice at my back, "she was tied up, stripped naked . . . Can't tell you how many guys went at her. They were lining up for their turns."

I spun around, backing up in the other direction as Kai inched toward me with a look in his eyes.

But then I ran into another body at my back and stopped. This time it was Will, his green eyes heated as he cocked his head down at me like a challenge.

What the hell were they doing?

I whipped my head around, seeing Damon close in, too, his black eyes looking like a void in the darkness of his mask.

Kai looked up, asking Will in a light voice, "I don't even think they caught them all, did they?"

"No," Will said playfully, "I think there's still a few running around loose."

"Like four."

I heard Michael's threat, and I jerked my head, widening my eyes as he closed in on my side, completing the cage.

Shit. My lungs emptied, my heart jackhammered in my chest, and I caught sight of the dirty mattress sitting on the floor.

Bile rose in my throat.

But then all of a sudden, laughter broke out, and I jerked my eyes up, seeing their bodies shaking with amusement as they backed away from me.

"It's just a crack house, Rika," Michael assured me. "Not a rape site. Relax."

They were kidding? I crossed my arms over my chest, scowling. *Assholes.*

My stomach was tight with knots, and I inhaled a few deep breaths to get my nerves under control.

I watched as they all squeezed kerosene on the walls and floors and around the debris, and even though it didn't take a genius to guess what they were doing, I kept my concerns quiet. I wasn't sure if I was having fun yet, but I didn't want to argue or try to stop them and lose the foot in the door I'd somehow gained.

Not yet, anyway.

"Fire up!" Michael called out. "Time to clean out the garbage."

They all came to stand next to me, all of us facing into the house, and I watched as they lit matches, the glow of the small fires lighting up their masks.

Michael's hazel eyes flickered in the light, and my heart skipped.

Digging into my middle pocket, I pulled out my matchbox and lit a match, the burst of flame consuming the tip.

I smiled to myself, looking around at all the shit on the floor and thinking about all the bad stuff that had probably happened in this house. Given the amount of drug debris lying around, I guessed violence had come with it, too. People had probably been abused here.

Maybe even children.

I turned my head right, seeing Michael watching me. Looking to my left, I saw Kai and Damon staring at me, as well. Will held up a cell phone, clearly recording what was about to happen.

I stared ahead, knowing what they were waiting for.

I tossed the match, the small ember bursting into a four-foot flame against the wall, and I let out a breath, feeling the heat against my body.

All of the guys then tossed their matches, the small house turning into an inferno of yellow and red. Heat flooded my veins, and I smiled.

"Woo-hoo," Will praised in a low howl, filming every inch of the living room going up in flames.

Slowly, we all turned and walked out of the house, Damon carrying the duffel that Will had carried in, his hands too busy recording the spectacle now.

Should he be doing that? You didn't really want evidence floating about when you broke the law, after all.

"Make the call."

I looked up to see Michael tossing Kai a phone as we all pounded down the stairs in the yard.

Kai took the phone and walked off, while I quickly glanced around, keeping my head down to make sure there were no witnesses.

The neighborhood still looked dead.

I watched Kai as he walked about twenty feet away and lifted up his mask, talking into the phone.

"Do you know what you're doing yet?" Michael asked Will.

He turned off the phone, stopping the recording, and stuck it in his pocket. "Not yet," he answered as Damon walked past him and stuffed the duffel into the back of Michael's car.

"All right, we'll do Kai, then Damon," Michael told him. "Figure it out by then."

Figure it out?

And then it hit me. Kai, Damon, then Will. Which meant Michael was done.

I turned, staring up at the house, the flames already visible through the second-floor windows.

"So each of you pull a prank on Devil's Night, and this was yours," I stated, finally figuring out what he was talking about. "Why?"

His eyes locked with mine through his mask, and I wondered why he never took it off. The others had peeled theirs away now that the stunt was done.

"I don't like drugs or drug houses," he admitted. "Drugs are a crutch for people too ignorant to self-destruct on their own."

I pinched my eyebrows together. "What do you mean? Why would anyone want to self-destruct in the first place?"

He held my gaze, and I thought he was going to answer the question, but then he walked around me, toward the car.

I shook my head, disappointed that I didn't seem to understand what he was trying to say.

"Let's go!" he bellowed, and everyone piled back into the car. I spared one last glance at the house, seeing it light up the night sky, and I smiled, hoping Kai had been on the phone calling the fire department.

He climbed into the driver's seat, and I opened the door behind him, ready to climb into my seat, but I was yanked back, and the door whipped closed right in front of my face.

My breath caught in my throat, and the next thing I knew my back was slamming into the car.

"Why did he bring you along?"

Damon scowled down at me, and I searched his face, confusion racking my brain.

"What?" I gasped out.

"And why did he take you into the catacombs today?"

What was his problem?

"Why don't you ask him?" I threw back. "Maybe he's bored."

His eyes thinned, glaring at me. "What did you two talk about today?"

What the hell?

"Do you interrogate every person Michael talks to?" I charged.

He shot into my face, growling out his whisper. "I've never seen him give a handheld tour of a fuck party before. Or bring someone along on Devil's Night. This is ours, so why are you here?"

I remained silent, gluing my teeth together. I had no idea what to say or even think. I was under the impression that Damon, Will, and Kai were on board with this when Michael picked me up earlier.

Were Will and Kai angry, as well?

"Don't think you're special," he sneered. "Lots of women get him. No one keeps him."

I held his eyes, making sure not to let him see me falter.

"Rika," Michael called. "Get over here."

Damon kept his eyes locked on me for another moment and then backed away, letting me leave. I sucked in a breath, realizing my heart was pounding like a bass drum. I dived around the back of the car to meet Michael on the passenger side.

He opened the door and climbed in, tossing his mask to Will and then turning his eyes on me.

"Come here." He held out his hand.

I inched closer and then gasped as he pulled me into the car, onto his lap, draping my legs across his.

What? I hooked a quick arm around his neck for support, my ass planted on his thighs.

"What are you doing?" I asked, shocked.

"We need the room in the back," he said, pulling the door closed.

"Why?"

He let out an aggravated sigh. "Your fucking mouth never stops, does it?"

I heard Kai snort, and I shot my eyes up, seeing him grinning as he turned the ignition.

Why had they switched seats? I could just as easily have sat on Kai's lap.

Not that I was complaining.

I let Michael pull me in, my back against his chest, and I blinked long and slow, soaking up whatever was rushing underneath my skin.

His hand rested on my thigh while his other texted on his phone, his thumb jutting out a mile a minute.

"Let's go," he told Kai. "Hurry up."

My jaw ached with a smile as Kai took off. I didn't know what the hell was next, but all of a sudden, I was having a lot of fun.

CHAPTER 9

ERIKA

Present

Anthropology of Youth Culture.

I walked into my first class of this course, already jaded that I'd set myself up for failure. I'd relate to it either too much or not enough.

Sure, I'd seen plenty of youth culture in my short years. The Horsemen in high school and the hierarchy they dictated. The mob mentality of the hazing events on the basketball team and whatever went on down in the catacombs.

The way the guys schemed as much as the girls, and the way we'd all been mirrors of our parents in some way. The few leaders and the many followers, and the only way you could be strong was if you weren't alone.

And then there was Devil's Night. The way much of our town looked the other way and let the youths have that one evening of mischief.

Youth culture in Thunder Bay was a snake pit. Tread lightly with no sudden movements or someone would strike. Unless you were one of the Horsemen, of course.

But that didn't mean I really knew anything of youth culture, either. My hometown population was largely wealthy and well-connected. That wasn't the average. How much of a threat would you be without money, connections, and daddy? Was the playing field more level without those perks?

That's what I was trying to find out. Without my family name and their money, without my connections and their protection, what was I capable of?

That's why I'd left Brown and Trevor and the culture I'd grown accustomed to. To find out if I was a follower or a leader. And I doubted I'd stop until I'd proven it was the latter.

I walked down the carpeted stairs into the auditorium, scanning the tan seats for a place to sit. Which was difficult.

The classroom was built for at least a hundred students in staggered seating like that of a movie theater, and it was packed. When I'd registered for this class, I was told it was only offered once every two years, so it looked like a lot of people scooped it up when they could.

My eyes fell on a few empty seats scattered about, and then I stopped, seeing a brunette with long silky hair dressed in a thin beige cardigan. Stepping farther down the steps, I glanced at her profile and stopped, recognizing her.

I hesitated, clutching the strap to my messenger bag. I didn't particularly want to sit with her.

But I looked around, seeing places filling up, and there were a few empty spots in her row, so I didn't have to be right next to her, I guessed.

I walked down the row, sliding past the legs of the other students, and slid into a chair, keeping an empty space between me and the guy to my right and also between me and the brunette on my left.

She glanced over and offered a small smile.

I smiled back. "Hey, you were with Michael the other night, right?" I broached. "At the elevator. We didn't get a chance to meet."

I held out my hand, and she narrowed her eyes, looking confused.

But then she relaxed, nodding and taking my hand. "Oh, that's right. The younger brother's girlfriend."

I breathed out a laugh, not bothering to correct her. She didn't need my life history.

"Rika," I told her. "Actually, it's Erika, but everyone calls me Rika."

"Ree-ka?" she repeated, shaking my hand. "Hey, I'm Alex Palmer."

I nodded, releasing her hand and facing the front of the class again.

Professor Cain walked in, with his graying hair, brown suit, and glasses, and immediately began unpacking his bag, taking out papers and setting up his projector. I dropped my bag on the floor, digging out my iPad and propping it up, so I could lay out the keyboard to take notes.

I tried to keep my eyes forward, but I couldn't help but take Alex in out of the corner of my eye. She was really beautiful. Her green eyes were exotic and piercing, and she wore skinny jeans and a tank top under her open cardigan. Her body was flawless and sexy, and her tan skin glowed.

I pushed my hair behind my ear, looking down at my own clothes. Black leggings with knee-high brown leather boots and an oversized white shirt with a burgundy scarf loosely tied around my neck.

I let out a breath. It didn't matter. Even if I had dressed sexier, I still wouldn't look like her.

"Move," a deep voice ordered.

I snapped my head up, my chest immediately caving, seeing Damon Torrance standing over me.

What the hell?

He glared down at Alex, his black hair gelled and his T-shirt just as dark as his hair and eyes.

I heard her shuffle, and I twisted my head, seeing her pick up her things and move a few chairs down.

My mouth hung open, and I narrowed my eyes. "What are you doing?" I demanded.

But he ignored me, brushing my legs as he pushed past me and sat down on my left.

"Hey, Rika," another voice called, and I turned back to my right, seeing Will Grayson take the empty seat on my other side. "How've you been?"

Both settled back in their chairs, and I felt them like walls at my sides. I hadn't spoken to them in three years, and I stared ahead, not knowing what the fuck was going on right now.

Déjà vu. They were here. They knew I was here. The hair on my arms stood on end, and it was like no time had passed. Three years ago was today.

I squeezed my fists, noticing the professor coming to stand in front of the class.

"Hello, everyone," he greeted, threading his tie through his fingers. "Welcome to Anthropology of Youth Culture. I am Professor Cain and . . ."

I shifted my eyes, the professor's voice trailing off as I felt Damon's arm lie across the back of my seat.

Cain continued to speak, but dread sat like a brick in my stomach. "What are you guys doing?" I asked them, keeping my voice low. "Why are you here?"

"Going to class," Will chirped.

"You go to school here?" I asked, staring at him disbelievingly before turning to Damon.

His eyes, so cold but so hot at the same time, were on me, as if the teacher and class weren't even here.

"Well, we did kind of lose time," Will mused, keeping his voice low. "I must say I was a little heartbroken not getting a letter from you the entire time we were away. The last night we were free, we all had a lot of fun, didn't we?"

No. No, we didn't have a lot of fun. I breathed hard through my nose and hurriedly folded down my iPad and reached over for my bag, getting ready to leave.

But Will grabbed my wrist, pulling me back. "Stay," he suggested in a light tone, but I could tell it was a command. "We could use a friend in class."

I yanked my wrist away, the skin burning where he'd gripped it. I pushed my desktop to the side, grabbed my shit, and shot out of my chair.

But then Damon grabbed the back of my shirt, and my heart skipped a beat as he pulled my ass back down into the seat, whispering, "Get up again, and I'll kill your mother."

I rounded my eyes, my breath turning shallow as fear scorched my skin. *What?*

A guy in the row in front of us turned his head, probably having caught that, and pinched his eyebrows together in worry.

"What the fuck are you looking at?" Damon scowled.

The guy's expression turned scared, and he quickly twisted back around.

Oh, my God. I dropped my stuff and just sat there, trying to figure out what to do. Was he joking? Why would he say something like that?

But then I stilled, remembering that my mother wasn't home. She was away. I'd tried calling her several times this past weekend, but then, a couple of days ago, I finally got a text from her saying she was joining Mrs. Crist on their yacht for a cruise for the next month. She was on her way to Europe right now, and our housekeeper took the opportunity to go visit family out of town. The house was completely empty.

I let out a small breath of relief, relaxing. He couldn't get his hands on her even if he wanted to. Not right now anyway. He was just fucking with me.

His arm snaked around my neck and pulled me toward him. I stiffened as he brought me in close.

"You were never part of our group." His angry whisper fell on my ear. "You were just pussy being groomed."

And then his other hand slid to the inside of my thigh, squeezing it.

I whimpered in shock and grabbed his hand, ripping it off me. He reached for me again, but I bared my teeth, slapping him away.

"What the hell is going on back there?"

I stopped, hearing the teacher's voice. Facing forward, I glared ahead, feeling eyes on us, but I refused to answer.

"Sorry, sir." I saw Damon smooth down his black T-shirt as he slouched in his seat. "Gave it to her nice and good this morning, but she still can't keep her hands off me."

Laughter broke out around the class, and I heard Will's quiet, self-satisfied chuckle next to me.

Embarrassment warmed my face, but it was nothing to the anger building under my skin.

What the hell did they want? This didn't make any sense. *This* was mine. This school, this class, this new chance to be happy . . . I'd be damned if I let them chase me off.

The teacher shot us a look of annoyance and then returned to his lecture about technology and its impact on youth. Will and Damon settled back into their seats, keeping quiet.

But I couldn't concentrate.

I just needed to make it through class. I just needed to get out of here and to my apartment and . . .

And what?

Who would I complain to? Michael?

Michael. He lived at Delcour, only one floor above me. The guys would be there. Frequently, probably.

Shit.

After years in jail, I would've thought they'd be long gone after that much loss of freedom.

But here they were. I guess this was more fun for them?

I dropped my gaze, seeing the tattoos scaling down Will's left arm. He hadn't had those when I last saw him. Giving Damon a sideways glance, I saw that his arms were still bare. I didn't know why I wondered if the guys had changed or not, but one thing was for sure. They were still very much the same.

Minutes passed, and eventually Damon moved his arm around the back of my chair again. I remained frozen as I focused ahead and tried to listen to the lecture that was turning into more of a rant.

"The problem with your generation," the professor preached, sticking his hands into his pockets, "is a bloated sense of entitlement. You feel owed everything, and you want it now. Why suffer the sweet agony of watching a television series just to find out the big reveal you've waited years to discover when you can just wait for the entire series to appear on Netflix and watch all fifty episodes in three days, right?"

"Exactly!" a guy on the other side of the room blurted out. "Work smarter, not harder."

Everyone laughed at the guy's dig.

Bloated sense of entitlement? What?

"I've been dreaming about those lips," Damon said low in my ear, bringing me back. "You know how to suck cock yet, Rika?"

I recoiled, my stomach rolling. But he pulled me back in.

He's just messing with you. Ignore it.

"But working hard builds character," the teacher continued to argue with the student. "You aren't born with respect and reverence. You learn patience and value through struggle."

I forced myself to listen, but then my breath caught in my throat when Damon's hand gripped my hair at my scalp and held me tight and still.

"Because when I shove myself down your throat," he whispered over my cheek, "you better know how to take it and love it."

I jerked my head away from him, growling under my breath. *Sick fuck.*

"Nothing worth having comes easy," a girl went on, backing up the professor's argument.

"Exactly," he agreed, pointing out his finger in excitement.

Jesus. I rubbed my hands over my face, unable to keep up. There was something I wanted to say, but I couldn't remember what it was.

Dammit, what was the professor talking about?

I sighed and shook my head.

"Yes?" I heard the professor call out.

When no one said anything, and Will and Damon had gone still, I slowly raised my eyes, seeing Cain looking directly at me.

"Me?" I asked. I hadn't said anything.

"You seem frustrated. Would you like to contribute to the discussion other than distract the class with your boyfriends?"

My heart sunk. Will laughed under his breath next to me, but Damon remained quiet on my other side.

I could just imagine what everyone thought.

I shifted my eyes from left to right, trying to recall what the hell the teacher had been talking about, and then I remembered the first point that had popped in my head before Damon whispered in my ear.

"You . . ." I took a deep breath and met the teacher's eyes. "You talked about an ungrateful generation whose lives revolve around the technology yours gave us. I just don't . . ." I paused. "I just don't think that's a useful perspective."

"Clarify."

I straightened in my seat, sitting forward, away from Damon's touch.

"Well, it's like taking your child to an auto lot to buy a car and being angry when they choose a car," I explained. "I don't think it's right to get aggravated with the public for utilizing conveniences that are made available to them."

He talked about my generation's "bloated sense of entitlement," but it went much deeper than that.

"But they don't fully appreciate the convenience of it in their lives," Professor Cain argued.

"Because it's not a convenience to them," I shot back, growing stronger. "It's their normal, because their frame of reference is different than yours was growing up. And we'll say it's a convenience when our children have things we didn't. But again, that won't be a convenience to them, either. It will be *their* normal."

Damon and Will remained unmoving at my sides.

"And furthermore," I went on, "this discussion isn't useful, because it won't change anything. You're angry because your generation has given mine advances in technology and then blame us for the altered reality? Where's the accountability?"

Will breathed out a quiet laugh next to me, while the rest of the room, including Damon, sat silently, as if waiting for whatever was next.

Professor Cain peered up at me, narrowing his eyes as the heavy silence wrapped around the room like a rubber band, making it smaller and smaller and smaller.

I felt like everyone was looking at me.

But as I waited for my skin to heat up with shame, it didn't. Instead, my skin buzzed with adrenaline, and I had to hold back a smile as I stared at the professor.

This feels good.

Maybe it was the bullshit with Damon and Will or the run-ins with Michael, but the end of my rope was in my hand, and I was grasping for threads. I just decided to let go.

I didn't drop my eyes. I didn't blush. I didn't apologize.

I owned it.

Crossing my arms over my chest, I sat back.

"She asked you a question," Damon spoke up, making Cain's face fall.

I blinked in surprise. What was he doing?

But Cain didn't respond, merely straightened his back and walked back around his desk.

"Let's think about that for next time, everyone," he called out, plastering a smile on his face for the class as he evaded the discussion. "And don't forget the reading assignment posted on my website. Have that ready for Wednesday."

The class began to rise, and I didn't hesitate. I grabbed my iPad, hurrying to make my escape, but Damon stopped me, getting in my face as he rose from his seat.

"No one fucks with you but us," he warned with a sinister smile.

And I steeled my jaw, stuffing my belongings in my bag and shooting out of my chair.

All that time away, everything they'd lost, and this is what they indulge in when they come back? Me?

I slung my bag over my shoulder and glared at him. "Your sense of humor sucks," I gritted out in an angry whisper. "It's a little early for Devil's Night pranks. If you ever threaten my mother again, even if it's just joking, I'll call the police."

I turned to leave, but he hooked my neck, and I came crashing into his chest. I gasped, my breaths shaking as students continued to filter out, seeming oblivious to what was happening.

"Who said I was kidding?" he whispered against my cheekbone.

I felt a body press into my back, and I knew it was Will caging me in.

I looked up at Damon, hardening my gaze. "What do you want?" I challenged. "Huh?"

He licked his lips, and I felt Will's breath on my neck.

"Whatever it is," he taunted, "I think I'm getting it."

But I shook my head, feigning boredom. "A child can pick the legs off a spider," I sneered. "What else you got?"

His eyes narrowed on me. "You're going to be a lot of fun, Rika."

He released me, and I immediately shoved him away, turning and pushing past Will. Hurrying up the stairs, I brushed past the other students to get away and barged out the door and into the hallway.

What the hell was going on?

Will, Kai, and Damon were all out of jail in Meridian City, and Will and Damon, at least, were seeking me out. Why?

Hadn't they done enough damage three years ago? Hadn't they learned their lesson then? They'd gotten what they deserved, and I couldn't say I was sorry. They'd fucked up and they'd pissed me off, so any sympathy I mustered over the years for them was minimal.

I just wished they'd quit while they were ahead. They thought I was an easy target, and they mistook my quietness for weakness, but I was no longer their toy.

They needed to move on.

I didn't have any more classes today, so I bolted from campus and rushed across the commons to my apartment a few blocks down the busy city street.

Walking into Delcour, I spotted Alex, the girl from class and the other night, waiting at the elevator.

"Hey," she greeted, turning to me and pushing her sunglasses up to the top of her head. "Are you okay?"

She must be asking because of Damon and Will.

I smiled weakly, hooding my eyes. "I think so. I used to go to school with them and be so curious about who they were. Now I just wish I was invisible to them again."

I turned my eyes, seeing the blue lights of the elevator descending.

"Well, I don't know Damon and Will all that well," she stated, "but I can promise you, you were never invisible to them."

I shot her a look, seeing her eyes scale down my body.

She knew them?

Well, I guess that made sense. If she was seeing Michael, she would've met his friends, I suppose.

Which reminds me . . .

"Don't you take the other elevator to his penthouse?" I asked her, pointing my thumb over my shoulder, indicating Michael's private entrance.

"Whose penthouse?" she asked.

"Michael's."

The elevator dinged, and the doors opened. She stepped in, and I followed behind absently.

"Yes, but I'm not going there," she answered. "I live on the sixteenth floor."

I watched as she pressed sixteen and the doors slowly closed.

She lived in the building.

"Oh," I responded. "Well, I guess that makes it convenient to see him."

"I see lots of men."

I raised my eyebrows. *Oooookay.* Whatever that meant.

I reached over and pushed twenty-one, holding the strap of my bag at my shoulder as the elevator approached its first stop.

"Women, too," she added, sounding cocky.

I stilled, feeling the heat of her stare on my neck.

"Do you like women?" she asked matter-of-factly.

My eyes rounded, and a laugh lodged in my throat. "Uh," I choked out. "Well, it's never really occurred to me."

Damn. Got to hand it to her. She knew how to get my mind off the guys.

She turned her head, looking at the elevator door and smirking. "Let me know if it ever does."

The doors opened, and she stepped out, calling over her shoulder in a taunting voice, "Hope to see you around, Rika."

And she disappeared down the hall, the doors closing behind her. I shook my head, clearing it. What the hell was that?

When the doors opened again, I stepped out, going straight for my apartment. Once inside, I locked the door and dug my phone out of my bag before tossing the satchel onto the sofa.

No missed calls.

I spoke to my mother every other day, and if she didn't have a signal, the yacht had a satellite phone. Why wasn't she calling me back? Damon's threat had me concerned now, and I wanted to make sure she was safe.

Pithom, the Crists' motor yacht, was usually docked in Thunder Bay. They'd hosted many parties there when I was growing up, but it was also perfectly capable of handling long ocean excursions. During the fall and winter months, Mr. and Mrs. Crist often took it to southern Europe for their annual excursion instead of traveling by plane. I guessed Mrs. Crist went ahead of her husband a little early this year and took my mother with her.

I dialed her number, the line going straight to voicemail.

"Okay, Mom," I said, annoyance thick in my voice. "It's been days. I've left messages, and you're making me worry now. If you were taking a trip, why didn't you call me?"

I hadn't meant to yell, but I was already frazzled. I pulled the phone away, hanging up.

My mother was flighty and not at all self-sufficient, but she was always available to me. She was always in contact.

Walking to the refrigerator, I dialed Mr. Crist's office and stuck the phone between my shoulder and my ear as I plucked out a Gatorade and twisted the top.

"Evans Crist's office," a woman greeted.

"Hi, Stella." I took a quick sip and replaced the cap. "This is Erika Fane. Is Mr. Crist in?"

"No, I'm sorry, Rika," she replied. "He's already gone for the day. Would you like his cell number?"

I sighed, setting down my bottle. Stella had worked for the Crists and been Mr. Crist's personal secretary my entire life. I was used to dealing with her, since she also handled most of my family's finances for Mr. Crist. Until I graduated from college anyway.

"No, I have his number," I told her. "I just didn't want to bother him on his private time. Could you please ask him to call me at his convenience when you speak to him next? It's not an emergency, but it is kind of important."

"Of course, dear," she replied.

"Thank you."

I hung up and grabbed my Gatorade, moving to the window to look out into the courtyard and the city beyond.

The sun was starting to set, thin slices of it peeking through the skyscrapers as I took in the clear sky and purple hues in the distance. The lamps outside in the garden, sensing the disappearance of sunlight, suddenly lit up, and I raised my eyes, seeing the windows of Michael's penthouse.

It was dark. I hadn't seen him in several days, not since the episode at Hunter-Bailey, and I wondered if he was off training or out of town. The basketball season would be starting in the next couple of months, but it wasn't uncommon to have exhibition or preseason games before the regular schedule began. He'd be very busy and most likely away a lot between November and March.

I turned on some music—"Silence" by Delerium—and took off my scarf and kicked off my boots and socks as I spread out at the kitchen island with my laptop, working on the assignments I'd accumulated today.

In addition to the anthropology class, I'd also started statistics as well as cognitive psychology today. I still had no idea what I wanted to do for a career, but since I'd already taken so many courses between Brown and Trinity that focused on psychology and sociology, I was pretty sure I'd declare my major soon.

The only thing I knew for certain was that I liked learning about people. The way their brains worked, how much was chemical and how much was societal, and I wanted to understand why we did the things we did. Why we made the decisions we made.

After I'd finished reading, highlighting more lines than I hadn't, I worked on the statistics problems assigned and then made myself a chicken Caesar salad as I finished a few chapters for my history class tomorrow.

By the time I was done, the sun had set, and I'd repacked my school bag for tomorrow's classes and hooked up my iPad to charge. Walking to the windows, I dialed my mother again and gazed outside, the city glittering with life.

The call went immediately to voicemail again, and I clicked *End*, dialing Mrs. Crist right after.

But she didn't answer, either. I left a message, asking her to call me, and tossed the phone on a chair in defeat. Why couldn't I reach my mom? She'd called nearly every day when I was away at Brown last year.

I glanced up, doing a double take and noticing Michael's apartment all lit up. He was home.

I twisted my lips to the side, thinking. I couldn't reach Mrs. Crist, and her husband was a busy man. I hated bothering him or even dealing with him if I had to. Michael was slightly less frustrating, and he probably had the number to *Pithom*'s satellite phone.

Spinning around, I headed out the front door in my bare feet and took the elevator down to the lobby.

I wasn't calling him. He'd just brush me off. I had a better chance if I asked him in person.

Stepping out of the elevator, I spotted Richard, the doorman, standing outside, and I quickly glanced around, looking for a desk clerk. It was after hours, so the lobby rarely had an attendant, but I was sure I needed a key card to get me into Michael's elevator.

I jogged toward the front doors, ready to sweet-talk Richard into giving me access, but then an elevator dinged behind me, and I turned around, seeing two tall gentlemen stroll out of Michael's elevator. They were huge, at least four inches taller than him, and even he was big. They half laughed together and half played on their phones as they walked through the lobby, one of them giving me a smile as he passed.

They had to be basketball players. Probably teammates of Michael's.

Shooting my gaze over to the elevator, I saw that it was still open, and I didn't wait. I hurried over, dived inside, and pressed the button for the doors to close. I didn't even check to see if Richard had spotted me, too scared I'd *look* like I was doing something wrong.

The doors closed, the elevator immediately began ascending, and I locked my hands behind my back, breaking out in a smile at the rush.

It felt like forever, my stomach flipping and my heart racing, but when the elevator finally stopped, it was like no time at all. I was here.

The doors opened, and I raised my eyes, steeling myself.

It was dim. Like a cave.

A gray wall sat just ahead, and despite the drumming in my chest, I stepped out onto the black hardwood floors and crept slowly to the left, the only way I could go.

It smells like him. Spice and wood and leather and something else that I could never pin down. Something that was just him.

Slowly walking down the small hallway, I heard Godsmack's "Inside Yourself" echoing through the penthouse, and I stepped into a large living area, taking in the beauty and the darkness all around me.

There were only dim lights on, and blue neon glowed from behind the black boards mounted along the walls. The living room dipped, and he had a whole wall of windows just like mine, but his was twice the length of my entire apartment. The thousands of lights of the city spread before me, and with the elevation, I could see more and more in the distance. It went on forever.

Everything inside was black and gray, and everything shined.

I walked into the living room, grazing my fingertips over a long black glass table he had sitting against a wall, feeling something tingle deep in my body.

But I stopped, hearing the pounding of a basketball. The sound heated my blood, bringing back so many memories. Michael was always dribbling a ball growing up. You could hear it echoing throughout the house.

I followed the sound as it led me to the railing off the side of the living room.

Of course.

A private indoor basketball court sat below in a sunken room, and while it wasn't as large as an average court or his court at home, I was sure it served its purpose anyway. There were two hoops, a pristine, shiny hardwood floor, and plenty of basketballs on racks.

It was state-of-the-art, like everything else in the apartment, and I didn't know why I wouldn't think Michael would have a court in his apartment. When he wasn't playing basketball, he was almost always carrying one. Playing was the only time he ever really smiled.

My eyes fell on him as he jogged and dribbled and then shot the ball, landing it right in the hoop. He wore long black mesh shorts and no shirt, sweat shining across his broad, toned chest and tight abs, and I watched as he spun around, grabbed another ball off the cart close by, and continued his drills.

The muscles in his long back flexed, and I watched his arms

tighten, every thick cord defined as he raised his arms again and shot the ball, sending it flying through the air.

A *ding* went off behind me, and I tore my eyes away from him, casting a nervous glance over my shoulder as I remembered that I wasn't supposed to be here.

Shit.

I tensed my legs, ready to run . . . but it was too late. Kai, Will, and Damon strolled in, immediately slowing when they spotted me. Their eyes locked on mine, and my heart dived into my stomach.

"You okay, Rika?" Kai asked, his gentle eyes from three years ago now cold and hard.

I swallowed. "I'm fine."

But his lips tilted in a knowing way. "You don't look fine."

He continued to approach me, and I watched as Damon and Will took seats on the couch, relaxing as they hooked their arms around the back. Damon blew out a cloud of smoke, and I recoiled into the railing, suddenly feeling caged.

It had been so long since I'd seen them all together. I wanted to leave.

For some reason, I thought they'd grow apart over the years, but here they were, together as if nothing had changed.

All of them were dressed in black suits, looking like they were heading out for the night, and I tucked my hair behind my ear, trying to find my voice.

"I'm just surprised, that's all," I told him, straightening against the railing. "It's been a long time."

He nodded slowly. "Yes, it's been a very long time since that night."

I blinked, trying to avert my eyes, but there was no point hiding my nervousness. He already knew I was uncomfortable.

"I just needed to speak to Michael," I said quickly.

He leaned into me, placing both hands on the railing at my sides and called over my head, "Michael! You've got a visitor."

His deep voice sent shivers over my skin. I didn't have to look behind me to know that Michael had seen me. I heard the basketball dribble to the ground, bouncing against the floor faster and faster until it eventually came to rest, making no more noise.

Kai brought his eyes back to me, his face an inch from mine as he looked down at me.

"I wasn't aware you all were in Meridian City," I said, trying to lighten the tense mood.

"Well, as you can imagine," he said, pushing off the railing and joining his friends on the couches, "we didn't want a lot of attention or fanfare. We needed some privacy to ease back into things."

Seemed reasonable. The whole town lamented their arrest and incarceration, and despite the proof of what they'd done, no one really hated them for it. It wasn't long before their deeds were forgotten and they were sorely missed. By almost everyone.

"Come on. Sit down," Will pressed. "We're not going to hurt you."

Damon tipped his head back, blowing smoke as he let out a dark, quiet laugh, probably remembering his threats to me in the classroom today.

"I'm fine," I asserted, crossing my arms over my chest.

"Are you sure?" An amused look crossed Will's face. "Because you're backing away from us."

My face fell, and I stopped, realizing I was, indeed, moving away from them. I'd been inching farther down the railing toward the wall.

Shit.

Michael climbed the stairs from his basketball court, wiping off his face and chest with a towel. His hair glistened with sweat, and his stomach flexed with his movements. I tightened my arms across my chest.

"What do you want?" he bit out.

Guess his temper hadn't cooled from the argument at Hunter-Bailey the other day.

I took a deep breath. "I haven't heard from my mother, and I was wondering if you could give me the number to the satellite phone on board *Pithom*."

Michael's chest still heaved from his workout, and he tossed the towel on a chair as he walked to the kitchen.

"They're in the middle of the ocean, Rika. Cut her a break."

He grabbed a bottle of water out of the refrigerator and tipped it up, gulping down the whole thing.

"I wouldn't have bothered you unless I was worried." I shot a quick glare at Damon for planting the seed in my mind. "If I can't reach her, that's one thing. But she hasn't called me, and that's unusual."

Michael finished drinking his water and set the bottle down on the island, planting his hands on the countertop before him. Raising his head, he stared at me, narrowing his eyes as if thinking about something.

"Come to a party with us," he commanded.

I heard a breathy laugh behind me, and I pinched my eyebrows together in confusion.

Was he playing with me?

"No," I answered. "I'd like the number to the satellite phone."

I heard shuffles, and one by one, each of the guys came up to the island, positioning themselves around me and watching.

Michael stood across from me, while Kai and Will leaned their forearms down on the counter to my left and right. I shot a sideways glance, seeing Damon with his arms crossed and leaning his shoulder against the wall between the living room and kitchen, staring at me.

They're just messing with you. That's what they do. They push, they intimidate, but they'd learned their lessons. They wouldn't cross the line.

"Come to the party," Kai chimed in. "And you can have the number."

I shook my head, letting out a bitter laugh. "Come to the party, and I can have the number?" I repeated. "Yeah, this isn't Thunder Bay, and I'm not as easy to push around as I was then, okay?" And then I turned my eyes on Michael. "Screw you. I'll get the number from your father."

I turned and stalked off, taking a left down the hallway toward the elevator. The doors opened as soon as I pushed the button, and I stepped inside, trying to calm my racing heart.

They still intimidated me.

And excited me. And challenged me. And knotted me up.

I'd kind of wanted to go to a party, but not with them.

The doors started closing, but just then a hand shot into the elevator, and I jumped, seeing the doors reopen. I sucked in a breath, staring wide-eyed as Michael reached in, grabbed my shirt by the collar with one hand, and pulled me out.

"Michael!" I shouted.

I stumbled into him, and before I knew what was happening, he'd grabbed my wrists and locked them behind my back, walking into me and forcing me backward, back down the hall toward the kitchen.

"Let me go!" I demanded, my lips brushing the tip of his chin.

"I don't know, guys," he teased over my head, "she still seems pretty fucking easy to push around. What do you think?"

Laughter greeted me as he forced me back into the living area.

Every muscle in my body was on fire, and the tips of my toes kept getting caught under his sneakers.

I twisted my body, trying to break his hold. "What the hell are you doing?"

I pushed against his chest and jerked my body to the left, tearing out of his hold with every muscle I could muster.

I stumbled, losing my balance, and fell backward, crashing to the floor. Pain shot through my ass, running down my legs as the fall knocked the wind out of me.

Shit!

Shooting my hands behind me, I pushed myself up and bent my knees, looking up at him as he advanced.

He stalked over and then stopped, towering over me. I immediately moved my hands and feet, crawling backward, away from him.

But then I felt something at my back, and I halted. I twisted my head, seeing a dark pant leg, and I didn't know if it was Damon, Will, or Kai, but it didn't matter. I was closed in.

Oh, no. I slowly raised my eyes, seeing Michael's lips tilt in a devious smile. I stopped breathing, seeing him lower his body to the floor, planting his knees between my bent legs and his hands at my sides.

My neck arched back as his face hovered over mine, but I tried to keep myself up as much as possible, no matter how close his body got.

"I thought you were one of us," he whispered, his breath caressing my lips. "I thought you could play."

I stilled, staring into his eyes.

You're one of us now. Will had said that to me on that night so long ago.

Michael's amber eyes searched mine and then dropped to my mouth, his breathing growing heavy as he stared at me like he was about to take a bite.

I wanted to cry. *What the hell was going on?*

Three years ago was nearly the happiest night of my life, and it quickly became the worst. And ever since then, Michael acted not only as if I didn't exist, but also, at times, as if he *wished* I didn't.

Now the guys were free, and they were all back together again. What did I have to do with any of this? What did he want with me?

"I don't know this game," I told him, barely audible.

He stared into my eyes, thinning his own as if studying me.

"All you need to know," he finally answered, "is that you can't tap out."

And he slid his body into mine, capturing my lips and rolling his hips into mine at the same time.

I cried out, but it was lost in his mouth. *Oh, my God.*

Every nerve under my skin fired with electricity, and his cock rubbed hard between my thighs. I could feel how thick he was, and I couldn't keep my body from responding.

I squeezed my eyes shut, feeling the little pulse in my clit throb as he ground and teased me. His lips pressed down hard, eating me up, his teeth nibbling, biting, and taking.

I breathed hard between kisses, relishing the feel of his tongue touching mine. Groaning, I steeled my arms behind me, staying up off the floor as I met his match and kissed him back, taking his bottom lip in my teeth and craving more.

Michael grabbed my hair, pulling my neck back before he trailed kisses down my throat.

I slowly opened my eyes and stilled. Kai was staring at me with a smug look on his face.

Dread crept in. How had I forgotten they were there?

But before I could push Michael off me, he pulled his mouth away from my neck and hovered over me, blocking out Kai and everyone else.

"We're going to a pool party," he said, his voice that had been thick with lust just a moment ago now gone cold. "We're going to pick you up in ten minutes, so have a swimsuit on."

My throat was dry, and I couldn't swallow.

"If you're not ready, we'll get you ready, even if it takes all four of us," he threatened. "And then, maybe, after the night is over, I'll feel like giving you the phone number."

He climbed off me and stood up, and I felt hands wrap around my arms and lift me off the ground.

And then I winced, feeling a hand wrap around my neck and pull me back into a hard chest as a whisper hit my ear. "You're a horny little bitch," Damon seethed. "You almost fucked him right here in front of us."

I ground my teeth together and glared ahead.

"The little fight you put up was cute, though," he said, sarcasm thick in his voice. "What else you got?"

And then he planted a hand on my back and shoved me forward, my feet stumbling to keep from falling.

I sucked in breath after breath, my stomach shaking and my nerves shot.

What else you got? He'd thrown my same words from today back at me. *Son of a . . .*

I squared my shoulders and charged straight for the elevator, not looking back.

Their game had changed. I didn't know why, and I didn't know what to do next, but I needed to think faster.

A lot faster.

CHAPTER 10

ERIKA

Three Years Ago

How's she feeling up there, brother?" Damon called from the back. "She can come and sit with me if she wants."

I heard Will's breathy laugh and felt Michael's hand tighten on my waist as I sat on his lap.

But he didn't respond. Michael wouldn't. From what I'd seen, he rarely indulged Damon's childish antics.

Kai sped ahead with his chin tipped down, shooting me casual glances. "I don't know. She looks pretty comfortable where she is," he told Damon.

And I just stared out the front windshield, half rolling my eyes at both of them. I didn't enjoy being the butt of a joke. I hadn't asked to sit here, after all.

But I couldn't say I was itching to rush back to my own seat, either. Butterflies fluttered in my stomach, heat covered my neck, and I had no desire to ever be anywhere else. My heart pounded so hard it hurt.

Every inch of my skin begged to feel his, and I wanted to turn around and straddle him and know what he felt like between my legs.

Gripping the support handle on the side of the window, I relaxed into his chest, feeling it rise and fall behind me.

He continued texting on his phone with his left hand, acting like I wasn't there, but the tension in his arm wrapped around my waist told me otherwise.

I spotted Kai stealing a sideways glance at me, something unreadable in his eyes.

"Have you decided what you'd like to do?"

I twisted my head back, looking at Michael. "Me? What do you mean?"

He finished his text, his eyes downcast at me and his warm breath falling on my face. "You get to pull a prank, too."

Will came up from behind, peeking over Michael's seat. "Think of the movie *The Crow*," he pointed out. "We could rob some stores, burn down the town, murder a young couple . . ."

I pinched my eyebrows together, not finding that funny.

Damon spoke up from the back. "She's a fucking lightweight. I didn't come all the way back to town this weekend to egg cars."

Will hooded his eyes, smirking at me. "That's so 2010. I'm sure she can come up with something better than that."

"I'm sure it won't be hard," I teased. "You haven't exactly set a high standard." And then I peered around at them, amusement pulling at my lips. "Is this all the Horsemen do on Devil's Night? Because I must say, you don't do the stories justice."

"Ohhhh, she did not say that!" Will howled, smiling.

Michael's sexy grin rose to the challenge. "Well, well, well, it seems Erika Fane is unimpressed, gentlemen."

Damon remained quiet, but I saw a flicker from the back as he lit a cigarette, and Kai smiled, focusing on the road but listening.

"You didn't like the fire?" Michael nudged, mischief in his eyes.

"It was cool." I shrugged. "But anyone could've done it. What was the point?"

I remained nonchalant, enjoying taking part in a conversation even if it was just teasing. Of course I wasn't trying to insult him.

Michael's eyes thinned, regarding me. "What was the point?" he asked, but I could tell he was just thinking out loud.

"Hey?" Michael called out. "She wants to know what the point was."

I heard laughter and turned to Kai, who had his arm steel-rod straight on the wheel as we sped down the road.

He glanced at me, waggling his eyebrows, but then he jerked the wheel to the right, and I yelped as all of us jostled in our seats. I shot out my hands, holding the support bar with both of them as we swayed from side to side, the car derailing onto a small, narrow gravel road.

I opened my mouth to speak, but I didn't know what to say. What the hell was he doing?

Before I knew it, he'd stopped the car, killed the engine, and turned off the headlights. The inside of the car fell completely silent.

"What the hell?" I burst out. "What are you doing?"

"What are *we* doing?" Michael corrected.

Kai turned his head to me, pressing his finger to his lips.

I was afraid to breathe.

We sat there for several seconds, and I was so confused, but I didn't want to annoy them with more questions. What were we doing here, in the dark, hidden on a gravel road? And I still didn't understand why I was on Michael's lap.

And then my ears perked up, hearing it.

Sirens.

Everyone in the car turned their heads to look out the back window, and within seconds, flashes of red, blue, and white flew past on the bit of highway we could still see. Two fire trucks and five police cruisers.

Will started laughing, his deep, boisterous bellow like it was Christmas morning.

The vehicles passed by, continuing down the highway, and the forest turned dark and quiet again.

I turned my eyes on Kai. "You called them? That's what you were doing on the phone."

He grinned, nodding. "Of course they think there's about five fires going on up there instead of just one."

Five? Why would he have lied when he called it in?

Michael must've seen the puzzled look on my face. "We needed as many police out there as possible."

"Why?"

But he just rolled his eyes at me, turning to Kai. "Show her."

Kai started the engine, and I grasped the support bar again as he backed out of the narrow inlet at top speed. I bounced around in Michael's lap until he wrapped his arm around my waist again, holding me still.

Kai shot the car into first gear and laid on the gas, speeding down the dark road as Nonpoint's "Bullet with a Name" filled the car.

He punched into third, fourth, and then fifth gear, and within seconds, I spotted four massive headlights ahead. I inched closer to the windshield, seeing that they were trucks.

Two of them. Dump trucks.

Will's excited noises sounded from the back, while Michael and Kai both put down their windows. I cast a nervous glance at Michael, and I couldn't explain what I saw in his eyes. Heat. Thrill. Anticipation.

His gaze fell to my lips, and his grip tightened on my waist.

"Hold on," he said softly.

I tore my eyes away, gripping the support bar, as I watched the front of the car drift into the middle of the road.

What was Kai doing?

My breathing turned shallow, and I shot my eyes up, seeing the two trucks spread apart to the outside, driving half on the road and half on the shoulder.

Their headlights shined brighter and brighter, and I breathed hard, seeing them get closer and closer.

And then all of a sudden, I widened my eyes, feeling Michael's finger graze my stomach, back and forth, nice and slow.

Oh, God.

I couldn't help it. I arched my back, pressing my ass into him and staring ahead at the trucks coming at us.

I heard his groan, and then his phone hit my ankle where he dropped it. His hand left my stomach and came up to wrap around the front of my neck, pulling me back to him as his other hand gripped my waist.

"Knock that off," he whispered in my ear, sounding out of breath. "You're driving me crazy."

His hand tightened around my neck, and I dragged my bottom lip in between my teeth, feeling my pulse throb in my neck and hearing it in my ears.

Fuck. I squirmed despite his warning.

The trucks started honking and the lights flashed at us, and I whimpered, fear racing under my skin and my stomach flipping again and again.

"Jesus," Michael whispered in my ear, slipping his hand under my sweatshirt to my stomach again. "You're about to come, aren't you?"

He breathed hard in my ear, and I squeezed my eyes shut, lights flashing, and then my breath caught in my throat and the trucks blew past, horns honking and gusts of wind bursting through the open windows, blowing my hair.

"Fuck yeah!" Will shouted, holding up the same phone from before and recording.

Damon laughed, and Kai slowed the car. Michael released his grip on my neck, everyone spinning their heads around to peer out the back window.

Kai stopped the car in the middle of the road, and I sucked in air, watching in confusion as the trucks both turned inward toward the road, stopping to face each other, grill to grill.

The headlights went dead, and the next thing I knew, one guy was jumping out of each cab and racing for us on foot.

The trucks were left blocking the road and the shoulders, leaving no room for anyone to get through. Ditches lined each shoulder, so driving off road wasn't a possibility, either, unless you had a pretty tough vehicle.

The back doors opened, and two young men rushed inside Michael's car, laughing and gasping for breath.

"Son of a bitch, that was awesome." The brown-haired one chuckled, climbing into the back with Damon.

Will slapped him on the back as he went, and then a blond one climbed in, taking my old seat. He pushed his hair off his forehead and tapped Kai on the shoulder, handing him two sets of keys.

"I set the alarm, so your uncle shouldn't know the trucks are missing until morning," he breathed out.

I recognized both of the boys. Simon Ulrich and Brace Salinger, both basketball players at my school.

So that's what Michael meant by needing the room and making me sit on his lap. We were picking up more people.

I dropped my eyes, narrowing them as I thought about what Brace said. The trucks belonged to Kai's family. His uncle owned a construction company, and they'd taken the trucks and just planted them in the middle of the road. That was Kai's prank for the night.

But . . .

I looked up at Michael, seeing his eyebrows rise in a challenge.

"You're blocking the road," I stated, finally figuring it out. "So fire and police can't get back."

The corners of his mouth lifted. "Are you impressed yet?"

After we dropped off Brace and Simon at a local diner, I moved back to my original seat, seeing no logical reason to stay in Michael's lap. Even though the last thing I wanted to do was leave him.

Unfortunately, I was more afraid he'd have to ask me to hop off, and then I'd be embarrassed that he was forced to ask.

Michael took over driving again, and we cruised back through his and my neighborhood, parking alongside the dark, quiet road about a mile from my house. We sat outside a huge iron gate, and I gazed at the tall stone wall, knowing it was the mayor's house on the other side.

Thunder Bay was a small community, maybe twenty thousand people, not counting the students who commuted from surrounding areas to attend Thunder Bay Prep. Our mayor had held his position for a long time, and as rarely as things changed in our town, it made sense.

Damon had left the car over half an hour ago as we all sat there with the engine running and the heat on, and I was trying very hard not to ask questions. Like, why were we waiting here? What was he doing in there? And, if it was something bad, should we just wait here like sitting ducks knowing the police might already be on their way?

Of course, several police officers were held up with the fire we'd distracted them with on the other side of town, but there were still a few left in the area.

"Here he comes."

Kai peered out Michael's window, and I followed his gaze, seeing Damon hop from a tree on the other side of the stone wall and immediately drop feetfirst to the ground.

He pulled on his hood and jogged to the car, opening Will's

side and laughing as he crawled over his friend's legs and fell into his seat in the back.

His cold sweatshirt brushed my cheek, but instead of the cigarette smoke I usually smelled on him, it was a subtle perfume.

"How was she?" Will asked Damon over his shoulder.

"Tasted better than a Popsicle."

I twisted up my lips. *Really?* We'd been waiting on him this whole time so he could get laid?

Over the years, I'd gauged that the guys definitely loved women, and they didn't hide it.

Being who they were and wielding the power they did, it was never hard to find girls up for a good time, and although I hated to accidentally overhear their comments and discussions and the crude way they talked about various conquests, I also kind of envied their freedom to do as they pleased without judgment.

Would they wait on me if I wanted to go get laid? Would they pat me on the back and ask me how it was?

No, they wouldn't.

They—or at least Will and Damon—would expect me to be a virgin, to open my legs only for them, and then not whine and cry when they never called me again.

And unfortunately, Michael was very much like Damon.

Never any girlfriends, never any commitment, and never any expectations. The only difference was Michael didn't talk about his dirty deeds. Damon made sure everyone knew.

"You guys could've come up," Damon suggested. "You like pussy, Rika?"

Anger heated my skin. I pulled my seat belt back on, not looking at him as I answered. "I'd take one to bed before your dick."

Will snorted, hunching over, and I heard Kai's quiet laugh in the passenger's seat in front. Michael made no move.

But a chill fell on the right side of my face, and I knew Damon was glaring at me.

"So who was it, then?" I asked, ignoring his temper.

"Mayor's wife," Will answered. "Trophy bitch, but oh so nice."

Jesus. An older, married woman? Damon had no limits.

"Actually, she wasn't home," Damon cut in.

Will and I jerked our heads around, confused. "So who were you with, then?" Will shot out.

Damon grinned, and lifted two fingers to his nose, sniffing. "I like virgins. So sweet."

Kai turned his head, scowling. "You didn't," he growled, apparently knowing something I didn't.

"Fuck off," Damon bit out.

I pinched my eyebrows together, looking around at the guys. "Who are you talking about?"

Damon held up the same phone Will had recorded the fire on and then tossed it to Will. "I got video," he taunted. "You want to watch?"

I straightened my back, turning back around. *Fucking lowlife.*

"You really are fucking stupid," Kai gritted out again and faced forward.

I stared at him in the front, wondering why he was so angry. Damon had pissed me off with his stupid remarks, but why was Kai annoyed with him? What could be worse than the wife of the mayor?

And then my eyes rounded, finally realizing who they were talking about. The only other person who lived in the house besides the servants.

Winter Ashby, the mayor's daughter.

Shit. That was his prank? Screw the mayor's daughter?

No wonder Kai was pissed.

But before I could confirm that's who they were talking about, Damon took out his cigarettes and called up front. "Let's go eat," he suggested. "I'm fucking hungry."

And Michael, who'd been silent the entire time, hesitated only a moment before shifting the SUV into gear and pulling back onto the road.

Cranking up the radio to "Jekyll and Hyde" by Five Finger Death Punch, Michael took us back into town and parked right in front of Sticks, a favorite hangout, bar, and pool hall frequented by nearly every kid in town up to the age of twenty-one. They served alcohol, but unless you were of age—or a star basketball player—you didn't get served.

It didn't matter, though. The music was great, the atmosphere dark, and it was big enough to accommodate plenty of people. It was the place to be if you wanted action on a Friday or Saturday night. Every time I'd tried to join my friends, though, Trevor showed up and hovered, so I rarely came.

We stepped out of the car, and I combed my fingers through my hair as I walked around the back of the SUV to meet everyone on the sidewalk. Damon flicked his cigarette into the street, and I crossed my arms over my chest, trying to keep warm.

"Fuckin' Anderson," Kai said under his breath. "I can't stand him."

I followed his gaze through the windows, immediately looking away again as soon as I saw who he was talking about.

Miles Anderson.

I stared at the ground, letting my hair fall over the side of my face, covering it. I couldn't stand him, either.

Uneasiness settled in my muscles until they were so tight and tense that I thought they would pop.

"Asshole's been talking shit since we graduated," Damon added.

I could tell none of them really liked the new captain of Thunder Bay's basketball team. Miles had taken over after Michael graduated, and he enjoyed no longer living in his shadow. He resented the Horsemen's power, charisma, and reach, and after they'd left for college, he wasted no time in trying to claim what was once theirs.

The only problem was he sucked as a captain. The team had a horrible year last year, and the more he failed, the more he pushed to prove what a man he was.

I shivered, forcing thoughts of what happened last spring out of my head. He might be the only person worse than Damon.

I eyed Michael, trying to hide my concern. "We're not going in there, are we?"

"Why not?"

I shrugged, looking away like it wasn't a big deal. "I just don't want to."

"Well, I'm hungry," Will chimed in. "And there's tail in there, so let's go."

I stared down the sidewalk, blinking long and hard, in part because of his crass remark and in part because I refused to budge and didn't want to explain why.

I had to endure Miles' presence at school, but I wouldn't on my free time.

I felt Michael approach. "What's the matter with you?"

His hard tone sounded impatient. Why wouldn't it be? He never coddled me.

I looked up at him defiantly, shaking my head. "I just don't want to go in. I'll wait for you guys out here."

Damon shook his head, looking at Michael. "I told you," he complained. "Fucking complicated."

I heaved an aggravated breath, staying frozen in my spot. I didn't care what Damon had to say about me. I cared more about not having to look at Miles fucking Anderson and him knowing he'd gotten away without a scratch.

He always had that power over me now.

But then I gasped, sucking in a breath as Michael grabbed my upper arm and force-walked me behind the SUV. He threw me off, letting me go, and I backed into the car as he advanced.

"What," he growled, "is your problem?"

A lump stretched my throat, and I chewed on my lip, not really wanting the rest of the guys to know.

Fat chance.

They followed us over, around the car, and stood next to Michael, staring at me and waiting.

Great.

I let out a sigh, squaring my shoulders and just blurting it out. "Miles Anderson slipped me a spiked drink at a party last spring."

I stared at the ground as they all just stood there, not saying anything.

Last March, I'd gone to a St. Patrick's Day party at a senior's house, and of course I hadn't gone alone. Noah and Claudia came with me.

We hung out, we danced, I had one drink, and the next thing I knew I was being slapped awake by Noah in a bathroom as he stuck his finger down my throat.

Maybe the guys didn't think that was a big deal. Who cared about some idiot girl who got roofied?

Michael shifted, inching closer. "What the fuck did you just say?"

I shot my eyes up, my blood heating at the sight of his cinnamon eyes looking like he wanted to tear me limb from limb.

But I stayed strong. "Astrid Colby, his girlfriend, actually did it," I explained. "She gave me the drink, but he was in on it."

Yeah, any confidence Michael had in me was probably gone now. I was weak, stupid, and a waste of time.

"What happened?" he demanded.

I swallowed through the lump in my throat, my voice shaky. "I went down quick," I told him. "I barely remember anything. All I know is what Noah told me. He'd broken down the door to a bedroom in the house where the party was. They had me on the bed, and my . . ." I paused, my stomach rolling with the thought as my eyes burned. "And my shirt was open."

Michael hesitated a moment and then pressed. "And?"

"And they didn't get that far," I assured him, knowing what he wanted to know.

No, I hadn't been raped.

"Noah had noticed me being led upstairs with them," I explained, "barely able to walk, and thankfully he got there before anything else happened."

"Why didn't you tell anyone?" he threw back, accusing me.

My chest shook, and I blinked away the tears pooling.

But it was no use. They came anyway, and I couldn't look at any of them as they started to fall.

"What the fuck is the matter with you?" he yelled in my face, and I winced. "Why didn't you tell anyone?"

"I did!" I cried, glaring at him through blurry eyes. "I told everyone! My mother called the school and . . ."

I trailed off, clenched my fists under my arms.

"So help me God . . ." he warned when I didn't finish.

I filled my lungs and forced the rest out. "And your father is partnered in three real estate ventures with the Andersons, so—"

"Goddammit!" Michael tore himself away, turning from me as he swore.

Kai shook his head, heat turning his dark eyes fierce. "Unbelievable," he gritted out.

I didn't need to explain further.

Yeah, I'd tried to fight back, tell my mother, the Crists, the school, even Trevor . . . but in the end, even despite the protests of my mom and Michael's, the business relationship between Michael's father and Miles' parents was more precious than my honor.

Miles was told to stay away from me, and I wasn't permitted to go to the hospital to take a drug test for evidence. The incident never went to the police or even left our respective homes. I had to look at him every day in school, knowing what he almost did to me and wondering, if he and his girlfriend had raped me, would I have seen any justice then?

I bowed my head, trying to hold back my silent sobs. God, I wanted to kill him.

"Stop crying," Damon ordered, glaring down at me.

He then looked up at Michael, his eyes narrowing. "What are we going to do?"

What are we going to do? What could we do? Even if the Horsemen had power in this town, they didn't hold any over their parents. Evans Crist had convinced my mother not to publicize the issue, and what was done was done. Astrid and Miles weren't going to be investigated, and if they were, there was no evidence now anyway.

Unless . . .

Unless that's not the kind of payback Damon was talking about.

Michael breathed hard, shifting back and forth, and then his eyes fell on me.

And I saw his chin lift and his eyes turn resolute. "Ask her."

I stilled. *What?*

He cocked his head, daring me as the rest of them slowly turned to me and waited.

What the hell? What was I supposed to do?

And then I realized what Damon had just asked. What are *we* going to do? It was my decision.

They'd all had each other's backs tonight, and now they had mine. But they weren't going to do my shit for me.

No, Michael never would. He'd never handled me lightly, and he was going to make me deal with this. And if I didn't, I might as well have them take me home now.

I bit down, glaring through the windows of Sticks again. Miles leaned into his girlfriend, wrapping her thighs around his waist as she sat on a stool, and kissed her while pawing her breast. She giggled, and he backed away with a smug smile on his face, having no care in the world as he walked up to the bar and got a pat on the back from a teammate on the way.

I glanced at Astrid again, seeing her laughing with her friends and fluffing her long red hair.

They thought they'd won. They didn't fear me.

And I locked my teeth together so hard it hurt.

I didn't know what I was doing, but fuck it.

Rubbing my knuckles along the corners of my eyes, I wiped away any remaining tears, making sure my mascara hadn't run.

Grabbing the back of my sweatshirt, I pulled it over my head, slipping my arms out, and tossed it to Kai. I mussed the hem of my tight gray tank top, bringing it up to show an inch of stomach, and fluffed my hair, trying to give it some temporary volume or sexy chaos or whatever.

"After you see me take him into the bathroom," I told them, checking the rest of my clothes, "give me a minute and then follow."

And then I looked up, checking for confirmation that they'd heard, and froze.

"What?" I asked in a low voice.

Four sets of eyes stared, their intense gazes falling down my body as if they'd never seen a girl before.

Kai tried to look away, but he kept stealing glances with narrowed eyes, as if he were almost angry, and Damon looked at me like I was naked.

Will's eyebrows rose, and then he shot Michael a look, forming an O with his mouth and blowing out a long breath.

But turning my eyes on Michael, I saw his jaw flex and his fists clench. Who knew what he was thinking, but he looked mad. As usual.

I rolled my eyes at them.

I guess it felt kind of good. In fact, I hadn't thought about my scar one time since I'd come out with them tonight. I never felt sexy, but what I liked even more was that it didn't take much to get their attention. No miniskirt, barely any makeup, and no games. I just took off my sweatshirt, and suddenly I wasn't a little girl anymore.

Of course, that fact wasn't difficult to forget when the tank didn't leave much to the imagination with the low-cut neckline. And given the temperature outside, I didn't even want to know what they could make out through the fabric.

Forcing a huge-ass smile to psych myself up, I grabbed Will's flask out of his hands and spun around for the door.

"Hey!" I heard him bark behind me.

But I was inside before he could protest further, the door closing and leaving them outside.

The warmth of the pool hall, smelling of wood and hamburgers, greeted me as soon as I walked in, and despite the warmer air, the change in temperature made my sensitive skin tingle. I felt my nipples grow harder, and my hands shook.

Maybe it was just nerves.

Scanning the area and trying to appear like I had no idea the person I was looking for was right at the bar, I tried to act casual. Several people looked up from their pool tables and small groups to see who had just entered. Some smiled and others jerked their chins in a hello before turning back to their conversations.

"Corrupt" by Depeche Mode played over the speakers, and I flipped my hair to the side, tipping up the flask and taking a small swig, trying not to wince at the burn coating my throat. I caught Miles' head turned toward me from the corner of my eye.

Holding the flask in one hand and sticking my other hand into the back pocket of my jeans, I walked down the aisle between the bar and the pool tables, forcing myself to smile and my hips to sway. I tried to look flirty, even though my heart was stretching my throat and sweat cooled the back of my neck.

Turning my head, I pretended to be interested in something happening at one of the tables and not watching where I was going.

And then I crashed into his arm, spinning my head back around and feeling the vodka from Will's flask splash my arm and seeing the blotches on Miles' shirt.

"Oh, my God!" I gasped, making a big show of wiping him off. "I'm so sorry. I—"

"It's okay," he cut in, running a hand down his shirt and then over his blond hair, fixing himself. "What are you drinking there, pretty girl?"

He took the opportunity and grabbed my waist with one hand, stealing my flask with the other and taking a drink.

His eyebrows shot up; he was probably surprised to actually find alcohol and not Kool-Aid in there. The perk about being the quiet girl was not many people really got to know you, which left you the advantage of surprise if you ever decided to switch gears in situations just like this.

I pinched my eyebrows together, trying to look worried and vulnerable.

"Please don't tell anybody," I pleaded. "Trevor and I got in an argument, and I just needed to relax."

Not that he'd tell anyone I was drinking. Everyone drank, but I wanted him to see me as easy prey. Miles and Astrid were aware I knew about the episode on St. Patrick's Day, even though I couldn't remember it, but I was hoping he would buy the fact that I was too drunk to care right now.

His lips quirked, and he handed me the flask. "What did you fight about?"

I dropped my head back, like the alcohol was getting to me as I moaned. "He thinks I belong to him, and I disagree," I played, bringing my eyes to him and giving him a "fuck me" look.

I saw the heat grow in his eyes and felt his hands hold my hips possessively.

"Holdin' out for someone else?" he whispered, getting closer to my mouth.

I licked my lips and hung a lazy arm over his shoulder, my hand dangling behind him. "Maybe," I taunted, forcing myself to sway in his arms.

"Can't really blame him, Rika," he spoke low, yanking my body into his. "I mean, look at you."

I smiled, forcing down the bile coming up from my stomach.

Stumbling backward, I groaned, acting like I was dizzy. "The room is spinning," I whimpered. "I think I need to splash some water on my face. Where's the bathroom?"

He took my hand, leaning in and whispering, "Come on."

I didn't bother looking back to see if his girlfriend or friends had seen. I knew they had, and hopefully Astrid would only be a moment behind.

Letting him lead me, I walked with him through the bar and around the corner to where the bathrooms sat. He pulled me into the men's room, and I immediately went for the sinks, turning on the water. Thankfully, the room was empty.

Leaning my hand on the side of the basin, I got my other one wet and patted my chest and neck, making a show of arching my back and flipping my long hair over the side.

Come on, guys. Get in here.

"Oh, that's better," I moaned, continuing to slide my wet hand around the back of my neck and letting it glide down my chest.

And Miles didn't waste any time. He came up behind me, his hands gripping my hips as he pressed himself into my ass.

"God, I bet you're a hot fuck," he breathed out, bringing up one hand to squeeze my shoulder at the neck while the other reached around to take my breast.

My breath shook and my mouth went dry.

Michael.

I kept going anyway, forcing a small laugh and pushing his hand away. "What are you doing?"

He grabbed for my tits again, growling low in my ear, "You

know what you want." And he reached down, fiddling with the button of my pants.

My pulse pounded in my ears, and I glanced at the door.

You're not a victim, and I'm not your savior. My eyes burned, and every inch of my skin crawled with fear.

Where were they? What the fuck?

I gritted my teeth and inhaled a deep breath. Breathing out slow and steady, I calmed down.

"You think that's what I want?" I said, trying to sound less nervous than I was.

My phone was in the car, and my keys were in my sweatshirt. I was naked in here. No weapons, and my only hope was to make it out of the bathroom.

I spun around, leaning my hands at my sides on the sink. And then my hand froze, falling on something small and sharp.

I held it as Miles dived in, kissing my neck and pawing my ass. "I know exactly what you're begging for," he replied.

I gripped the metal in my hand, realizing it was the pump for the soap dispenser on the granite top. It had a long metal spout that was thin and sharp. I tensed my arm, slowly and quietly wiggling it out of its hole until it finally popped off, and I hurriedly hid it behind my back.

"Get off me," I ordered, done playing.

But then he grabbed my hair, and I cried out as he yanked my head back. "Don't tease me."

He slipped his other hand in the top of my tank and squeezed my breast as he smothered my neck with his mouth. "You can cry, though, if you want to. Just get those fucking pants off."

I cringed, gripping the soap pump and raising my arm to bring it down across his face, but then the door burst open, and we both shot our heads up, relief flooding me.

But that was short-lived.

Astrid.

My chest caved and my eyes flared; I quickly hid my weapon behind my back again. She walked through the door and shut it behind her, looking like she wanted some trouble.

"So you think you can fuck my boyfriend, you little slut?" She held my eyes, looking half-amused and half-daring.

I loosened and retightened my fingers around the makeshift weapon in my hand, liquid heat pouring under the skin of my neck and chest.

Jesus, I was scared. *Michael.*

She walked over, hooking an arm around Miles' neck, and darted out her tongue, flicking his lips. He dived in for a kiss, tightening his hold on me, and I winced, pushing away from him and darting for the door.

But he caught me, throwing me back against the sink. My skin crawled, and I started to breathe hard and fast. *No.*

I wanted out of here. I wanted to go home. I wanted my mom.

Astrid leaned back, speaking to Miles, "You want her?"

He dragged his bottom lip between his teeth, jerking me into him like I was his dinner. "Fuck yeah," he growled, and I let out a small cry, feeling the ridge of his cock rub against me.

"Bend her over and give it to her from behind," Astrid ordered him. "And be rough. I don't like her."

He whipped me around, and I gasped as the room spun and he forced my head down over the counter.

Astrid hopped up on the sink next to me, whispering in my ear, "I like to watch him dick other girls."

I couldn't breathe. I tried to inhale, but my chest only shook more and more.

Miles reached around to unzip my jeans, and I screamed, my throat going raw as a surge of anger filled my muscles. I lashed out.

Shooting back upright, I pulled both arms back and swung

them straight across Astrid's face, slamming her into the mirror to my right.

The left side of her head crashed into the glass, quickly shattering it into dozens of splinters and shards.

I whipped around, hitting Miles in the side of the face, gouging his skin with the spout of the pump and ripping a line right down his cheek.

"Fuck!" he bellowed, shooting a hand to his face and stumbling backward.

"You bitch!" Astrid cried out. "You cut my face!"

I shot up, holding out my weapon in front of me and backing up to the wall as sweat broke out across my body. "Good, you sick fucks!" I raged, fury heating my face.

"Come here!" Miles yelled, and I cried out as he grabbed my arm and damn near ripped it out of the socket as he threw me to floor.

"No!" I shouted.

He came down on top of me, and I flailed my arms and legs as he grabbed my hands and restrained me.

"Well, shit, little one," a voice chirped above me, and I whimpered, seeing Miles stop and look up.

I sucked in short, shallow breaths, my heart thundering in my chest as I followed his hard look up at the door that had just opened.

Will stared down through his white mask, Michael, Kai, and Damon flanking him. "Looks like you fucked them up good without our help," he stated, glancing at Astrid, who had blood pouring down the side of her face by the sink.

They slowly entered the room, filling the space around us and shutting the door behind them. I locked eyes with Michael, seeing his narrow as they fell down to my unbuttoned pants.

"What are you guys doing here?" Miles bit out, getting to his feet. "Get out. This is private."

No one hesitated.

Michael reared up his fist and slammed it down across Miles' face, knocking the wind out of him as his body whipped to the side. Damon and Will immediately dived in, taking both of his arms and hauling his body back to the wall, pinning him there.

Kai grabbed me and brought me to my feet, and I darted out, catching Astrid as she tried to run for the door. Fisting her hair, I shoved her into the wall next to her boyfriend and fought to keep the relieved tears at bay.

"Don't you ever touch me again!" I screamed at her and then stepped over, jutting out and spitting in Miles' face. "Ever!"

He winced, blood trickling down his cheek from the gash I'd made.

My whole body shook as I backed away, the rush of fear cracking my face and making my heart ache. I dropped my eyes, seeing Miles' blood on my shirt.

"Go to the car," Michael commanded, Miles pinned to the wall in front of him. "We'll be there soon."

I sniffled, still fisting the soap pump as I snatched my sweatshirt out of Kai's hand and slipped it back on, covering the blood.

"What are you guys going to do?"

Michael turned from me back to Miles. "Make sure they understand," he answered.

CHAPTER 11

ERIKA

Present

We walked into a large white house on the outskirts of the city, all four guys ahead with me trailing behind. They didn't worry about whether or not I would run off.

I'd gotten in the car, after all.

When I'd made it back to my apartment after the confrontation, I'd seethed for about two minutes, a million fears running through my head. They liked toying around and playing games, and tonight, for some reason, I was the mouse hanging by its tail. Why?

As the minutes on the clock in my apartment ticked away, I couldn't calm down. They were coming for me, and who knew when they'd stop? I'd never wanted to see them again. Ever.

But it was obvious they were after something. They pushed people. That's what they did. And they'd keep pushing me until I started holding my ground and quit backing away.

What else you got?

What else did I have? I was taught to be brave by my father. Dip your toe in every ocean and try everything and anything. Learn, explore, take the world on . . .

And from my mom, I learned self-sufficiency. Of course, she'd taught me by default, but watching her showed me exactly who I didn't want to be.

And from Michael—as well as Damon, Will, and Kai—I learned to breathe fire. I learned to walk as if the path were carved for me and me alone, and to treat the world as if it should know I was coming.

Did I practice any of it? Of course not. I was a mouse, and that was why I got on my bikini and got in the damn car. I wanted to be different.

I wasn't tapping out this time.

The drive was quiet, and I spent the whole time focused out the window, happy that they'd turned up the music and killed any possibility of conversation.

After a valet took the car, they led the way into the house, and I followed in my black leather flip-flops, suddenly relaxing at the sight of so many people.

I wouldn't feel unsafe here.

The architecture of the mansion was modern—lots of windows and glass, as well as sharp edges and white everywhere. There were several levels with balconies, each jutting out of the house at varying lengths and widths, and as we strolled in, I could tell immediately that this was a Storm party.

Michael's basketball team.

There was sports paraphernalia sitting around, and several of the guests, including the ones I'd just arrived with, towered over everyone else.

A moment of alarm hit me when I saw all the guys in suits without ties, but then I calmed down again seeing the women, some in club wear and others in swimwear like me.

"Jake." Michael shook hands with a guy a few inches taller than him and then turned to me. "Erika, this is Jake Baldwin. A teammate. This is his house."

I offered a half smile, shaking his hand.

"Nice to meet you," he said, his eyes gentle. "You're very beautiful." And then he looked to Michael. "You sure you want the rest of the team to see her before you get a ring on her finger?"

Michael hooded his eyes, shaking his head as he brushed off his friend's joke.

"I dated his brother, actually," I told him. "We grew up together."

"Really?" He straightened, looking at me with more interest. "Well, I'd love to hear some basketball stories from his youth. Michael, as I'm sure you know, isn't much for sharing."

I grinned, knowing exactly what he was talking about. But then something caught my eye, and I looked over, seeing Alex. Will was pulling her up the stairs, a grin plastered on his face.

Alex was here? And why was she going off with Will?

I then saw Kai and Damon take their drinks and head out to the patio.

I turned back to Jake, blinking and remembering myself. "I . . ." I stammered. "I'm afraid there's not much I could tell you. I didn't watch his games in school. I'm sorry."

Michael's eyes narrowed just a sliver.

Yeah, I'd been to every basketball game he played in high school. No, I couldn't tell you a single play or what teams they beat. I wasn't paying attention to that.

Backing away with a small smile, I excused myself and left them alone. I was sure Michael didn't intend for me to hang on him all night, and I needed some space.

And maybe a drink, too.

I spent the next half hour or so wandering around the downstairs, acting like I cared about the artwork and the sculptures, before finally hitting the bar for a drink.

Thankfully the guys had left me alone and I hadn't seen them since we arrived. Taking my rum and Coke outside and feeling the alcohol slowly warm my blood, I noticed all of the people in the enormous pool. No one was swimming, but it was plenty spacious for lounging and enjoying the last bit of balmy summer air.

On the far end of the pool were rock cliffs and a waterfall display, and I cocked my head, peering over to notice what looked like a secret cave behind the falls.

Looking around, I noticed that the guys were still AWOL, so I quickly slid my shirt down my arms and my shorts off. Laying my clothes and sandals on a lawn chair, I grabbed my drink and slid into the pool.

The water reached my waist, and I fluffed my hair, bringing it over my left shoulder as I hung around the edge of the pool, sipping my drink.

Closing my eyes, I tilted my head back and finally felt the tension leave my face.

Finally.

"Hey," a voice greeted.

I popped my eyes open and looked up to see Alex, a bottle of Patrón and a couple of shot glasses in her hands. She wore a red bikini with several long, thin gold necklaces around her neck and big hoop earrings in her ears.

"You look a little happier than the last time I saw you," she observed.

I nodded, tipping my glass up to her. "This helps."

"Psh," she scoffed, setting down her things and hopping into the pool. "That's not a drink."

And she poured two quick glasses of the tequila, taking one for herself and handing me the other.

I fought not to turn up my nose, because hard liquor—not mixed with anything else—was agony for me.

However, I wanted to relax—for once—and I didn't fear the guys or any advantage they would take if I got buzzed. Between the four of them, they wouldn't need alcohol to subdue me, so if that's what they were after, I was as good as dead, anyway, drunk or sober.

I downed the shot, the liquid scorching my throat, and I squeezed my eyes shut, swallowing again and again as I tried to get rid of the taste in my mouth. I didn't think she'd brought limes, unfortunately.

God, I was a girl.

Blowing out a breath and getting over the pungent taste, I set the glass down, seeing her refill them.

"So I have to ask," I started, still forcing down the taste in my mouth. "What's with the 'I see lots of men' line?"

The corner of her mouth turned up in a smirk, and she turned around, handing me the shot glass, now full again.

"And I know Will took you upstairs before, and it was Michael the other night?" I went on, giving her a playful look.

She shrugged, looking guilty. "I know lots of men. As in, I get *paid* to know lots of men."

Paid? She got paid to know men and spend time with them?

And then my eyes widened, realization hitting. "Ohhh. Right."

She smiled, blushing as she took her shot.

She was an escort. A prostitute. Wow.

I followed her lead, taking the shot and trying anything to help me wrap my head around that one. Michael had been with her that night. He'd hired her?

"You can't tell anyone, though." She pointed at me, her voice thick with the burn of the alcohol. "My clients are mostly wealthy and well-known."

I set the glass down, stepping out a few inches away from the edge and brushing the surface of the water with my hands.

She had sex with men—and women, I thought, now remembering what she'd said in the elevator—and she got paid for it. And she lived in my building.

I wasn't sure if that was better than when I thought she was Michael's girlfriend.

I'd always been a little jealous when Michael had girls around when we were growing up. Even when I was little. I wanted him.

But over time, Michael's routine was something that never faltered. He took, he enjoyed, and at times, he dated. But no one ever became permanent.

But knowing she was just sex kind of pissed me off, too. She was only floors away at any given time, and he could call her up whenever he felt the need.

"Don't worry. I haven't slept with Michael," she spoke up as if reading my mind.

I pressed my lips together, shrugging. "Why would I care?"

She snorted. "By the way you were all tongue-tied with him the other night in your pajamas, I gathered you did."

I dropped my eyes, feeling the water pass between my fingers.

I could ask her why she hadn't been with him, when I'd seen her go up to his apartment, but I didn't want to care. It felt weird with her in the building and so close, but Michael wasn't mine, so it wasn't my business.

"And I haven't slept with Kai, either," she added, tipping back another shot.

"So Will and Damon, then?" I broached. "No offense, but I've never known them to have to pay for sex."

"Men who hire escorts aren't paying for the sex," she corrected. "They're paying us to leave when it's done."

Nice. I looked away, feeling bad for her.

"Some people aren't interested in forming attachments or having obligations, Rika," she explained. "I'm just a professional who'll show you a good time and then not expect anything afterward."

I nodded, not really believing her. You may be the good time, but you're also the dirty secret they hide.

She must've seen the judgment in my eyes, because she rushed to explain.

"It pays for school and pays for my apartment, and—no—I

don't want to do this for any longer than I have to, but I made my choice. I wish I didn't always have to do it, but I don't regret it. And sometimes"—she flashed me a playful smile—"it's fun."

I understood what she was saying, and I hadn't meant to look like I was judging her. She made her choices, and she owned them. In a way, I envied her confidence.

But I suddenly realized how happy I was to be born a Fane with all the securities that entailed.

Over the next twenty minutes, she took another shot while I finished my drink, and I noticed everyone slowly relaxing as their alcohol took effect. Suit jackets came off, more people got into the pool, and Alex and I were lost in the music and laughing.

The tequila had coursed through my body, warming my stomach and chest, and it felt so good to smile and lose control a little. My skin hummed as my head began to float, and she and I moved our hips to Calvin Harris's "Pray to God," barely noticing the couple making out next to us.

"I'm going to hit the bathroom," she yelled over the loud music, shoving the bottle of tequila in my hand. "Drink more. I'll be back in a minute."

I shook my head, laughing her off.

I watched her hop out of the pool and disappear into the house, but then I spotted Michael, Will, and Kai on the other side of the pool, watching me, and my smile fell.

How long had they been there?

They stood in a semicircle, drinks in their hands, and I wondered if they'd been watching Alex and me the whole time.

Cocking an eyebrow, I shot them a defiant look and turned around, setting down the bottle and making my way to the edge of the pool.

I headed toward the cave behind the waterfall, partly to escape their prying eyes and partly because I was curious.

The water cascaded down the rocks, splashing my arms and

chest as I waded through the pool to the far right side. I spotted a sliver of darkness behind the falls and moved around the rushing water, slipping through without getting drenched.

As soon as I stepped past the falls, though, butterflies hit my stomach and I smiled.

It was huge.

A secret pool hid behind the falls, and the water glowed with neon-blue light, much like the light in Michael's penthouse. Off to the right lay a bank, of sorts, where you could lie or sit down, or where people who weren't swimming could walk in, stand, and see the beauty inside without getting wet.

The whole place was exactly like a cave. The rock walls and ceiling glittered with little white lights, probably to look like stars, and I couldn't help the little groan that escaped as I tensed my thighs. I was turned on.

I wasn't sure if it was just the place, the drinks, or Michael. My senses had been overwhelmed today.

I waded farther in, enjoying the solace and the darkness, but then I saw Damon enter the cave and I stopped.

He'd walked straight through the falls, coming from the other side, and was drenched. He pushed his wet black hair over the top of his head, the wall of his chest, shoulders, and arms glistening with water. He must've either brought swim shorts with him or borrowed some, but I immediately took a step back, seeing that he was coming straight for me.

"I wish I could say I wasn't used to that reaction from women," he mused, noticing my retreat.

My hands fisted, and I licked my dry lips. "No, you don't," I contended. "I think you like it."

His lips curled, and I fought not to back away again. He wanted me to be scared. He counted on it.

"I'm not scared of you." I cocked my head, my heart racing despite my steel resolve.

The music blared outside, and between that and the waterfall, I doubted anyone would hear me if I screamed.

He stopped just in front of me, an inch between us. "Yeah, you are."

And then he wrapped his arms around my waist like a steel band and lifted me off the ground.

I grunted, planting my hands on his shoulders and pushing away. "Damon."

"I could tear you limb from limb," he threatened, his breath falling across my face. "And I wouldn't even break a sweat."

I pressed my hands into him, pushing harder and twisting my body left and then right. "Knock it off. Let me go."

"You know what I thought about in prison?" He took hold of my hair at the back of my scalp, and I gasped as he pulled my neck back, holding me tight and still with his lips only an inch from mine. "You . . . and our last night together," he finished.

He kissed me, soft but possessive, dragging my bottom lip out with his teeth. I jerked away, digging my nails into his upper arms as my heart hammered in my chest.

"Damon, fuck off," I bit out.

But he tightened his fist in my hair, brushing my lips with his. "Every time I was alone, I stroked my cock, seeing you in my head, taking it like a good girl."

I darted out my hand and took his neck in my fingers, squeezing as hard as I could and trying to push him away from my mouth.

He laughed as if he didn't notice. "You never told Michael what happened that night, did you?"

"How do you know I haven't?" I growled, baring my teeth.

He pushed his head in closer. "Because he would've killed me already."

I clenched my fingers around his neck, digging in my nails. "Then maybe I will tell him," I threatened. "Now, take your hands off me, asshole."

"Enough."

Michael.

I sucked in a breath, and Damon shot his eyes up over my head at the deep command.

I breathed hard, watching him sneer as he probably debated whether or not to challenge his friend.

I couldn't keep up. Two hours ago they seemed on the same page, and now Michael was reeling him in.

Damon finally released me, pushing me away, and I caught sight of the half-moon marks I'd made on his neck. He was bleeding, and I couldn't help the feeling of satisfaction that coursed through my chest.

Good. Maybe it wouldn't deter him, and maybe it would even turn him on, but he now knew I'd fight back. That was worth the risk of inciting him.

He left the cave, and I turned around, not even having to force myself to relax. I felt stronger already.

"You like all that attention, don't you?" Michael pinned me with a hard stare. "How badly are you begging for it, Rika? Does it even matter who gives it to you?"

I laughed to myself, climbing the small steps up to the spacious stone bank. "Ask Trevor," I taunted, pulling my hair up into a ponytail and very aware of how his eyes scaled down my wet body. "Even he couldn't keep up with how much I needed it. All the time. God, I love to fuck."

He tipped his chin down, a sick grin spreading across his face. Walking over to me, he backed me up into the cave wall, his gaze never leaving mine.

"Open your mouth," he commanded, lifting his rocks glass.

I hesitated for only a moment. I wouldn't let him see me falter. Little scared, timid Rika who couldn't manage to take a step without permission? She was gone.

I tipped my head back, opening my mouth.

Michael poured a drab of his brown drink into my waiting mouth, and I swallowed it, careful to hide the pain of the burn as it coursed down my throat.

"Tell me more," he urged, a challenge in his eyes.

I held his stare, diving in as I leaned against the wall, eyeing him. "I'd suck him off in the morning," I told him, keeping my voice low and steady, "taking him down my throat and getting him so hard, so I could ride his dick before school."

"Yeah?" Michael egged me on, a fire starting to burn in his eyes as he lifted the glass again. "Keep going."

I leaned my head back again, opening my mouth for the sip.

Swallowing it, I continued, softening my voice. "He'd make me come so good," I cooed. "His hands were all over my body, squeezing my tits as he bent me over the couch while your mother was in the next room." I hooded my eyes, seeing his gaze drop to my mouth as I licked my lips. "He had to put his hand over my mouth when I came, because it was so fucking hot I couldn't stop screaming."

"Mmm . . ." he responded, tipping up the glass again to feed me more and then setting it down.

"And his dick is built for my ass," I went on, curling the corner of my lips and playing with him. "When he slides it in, he owns me."

"Is that right?" Michael asked lightly, thinning his eyelids and wrapping one arm around my waist, holding my face with the other. "Tell me more." His breath fell across my lips. "I want to know everything my brother doesn't do to you, you little liar."

My chest shook with having him so close. I could almost taste his mouth. I parted my lips, feeling him hover, feeling him about to take his bitc, and I fucking craved it.

Michael.

"After he comes," he whispered, "and after he leaves you, leaves you wanting more and wanting everything you know only I can give you"—he snatched up my bottom lip between his teeth and let go—"is it my cock you think of when you slide those fingers in your pussy?"

I groaned, a rush of warmth hitting between my thighs, and my clit throbbed so hard, I had to be wet.

"Sometimes," I admitted in a whisper, forcing myself to hold his eyes.

He cocked his head. "Sometimes?"

I nodded.

His glare hardened, and I knew he felt challenged.

My heart raced, beating faster and faster, and I didn't know if my gamble was a huge mistake.

I only ever thought of him. Every fantasy, every orgasm . . .

Every time I was alone and touched myself, I only ever pictured him, his gorgeous eyes and body pinning me to a bed.

Or to a couch, a table, or the floor. It was always Michael.

But he had gotten my attention for far too long, and it was time for him to get jerked around. He wanted to play? I could play.

"Why did you lie to Jake?" he asked, suddenly changing the subject. "You watched the games in high school. You were at every one of my games."

I tensed. "You knew that?"

I couldn't believe he knew I attended every game. Even when he was in high school and I was still in junior high, I tagged along with Mrs. Crist, never missing a game until he went off to college.

"Why did you lie?"

I opened my mouth, searching for words. "I didn't," I finally forced out. "I said I never watched the games, and that was true. I just . . ." I swallowed the lump in my throat and looked back up at him, dropping my voice to a whisper. "I just watched you."

He held my eyes, his expression hardening. His breathing sped up, and his rich scent flooded my head as I closed my eyes.

"Rika," he whispered, sounding desperate as he grazed my bottom lip with the tip of his tongue.

Tingles spread over my face, and I felt higher than I ever had.

"When you think about me . . . 'sometimes,'" he added with amusement in his tone—he knew I was lying—"show me what you do to yourself."

I blinked my eyes open, looking at the heat in his eyes. My nervous heart pounded harder, but I fought to restrain my excitement, too.

I'd never done *that* in front of anyone, and I hesitated, worrying about all the other women he'd had. How experienced they were, and if he'd snicker and laugh at what I had . . .

And then I heard Michael in my head from what seemed like ages ago, in a dark room, the first time he got close . . .

Own it. Don't apologize for who you are. *Own it.* You can't win if you don't show up, right?

I held his eyes, intense and not blinking, as I slid my hand down into my bikini and between my thighs.

Michael ran a hand over the left side of my neck, and I faltered, not used to having anyone touch me there.

But he didn't seem to notice anything. He continued, threading it under my hair, holding me as his eyes dropped and he watched me move my fingers inside my black swimsuit.

His chest rose and fell quicker, and his hard gaze stayed trained on my hand as I circled my clit with two fingers.

My pussy started throbbing harder, and I whimpered, my insides flooding with heat as he watched me play.

"Take them off," he breathed out, eyes never leaving my hand.

I shook my head.

"Do it." He shook me, and I gasped.

Jesus. A rush hit my stomach, and the pulse in my fucking clit pounded harder.

I groaned.

"Please, Rika," he begged, kissing my lips and drawing them out with his as he pulled back. "I need to see."

I licked my lips and slipped my fingers under the straps at my hips and pushed the bottoms down, stepping out of them.

I caught his sudden intake of breath, and, without hesitation, I slid my hand back down between my thighs. I moved my fingers in and out, swirling the wetness up and over my clit as I leaned back against the wall, closing my eyes.

I arched my back and lifted my leg up, letting Michael grab it under the knee and hold it at his waist.

Much better now.

Rolling my hips in small movements, feeling his cock grow hard as I brushed against it inside his pants, I continued fingering and playing, hearing his breathing grow labored. He must've liked what he was seeing.

"Is this what you wanted?" I whispered, sliding two fingers inside myself.

"Yes," he choked out.

I smiled. Whether or not I thought I was sexy or just a stupid kid was irrelevant. Michael Crist was losing his grip.

"Sometimes I do other things," I taunted.

He snapped his eyes up to me, narrowing them. "What else?"

"I can't tell you." I licked my lip. "Maybe I'll show you sometime. Or maybe I'll do it tonight when I take off my clothes and crawl into my bed alone"—and I leaned in, whispering across his lips—"naked, hot, wet, and alone."

He exhaled, his lungs emptying. "Fuck."

And before I knew what was happening, he dropped to his knees, hooked my leg over his shoulder, and took my bare pussy in his mouth, assaulting me fast and hard with his tongue and teeth.

I cried out. "Michael!" *Oh, God.*

He sucked my clit into his mouth and then released it, rubbing his tongue over the sensitive skin again and again. I squeezed my eyes shut.

"Oh, shit," I choked out. "Fuck."

He dived in between my legs, eating me like he was starved.

I fisted the top of his hair, arching my neck as he nibbled, sucked, and licked, going around in circles and circles and then diving back in to claim me hard.

"Fuck, you've got a nice pussy," he whispered against my skin, looking up at me as he flicked my clit with his tongue. "You're a pretty girl, Rika. So soft and tight."

I sucked in air through my teeth and pressed myself into his mouth, watching him lick the length of me as he stared into my eyes.

And then he dived down and slid his tongue inside of me, and I groaned louder.

"Oh, God!" I moaned. "Michael, I need more."

"You want my cock?" he asked, dragging my clit through his teeth, an ache building deep and hard.

I nodded frantically.

"My cock or someone else's?"

"Yours!" I cried.

"You mean the only one you think about when you finger-fuck yourself, right?" he argued, sliding his two fingers inside me as he continued to circle my clit with his tongue.

"Yes," I moaned, feeling my orgasm build and gather deep in my belly.

"So you're a fucking liar, then, huh?" he growled, rubbing my nub harder and harder with his tongue as his fingers plunged in and out.

"Yes!" I fisted his hair tighter.

My muscles tingled and weakened, and I breathed faster and faster, feeling it coming.

I opened my eyes, staring at the ceiling as he ate me out, but then my head snapped to the left, seeing Kai.

My eyes widened, and my heart jumped into my chest. "Wha—!" I gasped, my orgasm building and building, and my head feeling dizzy.

He leaned his shoulder against the rock wall with his arms crossed over his chest, watching us with impassive eyes. He may as well have been watching the news.

I shook my head, wanting to tell him to get out, but then I groaned, tightening every muscle in my fucking body as the orgasm exploded inside me.

"Oh, God!" I cried, my body taking over as I rode it out and ground my pussy against Michael's tongue. "Oh, fuck!"

My clit beat like a drum, and I could feel the heat of my cum between my legs.

I heaved, trying to catch my breath as the bursts of pleasure inside my belly and between my thighs pulsed and spread and slowly dissipated.

My chest shook with aftershocks, and Michael's mouth slowed, licking me soft and slow.

He then kissed my clit nice and soft and looked up at me with a gloating curl to his lips.

"Does she taste as good as she looks?" I heard Kai ask, and I snapped my head up, remembering he'd been watching.

"Better," Michael answered calmly, staring up at me as if he'd known Kai was there the whole time.

I glared at Michael and then pushed him away, taking my leg down. Grabbing my bikini bottoms, I hurried back into them and made for the exit.

Back and forth, back and forth . . . Michael challenged me, and I met him, pushing back the whole time.

But in the heat of the moment, he got to me. He knew he was the only fantasy in my head, the only one I wanted.

And worse, Kai was challenging me, too. Their games had changed, and I was thinking faster, but not fast enough.

I brushed past Kai, and he turned his head over his shoulder, following me with his eyes.

"Run all you want, Little Monster," he said, sounding like a threat. "We're faster."

CHAPTER 12

MICHAEL

Present

I dragged my bottom lip between my teeth, every nerve in my mouth craving more of her. *Fuck, she tasted good.*

I stood up, seeing her disappear on the other side of the waterfall, and Kai turned his head back to me.

"You're eating off the community plate, brother," he charged, "and you're taking more than your fair share."

The corner of my mouth lifted, and I walked up to him. "You know," I said, hardening my tone, "this leash you keep trying to put on me is getting tighter. The day I start feeling the need to explain myself to you, I'll be dead. You got that?"

"I'll remember you said that." He pushed off the wall but kept his arms locked across his chest. "The same goes for Will, Damon, and me."

"What's that supposed to mean?"

But he only looked at me, a sinister smile in his eyes.

And for the first time, I didn't trust Kai. Yeah, I'd touched her when I'd told them all to leave her alone. I knew he was pissed, and he had a right to be.

But she'd surprised me. I came in to get Damon off her and

found myself losing control as soon as she opened that mouth. She got smart, and she didn't back down.

I saw the little monster again. The one who breathed fire and made people see her. I'd needed to touch her. I couldn't think past that.

But as much as Kai deserved revenge, there was no way in hell I was apologizing to him. I was, however, starting to fear him. Not for my sake, but for Rika's. I couldn't help the feeling that his premonition from Rika's first night in Meridian City was true, not only for Will and Damon but for Kai, as well.

Things never go according to plan.

Did they each have agendas I didn't know about?

"What about her house?" Kai spoke up. "Where do we stand on it?"

"I'm taking care of it."

"Where do we stand on it?" he demanded again.

But I got in his face, challenging him. "She's in Meridian City because of me," I gritted out. "She's at Delcour because of me, and she's isolated because of me. We're on the homestretch."

And then I walked out, proving one thing. He, Damon, and Will may have changed, but I hadn't.

I didn't explain myself.

By the time I'd made it out of the cave, Rika's clothes by the pool were gone. After a search of the party, and also noticing Alex's absence, I'd finally figured out she'd asked her for a ride and left without us.

Will and Damon had stayed at the party, and after the confrontation in the cave, I couldn't find Kai.

We needed to get this shit done so we could all get on with our lives.

I was constantly distracted from basketball, Kai was turning more and more inward, Damon was a ticking bomb, and I was pretty sure Will couldn't get through the day without a drink anymore.

I thought they'd slowly start reacclimating to life and the possibilities of what their futures held, but it was getting worse, not better. This bullshit needed to end, and I needed them back on track. Pretty soon, those three years away would just seem like a bad memory.

They'd been offered jobs, places within their families' circles to get their lives going again, but none of them wanted to even talk about it. Nothing existed beyond Rika and today. They didn't even want to see any family or spend time in Thunder Bay.

My friends—my brothers—were dead on the inside, and the more I thought about what she'd done to them—to us—the more I wanted to rip her apart. I only hoped what we were about to do would bring them back, though.

"Mr. Crist," Stella greeted as I strolled into my father's office on the top floor of his building.

I nodded, offering her a half smile as I walked past. She never tried to stop me, no matter if he was in a meeting or on a call. My brother and I rarely came down here, but the truth was, I think she was just as afraid of us as she was of my father. She didn't interfere with family.

Even if my father didn't like us here.

My mother, Trevor, and I learned early on that his life in the city, with us tucked away in Thunder Bay, was just how he wanted things. Family hanging around his work was a nuisance. He kept the two lives separate and didn't involve us.

And as much as I fucking adored my mother, I respected her less and less for staying married to such a prick.

To them, though, they had a good arrangement, I guess. He

gave her the money to buy anything, have the home she wanted, and secure the place in society she enjoyed. In return, she stayed respectable and gave him two sons.

They were both liars and cowards. My mother wasn't brave enough to demand the life she deserved, and my father would never open up himself to anyone. Not his wife or his sons. And he didn't have any friends. Not really, anyway.

In the spider's web of Thunder Bay, with its endless lies and secrets, its fake smiles and bullshit, I thought I'd found one person who was different. Who saw everything I wanted and craved it with me.

My brother was right. I'd seen that look in her eyes long before I even noticed her face or her body. That look of something being contained and wanting to claw its way out.

Rika and I had always circled each other, even before either of us was aware of it. And her betrayal was as close as I'd ever come to being gutted.

I walked straight for the door and opened it without knocking.

My father was seated behind his desk, the furniture polish of the dark mahogany tables and bookshelves hitting my nose and reminding me of a museum.

His lawyer, Monroe Wynn, sat across from him with his back to me.

"Michael." My father looked up, tapping his finger on his desk with a smile that didn't reach his eyes. "What a rare surprise."

I shut the door behind me, already feeling the air filter into my lungs like oil. He wasn't happy to see me, and I hated being in his presence. Our relationship died long ago, when I started standing up for myself, so his mock pleasure at the sight of me was merely for his lawyer's benefit.

"Monroe, you know my son," he offered, waving his hand between us.

Monroe rose from his chair and held out his hand. "Hi, Michael."

I took it and nodded once. "Sir."

I released his hand and crossed my arms over my chest.

"We're expecting great things from you this year," Monroe said. "Wife was mad enough I bought box seats for the season, so it better be worth it. Don't let us down."

"No, sir."

"He'll do his job," my father assured him. As if he had an ounce of fucking control. He hated my career and never supported it.

Monroe nodded, and I turned my eyes on my father.

Sensing the uncomfortable silence, Monroe finally grabbed his files and briefcase, his arms full as he turned to leave.

"We'll talk soon," he told my father.

He left the room, and my father leaned back in his seat, looking at me through annoyed blue eyes. He and my brother looked alike, with dark blond hair, pale skin, and a narrow jaw. Both of them stood at least three inches shorter than me. I inherited my height from my mother's side of the family.

"I'm surprised you even remembered where the building was," he sneered.

"Fair's fair," I retorted, leaning my shoulder against the bookshelf. "I'm here as much as you're home."

He leveled his gaze on me, looking unamused. "Have you talked to your mother?"

I nodded. "Yesterday. She's spending a few days shopping in Paris before heading to Spain. You're meeting her this week, correct?"

"As usual," he replied. "Why do you ask?"

I shrugged, shaking my head. "No reason."

Actually, there was a very good reason. I wanted to make sure he was leaving. And soon. Rika believed her mother was with mine on board *Pithom* off the coast of southern Europe.

No. Pithom was still docked in Thunder Bay, and my mother hadn't seen Ms. Fane since before she left for Europe, by plane, over a week ago.

Rika didn't know where her mother really was. I did.

And when my father joined my mother, Rika would have zero support around her.

My parents always left in the fall for several weeks to visit various friends and business partners out of the country. And while my father traveled extensively throughout the year, their annual excursion was always together. My mother was useful, with her charm, wit, and beauty, so he insisted she accompany him when he made the rounds in Europe every autumn. It was the one thing I knew I could count on.

The house in Thunder Bay was currently empty, with my mother having already left and my father staying here in the city, at the private fuckpad he kept on the other side of town.

At the very least he had the decency not to keep an apartment at Delcour and flaunt his sluts in a building he owned.

"Have you spoken to Trevor?" he asked.

But I just stared.

He breathed out a laugh, realizing that was a stupid question.

A young woman came into the office with an armful of file folders. She smiled at me, looking sexy in her bright blue dress and perfect blond hair.

Walking behind my father's desk, she placed the folders on top and reached over it, taking a Post-it and writing a quick note for him.

He didn't even try to hide his leering as he reclined in his chair and gazed at her ass as she bent over next to him.

"So why are you here?" he broached, and I didn't miss his hand disappearing up her dress.

She bit her bottom lip to stifle her smile.

I fisted my hands under my arms. God, I fucking hated him.

"To talk about my future," I replied.

He cocked his head, narrowing his eyes on me.

I hated this. I didn't want to deal with him for another second, which is why it'd taken me so long to deal with what should've been settled long ago. I hadn't wanted to come here.

His lips curled. Pulling his hand out, he gave the girl a pat on the behind. "Close the door on your way out."

She walked around the desk, casting one last glance at me before leaving the room.

He exhaled a heavy breath, peering over at me. "I seem to remember trying to have this conversation with you many times. You didn't want to attend Annapolis. You wanted to take a full scholarship to Westgate."

"They had a superior athletic program," I reminded him.

"You didn't want a future in this company," he continued. "You wanted to play basketball."

"I'm a professional athlete," I responded. "I've been in more magazines than you."

He snickered. "This isn't about making better choices, Michael. This is about you consistently defying me. Whatever I want, you do the opposite."

He stood up from his chair and took his glass of what I assumed was his usual Scotch and stood next to his floor-to-ceiling windows overlooking the city. "As you grew up and became a man, I thought you'd be more agreeable, but you haven't stopped. At every turn of the hand, you—"

"Back on topic," I cut in, straightening my stance. "My future."

We'd had this conversation—or fight—several times. I didn't need a rehash.

"Fine," he allowed. "What do you want?"

"You were right," I admitted, swallowing the bitterness in my mouth. "In ten—fifteen—years I'll be looking for college coaching positions, and as I look ahead, my career loses its luster. It doesn't have a future."

He inhaled a deep breath, looking as if he liked the sound of that. "I'm listening."

"Let me try something on for size," I suggested. "Let's see what I can do with some of your interests."

"Like what?"

I shrugged, pretending to be thinking, as if I hadn't come in here with a plan. "How about Delcour and fifty thousand shares of Ferro?"

He laughed at my audacity, which was exactly what I wanted. I knew he wouldn't go for it.

"Fifty thousand shares would make you a partner," he pointed out, setting down his glass and taking a seat again. "Son or no son, you don't get those kinds of perks just handed to you."

He fanned out his suit jacket, leaning back in his seat and pinning me with a stare. "And not in Meridian City," he demanded. "If you embarrass me, I'd like it less visible."

"Fine." I nodded. "What about . . . Fane, then?"

Rika's family had given their jewelry store the family name when it'd been opened years before she was born.

He pinched his eyebrows together, looking suspicious. "Fane?"

Shit. I'd moved too fast. He was going to say no.

I shrugged, trying to downplay it. "Everything is tucked away in Thunder Bay, isn't it? Out of sight? Let's see what I can do with the shop, the house, and the Fanes' holdings."

"Absolutely not," he answered. "All of that will be your brother's someday."

I stilled. *Trevor's?* Not Rika's?

In his will, Schrader Fane had named his daughter as his sole heir. Rika would inherit everything upon either her graduation from college or her twenty-fifth birthday, whichever came first.

Mr. Fane had named my father, Rika's godfather, the trustee until that time, which had been just fine with Rika's mother. She took no interest in business, nor was she capable of even running her own household, let alone a multimillion-dollar estate.

If everything went to Trevor, though, that meant—

"You must realize by now that they will eventually be married," my father told me when I didn't say anything.

Married.

My muscles ached, every single fucking one tight as I stared at my father and fought not to lose my shit.

What did I care anyway? She and Trevor deserved each other, and I was sure we'd be more than done with her by then.

"Makes sense," I agreed, trying to unknot my stomach.

"It'll be some time after they both graduate," he told me. "We can't have her spreading her wings too wide and taking off. He'll marry her, put a Crist baby in her, and everything Fane will be ours, including little Rika. That's the plan."

And I'd bet everything I had that she wasn't aware of any of this, either. Sure, we all knew the family had been trying to push Rika and Trevor together, even though she'd broken it off.

But there was only so much a person could take. They'd continue to pressure her, including Trevor, and Rika would eventually fold.

"She doesn't love him," I pointed out, wanting to burst his little bubble.

He raised his eyes, meeting my challenge. "She'll take him back, and she'll marry him."

"And what if he can't get a baby in her?" I argued.

Rika didn't want Trevor. They might get her down the aisle, but there was no guarantee she'd be pliable in the bedroom.

"If he can't," he said, looking at me pointedly, "then maybe you will. As long as it's a Crist, I don't really care."

He tipped up his glass, taking another sip. "Hell," he continued, a hint of a grin on his face, "I'll do it if I have to."

Motherfucker. Her life was already as good as over.

I fixed him with a sarcastic smile. "So you need me, then."

"Yeah, but I don't trust you," he retorted.

"But I am your son," I shot back. "And I know that scares you, because you can't control me, but you know why that is? Because we are exactly the same." I tipped my chin down, challenging him as I stood my ground. "The same qualities you hate in me are the ones you prize in yourself. And whether or not you want to admit it, you respect me a lot more than you do Trevor."

I kept my arms folded across my chest as I approached his desk.

"It's time I joined the family business," I stated. "I'll keep nothing. Fane belongs to Rika, as well as her property and finances, when she graduates college. That's in her father's will and can't be changed. Let me manage it until she and Trevor are ready."

He narrowed his eyes, turning it over in his head.

What did he have to lose? I couldn't keep anything. The law protected Rika. And as far as my father knew, I had no reason to mismanage her estate. Why would I want to seize her house, close down the business, freeze her assets . . . ?

"Fane," he said, finally coming to terms with the idea.

"And the house and all their other holdings," I reminded him. "And if I do well, I get Delcour and the fifty thousand shares."

I didn't give a fuck about Delcour and the shares, but I wanted to keep up the pretense that the Fane estate wasn't the real prize.

He paused but finally nodded, accepting the deal. "I'll have Monroe change over the power of attorney and fax you the papers later today."

And then, looking at me sternly, he pointed out, "You're getting a chance because you're blood, Michael. And only because you're blood. If I were you, I'd prove my worth by not fucking this up. You might not get a second chance."

I kept my smile to myself. I wouldn't need a second chance.

I turned and walked toward the door, ready to leave, but then I stopped.

"Why not me?" I pivoted back around, looking at him. "Why didn't you consider me to marry her?"

"I did," he answered. "You're too volatile, and I need her happy and pliant. You'd make her miserable."

I cocked an eyebrow, looking away. Well, he was right, wasn't he? I had every intention of hurting her beyond repair.

But he didn't know that. He was reading into something else. Knowing nothing about the bad blood between Rika and me, my father thought I wasn't good for her.

I walked out of the office, slamming his door closed behind me with a loud *thud*. Anger coiled in my gut, and I hardened my jaw. It didn't matter. *None of it matters*, I reminded myself.

He thought he'd secure the Fane money and connections and that he would control everything through Trevor. He had no idea that I was going to drive everything into the ground.

And he had no idea that my plans had just now changed. He and Trevor would never get their hands on her. I'd see her dead first.

I stepped into the elevator, pushing the button for the lobby and feeling my phone vibrate inside my suit jacket.

Pulling it out of my breast pocket, I clicked on a text message from Will.

No more house.

And my eyes rounded, seeing a picture of the foyer of the Fanes' home covered in flames.

What the fuck! My heart filled my throat, and I stopped breathing. They'd acted without me.

We planned to take the house, not burn it down!

I worked quickly, dialing the security office at the community. The night guard answered immediately.

"Ferguson!" I growled. "The Fanes' house!"

"Yes, sir," he rushed out. "I already called 911. Fire trucks are on their way."

I hung up and instantly twisted to the side, slamming my fist into the elevator wall. "Goddammit!"

CHAPTER 13

ERIKA

Three Years Ago

I should've beat the shit out of them. Miles and Astrid were ugly and vile, and I couldn't believe what they'd tried to do to me in there.

I fisted my hands as I sat in Michael's car, waiting for the guys to come out of Sticks.

Astrid and Miles deserved so much more than they got. Tears welled as I chewed on my thumbnail and stared out the window, holding my cries back.

They would've raped me in that bathroom. And they would've gotten away with it.

Rage fired under my skin, and I wanted to go back in and hit them until they understood. Until they knew I wasn't a victim.

I moved to open the door, but I looked up and stopped, noticing the guys coming out of the pool hall.

They still wore their masks, and I spotted several people inside following them with their eyes.

Everyone knew who the Horsemen were and probably had no doubt about the shenanigans they were up to tonight. While interested, onlookers wouldn't interfere.

Michael and Kai slid into the front seats while Damon climbed in Will's side, dropping into the back as usual. Will followed, sitting down next to me and slamming the door, and I noticed that the sleeve of his sweatshirt was torn. There must've been a struggle.

I almost started to worry if he was hurt, but he was laughing his ass off.

"What did you guys do?" I asked.

Everyone pulled off their masks, setting them aside, and I watched Will wink at me and shoot me a dashing grin.

"Hold out your hand," he instructed.

My stomach sunk. *Shit.* What now?

Reluctantly, I inched out my left hand and watched as he laid something soft and red across my palm, the strands spilling over the sides like a scarf.

He removed his hand, and my eyes rounded.

"Oh, my God," I gasped, horror heating my blood. "Is this . . ." I breathed out, trying to wrap my head around it. "Is this from them?"

In my hand sat a bloodied tooth and a thick rope of long red hair.

I cringed, acid burning my throat as the weight of what was in my hand suddenly went from nothing to a thousand pounds.

"We took a souvenir from each," Will explained.

Kai spoke over his shoulder from the front seat. "They won't ever touch you again."

"They'll never even look at you again," Damon chimed in from the back.

"But won't they tell someone?" I knew I sounded worried, but my hand was shaking, desperate to get rid of the shit in it.

"Who they going to tell?" Michael started the engine and peered at me in the rearview mirror, smirking. "My dad is in three real estate ventures with the Andersons."

I sat there frozen as realization hit. *Holy shit.* He was right.

The law might have failed to protect me, but it also worked the other way around. Who were Miles and Astrid going to tell to get justice now?

I let out a smile. *No one.*

"A thank-you might be in order," Damon said behind me.

"I . . ." I stared at the tooth again, its bloodied root growing cold on my hand. "I'm just a little weirded out." I offered a nervous laugh.

"You would've been a lot more weirded out waking up naked with the cum of ten guys spilling out of you at that party," he retorted. "Not to mention what they were going to do to you in that bathroom."

I dropped my eyes, the horror of what he'd said hitting me as I stared at the tooth and hair.

"Yeah," I whispered, in complete agreement.

Last spring, passed out on that bed, what would've happened to me after they were done? Would they have invited more to come in and hurt me, one after the other? Pictures? Videos? How many people would've violated me?

I clenched my teeth, suddenly wanting them to hurt more. I wanted to kill them. No one should hold the power to change your life forever.

I closed my fist around the objects. "Thank you."

I heard the click of Damon's lighter and then an exhale as he blew out smoke. "Your attempt to strong-arm them was cute, though."

I rolled my eyes, opening the door and quickly disposing of the tooth and hair in the stream of water flowing to the gutter. The remnants of their assault disappeared into the void.

There was nothing wrong with my attempt. Maybe I didn't chop off body parts, but I'd defended myself. What more did they want?

Slamming the door, I wiped my hand on my black sweatshirt, thinking I should definitely burn my clothes after tonight.

As if sensing my questions, Kai peeked over his shoulder, speaking to me. "When you want to make an impression and you think you've gone far enough, go a little further. Always leave them wondering if you're just a little bit crazy, and people will never fuck with you again."

I nodded, understanding. I wasn't sure if I could ever do what they had done, but I knew what he was saying. When your enemies didn't know your limits, they don't press them.

Michael pulled away from the curb, rounding the corner down Baylor Street.

"What took you guys so long?" I finally asked, remembering that they'd waited far longer to come in after me than I'd told them to.

"We waited for his girlfriend to follow," Will answered.

"Don't worry," Kai assured me. "We wouldn't have waited too much longer. You did good."

I stared out the window, seeing teens laughing and joking around on the sidewalk outside the theater as we passed. Halloween decorations—ghosts with flowing white gauze—blew in the breeze as they hung from the streetlamps. Orange leaves spilled down from the trees, and I could smell rain coming.

"Let's go find some food away from the scene of our latest crime," Will joked, reaching up front and cranking up Drowning Pool's "Bodies."

He started rocking out to his air guitar as Michael took a right onto Breckinridge, circling the town square. I glanced over, always enjoying the sight of the park in the town center. The small pond glittered with the white lights from the trees surrounding it, and orange bulbs had replaced the usual white ones in the lanterns, bringing a festive feeling to the square. Halloween flags danced off poles hanging outside the shops along with jack-o'-lanterns and more decorations.

"Hey, stop!" Will shouted. "Stop!"

"What?" Michael called, slamming on the brakes and making all of us jerk in our seats.

Will rolled down his window, and Michael turned down the music, waiting.

"She finished it," Will said, gazing into the park.

I cocked my head, trying to see what he was seeing, but I wasn't sure what we were looking at. I glanced to my right, seeing Fane, my family's store, across the street. The glass display cases were all lit up, and even from here, I could see jewelry glittering.

I turned back, seeing Will still staring out the window in silence. He then twisted his head, holding his hand over his shoulder to Damon.

"Give me a bottle," he ordered.

"Why?"

"You know why," Will shot back, and I blinked, surprised at his suddenly sharp tone. "Give it to me."

"Not out in the open like this," Kai argued.

"Screw that." Will shook his hand at Damon, urging him. "Now!"

What the hell was going on? I saw Damon shoot Michael a quick glance through the rearview mirror as if still not sure.

"Give him a bottle," Michael said quietly.

My heart skipped a beat as I wondered what he was going to do. If Kai was nervous, whatever it was wasn't a good idea. And if Damon was nervous, it definitely wasn't a good idea.

Will slid his mask back on his face and pulled his dark hood over his hair before reaching over, sticking his hand in the center pocket of my sweatshirt, and pulling out my matches. Then, taking a bottle of liquor and a cloth from Damon, he swung his door open and hopped out.

"Jesus," Damon said, sounding suddenly worried as he shouted after him. "Fuck that bitch. I don't even know why you care!"

But Will didn't seem to hear him. He kept walking, fiddling with the materials in front of him.

Who were they talking about?

"Let's go," Michael said, opening his door and climbing out.

I watched as they all pulled on their masks and hoods and slammed their doors shut.

I clutched the handle, not sure I wanted to follow. They didn't all seem on board with what Will was going to do, and I didn't have a mask.

"Come on." Michael peered through Will's open window. "We all go. It's the rules."

Ooookay. All for one and one for all, then? But that wasn't really true. Damon had gotten away with doing his prank in private, but I guess, since it was a very private thing he was doing, I wouldn't want to be around for that anyway.

I hesitated, blowing out a sigh and yanking my hood up.

I climbed out Will's side and walked briskly next to Michael, stuffing my hands into my sweatshirt.

Scanning the area, I noticed several bystanders, teenagers and couples, and they were all staring at the men in masks. I kept my head down, trying to be invisible.

I spotted Will with a rag now stuffed in the bottle of alcohol as he, Damon, and Kai headed for what looked like the Witch's Hat Gazebo in the park.

What?

"Why's he going after the gazebo?" I asked Michael.

"Because he's in love with the girl who built it," he replied, "and she can't stand him."

I pinched my eyebrows together, confused and not caring who saw my face anymore.

"Emmy Scott?" I shot out, wanting to laugh.

"What?" Michael looked at me, not sharing the joke.

"Well, she's not . . ." I trailed off, thinking of moody little Emory Scott in her black-rimmed glasses and overalls who never wore a stitch of makeup. "Well, she's not really his type, is she?"

I couldn't believe it. This had to be a mistake. Will had only ever been seen with girly-girls in short skirts with perfect hair.

Girls who knew how to flirt. Emmy Scott was . . . well, kind of a nerd, in everyone's opinion, including her own.

We stopped as we neared the gazebo, and I turned my head, seeing Michael's piercing eyes lock with mine.

"We want what we want," he explained, the weight of his soft words meaning more than I think he intended.

And my heart started beating faster.

I glanced over to the guys, seeing Damon hold the bottle as Will lit the cloth, and I shook my head.

"I don't like this," I whispered, keeping my head down again. "Emmy's a good person, and she worked her ass off on that gazebo. It was her senior project for social science. It got her into Berkeley."

She'd built the gazebo a year ago last summer, and while she might have been thrilled to get out of here and go off to college, she'd certainly put everything she had into that gazebo, as well as a few other little projects she'd built around town.

Michael tipped his chin up. "He'll make it right," he assured me. "Let him go through his shit."

And then, before I could say anything, I saw a flash of light fly through the air. I held my breath as the bottle crashed into the gazebo, an explosion of flame bursting forth and drowning every inch of wood in fire.

"Oh, Jesus." I shot my hand to my forehead, guilt filling me up. "I'm not watching this. This is a dick move!"

I spun around, but Michael grabbed my arm. "You stand with us or you can go home," he warned.

I yanked my arm out of his grasp, scowling up at him.

I didn't want to go home.

But this wasn't fun, either. They were being assholes, and if I didn't stand my ground, he'd always see me as weak.

I stalked off, back toward the street to where the car sat.

Screw them. I'd find an open business and call Noah to pick me up.

Pulling open the car door, I dug inside the back pocket of Kai's seat, where I'd stuffed my phone, and pulled it out, slamming the door.

The fire blazed only a short distance away, and several excited voices rang out around me.

"Oh, shit!" someone called, noticing the blaze.

There were more gasps and a few excited laughs. Certain people knew what to expect on Devil's Night and had probably been waiting for it.

I ignored them and swiped the screen of my phone, dialing 911. Maybe the fire trucks had gotten back through.

I hesitated a moment, not wanting to get the guys in trouble, but then I remembered that they didn't get in trouble.

Fuck it. I pressed *Call*.

"Stop!"

I jerked my head up, seeing Officer Baker across the street in the park. My stomach dropped.

Oh, no.

He was headed straight for the guys. With his hand on his firearm, he slowly approached where they all stood together now. "Hands in the air! Now!"

I ended the call, knowing he'd probably called it in already.

"Shit!" I heard Will growl. "Dammit!"

"Hands up! Now!" Baker bellowed again. "You little shits are done for the night! I'm taking you in!"

"Son of a bitch," I breathed out, stuffing my phone in my sweatshirt.

Michael's hands went up first, slowly followed by everyone else's.

"This really ruins our night, Baker," Will joked, and I heard the rest of the guys erupt in laughter.

"Down on the ground!" the officer shouted, ignoring their teasing. "Slowly."

"My father's going to have my head," Kai grumbled.

My pulse raced, and I watched as they all lowered to the ground and a crowd of spectators gathered around the scene.

It wasn't the first time the guys had gotten taken in. Baker would probably just keep them for the night so they didn't do any more damage and then release them in the morning.

But then I shot my eyes back and forth, noticing several people take out their cell phones and begin recording.

"Take your masks off," the officer ordered.

My jaw dropped open as I breathed hard. *No.*

Not with everyone fucking recording! Michael would be discovered, and he'd lose his spot on the team. Not that I cared.

Okay, yes. I fucking cared.

I shot my head around, twisting from side to side and looking for something—anything—to do. Something to distract the cop.

And then I froze, seeing the store windows of Fane.

My heart in my throat, I didn't stop to think.

Just do it.

Lunging for the rear of the car, I opened it and dug out a crowbar. Slamming the back door closed again, I pulled my hood down over my eyes and ran up to the display case, which showed off a glittering set of ruby earrings with a matching necklace and a ring, probably worth more than a quarter of a million dollars.

Yeah, my family didn't fuck around when it came to jewels. We were worth as much as, if not more than, the Crists.

I raised my arm, wincing with fright at what I was about to do. "Shit," I whimpered.

And I just swung.

The crowbar crashed through the glass, the lights and alarms immediately blazing, filling the town square with an onslaught of noise.

I was just about to run, knowing the cop would come after me in preference over them, but then I quickly realized that I'd be leaving the jewels unprotected.

Grabbing the shit out of the case, I held it tight in my fist, the stones cutting into my skin, and I bolted.

"Oh, fuck! Really?" I heard Will's excited voice and then a huge, boisterous laugh.

"Go! Get in the car!" someone else shouted, but I was too far gone to make out the voice.

I darted around the corner, down the street, and then I took another quick left, racing into one of the quieter, less ostentatious neighborhoods as I tried to lose the cop.

I didn't know if he was after me, but hopefully he would think I'd kept going down Breckinridge.

I ran as fast as I could, pushing with every muscle in my legs, the crowbar in one hand and the jewels in the other.

Noah didn't live far from here, so I could make it to his house.

Shit! What the hell had I done?

No matter how much I covered my face, somebody was still bound to recognize me, not to mention the cameras around the store. And then I'd have to return this shit, and my mother would know.

I ran hard, the cool air pouring in and out of my lungs as sweat glided down my back.

"Rika! Get in!" a voice yelled behind me.

I spun around, seeing Kai with his head stuck out the window as Michael raced his G-Class up the dark street.

He slowed alongside me, and I shot out, grabbing the door handle and opening it. I jumped inside and slammed the door. Michael laid on the gas and sped down the street.

"Woo-hoo!" Kai slid the top half of his body out of his window, screaming into the night air.

"You robbed your own fucking store, Rika!" Will laughed and

grabbed fistfuls of my sweatshirt, shouting into my face. "You're the fucking king, baby!"

He released me, hysterical with laughter and smiles.

Tipping his head back, he howled up to the roof of the car, the rush of fear and excitement probably too much.

I breathed hard, heat overcoming my entire body, and I felt like I was going to throw up.

I glanced at the rearview mirror, running my hand through my hair in worry and seeing Michael staring at the road with a small smile on his face. He raised his eyes, as if knowing I was watching him, and I could see something different there.

Maybe respect, or maybe awe.

Or maybe he finally thought I was worth a damn.

I dropped my eyes, forcing myself to relax, a small smile finally peeking out.

"Thanks," a low voice said behind me.

I turned my head to see Damon, his arms resting on the top of the back seat as he stared at me.

I nodded, knowing that probably wasn't a word he said often.

"Yo, turn it up!" Will shouted. "That's her. Monster."

He flashed me a smile as Skillet's "Monster" filled the car, pumping through my veins.

Will started singing, then slid out of his seat, and I shook with laughter as he straddled me, giving me a lap dance to the music.

"To the warehouse," he commanded, holding out his fist. "Let's get fucked up."

CHAPTER 14

ERIKA

Present

I gripped the steering wheel, racing down the dark highway as I held the phone to my ear.

"Mom, where the hell are you?" I burst out, my heart thundering in my chest.

The line kept ringing and ringing, and even though I'd called her several times since I got the call about the house, she still wasn't answering.

I'd even tried our housekeeper, but I couldn't reach anyone.

Goddammit, why hadn't I gotten the satellite number from Michael the other night? I'd just grabbed Alex and begged her to take me home, even though I'd had to drive because she'd had too much to drink.

Turning the wheel to the right, I curved around the bend, hitting *End* on the call and throwing my phone onto the passenger seat.

"Please," I breathed out, my face cracking as I held back the tears. *Please let it be okay.*

The fire trucks got there in time. They had to have.

Ferguson had called me over an hour ago, telling me that my parents' house was on fire and that he'd called the fire department. They were already there, but he couldn't get ahold of my mother or our housekeeper, both of whom were supposed to be out of town.

I didn't hesitate. I jumped in the car and left the city, speeding down the highway. Finally, after an hour of driving, I'd entered the dark, quiet roads of Thunder Bay.

It was after ten at night, after all.

Coming up on the left, I spotted the community entrance and pushed down on my horn, blaring it again and again and again.

Ferguson opened the gate, and I raced through, not even slowing down to talk. My headlights fell across the black road as I wound through the spacious forest, spotting gates and homes, lanterns and driveways, melting into the landscape.

Passing the Crist house, I didn't even spare a glance. I raced right past, clicking the remote for my own gate as it came up half a mile down the road.

Jerking the steering wheel to the left, I charged into the driveway and immediately slammed on the brakes.

Turning off the car, I jumped out, gasping as my chest shook.

"No, no, no . . ." I stared through blurry eyes up at the house.

Black soot spilled over the window frames, and I could see the curtains in the upstairs' windows hanging in shreds.

The front door was gone, the roof was black, and the foliage surrounding the house was burnt up. The house stood dark and beaten as the smell of fire filled the air and black smoke drifted up from a few remaining embers.

I couldn't make out anything from the inside, but it looked gutted.

I shot my hands into my hair, tears spilling over as my face broke. I sobbed, struggling for breath as I broke out in a run, racing up to the house.

"Mom!"

But someone's arms engulfed me, holding me back.

"Let me go!" I struggled and fought, twisting my body away from them.

"You can't go in there!" he shouted.

Michael.

But I didn't care. I broke through his hold, shoving his hands away and bolting into the house.

"Rika!"

I raced into the house, barely taking in the black floors, carpets, and walls. I rounded the banister, feeling the grains of soot under my palm as I grabbed it for support.

"Miss!" a man yelled, and I briefly noticed firefighters walking about.

I ignored them and leapt up the stairs, the floorboards under the soaked carpet shaking with my weight and warning me with their creaking, but I didn't fucking care.

The whole goddamn house could fall on me.

"Mom!"

But wait . . . she's not here. She's away, remember? Relief flooded me as I reached the second-floor landing. She's not here.

I dived into my bedroom, the pungent stench of the smoke filling my lungs as I went straight for my walk-in closet. I fell to my knees, coughing, as I rummaged in the corner for a box.

Water dripped on my back from the doused clothes hanging above me. The fire had been in here, too. *Please, no.*

I flipped off the top of the box and dug in, my hand wrapping around another hard wooden box, this one smaller. I pulled it out.

Water immediately spilled out of its corner.

My heart broke. *No.*

Wrapping my arms around it, I hugged it to my chest and hunched over, sobbing. It was ruined.

"Stand up."

I heard Michael's voice behind me, but I didn't want to move.

"Rika," he urged again.

I raised my head, trying to force in deep breaths, but all of a sudden dizziness racked though me, and I couldn't breathe. The air was too thick.

I should've taken the box with me. It was stupid to leave it here. I thought I was trying to be strong, letting the past go and leaving it behind. I should never have left without it.

I opened my eyes, barely seeing anything through the blur.

Why was Michael here? He'd been here when I got here, which meant he'd found out about the fire before I had.

Slowly, all the control I'd fought to assume over my life was getting taken away from me. Being duped into living at Delcour, finding Will and Damon in my class, the constant threat of his friends hanging over my head, and then there was Michael. I had no control around him.

And now my house?

A weight sat on my chest, and I drew in hard, shallow breaths as I looked up at him. "Where is my mother? Why can't I reach her?"

Holding his eyes, I started coughing again, the air like poison every time I tried to take a breath.

"We need to get out of here." He reached down and pulled me up, knowing that the smoke was getting to me. "We'll come back tomorrow after the fire department's assessed the damage and made sure it's safe. We'll stay at my parents' house tonight."

A lump stretched my throat, but I didn't even have the energy to swallow it down. I squeezed the box to my chest, wanting to sink away.

I didn't fight as we left the room. I didn't fight when he put me in his car or when I saw him pass his parents' house and take me into town.

I couldn't fight him tonight.

A re those the matches you told me about?" he asked, gesturing with his chin to the box on the table. "The ones your father collected from his trips?"

I dropped my eyes, seeing the damp wood of the cigar box, and nodded. I was still too deflated to say anything.

After we'd left the firefighters to keep working at the house, he hadn't taken us back to his parents' place. He'd driven into town and stopped at Sticks, and even though I didn't want to see anybody, I welcomed a drink.

I followed him in, and thankfully, he hid us in a booth and ordered us a couple of beers. The waitress gave me a quick glance, knowing I wasn't twenty-one, but she wouldn't argue with him.

No one ever did.

The bar was nearly empty, probably because it was a school night, and because the college kids had all left town to go back to school by now. A few older patrons sat at the bar, some people played pool, and others loitered around, drinking, talking, and eating.

Slowly easing back into the chair, I touched the box with shaky hands and flipped the clasp on the front, lifting the lid.

Tears sprang to my eyes, and I looked away.

Ruined. Everything was ruined.

Most of the matchbooks and little boxes were made of paper, and even if the matches dried out, the containers were split, torn, and shriveled. The damp cardboard dripped with water, discolored and broken.

I reached over and picked up a little glass jar. The matchsticks inside had a green tip, and I still remembered my father returning from Wales saying he'd found them in a seaside shop in Cardiff.

I smiled sadly, holding up the jar. "These are my favorite," I told Michael, leaning over the table. "Listen to the sound."

I jiggled the jar next to his ear, but then my face fell as I heard the heavy clumping instead of the light, familiar sound of the wooden sticks tapping the inside of the glass.

I lowered myself back down into my seat. "They don't sound the same now, I guess."

Michael stared at me, his huge frame and height damn near taking up the whole bench on his side of the booth.

"They're just matches, Rika."

I cocked my head, my eyes narrowing with ire. "They're just matches?" I sneered. "What do you treasure? Is anything precious to you?"

His expression turned impassive, and he remained silent.

"Yeah, they're just matches," I continued, my voice growing thick with tears. "And memories and smells and sounds and butterflies in my stomach every time I heard the car door slam outside, telling me that he was home. A thousand dreams of all the places I'd have adventures someday." I took a deep breath, placing my hand on top of the box. "They're hopes and wishes and reminders and all the times I smiled, knowing he'd remembered me while he was gone."

And then I looked at him pointedly. "You have money and girls, cars and clothes, but I still have more than you in this little box."

I turned my gaze out to the pool tables, seeing him watch me out of the corner of my eye. I knew he thought I was being silly. He probably wondered why he was still sitting here with me. I had my car. He could've just let me crash at his family's house tonight and gone back to the city himself and to whatever date or function he was dressed up for.

But the truth was, I wasn't being silly. Yeah, they were just matches, but they were also irreplaceable. And the things that were irreplaceable in life were the only things of value.

When I thought about it, there actually weren't a lot of things or people in the world that I loved. Why had I left them here?

"They think the fire started near the stairs," Michael said, taking a drink of his beer. "That's how it traveled to the second floor so fast. We'll know more tomorrow."

I stayed silent, watching as the waitress set down two shots.

"You don't care?" Michael broached when I didn't say anything.

I shrugged, the anger numbing the sadness. "The house doesn't mean anything," I said in a low voice. "I was never happy there without my father anyway."

"Were you happy at my house?"

I shot my eyes up, locking with his. Why was he asking that? Did he actually care? Or maybe he knew the answer.

No. No, I wasn't happy at his house. Not without him there.

In middle school and high school, I'd loved it. Hearing the basketball bounce through the house as he walked around, feeling him in a room and not being able to concentrate on anything else, running into him in the hallway . . .

I loved the anticipation of just being around him.

But after he left for college and barely ever made it home, the Crist house became a cage. I was constantly circled by Trevor, and I missed Michael so much.

Being in his house when he wasn't there was the loneliest I'd ever been.

I dropped the jar back into the box and snapped it shut, turning my head to the jukebox along the front windows.

"Can I have some money?" I asked, turning back to him.

I'd left my bag in my car.

He reached into his pocket, taking some bills off a clip. I reached over without hesitation and took the five I spotted, climbing out of the booth and carrying my beer with me.

Chills broke out down my arms, and I remembered that I was still in the jeans and white tank I'd changed into when I got home from school earlier. Having jumped into the car in such a hurry, I hadn't grabbed a jacket.

Michael was in a black suit and a white shirt, open at the collar, and I wondered if he had been coming from somewhere or was going somewhere.

It didn't matter. He could leave. I could take care of myself.

I took sips of my beer as I fed the machine the five dollars and began choosing music.

A girl's laugh sounded behind me, and I twisted my head, recognizing Diana Forester.

She was hanging on our booth, with her hand on her hip and a coy smile on her lips as she talked to Michael.

Jesus.

They dated in high school, although I wouldn't call it dating exactly. Kai and Michael shared her. And I only knew that because I'd seen them both kissing her in the media room one night. I'd bolted before I saw anything else, but I could definitely guess what went down.

Life past high school wasn't so hot for her. Last I heard, she was helping her parents run the bed-and-breakfast they owned here in town.

He nodded at whatever she was saying, a slight tilt to his lips, but it looked like he was just indulging her.

Until she leaned down, and I thought I saw his eyes flash to me for a brief second before he smiled wider at her and reached up, touching her blond hair.

My neck and face heated, and I spun back around.

Asshole.

Even if I never tried to, I had expectations about the man I thought he was, and I needed to knock it off.

Was I going to be the third wheel in the house tonight when he brought her home? Would I be the one sitting uncomfortable and silent a few rooms down the hall?

I was done pretending and acting like shit didn't bother me. I was mad. *Own it.*

Punching buttons, I loaded only one song even though I'd paid for twenty. Downing the rest of the beer, I headed back to the booth.

Sliding the empty bottle across the table, I saw Diana jump as if she hadn't known I was here.

"Oh, hey, Rika," she chirped. "How's Trevor? Are you missing him a lot?"

Trevor and I weren't dating. Guess she didn't get the memo.

I sat down, crossed my legs, and folded my hands, laying them on the table. Ignoring her question, I stared at Michael. He was fucking with me, and I cocked my head, holding his amused eyes.

I hadn't asked to come to Sticks, but he'd brought me here. He didn't get to lock in his one-night stand with me in tow. Not tonight.

The uncomfortable silence thickened, but the more I held my ground, challenging him to get rid of her, the stronger I felt.

"Dirty Diana" by Shaman's Harvest began playing, and I smirked.

"Well . . ." Diana spoke up, touching Michael's shoulder, "I'm so glad I ran into you. You barely make it home anymore."

But Michael ignored her, still holding my eyes.

He cleared his throat, squinting at me. "Interesting song."

I fought not to laugh. "Yes, I thought Diana would like it," I replied cheerfully and then looked to her. "It's about a woman who jumps into bed with men that aren't hers."

Michael dropped his eyes, laughing under his breath.

Diana scowled, cocking an eyebrow as she shifted away. "Bitch."

And then she turned around and left.

I locked eyes with Michael again, my body rushing with liquid heat. It felt good to stand up to him and his antics.

"Why are you always messing with me?" I demanded.

"Because it's fun," he admitted, "and you're getting so good at it."

I narrowed my eyes. "Why are your friends messing with me?"

But he just stayed silent.

I could see the challenge in his eyes. He knew they were fucking with me, and instinct told me to be afraid, but for some reason . . .

I wasn't.

The pushing and shoving, the head games and the mind-fucks . . . everything twisted me up and tore me down so much that when I finally got tired of stumbling and falling and backing down, I found that it felt really good to play.

Michael leaned back in the booth, resting against the corner and looking out at the bar.

"So if Diana is 'Dirty Diana,' what about Sam?" He tipped his chin. "The bartender. What's his song?"

I turned my eyes away, finding Sam Watkins behind the bar, working alone. He was taking down bottles of liquor, wiping them off, and replacing them.

"'Closing Time,'" I guessed. "By Semisonic."

Michael snickered, looking at me like I wasn't even trying. "That's too easy." He took a drink of his beer and nodded to some-one else. "Drew, at the bar."

I inhaled a breath, trying to relax. Looking over at Drew Hale, I saw a middle-aged judge who was well-connected but not par-ticularly rich. His shirtsleeves were rolled up, and his suit pants were wrinkled. He was in here a lot.

"Hinder. 'Lips of an Angel,'" I tossed out, turning to Michael. "He was in love with a woman, they broke up, and he married her sister on a whim." I looked down, my heart going out to him a little. "And every time I see him he looks just a little worse."

I couldn't imagine how hard it was to see the woman you loved all the time and not be able to have her, because you married the wrong woman.

Blinking, I looked up, seeing Michael. And all of a sudden, it wasn't so hard to imagine.

"Him," he continued, gesturing to a heavyset businessman sit-ting at a table with a younger woman. She had platinum hair and heavy makeup. He wore a wedding ring, and she didn't.

I rolled my eyes. "'Seventeen.' Winger."

Michael laughed, his white teeth shining in the dim booth.

He went on, jerking his chin to a pair of high schoolers playing pool. "How about them?"

I studied them, checking out the black hair hanging in their eyes, the black skinny jeans and T-shirts, and their scary black boots with five-inch-thick soles.

I smiled. "Closeted Taylor Swift fans. I promise."

His chest shook as he laughed. "And her?" He nodded.

I twisted my head over my shoulder, seeing a beautiful young woman leaning over the bar. I could see a good bit of thigh going up her skirt, and when she leaned back down again, I saw her pull her mouth away from a drink and take hold of the straw, dipping it in and out of a milkshake.

I couldn't help but laugh as I turned back around, singing, "My milkshake brings all the boys to the yard . . ."

Michael choked on his beer, a drop of it spilling out of his mouth as he tried not to laugh.

I picked up my shot of whiskey the waitress had left before, swirling the amber liquid in the glass.

I hadn't felt anything from the beer, but for some reason, I hadn't really needed it. My body felt warm now. I was relaxed, despite what had happened to the house, and I felt something building in my gut. Something hot that made me feel ten feet tall.

Michael leaned in, his voice turning low and heavy. "And how about me?"

I swallowed, still studying my drink. What song described him? What band?

That was like trying to pick one food to eat for the rest of your life.

"Disturbed," I said, naming the band and still looking down at the glass.

He said nothing. Only remained still before finally sitting back and tipping his drink up to his lips.

Butterflies swarmed in my stomach, and I kept my breathing even.

"Drowning Pool, Three Days Grace, Five Finger Death Punch," I continued. "Thousand Foot Krutch, 10 Years, Nothing More, Breaking Benjamin, Papa Roach, Bush . . ." I paused, exhaling nice and slow despite the way my heart drummed. "Chevelle, Skillet, Garbage, Korn, Trivium, In This Moment . . ." I drifted off, peace settling over me as I looked up at him. "You're in everything."

His eyes held mine, as mine narrowed with just a hint of the pain I'd felt while longing for him all these years. I didn't know what he was thinking or if he knew what to think, but now he knew.

I'd hid it, pushed it down, and acted like it wasn't there, but now I'd owned it, and I didn't care what he thought. I wasn't ashamed of what was inside me.

Now he knew.

I blinked, lifting the glass to my lips and downing my shot. Leaning over, I swiped his and slammed it down, as well.

I barely felt the burn in my throat. The adrenaline overpowered it.

"I'm tired," I told him solemnly.

And then I got up and left the booth, knowing he'd follow.

CHAPTER 15

ERIKA

Present

The house scared me at night. It always had.

A light wind blew outside and bare tree branches scraped against windows in various rooms as I crept downstairs, passing the ticking grandfather clock in the foyer.

Its sound echoed through the vast house and always reminded me that life went on while we slept. *Tick-tock, tick-tock, tick-tock . . .*

Kind of a scary thought, actually. Creatures stirred outside, trees sat patiently in the forest, and danger could be lurking right outside the front door, mere feet away from our vulnerable spots in our warm beds.

And the Crist house held that same mystery. There were too many dark corners. Too many nooks to hide in and too many dark closets hidden in dormant rooms lurking behind closed doors.

The house was heavy with secrets and surprises, and it scared me, which was probably why I always found myself wandering around at night.

I enjoyed the fear of the silent darkness, but it was something else, too. You became aware of things under the shroud of night that you didn't see in the light of day. The things people hide and how lax they become with their secrets when they think everyone is asleep.

In the Crist house, the most interesting hours would often be after midnight. I'd learned to love the sound of the house being shut down and locked up. It was like a new world was about to unfold.

My bare feet didn't make any sound as I walked into the dark kitchen and headed over to the pantry.

This was where I'd first found out that Mr. Crist was scared of Michael. It had been the middle of the night, and Michael had been sixteen. He'd come into the kitchen to get something to drink and hadn't noticed me on the patio outside. I'd gotten up to watch the rain under an awning with a stash of Fruit Roll-Ups Mrs. Crist had bought me. I remember it clearly because it was my first night in the new bedroom she'd decorated just for me for when I slept over.

His father walked into the kitchen, and I couldn't make out what they were saying, but it turned heated, and Mr. Crist slapped his son across the face.

I hated it, of course, but it wasn't something I hadn't seen before, unfortunately. Mr. Crist and Michael didn't get along, and it wasn't the first time Michael had been hit.

But this time was different. He didn't take it quietly. He immediately lashed out and grabbed his father by the neck. I stared in horror as Mr. Crist struggled. Something had come over Michael, and I'd never seen him act like that before.

And as second after second passed, it was clear that Michael was too old for his father to push around, and now Mr. Crist knew it.

I watched as his father started to choke and cough.

Michael eventually let go, and his father stormed out of the kitchen. The incident lost Michael his car and his allowance, but I didn't think Mr. Crist ever touched him again after that.

Opening the pantry door, I turned on the small light and walked down to the third column of shelves, finding the peanut butter.

Holding it to my chest, I gazed around, spotting the half-full bag of mini marshmallows on the top shelf near the corner.

I smiled, walking over and arching up on my tiptoes, trying to pinch the bag between my fingers and grab it.

But then an arm reached out over me, snatching the bag, and I jerked my hand down, sucking in a quick breath.

"I thought you were tired," Michael said, holding out the bag to me.

I swallowed to wet my dry mouth and turned, peering up at him. He was dressed in black lounge pants with no shirt, and his hair looked wet, probably from a shower.

I wanted to groan at the ache between my legs. *God, he drove me crazy.*

With everything that had happened tonight, I hadn't had a chance to slow down enough for it to occur to me, but . . .

The last time I saw Michael alone was in the pool cave. I tensed my thighs, the little pulse in my clit suddenly beating harder at the memory and wanting a whole lot more of whatever he did to me in there.

Thankfully, he hadn't mentioned it.

After we'd arrived home from Sticks, we'd both gone our separate ways. I went to my room and hurriedly dialed the number for the satellite phone he'd finally given to me on the car ride home, unfortunately not getting an answer.

After calling a few more times with no luck, I decided to try again in the morning. She was fine. Damon had just scared me with the threat, which was probably all he was trying to do to begin with.

I then crawled into a hot bath and slipped into some pajama shorts and a white cami. But I was no longer tired. Since I hadn't eaten since breakfast that morning at my apartment, I went downstairs in search of food.

Brushing past Michael, I left the pantry and set the provisions down on the island, trying to get away from him.

No such luck.

He came to my side and stood next to me, grabbing the loaf of bread and taking out two slices for me and two for himself.

Guess he was hungry, too.

I let out a frustrated breath and spun around, sliding two plates out of the cabinet while he opened the refrigerator and dug in one of the drawers for something.

We didn't speak as we busied ourselves making sandwiches. I dug into the marshmallow bag for a handful and poured them onto the peanut butter I'd already spread while he unscrewed a pickle jar. I stopped what I was doing, twisting up my lips as he laid slices across his peanut-butter sandwich.

Gross.

"That makes you so much less attractive," I said, wincing.

He snorted, and I watched as he replaced the top slice of bread and picked up the sandwich, bringing it to his mouth.

"Don't knock it 'til you try it." And he took a huge bite, grabbing his plate and walking around me.

I shook my head, amused.

"Let's watch a movie," he said as he left the kitchen.

I popped my head up. *A movie?*

"And grab a couple of waters before you come," he shouted from the hallway.

I cocked an eyebrow. The only time Michael and I had ever watched movies together was when Trevor was in the room, too. Otherwise I was too scared to invade Michael's space.

I exhaled a sigh and turned around, taking two bottles of water out of the fridge. Grabbing the rest of my food, I left the kitchen, my arms full.

The media room was dark, lit only by the light of the seventy-inch flat-screen hanging on the rock wall ahead of me.

As beautiful as the house was, it was this room I liked best.

There were no windows, as it was buried in the center of the house, and all the walls were made of stacked stone. It gave the room a cave-like feel, and it was usually the one Michael and his friends hung out in when he lived here.

In the center of the room sat a three-sided brown suede couch. Huge and comfortable, it had throw pillows and a large matching ottoman sitting in the empty space in the middle.

Michael carried his plate to the couch and tossed the remote aside, sitting down with his back to me.

My blood started to heat, and my hand with the plate shook. It almost felt easy. Like just a relaxing night watching TV.

Too easy. I couldn't relax around him. I knew better.

I walked into the room and rounded the couch, tossing his bottle of water on the seat next to him and taking the right side of the sofa, perpendicular to him.

I sat cross-legged, facing the television and eating while he surfed.

"That looks good," I spoke up, seeing *Alien vs. Predator.*

"That looks good?" he mocked in my voice, and I turned my head toward him.

He was slouched back on the couch with his left arm tucked behind his head and his long, tight torso looking so smooth and beautiful. I once saw a girl straddle him as he sat like that, and I turned away, feeling the ever-present longing I wished would go away.

"You've already seen it, Rika," he argued. "I saw you in here watching that movie back in high school. At least twice."

Twenty-one times, actually.

I liked horror movies, but I also enjoyed sci-fi, so the Alien and Predator franchises were a big hit for me.

And then when they combined them and made *Alien vs. Predator*? Holy shit.

"Fine by me," Michael allowed, clicking on the channel, the

movie starting just as the team of archeologists had gotten to Antarctica.

The hair on my arms stood up, and my toes curled. I held the sandwich with both hands, taking small bites as I watched the screen. I could hear Michael biting into his sandwich and uncapping his water, and by the time the alien queen had started laying eggs, I had spread out on my stomach, leaning up on my elbows as I held the sandwich and chewed.

My stomach tightened, hearing the alien queen's heavy breathing. Her hissing echoed through the surround sound, and when the team of scientists entered the sacrificial chamber, unaware of all the alien eggs in the room that were about to hatch, I put down my sandwich and pushed it away. Grabbing a throw pillow, I crouched down behind it, peeking over the top.

And locking my ankles in the air, I winced as the eggs began to open.

Long legs crawled out of the opening, the music got faster, and the creature lurched, flying through the air toward a woman's face.

I shot my head down, burying it in the pillow as the shot cut to a new scene.

I twisted my face to the side, laughing as I peeked over at him. "That part always freaks me out."

But he wasn't paying attention to the TV. His eyes were on my legs.

I immediately warmed. Had he been watching the movie at all?

He still sat back on the couch, relaxing, but his eyes were trained on my body, and I could only imagine what he was thinking.

And then, as if realizing I'd just spoken, he finally raised his eyes, meeting mine, and then shot his gaze back to the screen, ignoring me.

I slowly turned back, too, and even though I wondered if he was still looking at me, I made no move to sit up or grab a blanket.

Over the next hour I continued to hug my pillow as the predators hunted the aliens and slowly all of the archeologists became collateral damage. I felt Michael's eyes on me from time to time, but I didn't know if it was real or just my imagination.

But every time a predator lurked in the dark or an alien crept out of a corner, I could feel the heat of his stare, and I gripped the pillow tighter and tighter until, by the end of the movie, my fingers ached.

"You like to be scared, don't you?" I heard his voice behind me. "That's your kink."

I twisted my head to the side, narrowing my eyes as the credits started to roll.

Like to be scared? I enjoyed scary movies, but it wasn't kink.

He placed his palms on his thighs, leaning his head back and watching me. "Your toes curled every time the aliens and predators came on the screen."

I dropped my eyes, lowering my legs and slowly sitting up.

All the movies that I enjoyed the most came to mind—the slasher flicks, like *Halloween* and *Friday the 13th*—and I noticed how tight my stomach muscles were. I took a deep breath, forcing them to relax.

Yeah, okay. I liked the way my heart pounded harder, and I loved the way my senses were sharper when I was scared. The way every simple *tick-tock* in the house became mysterious footsteps, or the way I was hyperaware of empty space behind me as I sat on the couch, feeling like someone was lurking back there.

I enjoyed the fright of not knowing what was coming and from where.

"When we used to wear the masks," Michael said, dropping his voice to a near whisper, "you liked it, didn't you? It scared you, but it turned you on."

I raised my hesitant eyes and tried not to let out a laugh. What was I supposed to say? That the fact that they'd looked like monsters got me hot?

I shook my head clear and stood up, saying in a quiet voice, "I'm going to bed."

I grabbed my phone and took a step, but Michael's voice stopped me.

"Come here," he said softly.

I turned my head, narrowing my eyes. *Come here?*

He sat up, resting his forearms on his knees and waiting, while I shifted on my feet.

He was always playing games. I didn't trust him.

But the temptation to engage was too great. He was right. I was getting good at it, and I kind of liked it, too.

I took slow steps, holding up my chin to steel myself.

When I reached him, he placed a hand on my hip and pulled me in between his legs. I gasped as he fell back against the sofa again, pulling me in with him. I shot my hands out, planting them on both sides of his head on the back of the couch, keeping myself upright as I leaned into him.

"Say it," he breathed out, holding my hips with both hands now. "It turned you on."

I closed my mouth and shook my head, looking down at him with a challenge.

"I know it did," he maintained, a fire in his eyes. "Did you think I couldn't see how tense your body would get or how your nipples got hard through your shirt when you saw me wearing it? You're a little twisted. Admit it."

I folded my lips between my teeth, turning my head away.

But then he tipped his chin up and caught my nipple between his teeth through my tank top, and I closed my eyes, letting out a small cry.

Oh, God!

The heat of his mouth swooped into my stomach as he released my nipple and then snatched it up again, dragging it out between his teeth.

"I've got the mask upstairs," he taunted, kissing and nibbling on me through my shirt. "I can get it if you want me to."

No. No, I wasn't like that.

I pushed away from him, but he held me firm.

"Michael, let me go."

But then I felt my phone vibrate in my hand, and I quickly glanced at the screen, seeing no name with the number. Reading the number, though, I noticed that it was his mother's. *That's strange.* I thought I had her number saved in my contacts.

But I let it go, remembering that my mom was with her. I needed to take this call.

Planting my fists on Michael's chest, I shoved him away. "Get off me. Your mom's calling."

All he did was laugh, though, and my face fell.

He grabbed my arm and threw me down onto my stomach and came down on my back, pinning me to the couch.

I breathed hard and fast, feeling his cock press against my ass as he snatched my phone out of my hand.

I stared wide-eyed as he placed it a few inches in front of me, his finger hovering over the green *Answer* button.

"Michael, no," I rushed out, panic making my lungs ache.

But he swiped the screen anyway. The ringing stopped, and I heard silence as she waited for me to say something.

"Say hi," he whispered in my ear.

I shook my head, too scared for her to hear my voice.

But then he put his hand over my mouth, forced his hand between me and the couch, and dived into my pajama shorts, sliding his fingers inside me. I let out a muffled scream.

Fuck!

I squirmed and tried to reach out my arms to hang up the phone, but he released the rest of his weight on me, pushing me down to where I could barely breathe.

"Shhh . . ." he cooed.

He brought his fingers out of my pussy and began rubbing them over my clit so slow and so soft I couldn't help but shake.

I heard his mother give a hesitant "Hello?" on the other end, but I couldn't catch my breath.

"Say hi," he whispered again, but this time his voice was thick and wet like he was fucking me.

He removed his hand from my mouth, and I licked my lips, swallowing the dryness and trying to find my voice. My heart thundered in my ears, and I winced, holding back the groan I wanted to let out at what his fingers were doing to me.

"Hel . . . hello, Mrs. Crist," I choked out.

Oh, God. The pleasure of his fingers rubbing me in circles slowly crept into my belly, pooling and building into something I knew I wasn't going to be able to control for long.

"Rika!" she chirped, sounding happy. "I'm so sorry to call so late, but there's a time difference here. I wanted to check in before I got underway today. How's everything going there?"

I opened my mouth to answer, but Michael fisted my hair and jerked my head to the side, diving into my neck with his teeth.

My scar! I stilled, waiting for him to feel it or see it and switch sides, but he didn't. He nibbled and bit, sweeping the tip of his tongue up the nape of my neck, not leaving a single inch that hadn't been touched by his mouth.

"Rika?" she prompted.

Oh, yeah. She'd asked a question. What had she asked? No, wait. I had a question. I'd been trying to get ahold of her. Wha—?

"Yes, um . . ." But I lost my train of thought as Michael slid two fingers back inside me, pumping in hard, steady thrusts.

"Are you scared?" Michael growled low in my ear. "I'll bet you are, and I'll bet you like it. I'll even bet this is the best sex you've ever had, and my dick's not even inside you yet."

"Rika?" Mrs. Crist called again, this time more urgent.

But I gasped, the rush of heat on my skin as he devoured my neck again sending waves through my body.

"Your pussy is so fucking wet." He drew out his fingers, swirling their wetness around my clit in quick circles. "So soft and tight."

I groaned, starting to grind into his hand.

"Yes," I moaned. "Yes, Mrs. Crist. Thank you for checking in. So far, so good here."

I heard Michael laugh in my ear, probably at how ridiculous I sounded.

"Oh, good, dear," she replied. "Have you run into Michael at Delcour? I told him to keep an eye on you in case you needed anything."

"Do you need anything?" he teased in a light voice, rubbing the thick, hard ridge of his cock into my ass. "Is that what your tight little pussy is begging for?"

"Yes," I breathed out, my clit pulsing harder and harder and my stomach hot with lust.

And then my eyes rounded, realizing she'd heard that.

"Um, yes!" I burst out, trying to cover it up. "I've seen him a couple of times."

"Good," she responded. "Don't let him push you around. I know he seems unpleasant, but he can be nice."

His kisses and bites spread up my neck and over to my cheek, making me shiver. "I am being nice to you, right?" he whispered, dragging his teeth across my jaw. "Yeah, she'd cut my fucking hand off if she knew just how nice I was being right now."

And with that he slid his fingers back in and pumped, rolling his hips into my ass, grinding his dick on me as his body weighed on my back.

Fuck! My thighs were on fire, and I gripped the sofa cushion, needing a release.

"No worries, Mrs. Crist," I gritted out, squeezing my eyes shut. "I can handle him."

"Can you?" he mocked in my ear.

But Mrs. Crist kept going. "Glad to hear it. Now, study hard, and I'll be coming back with lots of presents before Thanksgiving."

I couldn't take it. I rolled my hips again and again, riding the couch.

"You ready to come, you little brat?" Michael taunted. "Tell me how much you love it. Tell me my mask got you fucking wet."

I turned my mouth to him, whispering desperately, "Please hang up the phone."

He smirked, dropping his full lips to touch mine. "Don't worry," he breathed over my mouth. "She never notices anything. My father is faithful, Trevor is good, and I can be trusted. I'll look out for my little brother's girlfriend and keep her nice and safe in the light of day and not violate the fuck out of her in the dark."

I should've been mad about the "brother's girlfriend" remark, but I didn't give a shit right now.

And then he closed his eyes, groaning with the dry humping he was doing. "My mother never peels back the curtain, Rika."

I let my forehead fall to the couch, feeling the orgasm build. Every hair on my body stood on end, and my heart was jackhammering in my chest as I breathed in and out, faster and faster.

"Say it," he demanded.

But I shook my head, clenching my teeth to not cry out. Oh, God. *I'm coming.*

"I'm really sorry, Mrs. Crist," I groaned. "Someone's at the door. I have to go, okay?"

And I yanked my arm free, high on rage and energy as I hurriedly swiped the *End Call* button.

I threw my head back, whimpering, "Oh, God." Grinding harder, I fucked his hand, needing to come so bad.

But then he pulled his fingers out of my panties, and I shot my head up, confused.

What the hell?

He flipped me over and then came back down on me again, pinning my hands above my head.

The throbbing between my legs ached, and the orgasm was right there. Shit!

"Michael, no!" I cried, squirming underneath him. "Oh, God, why did you stop?"

The weight of his body between my spread legs felt so good. I rolled my hips, chasing the orgasm.

"Don't you fucking grind on me," he growled. "You don't get to come until you tell me the truth."

"What truth?" I burst out. "You mean what you want to hear?"

Jesus! Did he ever stop?

"Being scared turns you on, doesn't it?" he pressed.

No. Screw him. He needed to know he couldn't push me around and do this to me anymore.

I clenched my teeth and scowled, shaking my head.

No, Michael. Your mask doesn't scare me. It didn't get me hot, and I hated it when you wore it.

His piercing eyes turned angry, and I saw his jaw flex. He pushed up off me and looked down with contempt.

"Go to bed," he ordered.

And I fought to hide my smile as I peeled myself up off the couch. My body was tight and tense, and I was so fucking needy, I ached.

But I'd won. He hadn't gotten what he wanted.

I stormed out of the media room and made my way down the hall, running up the stairs to the second floor. I wasn't trying to get away from him, but I was fucking angry and pleased and turned on, and now I had energy to spare.

Slamming my bedroom door closed behind me, I crashed onto my bed and buried my face in my pillow. But the cool fabric of the fresh sheets did nothing to soothe my burning skin.

I was a wreck.

I needed him deep inside, to feel him and taste him and see him lose control over me for once.

I wanted him to use me and fuck me and go at me with a desperation he never showed for anything or anyone.

How did he manage to stop just then? He wasn't a machine. I hadn't mistaken what I'd seen in his eyes and the heat I'd felt from his mouth. He wanted me, didn't he?

I let out a sigh, trying to get my breathing to even out.

Circling, circling, circling . . . He pulled, I pulled. He pushed, I pushed. We fought and played, toyed and challenged, but he never gave in. We never came together, fused, and seized what was there.

And I was so tired. There was something holding him back.

I stared at my alarm clock, wondering if I should even bother to set it. I had classes tomorrow, but I wouldn't make it. I knew that. It was already after two in the morning, and I still hadn't slept.

I gazed at the red numbers, wondering what I was going to do. Would he act like none of this had happened tomorrow?

But then I blinked, my brain going on alert. The numbers on the screen disappeared, the clock went dead, and I jerked my head up, pinching my eyebrows together.

What the . . . ?

I turned around to see the small lights along the bottom of the bathroom walls—which were always kept on as a type of nightlight—dark, as well.

I pushed myself up, turning the knob on the bedside lamp, but that didn't work, either.

"Shit."

I twisted my head, looking out the window and seeing a light breeze. It wasn't anything major, but the power could've gone out, I guessed.

Climbing off the bed, I walked to my door and opened it a crack. The hallway was nearly pitch black. I couldn't see five feet in front of me.

My heart started to race, and I inched the door open all the way, peering out. "Michael?"

But the only sound I heard was the low howl of the wind outside. My toes curled into the carpet.

Stepping out of my room, I walked slowly, looking around and keeping my ears peeled as I made my way down the hallway.

"Michael?" I called again. "Where are you?"

I clenched my fists, the eerie darkness of the house vibrating off every inch of my skin. I felt like someone was behind me and I was being watched.

The grandfather clock chimed the quarter hour, still working since it ran off a battery, and I stepped lightly down the stairs and into the foyer, twisting my head from side to side and breathing hard.

But then someone grabbed my arm, and I sucked in a sharp breath. A large, dark form picked me up and wrapped my legs around his waist, holding me tight.

"No!" I cried out.

He slammed me into a wall next to a small table, the mirror above it shaking as I gripped his shoulders and he dug his fingers into my thighs.

I stared wide-eyed, coming face-to-face with a vicious red mask.

Michael.

The dark, violent gouges sent shivers down my spine, and his eyes stared out through the small holes like a chained monster. I stopped breathing.

Fear swirled in my gut, warming my insides and making every

muscle clench. I tightened my thighs around his waist, feeling the slickness between my legs and my nipples chafe against my tank top.

Oh, God. He was right.

My eyes burned, and I wanted to cry. *Goddammit, he was right.*

I locked my ankles behind his back and held his shoulders as his hazel eyes stared at me. He wore jeans and a black hoodie, just like in the past.

I stared into his eyes and slowly slid my arms around his neck, the drumming in my chest charging every muscle in my body, making me strong.

"Yes," I breathed out, bringing my lips close to his mask and taunting him. "Yes, it turns me on."

And then I dived down, burying my lips in his neck and devouring him.

He let out a breath, digging his fingers into my thighs as I went at him, nibbling and biting. I caught his hot skin between my teeth, sucking on him and kissing, before reaching up and flicking his ear lobe with the tip of my tongue.

Moving down his neck, I left soft, urgent kisses and grazed his skin with my nose, smelling his body wash. Like spice and man, and I nudged my head in more, forcing his neck to arch back as I kissed his throat, trailing the tip of my tongue up to his jaw.

"Rika," he warned in a hard voice.

But I didn't care.

I could hear his heavy breathing through his mask, and for a moment, I thought he was going to stop me, but I sucked in a surprised breath as he hoisted me up and slammed me into the wall again, holding me tighter.

"Fuck," he gritted out.

His hand slid down between our bodies, and I let out a moan, flattening my back against the wall and giving him room as he unfastened his belt and jeans.

Hell yes.

Reaching down with one hand, I pulled my tank top over my head, throwing it to the floor.

I tightened my hold around his neck and pressed my naked breasts against his black sweatshirt.

He worked quickly, dragging off my pajama shorts before his greedy hand slipped under the lace of my pink panties and pulled them, ripping them clean off my body.

He then grabbed hold of his cock, taking it out of his jeans and positioning his hips just right.

"So you like the mask. You're pretty fucking sick, aren't you?" he teased.

I nodded, a smile peeking out. "Yes."

He stroked my bare pussy with the head of his dick, dragging it up and down my slit.

"Just like me," he whispered.

And then he thrust his hips between my thighs, and I cried out as he slid his thick cock, inch by inch, inside of me, burying himself in my wet pussy.

"Oh, God," I panted, arching my back. "You're so hard."

My skin was stretched, and it hurt a little, but it was too fucking good, too. His tip rubbed so deep up inside me I could feel him in my stomach.

I dug my heels into his back and pressed my body into his, holding him close as I started to ride him, meeting his thrusts again and again.

"That's it, baby," he growled low.

He thrust, forcing my back up the wall again and again, and I hung on for dear life as he pounded and fucked.

I whimpered, fisting his sweatshirt in my hands. "Michael."

He jerked me into him, going faster and harder, and the feel of him sliding in and out of me, finally taking me, was doing nothing to ease my need. I was hungrier.

I dived into his neck, breathing against his skin as I grazed my lips back and forth, whispering, "They all thought I was a good girl, Michael." I dragged his lobe through my teeth. "But there's so many bad things I want to do. Do dirty things to me."

"Jesus," he gasped, hooking an arm under my knee and yanking my ass into him, fucking harder as he let his head fall back.

"Yes!" I cried out, his cock hitting deeper and my thigh aching from where his hand gripped it.

Fire started to pool in my belly, and my orgasm crested.

"Michael," I moaned, rolling my hips and riding his fucking cock as I grunted and panted. The house was filled with our breathing and groaning and the sound of his skin hitting mine.

Pleasure built between my legs, my muscles burned, and then I squeezed my eyes shut, letting him fuck me as my orgasm opened up and spread apart, bursting inside my womb and flooding my body and brain with heat and euphoria.

"Fuck!" I cried out. "Michael!"

My loud moans echoed in the great foyer, and my clit throbbed and my pussy tightened around him, trying to keep him there. He pounded into me, and I tightened my arms around his neck again, riding it out.

My head felt like it was drifting in a cloud, and I went limp, letting my forehead fall to his shoulder as the orgasm racked through my body.

"Such a beautiful little monster," he whispered, his chest heaving.

He reached around, grabbing the chin of his mask, and ripped it off, letting it fall to the floor. His thrusts slowed and his arms tightened around my body, which had now become deadweight.

I blinked my exhausted eyes, looking up at him and seeing the hunger still in his.

He slowly let me down, letting my feet come back to the floor as he peeled off his sweatshirt and dropped it to the floor.

His hair was matted with sweat, and he ran his hand through it, making it stick up, looking sexy. His broad chest shined with a light layer of sweat, and I let my eyes fall, seeing his cock still hard and sticking straight up at me.

"You didn't come," I said quietly.

The corner of his lips curled, looking threatening. "We are far from done."

CHAPTER 16

MICHAEL

Present

I screwed up.

I wanted her, and I wanted her to myself tonight. It was done, and it couldn't be undone, so fuck it. I was going to enjoy this.

I slid my hands down over her ass and squeezed, bringing her body into mine.

Her soft tits pressed against my chest, and I felt the brush of her hard nipples against my skin.

Goddamn, she had a beautiful body.

Smooth, toned skin, still tan from her time on the beach this summer, and her breasts were full and round, sticking straight out at me like they were begging for a little attention.

I leaned down, running the tip of my tongue up the length of her scar, feeling the jagged, thin line curve upward and give way to the smooth skin under her ear.

It never escaped my attention how she hid it around my brother, as if it made her less beautiful.

No. Our scrapes and bruises, tattoos, scars, smiles, and wrinkles told our stories, and I didn't want a pristine piece of wallpaper. I wanted her and everything she was. At least for tonight.

She finally leaned her head back, relaxing and letting me do whatever I wanted.

A shiver ran down my spine. It had been so hard not to come before.

She'd had me jacked up too much for too long, and I'd nearly lost control. I hadn't really planned this, after all.

At least not beyond scaring the shit out of her and antagonizing her with the mask.

But when I'd held her, she'd tightened her thighs around my waist, the fear in her eyes turning to lust, and I was knocked on my ass.

She was going for it, and I couldn't believe it. I'd never met anyone like her. She rose to every challenge.

Pulling back, she eyed me warily. "You're not going to dump me outside now, are you?"

I nearly snorted. "Don't you trust me?"

"Have you ever given me reason to?" she challenged in a suddenly serious tone. "I know you've always got something up your sleeve."

I narrowed my eyes on her, amused. Sure, I had things up my sleeve. Ideas.

I might have tried to ignore her over the years, but a fantasy or two had crept in, unfortunately, and while having them made it more difficult to be around her, they'd kept me hot. They'd kept me angry and ready.

I held my head up, looking down at her. "Do you still have school uniforms here?"

She cocked her head just a little, looking suspicious, before she nodded.

"Go get one on." I brought my hands up, running them up and down her arms. "Everything. The tie, the vest, the skirt, everything."

"Why?"

I smiled to myself, stepping aside to let her go to the stairs. "Because you can't win if you don't play."

She glared, and I gave her a light slap on the ass, urging her up the stairs.

The longer we talked, the more I'd come to my senses. Or the more her standing naked in front of me would just make me take her right here on the floor.

And I had something better in mind.

What are we doing?" she asked, peering out the windshield. "Why are we here?"

I pulled up in front of St. Killian's, the headlights shining in the darkness and landing on the broken stained-glass windows and the eerie blackness inside. The dilapidated stone of the structure was surrounded by fallen autumn leaves, and the only sound was the wind howling through the trees overhead.

My stomach knotted with anticipation, and a drop of sweat glided down my back.

This was my favorite place.

It was weighted with history and filled with a thousand corners and small spaces. As a kid, I'd climbed around inside, exploring and getting lost for hours.

I shut off the car, the headlights going dead, and I stepped out, the smell of earth drifting through my nostrils. This place felt more like home than any other.

Slamming the door shut, I gripped my mask in my hand and watched Rika climb out of the G-Class. Her nervous eyes kept glancing up at the dark and silent cathedral, and her chest rose and fell faster.

She was scared. *Good.*

I let my eyes fall down her outfit once again, having got a good look before we left the house, too.

She wore her navy-blue-and-forest-green plaid skirt and a white blouse fitted with a matching plaid tie under a navy-blue vest. On her feet were black flats. She'd even combed out her hair and put on a little makeup to freshen up.

I think she had an idea of what was in store when I told her to wear the outfit, but she was definitely surprised when I told her to get in the car.

And now . . . a little frightened.

I gazed at her legs, my cock swelling at the memory of how smooth they were and how warm it was between them.

My heart started to race.

"Let's go down to the catacombs." I nodded toward the cathedral. "No blindfold this time."

I smirked, keeping my expression hard. I didn't want her to feel safe.

She dropped her chin, searching the ground for a way out. Should she say no? Should she ask another question I wasn't going to answer?

Or would she play?

She raised her eyes and swallowed, a look of defiance crossing her face. And I held back a smile, seeing her turn and start walking toward the side entrance.

Lifting up the mask, I slid it down over my face and walked slowly behind her. Stalking, not following.

I stared at her back, taking step after step, slow and steady as she walked briskly, stumbling over rocks and uneven ground. She twisted her head, looking over her shoulder, and her face fell as she took notice of the mask.

But she turned back around quickly and kept walking, rolling with it.

My breath filled the inside of the mask, and I could feel a light layer of sweat breaking out over my forehead.

The backs of her thighs, the few inches I could see, were making my hands ball into fists. I wanted to slide my fingers up the back of her skirt and touch skin that I knew felt like butter.

The top of her hair glowed in the soft light from the moon, and every time her nervous glances over her shoulder hit me, it made my heart beat faster.

I'm going to make you scream.

She stepped slowly into the cathedral through the door, now hanging on its hinges, and stopped, looking around.

But we weren't sightseeing. I planted my hand on her back and shoved her forward.

"Mich—" she gasped out, losing her voice. She jerked her head around, shaking it as she breathed hard. "I don't think we should—"

But I immediately reached out and grabbed her neck, cutting her off and shoving her again.

"Michael!"

Her breaths rushed in and out loud and fast, and she hurried away from me, her eyes wide with fright. She swallowed, holding my stare, and I could tell she was definitely fucking scared now.

Then I narrowed my eyes, seeing her hand absently drop to the inside of her thigh.

Jesus. She was so fucking turned on, she was about to rub one out right here. She quickly pulled her hand away, probably realizing the impulse she'd had.

I jerked my head toward the entrance to the catacombs, remaining silent. She hesitated, shifting her eyes from side to side, but turned anyway and started walking.

She didn't trust me. But she wanted to.

We reached the entrance, cool air drifting up and seeping through my jeans and hoodie.

She paused. "There's no . . ." She twisted her head to the side, talking to me. "There's no light."

I stood behind her, looking down at the top of her head and waiting. I didn't care if there was any light.

She seemed to realize that when I didn't say anything. Taking a deep breath, she stepped down, slowly finding the next stair as she grazed her hand along the wall to our right, using it to guide and steady her.

With every step she took, my cock grew harder.

Reaching the bottom of the stairs, she turned her head again, looking to me with a question in her eyes. It was nearly pitch black down here, some moonlight seeping in from cracks in the ceiling.

The chilled silence of the tunnels to the left and right closed in on us like walls, and I wondered if there was anyone else down here.

Walking into her, I forced her forward into the vault ahead of me. The same room I'd taken her to three years ago.

Her footsteps picked up, and she entered the chamber ahead of me, her fair hair the only thing I could make out in the darkness.

"Michael?" she called. "Where are you?"

Taking out a lighter, I pushed the button and lit the small candle on the wall sconce by the doorway.

The soft glow barely filled the room, but it was enough to see her.

I stalked toward her, noticing that the mattress that was here last time was now gone and replaced with a small wooden table.

"Are there people down here?" she breathed out. "I hear something."

I kept approaching her, grabbing the string from my hood and pulling it out.

The wind blew through the cracks and crevices, making it sound as if there were whispers in the tunnels, but she didn't realize that's all it was. Her senses were heightened because of the fear.

"Michael?"

I grabbed her hands, hearing her small cry as I wrapped the black cord around her wrists, binding them together and tying a knot.

"Michael, what are you doing?" she demanded. "Say something!"

I took her bound arms and pulled them over her head, hooking them over another sconce high on the wall. She was forced onto her tiptoes, her body now long, tight, and stretched out.

"Michael!" She twisted and squirmed.

I stood flush with her and looked down into her eyes as I reached down and grabbed the bottom of her little sweater vest and the white shirt that peeked out of the bottom of it. Lifting both, I pulled them up, including her bra, and pushed them over the top of her breasts to sit high on her chest.

"Michael, no!" she protested. "I hear something, and I'm cold."

I dropped my eyes, looking at her perfect breasts, a little more than a handful, and her nipples as hard as bullets. "I can tell."

I dived down, ripping the mask off and taking one of her breasts, cupping it in my hand and covering the nipple with my mouth.

I wrapped an arm around her, holding her close as she squirmed in my hold.

Flicking the hard bud with my tongue, I played, nibbling the soft skin around her nipple and eating her up as I enjoyed free rein to touch and fondle her.

I groaned.

Shifting my head to the other side, I snatched up her other breast and left deep, hungry kisses everywhere, taking her into my mouth and dragging her sweet skin out through my teeth.

Her body shifted, and she dropped her head back, moaning.

I stood upright and grabbed her hair in one hand, reaching down with my other and slipping my fingers into her panties.

Flicking her mouth with my tongue, I looked down into her blue eyes. "Not so cold now," I teased, my fingers engulfed in heat. "You're nice and hot down here."

It was spilling out of her, she was so wet.

Taking my hands off her, I backed away and gazed at her beautiful form.

One of her shoes had fallen off, and the other one was only half on. Her smooth, flat stomach and tits were on display as she stood completely helpless just for me.

Dropping to one knee in front of her, I looked up, locking eyes with her, and slid my hands under her skirt. My cock twitched at the feel of the pink lace panties she had on. Light pink.

So sweet.

Lifting up her skirt, I tongued her clit through her panties, feeling the hard little nub through the fabric.

"Oh, God!" she cried.

Pulling the lace aside, I hesitated for only a moment, taking in her bare pussy and flawless skin before I covered her with my mouth, sucking on her clit and dragging my tongue up her length.

Pushing up her thighs, I lifted her feet off the ground and dived in, burying my tongue in her cunt.

"Please!" she begged, moaning and trying to twist out of my hold. "Michael, no."

I flicked her clit one more time and pulled back, grabbing her panties and pulling them slowly down her legs.

"You told me no?" I challenged. "You don't like a little tongue in your pussy?"

Her body shook, and her breaths were shallow. "Yes," she murmurs.

I stand up, tossing her panties to the side, and then reached to grab her wrists, pulling them off the sconce. "Yeah, I know you liked it," I bit out. "And you're damn well going to get it."

I palmed my cock through my jeans, feeling it ache with the release I hadn't yet had. My pulse throbbed in my neck, and I grabbed her arms, whipping her around and pushing her down on the ground.

"Michael!" she shrieked, landing on her ass with her hands still tied in front of her.

I lowered to my knees, kneeling above her as I pulled off my hoodie and T-shirt.

"You may think I fuck with your head," I said, looking down at her as I unbuckled my belt and unfastened my jeans, "but you don't know what you've done to me all these years."

I came down on top of her, forcing her legs apart as I pushed her arms back over her head and held her down with one hand.

Rolling the condom on, I dragged my cock up across her wet slit, finding her hot entrance.

I breathed hard, whispering over her lips. "You don't know."

And I thrust my hips, sliding my cock inside of her tight pussy.

"Oh, God," she groaned.

I leaned down, holding my body flush with hers as I slid out and back in again, picking up pace.

"You're so fucking hot inside," I growled, taking her lips and kissing her deep and hard. Her tongue brushed mine, sending a jolt straight to my cock.

So fucking tight. I slid my hand underneath her ass, holding her in place as I drove her into the dirt and fucked her.

"Goddamn," I gasped out, thrusting my hips again and again and again, pounding into her harder and faster.

Her tits bounced back and forth as I slammed into her, burying my cock up to the hilt every time.

She whimpered, her moans getting louder and louder, and I felt her clench around my cock, squeezing me like a steel band.

My abs tightened as I felt my blood rush to my groin and the heat build in my dick.

"Rika, fuck," I groaned. I was coming.

Leaning my head into her neck, I kept pounding her as I spoke in her ear. "Come on, you little slut," I growled low. "You're such a good fuck. Spread those legs for me."

She squeezed her eyes shut, sucked in a breath, and threw her head back, my dirty words sending her over the edge.

"Oh, Michael. Oh, God!" she cried out, stilling as I thrust harder and harder.

I squeezed her ass in my hand and pinched her jaw between my teeth. "Goddamn, Rika. So fucking good."

Leaning up, I watched her beautiful face as I dived inside of her wet heat over and over again. A blush spread across her cheeks, and she pinched her bottom lip between her teeth, enjoying every inch.

My dick swelled, and then I thrust one more time before pulling out of her, taking my cock in my hand, and stroking it up and down until I spilled.

My cum shot out, falling across her bare stomach and tits, and I tightened my abs, the pleasure too much.

I'd never seen anything so fucking hot.

Every muscle in my body warmed, and the fucking release went to my head and filled every inch of my skin.

I tried to catch my breath and sat back on my heels, tucking my cock back in my jeans.

But gazing down at her, I damn near wanted to go again. Her hands were still bound above her head, her tits looked entirely too inviting, and her schoolgirl skirt was pushed up.

She blinked up at me, a small smile on her face. "Can we do that again?"

I reached over, grabbing my sweatshirt to clean her up and laughing under my breath.

Such a little monster.

I sat in the chair next to the bed, my elbows resting on the tops of my knees as I leaned over, watching her sleep. "Deathbeds" by Bring Me the Horizon played softly from the iPod on the nightstand, and I balled one of my fists inside the other, last night playing over and over in my head.

She'd passed out in the car on the way home from the cata-combs, and I brought her in, undressed her, and put her in my bed.

Why had I put her in my bed?

Her leg peeked out of the gray sheets she was wrapped up in as she lay on her stomach with her head facing me. Her hair was all over the pillow and covering her eyes as her naked form lay silent and unmoving, only the small rise and fall of her body telling me that she was breathing.

She was worn-out. It made sense. She'd been through the ringer last night.

I turned my head, seeing the sunlight shining through the win-dows out of the corner of my eye. Gritting my teeth, I turned back to her again. I wasn't ready for the day to start. I wasn't ready for the night to be over.

The edges of her feet and calves had smudges of dirt. Her hair was matted with a bit of the dark soil from the catacombs as well, and I knew she had bruises on her hips from our round two down there.

Bending her over that table had been nice.

Her wrists had a burn from the string I'd wrapped around them, and I could make out the small red mark where I'd bitten her jaw. I didn't think I'd done it that hard, but she had the mark to prove it.

And she'd never looked sexier. Ever.

Her clothes lay in a filthy heap on the floor, including the lacy pink panties I'd had so much fun removing, and I dropped my eyes, wanting nothing more than to stop time.

I'd never been with a woman who fed my lust like she had. I'd never role-played, worn my mask, played games, or anything like that with anyone. Fuck, feed, kiss, lick, moan, pump, come, and repeat. I'd gotten so fucking lost.

But Rika was . . .

I leaned back in the chair, running my hand through my hair and unable to take my eyes off of her.

She said she didn't trust me, but I knew it was a lie. I'd be willing to bet I was the one person she trusted the most.

She and I were the same, after all. We fought shame every day, struggling with who we could let see the real us, and we'd finally found each other.

Unfortunately . . . we were fucked.

My phone buzzed from its charger on the nightstand, and I closed my eyes, trying to ignore it.

I wasn't ready.

I wanted to draw the blinds, pick her up, and put her in a bath. I wanted to see her ride me out by the pool and play more games with her. I wanted to pretend that I wasn't missing practice right now, that my friends weren't waiting for me . . . and that Rika's world wasn't about to fall apart.

But my phone buzzed again, and I leaned forward, burying my head in my hands.

Rika.

The walls were closing in.

I shouldn't be able to look at her. I shouldn't love to touch her, and I shouldn't need to feel her wrapped around my cock every second since I'd first had her last night.

She wasn't mine. She would never be mine.

And I shouldn't want her.

I stood up before leaning down and studying her pretty face.

Fuck you, Rika.

Fuck you. I can't choose you. Why did you do this to me?

I turned my head, reaching over to the nightstand and taking my phone. I had several missed calls, but I didn't bother listening to the voicemails or checking the texts.

I just typed one to Kai instead.

Finish it.

And I straightened, glaring down at her as I set the phone back
down.

Now it was done. And there was no going back.

CHAPTER 17

MICHAEL

Three Years Ago

I turned into the gravel parking lot, the night lit up with the head-lights of all the other partiers arriving. The warehouse had been abandoned long ago, but since it hadn't been slotted for use or torn down yet, we confiscated it every chance we got to let loose and raise a little hell.

People brought kegs and liquor, and the town's wannabe youth DJs set up their systems, filling the night with rage and noise so loud we couldn't think even if we wanted to.

This was what I'd been waiting for.

Sure, I wanted to see how she'd hang with my friends. Could she keep up? Could she even manage to make a dent in our world?

But what I really wanted was to get her away from my family, her mother, Trevor, and to just see her relax. I wanted to see who she was when she stopped caring what everyone else thought or expected of her.

When she finally realized that my opinion was the only one that mattered.

And even though she was always the one to watch me as we grew up, that didn't mean I wasn't always aware of her, either.

I still remembered the day she was born. Sixteen years, eleven months, and eighteen days ago. That crisp November morning when my mother let me hold her and then my father immediately took her out of my arms and laid her next to Trevor, who was just a baby then, too.

Even at three I understood. She was Trevor's.

And I just sat there, wanting her back, wanting to see the baby, and wanting to be included in the fun, but I didn't dare approach my father. He would've pushed me away.

So I didn't care. I made sure never to care.

So many times growing up I tore my eyes away from her. I made sure not to think about it when she and Trevor hung out or had classes together because they were the same age, and I made sure not to notice her in a room or feel her next to me. I made sure not to talk to her too much or be too nice and let her in.

She was too young.

We didn't travel in the same circles.

My father would force me away from her. He took away everything that made me happy. Why bother?

And when those excuses ate me up inside and turned anger into resentment and resentment into hatred, the day finally came when I really didn't care anymore.

It didn't seem to faze her, though. The more I pulled away and treated her with impatience and distance, the more she pulled closer.

So instead, I stayed away. I went off to college, and I rarely came home. I hadn't seen her in months before I walked into that classroom today and saw her sitting there, looking so grown-up and beautiful, like a fucking angel. I couldn't help it. I walked up to her, wanting to pull her up and take her with us, but when she raised her eyes, meeting mine, I knew I couldn't.

I wouldn't stop if I did. I wouldn't be able to give her back.

Why her? Why, despite my mother, who always loved me, and my friends, who always had my back, was it Erika Fane who put the air in my lungs or made my blood run hot? She always got to me.

And then when she showed up at the cathedral today, I was

done denying the need to be close and done pushing her away. To hell with it. I might or might not let her in when all was said and done, but let's see where the night took us.

I wasn't disappointed.

She had a lot of guts, and my friends liked her, even though I could tell Damon was still trying to give her the cold shoulder. She was one of us.

"Goddamn, I hope someone has grills going inside," Will complained as I pulled into a parking space. "I'm still fucking hungry."

I kept my smile to myself. Every time he'd tried to eat tonight, we'd gotten sidetracked, and now we were too jacked up and wanted to drink.

I shut off the engine and everyone climbed out, Damon and Kai pulling off their sweatshirts and tossing them onto their seats, while Will gathered the masks and secured them in the duffel in the back of the car.

Glancing over, I saw Rika stuff the jewelry under her seat, probably realizing it was safer in the car, and then slammed the door, walking toward the rear.

"Come here, Little Monster." Will pulled her around the back of the car.

I watched them over my shoulder, seeing him raise his hand to her face, and it appeared as if he was putting something on it.

He dragged his fingers down her skin, and then I spotted what was in his hand. Shoe polish. We kept it in the duffel in case a mask broke on one of our escapades and we needed to improvise.

He finished and grinned at her. "War paint," he explained. "You're one of us now."

She turned around, a small smile on her face. A smudgy black stripe traveled from the left side of her forehead diagonally down her face, across her nose, and ended on the right side of her jaw. I crossed my arms over my chest, ignoring the rush in my chest. She looked badass.

A few drops of rain landed on my face, and I heard excited laughter and yelps around us as people scurried through the parking lot, trying to get inside before the downpour started.

Rika tipped her head back, cool drops glistening on her cheeks and forehead as her lips spread in a smile.

"Let's go!" Kai yelled.

I turned and walked toward the warehouse, Kai and Damon at my sides while Will and Rika followed.

Entering the massive building was like stepping into a different world. The warehouse had been gutted years ago and the steel beams fifty feet above our heads were rubbed raw of their paint by weather and time. Barely any walls remained, and the dilapidated roof had several large holes, making it easy for the rain, getting heavier by the minute, to pour in.

We walked in slowly, taking in the chaos that resembled a small, postapocalyptic underground city.

However, despite the darkness, the raw feel of the unclean and cold metal, and the bonfire raging to the left as people danced to "Devil's Night" by Motionless in White, the madness here was better than any frat house party I'd attended at college.

No one cared what they looked like. They were going to get dirty anyway. Everyone, including the girls, wore jeans and Chucks, and you didn't really care about conversation, either, because it was too loud to talk. No airs, no drama, no masks. Just music, rage, and noise, and eventually, when the high hit you just right, you'd find a girl or she'd find you, and you'd disappear upstairs for a while.

People greeted us as we walked in, and without our asking, four Solo cups of beer showed up, a young girl smiling as she handed them off to us.

"We need one more," I told her and handed mine off to Rika.

But before she had a chance to take it, arms circled her waist and she was pulled off the ground.

She gasped and then broke into laughter as her friend Noah,

whom I remembered hanging around her when we were in high school, bounced her up and down in his arms.

I tensed, wanting to take his fucking hands away, but then I remembered that not only were they friends, but he was also the reason she hadn't suffered more at the hands of Miles and Astrid at that party in the spring.

So far, he had my trust.

"Well, what the hell, Rika?" he bellowed, putting her back on her feet. "You said this week that you didn't want to come out tonight." And then his eyes snapped up to us, and he narrowed them as if just realizing. "You're here with them? Are you okay?"

I nearly snorted. Turning around and leaving them to catch up, the guys and I walked off to find our table. A few teenagers were sitting at it, but as soon as they saw us approaching, they scurried out of the semicircle booth that sat right in front of the makeshift dance floor, offering a perfect view.

Damon grabbed the remaining kid, who trailed behind his friends, and yanked him out, sending him stumbling forward.

I hooked my arms around the back of the booth, four more beers showing up at our table just in time, as Will finished his.

The rain, glistening in the utility lights that were set up around the room, fell lightly through the roof, slowly wetting the hair of the dancers on the floor.

Casting a quick glance over my shoulder, I saw Rika and Noah joined by another friend—a girl—whose name I didn't remember. And then my eyebrows nose-dived, seeing Noah hand Rika a drink.

But she waved it off, refusing it.

I turned back around, scowling ahead. *Good.* If that little lesson with Miles and Astrid hadn't taught her to get her own damn drinks—or at least get them from me—then I was going to beat her ass. The last fucking thing I ever wanted to imagine was what almost happened to her while I was away at college.

We drank our beers, leaning back, relaxing, and watching the action around us. Damon lit a cigarette and stared at the floor ahead, watching a girl dance as she eye-fucked and taunted him. Will pulled off his sweatshirt and poured beer after beer down his throat, while Kai kept turning his head, stealing glances toward the door where we came in. I knew he was watching Rika.

The muscles in my arms tightened, and I stared ahead, trying not to care. *No one comes between friends.* Least of all a woman.

I heard light laughter and looked up, seeing Rika round the booth and pull her sweatshirt over her head. She wore a huge smile as she tossed it at the empty space next to me and followed her friends as they pulled her to the dance floor.

I breathed harder.

That tank top was killing me.

I could still make out a few small bloodstains from Miles, but they were barely noticeable in the dimness of the surroundings.

A good inch of her toned stomach showed, and the thin straps of her gray tank barely gave her tits any support. It left almost nothing to the imagination, showing off her ample chest and sexy fucking body.

Her hair flowed down her back, and her round ass was perfect in her jeans. I could almost feel her straddling my lap.

Fuck.

Lightning hit low in my stomach, getting me hard, and I grunted under my breath, trying to clear my fucking head.

Laurel's "Fire Breather" started, and she and her friends made their way to the middle of the floor, right under the hole in the roof where the rain drifted in.

The slow, sonorous tune wrapped around my dick, filling it with heat as I watched her move to the beat, pumping her hips and arching her back like she knew exactly what would jack me up and get me ready.

Damon tore his eyes away from the girl on the floor, breathing out a cloud of smoke as he started watching Rika instead. She laughed, letting that friend of hers rub up on her as they both moved in sync, lost in the music.

I might be jealous if it wasn't so hot. And he didn't have a chance with her anyway. Her little glances at me across the breakfast table had more heat in them than the way she smiled at him.

Will leaned his elbows on the table, watching her, as well, and I didn't spare a glance at Kai to see if he was staring. I knew he was.

Who wouldn't?

The deep beat filled the room, carrying into the rafters, and I watched as she rolled her hips nice and slow, sliding an arm around his neck behind her as her girlfriend came up in front of her, and the three of them started grinding together.

I shifted in my seat, liquid heat rushing to my groin.

"Holy fuck," Damon breathed out, turning around to face us.

Will's wide eyes glanced to us, as well, and I could tell he was as turned on as I was.

"There's no way Trevor can handle her," Kai stated.

A grin tugged at my jaw, but I didn't let it loose. *No.* My brother wouldn't have the slightest clue what to do with trouble like that. He could never give her what she needed.

I stared at her, seeing her hips sway in small, sexy movements to the music, and then she laughed, pulling out and switching places with the girl. The light rain falling through the roof made her skin glisten, and she closed her eyes, holding her hands up in the air and losing herself to the music once again.

"Michael?" I heard Kai's voice. "You're looking at her like she's not sixteen, man."

I shot him a look, a little amused, before turning my eyes back to Rika.

It wasn't a warning, simply a tease. This suburb wasn't the least bit exciting, and teenagers didn't have much else to do except fuck every chance they got. We'd all had sex long before we were eighteen.

And we were *all* looking at her like she wasn't sixteen.

"Well, you know what I say?" Damon chimed in, blowing out a stream of smoke. "As long as they're old enough to crawl, they're in the right position."

Will scrunched up his face. "Aw, you're sick!" he said, laughing.

I shook my head, ignoring the stupid remark. Damon was fucked up.

Sure, he was joking.

But there was also always some truth to anything he said. Women were as inanimate as rocks to him. Something to be used.

Will and Damon finished off a few more beers, and people came over to say hi and catch up. Since I'd been away all summer, training and traveling, I hadn't seen anyone in a long time. Hopefully spirits were higher now with the Devil's Night festivities to give everyone a small high and remind the team who they used to be.

I set down my drink, listening to Will and Kai talk to a few people standing around the booth, but when I glanced up to check on Rika on the dance floor, I instantly grew uneasy, seeing that she was gone.

Scanning the area, I found her friends still dancing, looking like they were getting pretty hot, and then I turned my head, finally spotting her climbing the stairs to the next level.

Just then, she turned her head, locking eyes with me over her shoulder as she continued to climb. I stood up on the seat and hopped over the back of the booth, landing on the floor.

I kept my eyes on her back as I followed her up the stairs, past loiterers standing about, and turned right, making my way up another set of stairs. The space was now completely empty of people and prying eyes.

The metal grate flooring under me led to a large window near the left corner, and I saw her standing there in the dark, gazing out into the night with the music and noise two stories below and far away from us.

What the hell was I doing?

"I like my house from here," she said quietly. "You can see the lanterns. It looks almost magical."

I came up to stand behind her, looking out into the darkness. Sure enough, you could make out our homes in the distance since they sat at a higher elevation. The houses weren't visible, shrouded in trees as they were, but the estates were well-lit and clear. In reality, it was about a half mile between her house and mine, but from here it looked like only a few inches.

"Thank you for tonight," she offered. "I know it doesn't mean anything, but I felt good for the first time in a long time. And excited, scared, happy . . ." She trailed off and then finished in a quieter tone, "Powerful."

I looked down at her, shadows of rain dancing across the light hair on top of her head.

Rika was a lot like I was a few years ago. Confused, caged, and corruptible. The most valuable lesson anyone learns in life should be learned as early as possible. That you don't have to live in the reality someone else invented. You don't have to do anything you don't want to do. Ever.

Redefine normal. None of us know the full measure of our power until we start pushing our boundaries and pressing our luck, and the more we do, the less we care what others think. The freedom feels too good.

I breathed in the hint of perfume her body still held, feeling high with need. God, I wanted to touch her. It had been building all night.

"I wonder what it's like to be you sometimes," she admitted. "To walk into rooms and have respect. To be so loved by everyone." And then she turned her head to the side, looking up at me with those big blue eyes, begging me. "To want something and take it."

Jesus.

"You were watching me on the dance floor," she whispered. "You never look at me, but you were watching me tonight."

Pain twisted my gut as I struggled to resist, but it was no use. I slid my hand around the front of her neck anyway and pulled her back into my chest, holding her tighter than I should.

"How can I not?" I breathed in her ear, squeezing my eyes shut. "You're getting very hard not to notice."

She whimpered, arching her body and pressing her ass into my cock. I opened my eyes, seeing her tits jut out, and I couldn't take it.

Moving my hand into her hair, I fisted it at the back of her scalp and pulled her head back to me, her full, parted lips begging for mine.

She moaned, sending all of my blood straight to my dick.

I should tear away. She was only sixteen.

Fuck.

I hovered my lips over hers, sliding my other hand over her chest and feeling her jerk when I cupped her breast with my hand.

"Michael," she groaned, breathing hard and squeezing her eyes shut.

"So soft," I whispered over her lips, feeling the warmth of her breath as I kneaded her in my hand. "My brother thinks you're his . . . and all I ever did was try to deny that I wanted you for my-self."

She licked her lips, trying to dart up and catch mine, but I pulled back, hiding my smile as I played.

"Michael," she whined, sounding desperate.

"Is that true?" I pressed. "Are you his?"

She dragged her bottom lip between her teeth, shaking her head. "No."

I darted out, catching her bottom lip between my teeth and sucking it into my mouth. I exhaled hard, my cock growing in my jeans as I went crazy, kissing a trail over her cheek and to her ear, getting lost in her scent and warmth.

But as soon as I dived into her neck, she jerked away, capturing my lips with hers and kissing me deep and hot. God, she tasted sweet.

"Such a good girl," I growled in a whisper, flicking her lips with my tongue. "Say it, Rika."

"I'm a good girl," she panted, her voice shaky.

"And I'm going to fuck you up," I finished, taking my hand off her breast and gripping her hip.

Diving down, I covered her lips with mine, eating her up and tasting her, her tongue meeting mine in more heat and fucking lust than I had ever felt for anyone.

My body was on fire, and I was gone. Completely lost in her mouth and the way the buzz under my skin traveled across my face, down my neck, warming my chest.

So many times of needing to be close to her, talk to her, see her smile at me, and now I had her in my arms, I never wanted to let her go.

Nothing—nothing—had ever felt this good.

She nuzzled into my body, sucking my bottom lip and giving it to me good.

"I know what you feel like now," she teased, hovering an inch below my lips and remembering what I'd said today at the cathedral.

I grinned, jerking her ass into me and hearing her moan at what she felt. "You haven't felt anything yet."

Turning her around, I lifted her by the backs of her thighs. She grabbed my shoulders as I lifted her up and guided her legs around my waist.

Walking to the corner, I sat her down on the railing with the wall not far behind her. She wrapped her arms around my waist as I pressed myself between her legs.

Rubbing her body up against mine, she flicked my top lip with her tongue and then left my mouth, trailing kisses and small bites down my jaw and neck.

"Jesus," I gasped out, moving a hand to her breast again, my heart pounding like a fucking drum.

Sliding her hands under my sweatshirt and shirt, she ran her fingers up my abs, making me shiver.

"The car," she gasped out, reaching for my belt and trying to work it open. "Please?"

I gripped her hips tighter, blinking long and hard. "Rika." I struggled, taking her hands away from my jeans.

Shit.

"I want to feel you," she pleaded, taking my face in her hands and kissing me again.

But I shook my head. "Not in a car."

She pressed her chest into mine, speaking low against my lips, "I can't wait. I don't want to lose this moment. It doesn't matter where it is."

No, it didn't. But this was where shit got complicated.

I was only home for the weekend, and then I'd be going back to school. If we had sex now, it would just make everything more stressful for her when it came time to be apart.

And even though I had no intention of keeping my hands off her, going that far wasn't right. Not yet. She was too young.

"Come on," she taunted, a small smile peeking out as she nibbled my lips.

I shook my head. "What am I going to do with you?" I asked.

She smirked. "I can't wait to find out."

I laughed quietly, taking her ass in my hands and leaving a trail of kisses down the side of her face to her lips.

"We need to go slow," I told her.

"How slow?"

I pulled back so she could see the seriousness in my eyes. "I won't touch you until you're eighteen."

Her eyes rounded. "You can't be serious! That's more than a year away," she pointed out. "And you're touching me right now."

I cocked my head, my fingers tightening around her ass. "You know what I mean."

But she pulled me in, closing her eyes and resting her forehead against my lips. She looked as desperate as I felt.

"You've had sex with sixteen-year-old girls, Michael."

"When I was sixteen," I clarified. "And don't compare yourself to them." I took her face in my hands. "You're different."

Our lips met again and her fucking hands and body got possessive, rolling into me, feeling me, gripping me. She held my hips, pressing me between her warm legs, and I lost my breath, knowing how goddamn good it would feel inside of her.

"Christ," I breathed out, pulling my mouth away. "Stop it."

There was no way I was going to be able to stay off her for a year. She was almost seventeen. Maybe that was good enough?

"You won't be able to stop yourself," she whispered against my jaw, looking up at me with thoughtful eyes. "This is what we were built for, Michael. You and me."

She left soft, slow kisses along my jaw and down my neck, and I felt my arms break out in chills.

I wrapped my arms around her, holding her tight and looking down into her eyes. "We've got to keep this quiet, okay?" I told her. "Just for now. I don't want my family to know."

She looked at me, puzzled. "Why?"

"You're still at home, and they watch you like a hawk, Rika," I explained. "My father hates me. I'm away at school, and he'd use my absence as an advantage to work you over if he knew I wanted you." And then I threaded my fingers into her hair, holding her nose to nose. "And I do fucking want you."

I played with her mouth, nibbling her lips.

"But he wants you for Trevor or some shit," I continued. "If they don't know about us, they won't interfere. We need to wait until you graduate and you're out from under them."

She pulled away, looking pained as she pushed my hands down

off her. "That's a year and a half away," she argued. "I'm not asking for a relationship, but I . . ." She paused, searching for words. "I don't want to hide the way I feel, either."

"I know."

I hated it, too. If she were off at college with the freedom to come and go as she pleased and out from under the influence and pressure of my father and Trevor, it wouldn't be an issue.

Sure, let them know. I wouldn't give a shit what they had to say about it then.

But the day after tomorrow, I'd be a thousand miles away again, and with basketball season approaching, I wouldn't be home until winter break and then not again until probably summer. It would put her under too much pressure, and I didn't trust my father or Trevor. Especially Trevor.

"Believe it or not, it's best," I assured her. "My father would put pressure on you, and I don't want you dealing with it without me there."

There was disappointment but also a little anger in her eyes. She needed to understand that I wasn't trying to piss her off. Her age was an issue, and it made everything complicated.

And that also scared me, because I had no damn clue what she and I were.

All I knew was that we were the same. Did that mean I'd fall in love with her, marry her, be faithful, and live the same day over and over again in this fucking suburb?

No. She and I were built for something different.

I would piss her off, I'd be difficult, and I'd be just as much of a nightmare to her as a dream, but after nearly seventeen years of this pull with her, I knew one thing.

I would always circle her.

It never stopped. Even when we were kids, if she moved, I wanted to move. If she left a room, I wanted to follow. My body was always aware of where she was.

And it was the same for her.

I dipped down, brushing the strap of her tank top off her shoulder and trailing kisses over her skin.

"And I want you to stop sleeping at my house when I'm not there, too," I demanded. "I don't want Trevor trying anything with you."

I grabbed onto her lobe with my teeth, dragging it out, but I stopped when she didn't respond. I felt her go cold, not making a move or a sound.

Releasing her ear, I brought my head up and looked down at her, seeing her flex her jaw with clear displeasure written across her face.

"Anything else?" she snipped. "I have to shut up and be quiet while you act like I don't exist when I'm in the same room, because no one can know. Now you get to dictate when we have sex and now where I sleep?"

I straightened my spine, hardening my muscles. She had a point, but it was the way it had to be. I wanted my family ignorant so they wouldn't fuck with her, and there was no way I'd trust my brother not to try to crawl into her bed at night. No fucking way.

She tipped her chin down, shooting me a defiant stare. "I have to wait and pine for the rare weekend you don't have a game and happen to make it home," she continued, "while you get your drones at Thunder Bay Prep to watch me while you're gone, making sure to inform you of my every move."

My jaw tugged with a smile I couldn't help. She'd constantly surprised me tonight. She was a lot smarter than I thought she was.

Okay, maybe I'd planned on getting Brace and Simon to keep an eye out. Make sure no one fucked with her.

Or fucked with what was mine.

"And what about you?" she went on. "Will your bed be just as empty as mine all that time you're away—college parties, away games, spring break with the guys in Miami Beach . . ."

I narrowed my eyes, searching hers. "Do you think anyone would be as important as you are?"

She shook her head, shooting me a sarcastic smirk. "That's not an answer."

And she hopped off the railing, brushing past me.

But I reached out, grabbing her upper arm. "What do you want?" I asked, my voice turning hard. "Huh?"

Her expression suddenly turned sad, and she dropped her eyes. "I want you," she choked out. "Forever I've wanted you, and now I feel . . ."

She looked up, her eyes glistening.

"What?" I bit out.

"Dirty," she finally answered. "I felt like your friend tonight. You saw me, you liked me, you respected me . . . And now I feel like a simple, stupid girl—a dirty secret that needs to sit quiet in a corner and wait for your word to speak or move. I don't feel like your equal anymore."

I released her, letting out a bitter laugh as I turned away. "You're such a kid. A fucking kid."

Goddamn insecurities and tantrums. *It was a year.* She couldn't wait a fucking year?

"I'm not a kid," she stated. "You're just a coward. At least Trevor wants me more than anything else."

I exhaled hard, every muscle in my stomach tightening and burning as I glared at her.

I didn't think. I grabbed her by the arms and pushed her into the railing in front of the window, hovering down over her face, nearly nose to nose.

I breathed hard, wanting her so goddamn much, but I was pissed beyond everything right now. She had balls to throw that in my face.

Her face twisted up, and she whimpered, "You're hurting me."

And I realized my fingers were digging into her arms. I relaxed my hands, trying to calm down, but it was no use. She was right. I was a coward. I wanted everything and to give up nothing.

I wanted her waiting for me and only me. I didn't want to deal with the stress my family would put on her or me. I didn't want any opportunities for my brother to win her over while I was gone.

But what was she going to get out of me? Was I enough?

Or was my father right? Was I not worth a damn? Even if I just admitted it to myself, I'd hurt her.

She was too young, I was away all the time, and for the first time in a long time I didn't like myself. I didn't like my reflection in her eyes.

She had too much power over me.

I pushed off her, backing up. "This was a mistake," I bit out, scowling at her. "You're pretty, and you have a pussy, but other than that, you're not special. You're just ass."

Her eyebrows nose-dived, and her eyes pooled with tears; she looked broken.

No one made me feel like shit for who I was, and ripping out her heart wasn't going to be enough. It needed to be crushed, so she'd never pull that shit again.

I grabbed her shoulders, shaking her and hearing her cry out. "You hear me?" I growled in her face. "You're not special. You're nobody!"

And I released her, twisting around and charging down the stairs as my stomach rolled. My chest hollowed, and I sucked in air, struggling to breathe.

I couldn't look at her. I couldn't see her pain and face it.

So I bolted. Making my way over to the booth, I dug my keys out of my pocket and tossed them on the table.

"Make sure Rika gets home," I told the guys, unable to hide the anger on my face. "I'm walking."

"What the hell happened?" Damon demanded, seeing how pissed I was.

But I shook my head. "I just have to get out of here. Get her home."

And I left the three of them sitting at the table as I pulled the hood over my head and left in the rain.

CHAPTER 18

ERIKA

Present

Had to get back to the city. Your car is outside.

I stared down at the text Michael had sent me four days ago when I'd woken up in his bedroom alone.

Filthy, bruised, sore, and alone.

There'd been nothing from him since then, and I hadn't seen him, either. After our little trip to the catacombs, he must've gone over to my house and picked up my car for me before leaving and texting me from the road.

How could he have just left me like that?

I'd heard on the news that his team had gone to Chicago for an exhibition game before the regular season started, but I saw the lights in his penthouse on this morning, so I knew he was home now.

But despite the fact that I knew better, I was still hurt. Finally having him, feeling him inside me, was something I hadn't been able to push out of my head the last four days. It was better than I ever imagined.

He should've woken me to say goodbye. Or called to see how I was, at least. I'd just lost my house, and I still couldn't get ahold of my mother, even though I'd been dialing for days. I also had no luck getting ahold of Mr. or Mrs. Crist on their cell phones, either. If I didn't hear from anyone by tomorrow, it was time to go to the police. My mother never went this long without calling.

I stuffed my phone back in my purse, picking out one of the books of matches I'd put in there when I brought the box back with me from Thunder Bay. I slid open the lid and inhaled the scent, a quick moment of relief hitting me before it was gone.

Putting it back in my bag, I continued down the aisle of the used bookstore, perusing old sci-fi paperbacks and trying to distract myself.

I'd be damned if I was the one to call him.

"Hey," I heard a voice call out.

I turned, seeing Alex approach me with a hand in her jeans pocket and a smile on her face. "I saw you through the window and thought I'd say hi. How are you doing?"

I nodded. "Fine. You?"

She held up her hands and shrugged. "Every day's an adventure."

I laughed under my breath, turning back to the books. With her profession, I could imagine that it was never boring.

I turned my head again, looking at her. "Hey, thanks for the ride the other night. I know we just met and all, but—"

"Oh, it's no problem," she cut me off. "Thanks for driving. I don't usually drink so much."

Her eyes fell, looking absently at the books as she gripped the strap of her bag. Like me, she must've just finished with classes.

"Are you okay?" I asked.

She shook her head. "Just the usual. I'm hot for someone, and he won't touch me because I sleep with other guys for a living." She rolled her eyes. "What a baby."

I smiled with her, but it was kind of sad, actually.

"So he knows what you do, then?"

"Yeah," she replied. "He was at the party, which was why I was drinking. He won't even look at me."

"Well, you must know people," I guessed. "You must've made connections in your line of work? Friends? Maybe someone can get you a different job."

"There's nothing wrong with what I do," she retorted, her voice suddenly cold.

I stopped and turned to her, guilt creeping into my chest. That wasn't what I'd meant, but it probably sounded like it. I was just trying to see a solution in the situation.

She cocked her head, thinning her eyes with a challenge. "Someday I'm going to own a building like Delcour and drive a hot car like you," she told me, "and I will have gotten it all on my own. And I'll do it while flipping the middle finger at everyone—including him—who looked down on me."

Her voice was hard and strong, and even though I might not understand how she did what she did, I also knew I would never have to. I didn't know what it was like to make hard choices.

Her lips curled as she continued. "I'm going to fuck my way through school and anyone who doesn't like it can go to hell."

I pursed my lips, letting out a small grin. "Okay," I accepted and took the hint to shut up about it. "But before the hot car throws you, my life hasn't exactly been a party, either."

Her eyes softened, and she leaned forward, reaching out her hand and running a finger down the scar on my neck.

"I thought as much," she allowed.

And I stared at her, feeling like she knew without me having to say anything. It was weird. When I first saw her with Michael, I'd judged her. I'd written her off. She was a bimbo—brainless, chasing fame and money.

But I was the asshole. We weren't so different.

It's odd to see how no one is really human to us until we talk to them and realize there's barely any separation between who we are and who they are. She might have wanted what I had, and I might have wanted less, but we were still both struggling no matter the shoes we walked in.

"Well." She let out a breath and smiled. "I've got to run. Have a good weekend if I don't see you, okay?"

I nodded. "Yeah, you, too."

She turned around and walked down the aisle, disappearing around the corner.

I thought I'd made my first friend in Meridian City, and for the first time in five minutes, I hadn't thought about Michael.

Win.

I dug my phone out of my bag and checked the time. The Thunder Bay fire chief had been evading my calls all week, as well, about the cause of the fire in the house. I needed to get home and try to get through again.

Taking the three books in my hand that I'd already picked out, I walked to the front of the store, heading straight for the register.

The sales clerk rang up the items and put them in a bag. "Okay, that's thirty-seven fifty-eight, please?"

I swiped my card and handed it to her with my ID to verify.

But she didn't take it.

"Oh, I'm sorry." She looked at her screen, narrowing her eyes in confusion. "Your card's not working. Do you have another one?"

I shot my eyes down, seeing **Card Declined** on my screen, as well.

My heart started to beat faster and my entire face warmed; I was embarrassed. That'd never happened to me before.

"Oh, um . . ." I stammered, digging in my school bag for my wallet and taking out another card. "Here. Maybe you should try this one." I smiled. "I'm probably doing something wrong."

Which was a ridiculous notion. I was a skilled shopper and a proud graduate of the Christiane Fane and Delia Crist University of How to Spend Money. I knew how to use a damn card.

She swiped it and waited a moment before handing it back to me and shaking her head. "Sorry, hon."

My heart dropped into my stomach. "What? Are you sure your machine's working?"

She hooded her eyes, looking at me like she'd heard that one before.

"I'm sorry," I blurted out, completely baffled. "This is just so weird."

"It happens." She shrugged. "Struggling college student and all. We have an ATM over there if you'd like me to hold the books."

She pointed to the windows behind me, and I saw the machine sitting in the bookshop's café area.

"Thank you," I said, leaving the bag with her and walking briskly over to the ATM.

How could my cards not be working? I'd had one since I was sixteen and started driving. When I left for college, my mother let me get one in my own name to build credit. I also had my debit card, but our accountant preferred I use that for food and gas only to track my expenses a little better.

I'd never had a problem with any of them. Ever.

I swallowed the dryness in my mouth and slipped my card into the machine, punching in my PIN. I went to hit **Withdraw**, but I stopped, thinking better of it. I hit **Account Balance** instead, and my heart immediately thundered in my chest.

Zero.

"What?" I burst out, tears stinging behind my eyes at seeing my checking account balance. "This isn't right. It can't be."

I began pushing buttons, my hands shaking as I went back out and checked the balance of my savings account instead.

That balance also read zero.

I shook my head, tears pooling. "No. What the hell is going on?"

Grabbing my card out of the machine, I stormed out of the bookstore, leaving the books behind, and charged down the street. I rushed home as a thousand knots tightened in my stomach.

One card not working? Fine. None of my cards working and my bank account empty? My mind was racing.

Was the jewelry shop in trouble? Had our accountant not paid our taxes and our accounts were now frozen? Had we been in debt?

As far as I knew everything had always been fine. Mr. Crist had handled the business and properties, and whenever I talked to the accountant, our finances were in great shape.

I dug my phone out again and dialed our family's accountant, who also handled the Crists' accounts, but all I got was a message that he was gone for the weekend.

I continued down the street, sweat breaking out across my back as I tried dialing my mother, Mrs. Crist, and even Trevor. I needed to know how to get in touch with someone who could help.

But no one was answering. *What the fuck is going on? Why can't I get ahold of anyone?*

Richard, the doorman, saw me approach and immediately held open the front door of Delcour. I whisked through, ignoring his hello and making straight for the elevator.

Once I got upstairs and in my apartment, I dumped my bag and started up my laptop to log in to my accounts. I couldn't wait until everyone was back in the office on Monday. I needed to find out what the hell was going on now.

As I brought the Internet up, I dialed Mr. Crist's office, knowing he worked late and that his assistant would most likely still be there as well. It was only just after six.

"Hello?" I rushed out, cutting off the woman as she answered the phone. "Stella, this is Rika. Is Mr. Crist in? It's urgent."

"No, I'm sorry, Rika," she replied. "He left for Europe a few days ago to join Mrs. Crist. Can I leave a message for him?"

I dropped my head in my hand, gripping my hair in frustration. "No, I . . ." Tears started to spill. "I need to know what's going on. Something's happened with my accounts. I don't have any money. None of my credit cards work!"

"Oh, dear," she burst out, sounding a little more concerned now. "Well, have you talked to Michael?"

"Why would I talk to Michael?"

"Because Mr. Crist transferred power of attorney over to him late last week," she pointed out as if I should've known. "Michael is currently in charge of everything until you graduate."

I stilled, my eyes widening.

Michael? He controlled everything now?

I shook my head. *No.*

"Rika?" Stella asked when I didn't say anything.

But I dropped the phone away from my ear and ended the call.

Tightening my fingers around the cell, I hardened my eyes and clenched my fucking jaw so hard my teeth ached.

All the money my father left us. All the money we earned from our property and the shop. He had the deeds to everything!

I darted my hands out, swiping the laptop off the island and pushing it to the floor, where it tumbled and crashed.

"No!" I screamed.

My stomach rolled, and I felt sick. What the hell was he doing? I knew it was him, but why?

I wiped away my tears, anger charging through my veins now. I didn't care. Whatever he was up to and why he did it, God, I didn't care.

I hopped off the stool, slipped my phone in my pocket, and grabbed my keys from where I'd dropped them on the floor, racing out of the apartment. I didn't even bother grabbing my purse before I locked the door and took the elevator down to the first floor.

As soon as the doors opened up again, I charged out and headed straight for the front desk. "Has Mr. Crist come home yet?"

Mr. Patterson popped his head up from his computer and looked at me. "I'm sorry, Miss Fane. I can't tell you that," he said. "Would you like to leave him a message?"

"No." I shook my head. "I need to know where he is right now."

But he just frowned, looking regretful. "I am sorry. I'm not allowed to give out that information."

I heaved a breath and pulled out my phone, bringing up my pictures. Clicking on one of Trevor, Mr. Crist, and me in May, I flashed him the screen.

"Recognize the man in the middle with his arm around me?" I asked. "Evans Crist. Michael's father." My voice turned sharp. "*Your* boss. *My* godfather."

His face fell, and I saw his Adam's apple bob up and down. I'd never played the "I'm going to get you fired" card before, but it was all I had. Now he knew I knew the Crists, so why shouldn't I know where Michael was?

"Where is he?" I demanded, sliding my phone into my pocket again.

He straightened, dipping his head down and not looking at me. "He left about an hour ago," he admitted. "He and his friends took a cab to Hunter-Bailey for dinner."

I shoved away from the counter, rushing out the front doors.

Turning left, I ran down the city sidewalk, veering around other pedestrians and racing through crosswalks as I made my way down to the gentlemen's club several blocks from Delcour.

I breathed hard, a light layer of sweat covering my stomach and back as I finally jogged up the stairs of the old stone building, my legs burning from the rush I'd made to get here.

I was done thinking. Done wondering and pondering. He'd stolen from me and my family, and my blood was burning.

Fuck him.

I entered the building and stepped up to the front desk. "Where's Michael Crist?" I demanded.

The attendant, in his pressed black suit and midnight-blue tie, squared his shoulders and narrowed his eyes on me.

"Well, he's dining right now, ma'am," he told me, and then I caught the flash of his eyes to the wooden double doors to my right. "May I help—"

But I was gone. I charged for the doors, not waiting to be turned away or told what to do.

I grabbed both handles and turned the knobs, throwing the doors open.

"Miss!" the attendant exclaimed. "Miss! You can't go in there!"

But I didn't even hesitate. Screw their stupid "no women allowed" rule.

I walked in, my skin buzzing under the surface and my heart racing with a new high. I twisted my head left and right, vaguely taking in the room full of men in their fancy suits, with their clinking glasses and cigar smoke sitting in the air above their heads.

I finally halted, my eyes finding Michael, Kai, Damon, and Will sitting at a round table in the back. I stormed through the room, passing tables of onlookers and waiters carrying trays.

"Excuse me, ma'am!" one of them called as I shot past.

But I wasn't stopping.

I charged over, seeing Michael turn his eyes on me, finally aware of my presence, but before he could say anything, I reached down and grabbed the bottom of the tablecloth and yanked it off, carrying all of the glasses, plates, and silverware with it.

"Shit!" Will shouted.

Everything crashed to the hardwood floor, and Kai, Will, and Damon shot back in their seats, trying to avoid the mess of food and drink spilling everywhere.

I dropped the tablecloth and steeled my jaw, glaring into Michael's amused eyes as I stood up straight and demanded their fucking attention.

The chatter around the room had stopped, and I knew all eyes were on me.

"Miss?" a male voice charged, coming up next to me. "You need to leave."

But I didn't budge. I stared at Michael, challenging him.

He finally glanced at the man next to me and waved him off.

As soon as he was gone, I stepped up to the table, not caring who heard me or who was looking.

"Where is my money?" I growled.

"In my account."

But it wasn't Michael who answered. I looked to Kai, seeing a small smirk on his lips.

"And mine."

I twisted my head, turning my eyes on Will and seeing his cocky grin.

"And mine," Damon added.

I shook my head, trying to keep my body from shaking. "You've all gone too far," I breathed out, shocked.

"There's no such thing," Kai replied. "What we can do, we will."

"Why?" I burst out. "What did I ever do to you?"

"If I were you," Damon joined in, "I'd be more concerned with what we're going to do to you."

What? Why were they doing this?

Michael leaned forward in his chair and placed his forearms on the table.

"Your house is gone," he stated. "Your money and property? Liquidated. And where is your mother?"

My eyes rounded, realization slowly dawning as I saw the suggestion in his eyes.

My mother wasn't on a yacht. I'd been played.

"Oh, my God," I murmured to myself.

"You belong to us now," Michael declared. "You'll have money when we think you deserve it."

I narrowed my eyes, swallowing the lump in my throat. "There's no way you'll get away with this!"

"Who's going to stop us?" Damon argued.

But I looked to Michael, dealing only with him. "I'll call your father," I threatened.

He let out a laugh, shaking his head as he stood up from his chair. "I hope you do," he replied. "I'd love to see the look on his face when he realizes that the Fane fortune is gone, and Trevor will get you"—his heated eyes fell down my body before he continued "in less than pristine condition."

I heard Will laugh under his breath as the rest of them stood up, avoiding the mess on the floor.

Michael circled the table, coming around to stand in front of me. "Now, we've got spectators, and I don't like that." He glanced around the room full of gentlemen who were still watching us. "We're heading back to my parents' house in Thunder Bay for the weekend, and we'll expect you within the hour."

And he pinned me with a warning look, letting me know it wasn't a request.

I stopped breathing and watched as he walked away, through the dining room, followed by his friends. And without a single backward glance from any of them.

Thunder Bay? Alone with them?

I shook my head. *No.* I couldn't. I needed to get help. I needed to reach someone.

But I squeezed my eyes shut, fighting away the tears as I ran my hand through my hair.

There was no one. I had no one to turn to.

Who was going to stop them?

CHAPTER 19

ERIKA

Present

Climbing out of the car, I grabbed the baseball bat from the passenger's seat and shut the door. My pulse pumped violently, heat washing over my entire body and sweat breaking out on my forehead. I could barely breathe.

I'll be safe. Michael and Kai would go far, but they wouldn't hurt me. *I'll be safe.*

My mother was out there somewhere, God knows where, and she was the only reason I was here.

I walked toward the house, noticing that none of the lights were on, inside or out. The windows were black, and I approached the door, stepping into the shadows of the tree overhead as it blocked out the moonlight.

My hands shook. Everything was so dark.

My mother. *Don't back down, and don't leave until you get answers.*

If I called the police, it would take weeks to sort through the mess as they looked for her. She was on the yacht. She wasn't on the yacht. She was abroad, so of course it was difficult to reach her. *Give it some time, go back to school, and leave it in our capable hands.*

No.

Turning the handle on the door, I tightened all of my muscles, hearing the crackling of the packing tape stuck to the inside of my forearm.

The baseball bat was a decoy. If they thought they got one weapon away from me, they might not suspect I had another. Hence the Damascus blade I'd taped to the inside of my arm, under my sleeve, when I went back to my apartment to get my car earlier.

I forced in a deep breath and inched open the door, putting a foot inside the dark house.

A cold hand snatched my wrist and yanked me inside. I cried out, the door slamming behind me as the baseball bat was torn out of my hand.

"You came."

Will. I sucked in a breath as his arm came down in front of me and wrapped around my neck, putting me in a lock.

"That was really fucking stupid," he whispered in my ear.

He released me and shoved me forward, and I whipped around, gasping for breath.

Oh, my God. I immediately shot back, away from him.

He wore a black hoodie with the hood drawn, as well as a mask. But the mask wasn't like the ones they usually wore. This one was plain white, and I'd never seen it before.

I hunched down just an inch or so and kept my hands out, preparing for him to come at me again.

Holding up the bat, he took slow steps toward me. "What are you going to do with this, huh?" He held it to his groin and began stroking it as if it were his cock. "Yeah, that's what you like, isn't it?"

And then he shot out his arm, launching the bat off to the side of the foyer, the wood clanking against the marble floor.

Eyeing me through his white mask, he stalked slowly toward me.

I backed away. "No."

But then someone else came down on my back, and I screamed as he wrapped his arms around me.

"He may not be as big as that bat, but I am," a sinister voice threatened in my ear.

Damon.

I steeled every muscle, twisting and fighting against him as I tried to keep my forearm tucked close to me. I didn't want them to find the dagger, and I didn't want to use it unless I had to.

Unless I had the opportunity to run, because I wouldn't be able to take all of them at once.

"Hey, fuck you," Will shot out. "Rika's going to love me the most."

I sucked in short, hard breaths, my abs burning as I fought against his hold. "Fuck off, and let me go!"

Damon grabbed me by the back of my shirt and shoved me away, but it was straight back into Will's arms.

Will caught me, taking my ass in his hands and holding me to him. "Are you going to love me good, Rika?" he taunted. "Or would you like to try him first?"

He jerked his head behind me, gesturing to Damon before pushing me away from him again and sending me back to his friend.

The room was spinning. "Stop it!" I yelled. "Get off me!"

Where the hell was Michael?

Damon fisted my collar, bringing my face up to his, and I could hear his heavy breathing behind his white mask, which was identical to Will's. "I served the most time. She should get to feel me first," he told Will, and then looked to his right, speaking to someone else. "What do you think?"

Who—?

But before I had a chance to turn my head to see who he was talking to now, he threw me over to another white-masked man, and I gasped, instantly pushing against his chest as my bare foot got caught under his boot. I hadn't realized I'd lost a sandal.

"Stop it," I breathed out, shaking my head.

But the third man simply wrapped an arm around me and fisted the back of my hair with the other. I cried out, my scalp burning.

"Boys," he called out, "she won't even be able to tell us apart after a while."

And then he shoved me back to another one, my feet stumbling across the floor as I fought not to fall.

Kai. How could he do this?

"Hold her," he commanded as Will caught my upper arms and held my back to his front.

My arms and legs felt heavy, and my head was swimming. I couldn't get enough air.

"Stop it," I begged, fighting against Will's hold.

Kai knelt down in front of me and looked up as he began running his hands slowly up my legs, going around my calves and up my thighs.

"No!" I lashed out, kicking my legs with the small bit of energy I had left.

But he caught my ankles and squeezed them so hard the bones ached. "Got to make sure you're clean," he explained in a too-calm voice.

"Get away from me!" I bellowed. "Where's Michael?"

I jerked my head left and right, looking up the stairs and everywhere, but I couldn't see him.

He was here. He had to be here.

Damon leered behind Kai, watching me with his head cocked as if I were an animal being dissected in front of him. Will kept me flush with his body, his masked face nuzzling my neck.

"Got anything hidden here?" Kai asked, running his hand up the inside of my thigh.

But I lurched forward, growling, "Fuck you!"

Will laughed, tightening his fingers around my arms and yanking me back into him again.

"Why don't you just take off her clothes?" Damon suggested. "That way we'll know for sure."

"Hell, yeah," came Will's voice behind me.

I instantly recoiled, seeing Kai stand up, his dark eyes like deep black pools behind his mask.

"Let's set the mood first." And then he took out a remote from his sweatshirt and held it up, clicking a button.

I jerked as a motor-like sound started, and then I twisted my head, my stomach shaking with silent sobs as I watched the steel shutters descend over all the windows.

I shook my head, not knowing how to stop this. Any moonlight that had been streaming into the house slowly got smaller and smaller, the floor growing darker and darker. The house turned pitch black, and I watched as Kai and Damon disappeared in front of me, the room becoming as dark as oil. My legs started to shake.

"Why are you doing this?" I demanded. "What do you want?"

"Why are we doing this?" Will mocked in my voice.

And then they all joined in.

"Why are we doing this?"

"Why are we doing this?"

"I don't know. Why *are* we doing this?" Damon laughed.

And then I screamed as Will launched me forward into his arms. At least, I think they were his.

Damon caught me and pressed his body into mine, pawing my ass with his hands.

I planted my hands on his chest and tried to straighten my arms, grunting and choking on my breaths as I tried to push myself away from him.

"Get off me!" I shouted, my face burning with rage.

But he spun me around and shoved me into another set of arms. I stumbled in the darkness, light-headed and losing my balance.

The new guy wrapped his arms around me, and I clutched his sweatshirt to stabilize myself, acid bile rising in my throat.

"What?!" I choked out, trying to keep the fucking tears at bay. "What do you want from me?"

"What do you want from me?" Kai mocked, followed by the others.

"What do you want from me?"

"What do you want from me?"

And then I was shoved away again, another set of arms catching me.

"Stop it!" I yelled, and I raised my arm, coming down and catching him on the side of his mask.

"Oh, she's got some spit and fire," Will teased and pushed me to someone else.

My legs went limp, and I broke. Sobbing, I buried my hands in my hair on the sides of my head and curled my fingers, my nails scraping against my scalp so hard my skin stung.

I threw my head back. "Michael!"

"Michael?" someone called after me.

And then someone else singsonged, "Michael, where are youuuu?"

"Mi-chael!" the third one rang out, their voice echoing up the stairs and down the hall.

"I don't think he's coming!"

"Or he's already here!" Will taunted.

"Stop it!" I raged. "Why are you doing this?"

A head nudged my ear, making me jerk. "Payback," he said in a hard whisper.

"A little revenge," Will added.

"And restitution for time served," Kai finished.

Tears streamed down my face. *What were they talking about?* Where was Michael?

But then someone grabbed my hips from behind and pulled me into him, his arms circling my waist.

"You belong to us, Rika," he breathed out in my ear. "That's what's happening."

My eyes widened, and fire spread through my stomach as despair set in.

It was Michael's voice. *No.*

"You're Horsemen property now," I heard Kai say, "and if you
want to have money to eat, you'll be just as nice to us as you were
to Michael last weekend."

"He said you were a halfway-decent fuck," Damon chimed in,
"but we'll get you up to par."

"With some training!" Will boasted, sick amusement in his voice.

"But you won't like it," Kai growled next to me. "I promise you
that."

"And if you want college money—or rent money," Damon
threatened, "well then, you better be especially pleasing."

I hunched forward, feeling sick. I wanted to drop.

What the fuck?

"Hey, what are we supposed to do when we get tired of her?"
Will asked somewhere to my right. "We can't pay her for nothing,
can we?"

"Of course not."

"I guess we can just pass her around," Will suggested. "We've
got friends."

"Yeah, shit," Damon interjected. "My father loves the young
ones."

"He used to give you his sloppy seconds," Kai joked. "Now you
can return the favor."

Michael's arms tightened around me, and I heaved, trying to
clench my stomach to push down the vomit.

I raised my forearm, clutching the handle of the dagger.

"Come on, Rika," someone growled, grabbing me by the arms.

And I cried out as I was thrown across the floor, my shoulder
hitting the hard marble and the wind knocked out of me.

"Damon!" I heard a deep voice growl.

My face was wet, both of my shoes were gone, and I coughed

and sputtered as I struggled to turn over and see what was happening.

But a large body came down on top of me, and I fumbled, trying to push him away and crawl backward.

But he had me. His mouth was in my neck, and his hand was under my ass as he ground into me.

"You knew this was going to happen between us," Damon breathed out, biting my ear as he tried to pry open my legs with his other hand. "Open up, baby."

I screamed, my throat aching raw as I bellowed with everything I had.

I shot my arms up over us, went straight for my dagger, and ripped it off my arm. Bringing it down to my side, I lurched it forward and dug it into his body, on the side of his torso.

"Oh, shit!" he howled, pulling his hands immediately off me and launching backward. "Shit! Fuck! She stabbed me!"

I scurried away, my legs and hands going as fast as they could to get away from them. The blade fell out of my fingers, and my shirt was hanging down my arms, leaving me in my tank top. I spun around and got to my feet.

And ran.

I didn't look back, and I didn't hesitate. I raced through the house, entered the solarium, and threw open the doors, diving out into the night. My heart hammered in my chest so hard it hurt, and I felt eyes on me as I hit the grass and bolted across the vast backyard and through the trees.

Something wet coated my tank, but I didn't have to look down to know it was blood.

Droplets of rain hit my skin, my feet slid on the wet grass, and I fell to my knees a couple of times as I bolted. I had no idea where the hell I was going.

My mother was in danger, and I had no money. Who did I have to turn to?

The garden shed appeared ahead, and I slowed, suddenly feeling despair take everything I had left.

My mother.

They had an endless amount of money and power to hide this. There were no videos of their deeds this time to get them arrested.

I'd never find my mom, and I'd never get back everything my dad left me. Michael didn't care about his father or Trevor. He wouldn't listen to them when they eventually came back, and by that time, it might be too late for my mom.

I had nowhere to go. There was no one to help me.

Running my hands up and down my face, I wiped away the tears, wanting to scream in anger.

What was I supposed to do? Find a phone and call Noah? The only person I could probably reach?

And then what? Where would I go? How would I find my mom? There was no one to help me.

There was no one to help me but me. *You're not a victim*, his words came back, *and I'm not your savior.*

I turned around, looking back at the house and seeing the lights inside slowly come on. They were in there.

And once . . . I was one of them. Once, I ran with them, kept up with them, and stood next to them. I wasn't their victim, and I had their attention. I'd learned how to fight.

This was on me, and while I wouldn't make it easy for them, I wouldn't run.

I would never run.

I was built for this.

CHAPTER 20

MICHAEL

Present

F uck!" Damon growled. "I thought you checked her, man!"

"Just get in the kitchen!" Kai barked. "Goddammit."

I stood on the upstairs landing, my arms crossed over my chest and my white mask sitting on the small table next to me. I looked out the window over the large lawn, watching the small wooden building buried in the trees.

She was there.

I knew she wouldn't go far. Rika was a smart girl. She was scared and in survival mode, but she wasn't stupid.

After she'd fled, we'd grabbed Damon off the floor and sat him on a chair. I'd raised the shutters to let in the moonlight again, and then I'd gone upstairs to watch her run.

She'd scurried and fled, disappearing into the trees, but she didn't leave. There was nothing but cliffs back there and then a huge drop to a beach on the Atlantic fucking Ocean. She was barefoot, cold, alone, and without a cell phone.

What was she going to do?

And right about now, she was just realizing that.

"I'm going to go get her." Kai came up to my side, breathing hard.

But I shook my head. "Just leave her. She has nowhere to go."

"She'd be crazy to come back here!" he burst out. "After we just terrorized her like that?"

"Calm down," I bit out. "I know her better than you do."

I could see him shaking his head out of the corner of my eye.

He lowered his voice, but it was still thick with anger. "Michael, she could make it to a phone," he pointed out. "She could call a friend and eventually get ahold of your mother or father for all we know. The money isn't a big enough incentive for her to be pliant. We underestimated her."

I inhaled an aggravated breath and reached behind my head, pulling off my sweatshirt and T-shirt and dropping them to the floor. A layer of sweat covered my back.

"If she doesn't come back," I replied, "then keeping the money will have to be a big enough incentive for you and the others to accept that we've lost. We agreed that she had to agree to this."

I stared out the window, my heart creeping into my throat and my body growing hotter.

Don't come back, Rika. I knew she wouldn't run far, but I wanted her to. I'd fucked up. This wasn't how it was supposed to be.

We were going to make her ours. That was the plan. We'd make her feel what they felt when she destroyed their lives and tore us all apart. She'd be alone and have no control. We'd make her suffer.

But as soon as Damon jumped on her, I was on his back, prying him off.

I couldn't do it. I couldn't let them have her.

And then when she stabbed him and ran, I let her go, even knowing she wouldn't really have anyplace to go. I knew she would realize there was no other way out of this and that was simply the end of round one.

But I held out a small hope that she'd evade us. She'd make it off the property or hide or something until I figured shit out. There was no way I was going to be able to go through with this. She was mine.

"She'll be back," I told him.

"How can you be so sure?"

I peered over at him. "Because she can't say no to a challenge." And I turned back, looking out the window. "Just go see how bad Damon is hurt."

He hesitated a moment as if weighing his options and then walked off.

"Son of a bitch!" Damon howled from downstairs, and I heard a crash of dishes.

I didn't bother holding back my small grin. I couldn't believe she'd hidden a weapon on us. I was glad we'd given her the dagger, after all.

I closed my eyes and ran my hand over the top of my head. What the hell was I going to do?

How was I going to stop them?

Twisting around, I jogged down the stairs, spotting drops of Damon's blood on the floor as I walked past, heading toward the kitchen.

"Nothing you take from me will come easily!" a high-pitched shout raged through the house, and I stopped, recognizing Rika's voice.

It sounded staticky and distant.

"I won't come all the way out there to get you," I heard Will growl as I stood just outside the kitchen.

I clenched my fists. *The intercom.* He'd found her.

Every room in the house, including the garden shed, had an intercom. He must've figured out the same as me. She didn't have anywhere else to run.

"Oh, yes, you will!" she snarled back, challenging him. "You're the pack's dog. Come fetch, little dog!"

I couldn't help the curl of my lips. *Good girl.*

"You stupid fucking bitch!" Will barked. It was clear he was frustrated. Will never got mean.

Until he did.

But then another voice came in, smooth and threatening. "I'll come to get you," Damon chimed in. "And I'll want my blood back."

I ground my teeth together.

Stepping into the kitchen, I saw Kai opening and closing cabinets, probably looking for first-aid supplies, while Damon held a towel to the lower left side of his torso and leaned into the intercom on the wall.

"I will take it out of your ass before we leave that shed, Rika," he warned. "Don't run."

And then he stepped away and threw down the towel as Will began taping a huge patch of gauze over his wound.

It wasn't vicious—the blood seeping through the gauze was slow—but it was big. She'd slashed him good.

Will's bloodstained hands worked as Damon winced and picked up a cigarette he'd lit, taking a long drag.

"You're not going anywhere," I told him, walking in and diving down into one of the drawers on the island, pulling out the peroxide.

"Fuck you," Damon threw back.

He shoved Will away and flicked his cigarette in the sink, turning and charging out of the kitchen and into the solarium.

I shot out from behind the counter and caught his arm, slamming him into the wall. He struggled, and I immediately wrapped my hand around his neck, pinning him to the wall. My other hand pressed into the gauze over his fresh wound.

"Fuck!" he shouted, knocking my hands away, but I just came back in again. "Get off me!"

"We agreed."

"You agreed!" he argued. "I'm going to rip her in two!"

I twisted up my lips, having had enough. No one would touch

her unless she agreed to our terms. That was the deal we'd made, but now the deal was off. I wasn't on board with this anymore.

"I don't even know why you're here," he sneered, knocking my hand off his wound but making no move to get away. He turned his head, speaking to the other guys. "He got off scot-free—didn't serve a day—so why are we even involving him?"

I narrowed my eyes on him. "You think the past three years have been easy?" I charged. "I was the one to piss her off. She was mad at me that night, and you all paid the price. I had to look at her day after day . . . that lying, manipulative, vindictive bitch sitting two feet across the dinner table, knowing it was all my fault." I turned my head, looking between Kai and Will, and then back at Damon. "You're my brothers, more than family. You guys served the time, and I have the guilt for it. We all paid."

I let him go and backed away, watching him scowl at the air between us.

I'd felt like I'd owed them. I'd hurt her that night, pushing her away and being cruel, and it was my fault she lashed out. She had the phone. She posted the videos.

"Will, go get her," I ordered.

There was no way I'd trust Damon to be alone with her in that shed.

Will walked around me and stepped up to the solarium door, but then he stopped, looking out the glass.

"She's already coming," he said, sounding a little surprised.

What? I stepped to the side, following his gaze out the door.

Fuck.

Her lone figure trod slowly through the grass, her chin up and her shoulders squared.

"You were right," Kai said next to me, pleased.

I turned away, heading back into the kitchen while the three of them kept their eyes on her.

Gripping the edge of the counter, I heard the door open, and I watched them stay rooted in their spots as she calmly stepped inside, walking past them. She veered right, stopping at the entrance to the kitchen, and stared at me, her hard eyes doing a good job of masking the hint of hurt I noticed.

Her clothes were damp, and I could make out her white bra beneath her tank top.

"Where is my mother?" she asked.

Damon, Will, and Kai walked in around her, spreading out around the kitchen and turning to face her.

"Is she why you came back?" I asked.

Of course she would brave us for her mother. We'd counted on that.

"I'm not scared of you," she stated.

I nodded, crossing my arms over my chest. "I think you believe that."

Looking at her now, her hair dotted with crystals of water, Damon's blood on her hands and the bottom of her tank top, and the resolute look in her eyes, I'd never been surer of anything.

No, she wasn't scared. She'd given in to it. She was owning it. *Run or play.* Fuck it.

"Where is she?" she pressed again.

"You get answers when you confess."

"And submit," Will added.

"To what?" she gritted out, turning her fierce eyes on him.

"To us." He came around her, looking her in the eye. "All of us."

"Your tantrum cost us three years, Rika," Kai charged, baring his teeth. "And it wasn't easy time. We were hungry and threatened and miserable."

"And now you're going to know what that feels like," Damon added, leaning on the wall and holding his stomach as he glared at her.

Kai hovered down over her. "You're going to learn how to shut up and look down when I enter a room."

"And you're going to learn how to fight and resist, because that's what *I* like," Damon countered.

"But with me," Will came in close, making her jerk, "you'll want it."

She shook her head. "Tantrum? What tantrum? I don't know what you're talking about."

"You come when we say." Damon leaned a hand on the island, tensing in pain. "You leave when we say. And as long as you do as you're told, your debt to us will be paid. Your mother will be safe, and you'll have money to live. You got that?"

"You're ours," Kai told her. "You owe us, and this has been a long time coming."

"Owe you for what?" she shouted.

"We took you with us that night," Will charged. "We trusted you!"

"Never trust a fucking woman," Damon grumbled, reciting his father's words no doubt.

"And I was supposed to trust you, too!" she shot back. "And what did you guys do to me?"

She glared between Damon, Will, and Kai, and I stilled, wondering what the hell was going on.

"What is she talking about?" I demanded.

But Rika ignored me, pushing forward.

"You served three years? Well, I'm not sorry for you," she growled. "You guys screwed up, but surprise, surprise, you actually had to pay a consequence for once. You've never had to own up to anything. There's no one to blame but yourselves."

"You don't know anything!" Kai bellowed, shouting in her face.

She shook her head, a spiteful smile in her eyes. "Really?" And then she shot her glare to Damon. "You were sent to jail for raping an underage girl. Winter Ashby, the mayor's daughter. The video was proof. What's there to explain?"

I blinked long and hard, the morning that the videos surfaced flooding back.

I'd woken up on Halloween, the day after Devil's Night, and discovered that some of our videos had been posted online for the whole fucking world to see.

Which, quite simply, led to my friends' arrest.

It had been stupid to record the videos in the first place, but we were always careful with it. We kept one phone especially for those nights when we wreaked havoc and wanted to keep a little souvenir. And back then, we thought we were untouchable.

Winter Ashby had been one of Damon's conquests. She'd willingly taken him to bed the night before, but she'd been underage, and her father was just as powerful as ours.

And he hated Damon's family.

Which was probably why Damon preyed on her to begin with.

There was no way her father would drop the charges. He saw an opportunity to take down a Torrance, and he did it.

I looked over at Damon, seeing his flat expression as he stared at her.

"There's nothing to explain," he replied calmly. "You have me figured out. I preyed on a young girl, and I don't even remember her face."

Rika thinned her eyes on him, probably expecting more of an argument, but that wasn't Damon's style. He didn't talk. He acted.

She then turned to Will and Kai, carrying on. "And you guys beat up a cop. Nearly to death. They found him on the side of the road."

Another video that had surfaced.

"That cop," Will shot out, moving into her space, "is Emory Scott's brother. Her abusive . . . older . . . brother, and you're damn right I beat the shit out of him!"

She pinched her eyebrows together. "Emory Scott?"

"Yeah," Kai joined in. "We caught wind of it earlier that summer, so we jumped him, and I don't care what you think. We'd do it again."

Rika knew Emory Scott—went to school with her—and she must've remembered Will burning down her gazebo on Devil's Night. He'd wanted her for a long time, so he fucked with her to get her attention, but when he'd found out she was being abused by her brother, Will, Damon, and Kai beat the crap out of him.

And Damon had recorded it on the phone.

Unfortunately, there were pieces where Will and Kai had flashed their faces to the camera. I hadn't been there because I'd been at a basketball camp for most of the summer.

The morning after Devil's Night, I woke up to a nightmare. My social media was flooded with messages, posts, and even a few news articles that had already been uploaded. Somehow, the videos from our phone had wound up online overnight, and everyone within a thousand-mile radius knew about us. Or my friends, anyway.

It wasn't long before the police were at their houses, putting them in handcuffs, and while we could get out of a lot of things, the realization soon set in that they weren't coming back. Damon had fucked with a connected girl, and Kai and Will were screwed, as well. You don't hurt cops, no matter what.

Damon was sentenced to thirty-three months for statutory rape, and Will and Kai pleaded down to twenty-eight months for assault.

And then . . . after all that . . . after everything I'd been a part of, as well, I'd escaped without a scratch.

No videos with me were posted, and even if they had been, my face wouldn't have been visible in any of them. I'd always kept my mask on.

It didn't take us long to figure out who'd uploaded the videos.

"You threw us under the bus because Michael had hurt you that night," Kai accused, "but did you really think we weren't going to come after you?"

Her brows still furrowed; she looked confused.

"Being a rat is one thing," Will interjected, "but betraying people who trusted you is unforgiveable."

"Betraying?" she breathed out, and then looked to me, a question in her eyes. "What . . . ?"

But Will just kept going. "You're going to make amends," he commanded. "And if you don't, then maybe we'll go dig your mother out of whatever hole we stuck her in to take your place. I'm sure she's a good fuck. She landed your dad, after all."

Rika's eyes flared, and she lost it.

Letting out a growl, she drove forward, launching her body into Will's and shoving him backward, her hands pushing against his chest, the power of her whole body sending him stumbling back onto his ass.

Shit.

He landed, and I dived around the island, seeing her immediately jump on him and straddle him, her fists flying down on his face as he shot out his hands, trying to shield himself from her.

"Fuck!" he yelled, swinging his arm and knocking her to the floor.

Before either of them had a chance to launch into another attack, I came in front of her, blocking both of them and pulling her off the ground.

She bared her teeth, seething, and tried to dart around me, but I cut her off, shaking my head.

I stared into her eyes, noticing the way she took a step backward, away from me.

Dropping my eyes, I curled my fists. *I can't hurt her.* I couldn't do this.

I no longer cared what she did to us all those years ago or why she did it. I didn't trust her, but I . . .

I couldn't hurt her.

I turned and faced my friends, keeping her behind me.

"Goddammit!" Will barked as Kai gave him a hand, pulling him off the ground.

He wiped his finger under his nose, pulling it away and going back in a couple more times, looking at his fingers.

He was bleeding, and his eyes were watering.

Damon still stood over by the island, pinching a lit cigarette between his fingers and blowing out a cloud of smoke.

Will sniffled, a bit of blood smeared under his nose as he approached me. "Move."

But I just kept my shoulders squared and held his eyes, staying put.

He watched me, shaking his head in warning. "Michael, don't do this."

When I didn't move, he reached around me, trying to get at her, but I shoved my hands into his chest, pushing him back.

They might try to kill me, but they wouldn't get to her otherwise.

"You're choosing her?" Kai charged. "After everything? She'll screw you over just like us. We trusted her, too."

"You trusted me?" she burst out, coming around and holding their eyes. "I was your friend? Do you normally kidnap your friends against their will and drive them out into the middle of nowhere for a little fun?"

I narrowed my eyes, my heart picking up speed.

And then I turned to look at my friends. "What the fuck is she talking about?"

CHAPTER 21

ERIKA

Three Years Ago

I bolted from the warehouse.

My stomach was in knots and tears streamed down my face, probably making the black stripe run, but I didn't care.

How could everything have felt so good one minute and so fucking horrible the next?

I ran down the stairs, holding my arms over my chest to keep warm. I glanced over to the booth where the guys had been sitting, but I saw that it was empty. Were they gone?

They just left me here?

I tried not to feel hurt that Kai, Will, and even Damon had abandoned me, too. Just like Michael.

I walked over, seeing that my sweatshirt was still there. I gritted my teeth and grabbed it, whipping it out of the booth and charging for the front entrance.

"Assholes," I growled in a whisper.

Slipping it over my head, I pulled up the hood and stuffed my hands into the middle pocket.

And I stopped, my hand immediately closing around a hard rectangular object. I pulled it out, seeing that it was the phone Will had been carrying with him all night. The one he recorded all their pranks on.

I glanced back inside, trying to figure out how I'd gotten the phone. But then I noticed how long the sleeves were and that the hem fell all the way to the tops of my thighs.

I had the wrong sweatshirt.

I cocked an eyebrow, stuffing the phone back into the pocket and making my way through the parking lot. Will must've taken mine accidentally.

He'd be lucky if I didn't toss his damn phone—and all their memories—in the trash.

The rain had calmed, only a light sprinkle now, but the chill crept into my bones, and I considered calling my mom to pick me up.

But I immediately tossed the idea. I didn't want her to worry about what I'd been doing out so late, since she believed I was sleeping at the Crists'. Plus . . . I couldn't face anyone. I needed to walk and be alone.

He'd almost been mine.

When he'd followed me upstairs in that warehouse, just like I'd hoped he would, I anticipated his touch the whole time. I begged for it in my head.

Just one touch, and I would know he wanted me like I wanted him, and I could be happy.

And then his hand came around my neck, and he pulled me into his chest, and I was his. It was done. Now I knew, and there was no turning back. No stopping.

Why did he ruin it?

He'd told me today in the catacombs that he wanted what he wasn't supposed to have. He wanted to live without rules and defy everyone else's expectations, and what did he do? He gave into them instead. He tied my hands and his.

He let the fear of his father and the threat of his brother hold us back, and what was worse, he wanted to put the same restraints on me that he was trying to shed.

I didn't want anything planned. That wasn't Michael, and it

wasn't me. I wanted the thrill and the playing, the drama and the fights, the passion and the craving.

I wanted to fucking frustrate him and drive him wild, but I couldn't do that when he tried to micromanage everything.

I wanted it all to be out of our control, because we had no choice but to dive in.

But that was short-lived. He pulled back, held back, laid down rules . . .

Fucking rules? How could he do that? That wasn't us. We weren't going to care what others thought, and we wouldn't ask permission.

And in the span of sixty seconds I went from being the heartbeat in his chest to feeling like nothing more than his little plaything, pliable and unimportant. I damn well knew someone like Michael Crist wasn't going to stay celibate for a year, waiting for me to turn eighteen, either. I knew he wanted me. I felt as much when he ground between my legs.

But just because he denied himself having me didn't mean he'd deny himself altogether. I wasn't that naïve.

Tomorrow he'd ignore me, and it would be as if this night had never happened. I'd want to be invisible in his presence, and even though I shouldn't be, I'd feel embarrassed around him.

I dropped my head, strands of my hair spilling out of the hood as I walked down the dark road, the glistening blacktop reflecting the moon's light.

I missed him already. And hated him.

A horn blared from behind me, and I whipped around, my heart jumping as I backed away, making sure I was off the road.

I stilled, seeing Michael's Mercedes G-Class, and waited as it pulled up next to me.

Damon drove.

"Come on," he told me. "Get in. We'll take you home."

I backed away, spying Kai in the passenger seat with his mask on. Will sat in the back, slouched down and looking two seconds from passing out. I didn't see Michael.

I shook my head. "It's not that far. I'm fine."

I turned to keep walking, but Damon called after me, "Michael told us to make sure you got home. I don't care what happened between you two, but we're not letting you walk. Get in."

Stopping, I looked ahead at the pitch-black night on what I knew was a six-mile walk. So they hadn't left me, then?

My anger softened. My pride might be hurt, but that was no excuse to be stupid.

I averted my eyes, not wanting him to see how grateful I was, and opened the back door, sliding into my same seat.

Damon immediately laid on the gas, speeding down the road as Combichrist's "Feed the Fire" played on the stereo.

I narrowed my eyes on Kai, noticing his mask and drawn hood and wondering why he was so quiet. Giving Will a sideways glance, I noticed his hooded eyes as he leaned against the headrest. Turning my eyes back up front, I looked up, seeing Damon watch me from the rearview mirror.

"Why are you wearing your mask?" I asked Kai.

But it was Damon who answered. "The night's not over yet," he replied in a teasing tone.

But I suddenly felt unease creep into my chest.

We raced down the lonely highway, getting closer and closer to my house, so I pushed my concern away. They might be heading out elsewhere for more fun, but they were taking me home. Damon was always creepy. It was just my nerves.

"You want him, don't you?" Damon stared out at the road. "Michael, I mean."

I stayed silent, hardening my jaw and turning my eyes out the window. Damon wasn't interested in anything but fucking with my head, and even if he did want to just talk, I had no intention of confessing to Michael's friends how big a fool I'd just made of myself.

"Shit," Will groaned, his tired body swaying with the car. "She's ready to ride a fence post with how horny she is for him."

Both of them chuckled, and I narrowed my eyes, trying to stay hard. They were laughing at me.

"Don't be an asshole, man," Damon joked. "Maybe she's just horny, period. Bitches have needs, too, after all."

Will breathed out a laugh, and I sat frozen, waiting for my house to appear. What the hell was going on? They didn't act like this with Michael around, and why wasn't Kai stepping in like he had every time Damon got out of line today?

I glanced at him in the passenger seat. He remained motionless and silent.

"We're just messing with you," Will drawled. "We do it to each other, too."

I turned, seeing him give me a lazy smile before he closed his eyes.

"You know, the thing about Michael . . ." Damon went on, cocking his head as he relaxed it against the seat, "he wants you, too. He watches you. Did you know that?" He glanced at me in the rearview mirror. "Man, the look on his face when he saw you dancing tonight."

But I was no longer paying attention. I did a double take, straightening as I stared wide-eyed out the window.

What the hell? The lanterns from my home and gate flew past the window, and I shook my head, dread knotting my stomach. They passed my house.

"Yeah," Damon continued. "He never gets that look over a girl. I'd say he was damn close to taking you home and popping that little cherry of yours."

My breathing turned shallow. "Kai?" I broached, ignoring Damon. "We passed my house. What's going on?"

"You want to know why he didn't take you home?" Damon cut in, continuing his one-sided conversation.

And then the locks clicked, and I sucked in a breath, squeezing the door handle. I shot a glance to Will, seeing his head bob as deadweight on his neck. He was passed out.

"He doesn't like virgins," Damon finished. "He never wants to be that important to someone, and it's a lot less complicated to fuck people who know there's a difference between sex and love."

"Where are we going?" I demanded.

But he ignored the question. "You saw the girl at the old church today," he mused. "You liked it, didn't you?"

I breathed hard, my mouth going dry as we turned down a dark gravel road.

"You wanted to be her," he stated. "Pushed down on that floor and fucked . . ."

My eyes burned, and I could barely breathe, my heart was beating so hard.

"You know why?" he went on. "Because it feels good. And we'll make you feel so good if you let us."

I darted my eyes to Kai, unable to stop the shaking in my chest. Why was he so quiet?

He wouldn't let this happen. *Please.*

"You know," Damon carried on. "When guys let a girl into their gang, there are two ways for her to be initiated."

He pulled the car to a stop, and I looked out the front windshield, seeing the headlights shining on trees ahead. There were no other lights, and there was nothing out here. It was dark and isolated.

"She either gets beat in." He shut off the car, killed the lights, and locked his dark eyes on mine in the rearview mirror. "Or fucked in."

I shook my head quickly, clenching my fists. "I want to go home."

He sucked in a breath through his teeth. "That's not one of the choices, Little Monster."

And then he and Kai, together, turned around to pin me with dark eyes.

No.

I immediately grabbed the door handle and began yanking again and again as I started to shake.

What were they doing?

"We can take what we want from you," Damon warned, opening his door. "One after the other, and no one would believe you, Rika."

And then he climbed out, and I watched him through my window as he came to my door.

He opened it, and I lurched back, crying out as he pulled me from the car.

Slamming the door shut, he shoved me against the car and pressed his body into mine. I shot my hands up, trying to hit him, but he caught my wrists and held my arms down by my sides.

"We're untouchable," he stated in a low voice. "We can do whatever we want."

I breathed so fast my stomach hurt. He was pressing into me too hard, and I could barely get any air in.

Kai came around Damon's back, having just gotten out of the car. He watched me through his silver mask.

"Kai, please?" I begged for his help.

But he just stood there, silent.

"He won't help you," Damon threatened.

And then he forced my hands over my head, pinning them to the car as I cried out.

He came in close, whispering against my forehead. "I'm going to feel so good." And then he slipped his other hand around my ass, squeezing it and bringing me in to press against his cock. "You know you want to ride this."

"Damon," I said, twisting my head away, "take me home. I know you're not going to hurt me."

"Oh, yeah?" He got in my face, his lips on my cheek. "Then why have you always been afraid of me?"

I remained silent, knowing he was right. Anytime I'd seen Damon coming down the hall at school, I switched to the other side. The one time I found myself alone with him in the kitchen when I was fourteen, I immediately left.

I had never talked to him before today, and I was right to have kept my distance. It took less than a minute for him to force himself on me in the cathedral this afternoon.

But I held out hope.

For a brief moment tonight, after I'd smashed the glass of the jewelry store and Damon offered the small thank-you, I thought he might see me differently. Maybe hold a bit of respect for me.

He held my wrists and continued pawing my ass as he left a trail of kisses along my cheek all the way to my ear.

"Damon, no!" I shook my head, fear sinking in as I jerked against his hold. "Let me go!"

But then his lips were on mine, pressing against my teeth, and his goddamn body was everywhere. I couldn't get out, and I could barely breathe.

I twisted away, crying, "Help!"

"He doesn't want you," Damon whispered, ignoring my protest as he brought his hand up to my breast, kneading it roughly. "But we do, Rika. We want you so bad. Being with us will be like having a blank check, baby. You can have anything you want." And then he bit my bottom lip. "Come on."

I jerked my head to the side to get away from him. "I'll never want you!" I growled.

But then I gasped as he grabbed me by the sweatshirt and flung me around, straight into Kai's arms.

"Kai," I breathed out, my heart racing as I clutched his sweatshirt and stared up into the dark holes of his eyes.

What was he doing? Why wasn't he helping me?

"Maybe you want him, then," I heard Damon say.

Kai's arms came down around me, and I shot my hands out, pushing away from him.

"Stop!" I yelled and raised my hand back up in the air and came down across his mask.

But all I heard was a laugh as he spun me around and shoved me forward, pushing me onto the ground.

I landed on my hands, pain shooting up my arms as I quickly looked up and spotted the cell phone from Will's pocket—my pocket—lying several feet away. It must've dropped out when I landed.

The damp, cold leaves poked my fingers as I dug them into the wet earth, and my knees were chilled from the ground. I quickly flipped over, trying to keep aware of where they were as I slowly crab-walked backward to get to the phone.

Kai and Damon stood a few feet away, watching me, but then I saw Kai launch and charge straight for me. I yelped as I reached for the phone.

But he landed on me, and I grunted, emptying my lungs as his weight knocked the wind out of me.

"You think you can hurt me, you fucking slut?" he whispered hard in my ear. "You can't hurt me. The devil always has my back."

"Get off me!" I screamed.

He grabbed the back of my hair and called to Damon. "Hold her arms!"

"No!" I cried, my stomach shaking as I let out my wail. Despair spread throughout my body, and I began shoving and squirming against him. "Get off!"

Kai grabbed my arms and pushed them up over my head, holding my hands to the ground.

Oh, my God. How could he do this?

He reached for my neck with his other hand to hold me still, and tears streamed down the sides of my face.

But then a loud voice pierced the air. "Enough."

Kai stilled and turned his head.

I continued to squirm under his weight, but I looked down under his arm to see who had stopped him.

Damon stood back with his fists at his sides and his eyes narrowed. He charged over, grabbing Kai off me and shoving him away.

And then he dived down, dragging me up by the sweatshirt. "Stop crying," he ordered. "We weren't going to hurt you, but now you know that we can."

He grabbed me by the back of my hair, and I gasped as he brought me in, his warm breath falling across my face. "Michael doesn't want you, and neither do we. You get that? I want you to stop watching us and stop following us like a pathetic dog begging for someone to notice her." And then he shoved me away, disdain written all over his face. "Get a fucking life of your own, Rika, and stay the hell away from us. No one wants you."

I backed away, looking at both him and Kai and wondering why they were doing this.

A pathetic dog. Was that how Michael saw me?

Tears filled my eyes, but before they had the pleasure of seeing me break, I twisted on my heel and took off. Into the forest and toward home as fast as I could away from them.

I let the pain of the last couple of hours go and barely saw the world around me as I cried the entire way home.

Alone, so no one could see.

CHAPTER 22

ERIKA

Present

S he's lying."
I looked over at Kai, his narrowed eyes glaring at me.

Michael stood with his arms crossed over his chest, a flat expression on his face.

"Kai was with me," he stated. "He caught up to me at my house almost as soon as I got home, and we got drunk while watching game footage the rest of the night. He wouldn't have had time to take you out into the middle of the fucking woods."

I shook my head. "No. That's not right. He was there!"

"She's making it up to save her own ass," Damon chimed in, stepping up next to his friends.

"And I certainly don't remember that," Will added. "There was the warehouse and then nothing. I was drunk off my ass."

Michael looked away, shaking his head almost regretfully. "Just admit it. You leaked the videos, and we know."

My heart flipped in my chest. "What? Leaked the videos? You think . . ." I trailed off, scanning the air in front of me.

We trusted you . . .

Your tantrum cost us three years . . .

You owe us, and this has been a long time coming . . .

I closed my eyes, my lungs emptying. All this time they'd thought . . .

I looked at them again. "You think I posted the videos that got you arrested? That's why you're doing this?"

Oh, my God.

Michael leaned in and grabbed me by the back of the hair. I let out a small cry, sweat breaking out on my forehead.

"You had Will's phone," he charged.

But I shook my head. "I didn't! I would never have done that."

"You had the phone because you had Will's sweatshirt," he argued. "Damon saw you with it. Say it!"

"Yes!" I gritted out. "Yes, I had the phone, but it fell out of my pocket when I was fighting with them!"

"You weren't fighting with them," he growled, his voice stinging my ears. "Stop lying!"

"I swear!"

He shoved me away, and I curled my fingers into my palms. None of this made any sense.

"You're already caught," Will said. "Michael says Kai was with him. That's how we know you're making all of this up. He wasn't even there."

I slammed my fists down. "He was! You all were, except Michael! You were passed out in the car, Damon was threatening me, and Kai grabbed me. When I hit him, he just laughed and said, 'You can't hurt me. The devil always has my back!' You were all there, and the phone fell out when I was on the ground!"

"'The devil always has my back?'" Kai repeated, looking confused. "I didn't say that. I've never even heard that before!"

I shook my head, closing my eyes in despair.

"I have."

Everyone stilled and turned their eyes on Michael.

"My father," he said in almost a whisper, looking uneasy. "He says that."

Heat spread over my exhausted body, and I forced myself to take deeper breaths as I watched him turn his dark stare on Kai.

"Trevor," he said in a low voice.

Kai's stare hardened, and Will inched in to find out what was happening.

Trevor?

I thought back to that night. Trevor in Kai's mask. Would he do that?

Michael turned around, and I saw Damon lock eyes with him.

"What?" he snapped.

"Will was drunk as shit," Michael challenged. "But you weren't. You took her into the middle of nowhere instead of directly home, and you knew it was Trevor under that mask."

Damon blew out a stream of smoke and ground out his cigarette on the island. "You're taking her side?"

"You're the one lying to me," Michael replied.

He shook his head as his friends all turned to face him. "This changes nothing."

They waited while he stood there, and I looked over at him, completely numb. Damon never pretended to be my friend.

I felt nothing.

But Trevor . . . ?

He'd played me for a fool. That's why he'd whispered that night. So I wouldn't recognize the voice.

You think you can hurt me, you fucking slut?

All these years I'd been unaware. How he must've enjoyed that.

Damon hooded his eyes, looking bored. "Kai left almost immediately after you did that night," he told Michael. "That's when Trevor showed up. He was looking for Rika, and he wasn't happy. Someone told him that she was with us, so he came to get her."

I walked around, standing next to Kai.

"We had words," Damon continued, "but then I realized that

we could help each other. He wanted Rika away from us, and so did I. We decided to fuck with her."

"What was your problem with me?" I demanded.

"You had no business with us." He pinned me with a scowl. "Women always complicate shit. Michael couldn't take his eyes off you, and Kai was starting to notice you, too."

Kai straightened next to me, shifting uncomfortably.

"It was only a matter of time before you tore us apart," Damon bit out. "You're fucking pussy and nothing more."

Michael lunged.

He charged for Damon and slammed his fist across his face, sending Damon flying back and crashing into the stove.

He didn't come back swinging, though. He just stood there, blinking long and hard and breathing fast. Either he was in too much pain from the wound or he knew when he was outnumbered.

He swallowed and stood up straight again, continuing like nothing had happened. "We went out to your car and got the masks. If she thought it was Kai, Will, and me together, she'd get the shit scared out of her and never come around us again. Will was piss-drunk, so we put him in the car and went in to get her, but she'd already left. We caught up to her on the road."

"And you left my sweatshirt in the booth," Will chimed in, "along with the phone."

"Which I found and wore on the walk home," I added.

Christ.

"And then Trevor found the phone when she lost it in the struggle," Kai finished.

"So she says," Damon snapped. "We can't trust her."

"I trust her a hell of a lot more than I do you!" Michael bellowed.

"Yeah, fuck you," Damon growled. "She's a worthless fucking cunt, and I'll show you exactly what she's good for!"

Damon shot out from around the island and moved to pass Michael. I instantly backed up, steeling my jaw as he came at me, but Michael grabbed him and threw him against the counter.

Damon howled, holding his wound, but before he could straighten up again, Michael threw a right hook across his face, sending him flying to the floor. He crashed, and Michael came down on him immediately, grabbing his hair and raising a fist in the air.

"You choosing her?" Damon choked out, reaching up to grab Michael around the neck. "Huh? You choosing her over your friends?"

Michael's fist came down over Damon's jaw, but then Kai and Will were on him, trying to pry him off as he fought against their attempts.

Damon's face turned red as he raged up at Michael. "You're no better! What'd we bring her here for, huh? She's nothing! And she's making you weak!"

Michael lunged for him again, tearing out of Will and Kai's hold, but I didn't stick around to see what happened next.

I ran out of the kitchen and raced through the foyer. Slamming into the wall next to the door, I opened the keypad and punched in the code, unlocking the front gate. Digging my keys out of my pocket, I reached for the front door and pulled the handle. But then something hit the door, and I gasped as it was pushed out of my hand and slammed shut again.

I jerked my hand back as I watched the basketball that had hit the door bounce to the ground and roll away.

"You're not leaving," Michael's voice came behind me.

I reached for the door again, but he came and grabbed my arm, whipping me around.

"Let me go." I tried to yank my arm free. "I won't stay here!"

"We're not going to hurt you," he gritted out, and I could see blood on the knuckles of the hand he had wrapped around my arm. "No one is going to hurt you. I promise."

"Let me go!"

But then I straightened, rearing back as I looked over his shoulder at what was coming behind him.

Michael turned around, facing Damon. He wiped blood away from the side of his mouth as he charged toward us.

"Get out," Michael ordered.

Damon shot him a scowl and then locked eyes on me, grabbing the door handle as Michael pulled me out of the way.

He stared into my eyes, and what I saw there was no longer dead. His glare coursed right through me and coiled around my neck.

Yanking open the door, he left the house, slamming it behind him.

I let out a breath, my shoulders dropping.

But then I felt a hand brush my cheek and heard Michael's voice. "Are you okay?"

I jerked away, slapping his hand off me. "Fuck you."

He dropped his hand and straightened, keeping his distance. He knew he'd fucked up. What they'd done tonight was unforgivable.

"Fucking Trevor," Will grumbled, charging into the foyer. "I can't believe it."

"He always hated us," Kai added, coming in behind him.

Michael exhaled and turned away. Walking over to the stairs, he sat down and buried his head in his hands, looking completely defeated.

Yeah, it must be a bitch to realize you wasted three years hating the wrong person.

Chills broke out over my skin, and the heat that had covered my body before was now gone. The wet clothes stuck to me, and I shivered.

All this time, I thought I was insignificant to him. A stupid kid, barely worth his time. A mistake he'd made one night long ago that he barely remembered. But now I knew that not only was that not true, but he'd spent three years planning how to hurt me?

And he was going to let his friends hurt me, too.

Tears welled, and I clenched my teeth, hardening my jaw, to keep them away. He didn't fucking deserve them.

Stepping slowly toward Michael, I demanded, "Where is my mother?"

He combed his fingers through his hair and looked up, his eyes weary. "California," he answered. "She's in a rehab in Malibu."

"What?" I blurted out.

Rehab? My mother would never agree to that. She wouldn't leave the safety of her home or friends. She wouldn't leave what was familiar.

"I had a judge sign a court order, forcing her stay," he clarified as if reading my mind.

I inched closer, narrowing my eyes on him. "You forced her?"

"What everyone should've done a long time ago," he argued, his voice firm. "She's fine. Perfectly safe and taken care of."

I turned my head away, closing my eyes and running a hand over the top of my hair.

Rehab. So they weren't hurting her, then.

But . . .

But if Michael wanted to hurt me—if he thought I'd betrayed him—why would he do something that would ultimately help my mom? Why not just lock her in a basement somewhere like I'd thought?

I crossed my arms over my chest. "Why haven't I been able to get ahold of anyone?"

I now knew why my mother had been unreachable. She probably wasn't permitted a cell phone in rehab. But Michael's mother, his father's cell phone, Trevor, our housekeeper who was out of town . . .

"Because you haven't been calling anyone," Michael admitted, looking up at me with a flat expression. "During Trevor's party, Will went into your car and took your phone, replacing everyone's numbers under their names. You've been calling a fake phone we set up."

My fists curled under my arms, and I dropped my eyes, seething. I couldn't fucking look at him.

How had all this happened? Why hadn't they confronted me sooner?

"We were so sure it was you," Will chimed in. "I woke up, saw the videos online, and I panicked, realizing I'd left the phone in my sweatshirt at the warehouse."

He could barely look at me.

"And then Michael saw the sweatshirt hanging on a kitchen chair the next morning, and we finally figured out through Damon that you'd worn it home. You were mad at Michael, feeling rejected, so we . . . we just . . ."

He trailed off, the rest not needing to be said.

I glared at Michael. *All this time.* All these years he could've confronted me . . .

But that was him, I guess. He pushed forward no matter who it hurt, always believing he was right and never apologizing. At least I could see the regret in Kai's and Will's eyes.

With Michael, nothing. The more mistakes he made, the taller he tried to stand, so no one could see over him. So no one could see anything but him.

I shook my head, my eyes burning as I stared at him. *Say something!*

How could he just sit there after everything we'd . . . ?

I'd trusted him—shared parts of myself I'd never come close to sharing with anyone else—and this is what had been going through his mind every time he whispered in my ear or touched me or kissed me or . . . ?

I squeezed my fists so tight my nails dug into my skin.

"I want to leave," I told him, tears still thick in my throat.

"No."

"I want to leave," I repeated, hardening my tone.

"You can't." He shook his head. "I have no idea where Damon is. We'll all go back to the city tomorrow."

I ground my teeth together. *Goddamn them.*

I stomped past him, up the stairs toward my room. I couldn't stand the sight of any of them.

"So what do we do now?" I heard Kai ask behind me.

"Let's get fucked up," Will breathed out.

And I ran to my room, locked the door, and wedged a chair under the handle.

CHAPTER 23

ERIKA

Present

I had no intention of staying. I didn't care what their story was or what they had to say. I wanted my life back.

And if I thought I was in danger at my apartment, Alex lived on the sixteenth floor, so I could crash on her couch for a night or two. I wasn't safe here. I knew that.

But as I leaned down on the bathroom sink, feeling my chest shake with tears that weren't falling, I raised my eyes and looked at myself in the mirror.

My tank top clung to my skin, wet and dirty with splotches of Damon's blood, and my hair hung cold and stringy along my cheeks. My damp jeans hugged my thighs, chilling me to the bone, and I curled my fingers into the side of the sink, feeling Damon's blood thicken under my nails, wedging deeper and deeper, until it was the only thing I noticed.

I closed my eyes, feeling my heart pick up pace again.

I'd fought back. I'd hurt him.

And I hadn't run. Not like three years ago in the forest.

Being scared wasn't a weakness. But letting it force my head down and my voice quiet was. Fear wasn't the enemy. It was the teacher.

I hated Michael, and tomorrow, after I got everything back from him, I was leaving. No more Delcour, no more Meridian City, and no more Thunder Bay. I couldn't wait to get away from everything that had hurt me.

Chilled and shaking, my muscles exhausted from everything that had happened tonight, I didn't think. I stood up straight and slowly lifted the tank top over my head, peeling off the rest of my clothes and dropping everything to the floor before I turned to start the shower.

Just a few minutes.

I stepped in and sat down on the sandy-colored shower floor, right under the hot spray. Steam filled the small enclosure, and my hair was immediately drenched, falling down my back as I tipped my chin up and let the hot water cover my face.

Tingles spread over my body, and my heart began to calm as I hugged my legs and felt everything grow warm again.

Michael.

He'd done all of this. He'd been in charge. He'd told me to come here, and out of love for my mother, I did.

He'd trapped me, blackmailed me, and put his friends on me.

I hate him.

I worked vigorously, washing my hair and body, and then I used a file to dig Damon's blood out of my fingernails. Getting out of the shower, I dressed in shorts and a sleep shirt and checked my bedroom door again to make sure it was locked before going to dry my hair.

But as soon as I was done—and I'd turned off the hair dryer—I noticed a vibration under my feet.

And my ears perked, hearing an indiscernible beat coming from downstairs.

Was that music?

I set the dryer down and walked toward my door. Leaning my ear into it, I heard a short, fast rhythm and then a few howls.

What the fuck?

Tossing my brush on the dresser, I pulled the chair away from where it was lodged under the handle and cracked open the door.

Loud music immediately hit me, and I could hear voices and laughter.

A lot of voices and laughter.

Leaving the door open, I dashed over to my window and looked out at the driveway.

It was flooded with cars.

"I don't believe this," I said to myself.

Whipping around, I charged out of my room and down the stairs, taking a look around at all of the people.

I clenched my jaw. *What the hell was going on?*

Some of them I recognized from being a couple of years behind me and still in high school, some were college students home for the weekend, and others I had no idea. Maybe people from neighboring towns? Locals?

They walked around with Solo cups, talking and laughing, and some even tried to call out to me to say hi, but I just ignored them.

I stormed through the house, going in and out of rooms, trying to find Michael. The finished basement and media room were packed full of people I barely recognized, and I couldn't find any of the guys in the kitchen or on the patio, either.

I spotted Alex chatting with a couple of guys by the pool, but I didn't have time to wonder how she'd gotten here so fast.

Where the hell was Michael?

The court.

I charged for the other end of the house, already hearing the pounding of a basketball coming from Michael's huge indoor basketball court.

Swinging open the large double doors, I heard the squeaks of tennis shoes running across the polished wooden court floor as the echo of a basketball drifted up to the rafters. Several guys raced on the court with their shirts off, and I recognized a few of them. They were seniors now at Thunder Bay Prep.

Looking to my left, I spotted the carpeted hangout area, complete with couches and a refrigerator. Michael and Will sat on the large sofa, a sea of bottles and cups on the table before them, while Kai sat in a cushioned chair, looking anything but relaxed. His elbows rested on his knees, and he held the rim of a red cup between his fingers.

Stalking over to them, I stared disbelieving at the sight before me.

A party? They were fucking drinking?

"This isn't seriously happening right now, is it?" I snapped, stopping in front of the table and looking over at Michael.

He raised his eyes but kept quiet.

"You kidnap my mother," I started, "burn down my house, steal my money, lure me here, and then attack me."

"We're really sorry," Will spoke up right away, sounding sincere.

What?

I opened my mouth to retort, but I was too stunned. I almost wanted to laugh. They were sorry? That was supposed to fix everything?

Will leaned forward and poured some alcohol into a rocks glass and held it up to me.

"Do you want ice in your tequila?" he asked in a gentle voice.

But I darted forward, slapping the glass out of his grasp and sending it flying to the ground. The tequila splashed across the carpet, making a couple of the girls standing nearby scurry away.

Breathing hard, I tipped my chin down and glared at Michael. "Tomorrow you're going to put me on the phone with my mother," I ordered. "You're going to give me back every cent and schedule a contractor to start restoration on my house, which you will pay for! Do you understand?"

"We were going to anyway," he replied, and then looked at me curiously. "But I'm curious. What happens if we don't?"

I stood up straight, folding my arms over my chest and curling my lips.

"Did you ever find the phone?" I asked. "There are a lot more videos on there, huh?"

Michael's face slowly fell at my insinuation, and he sat up, resting his forearms on his knees. "You're lying."

I held up my hand, inspecting my nails. "Maybe." I shrugged. "Or maybe I know where Trevor hides everything important to him. And maybe I know what the combination is, and maybe I'm willing to bet that, if he hasn't destroyed the phone, then it's in his special hiding place." I looked straight at him, unable to hide the amusement I felt. "And maybe if I don't get what I want, I won't be nice and open up the safe for you."

Anger crossed his face, and I could tell he was thrown for a loop. They'd assumed the phone was gone. They'd assumed they were safe.

But from the look in his eyes, there was more on that phone that could hurt them.

Kai and Will sat frozen, their ease now apparently sucked away.

"You're threatening us?" Michael's menacing tone made my stomach flip.

"No," I answered. "That's what you did to me. I'm simply playing your game."

He inhaled a long breath and sat back. "Fine," he bit out. "Mom, house, money. Easy enough."

Then he snapped his fingers to a group of girls to his left, calling one over. A blonde in a tight blue dress falling just a few inches below her ass sauntered over and bit her bottom lip, trying to hide a smile, as Michael pulled her into his lap.

My heart sunk.

His hand snaked around her waist and held her close to him as he looked at me the same way he did growing up. As if I were in the way.

"Now, go to bed," he ordered. "It's late."

I tensed, half-expecting to hear Will laugh at the remark, but both he and Kai sat silently, looking at the floor.

Refusing to let him see me falter, I raised my chin and turned, walking out of the court as the pain and anger dropped like an anchor into my stomach. It sat there like a brick, and the weight was too much. I couldn't feel anything anymore.

Too much.

I'd been terrorized tonight for no reason, and not only had he not apologized; he was doing everything he could to hurt me more.

Did he feel anything?

I passed partiers and crossed into the foyer, racing up the stairs and into the solitude of my bedroom.

Keeping the lights off, I closed the door and locked it before walking over to my bed and sitting down. I dropped my head and closed my eyes.

I wanted to leave.

I didn't care about the money or the house. They should be coming to me, begging to make it right.

A knock sounded on the door. "Rika?"

I popped my head up, hearing Kai's voice and seeing a shadow in the light underneath the door.

"Rika," he said, knocking again. "Open up."

The pulse in my neck throbbed. I stood and walked over to the door, turning the handle to make sure it was locked.

"Stay away from me, Kai."

"Rika, please," he begged. "I'm not going to hurt you. I promise."

I shook my head. *Not going to hurt me. You mean any more than you already have?*

Twisting the lock, I cracked open the door and saw Kai standing there, dark and tall, dressed in a pair of jeans and a gray T-shirt. His eyebrows were pinched together, and there was a sea of pain in his eyes.

"Are you okay?" he asked, sounding timid.

"No."

"I won't touch you," he promised. "I wanted to hurt you because I thought you hurt me, and now I know that's not true."

"So does that make everything all right?" I glared at him, anger coursing through me. "The stress and the fear you put on me?"

"No," he rushed out. "I just . . ."

He dropped his head, looking like he was struggling to find words.

He looked weary.

"I just don't even know who I am anymore," he nearly whispered.

I dropped my hand from the doorknob, surprised by what he'd said. It was the first real moment I'd had with any of them in years, and he wasn't playing with me.

I turned and walked to the bed, sitting down at the end.

Kai stepped into my room, filling the doorframe and blocking out the light from the hall.

"That night three years ago . . ." I began, speaking softly, "I felt so alive. I needed the chaos and the anger, and you guys seemed exactly the same. It was a really good feeling not to be alone anymore."

My eyes watered, thinking back to how, even for a little while, I felt like I belonged somewhere.

"I'm so sorry, Rika. We should've made Michael confront you all those years ago." And then he exhaled a shaky breath and ran his hand through his hair. "Your house. Jesus Christ," he said, as if just realizing the full measure of what they'd done.

I clutched the blankets at my sides and stared at the carpet.

Well, that was one apology, at least.

I shrugged, allowing him a little consolation. "With you in jail and unable to confirm that it wasn't you in the mask instead of Trevor, we may never have realized what had actually happened anyway."

I wasn't sure why I wanted him to feel better, but even if Michael had confronted me, it was my word against Damon's, and seeing as how I had the sweatshirt, it made sense that he would trust his friend.

But he still should've confronted me. What were they hoping to gain with revenge, other than pleasure in someone else's torture? Would it accomplish anything, take away what happened, or move their lives forward? Had their worlds become so small in prison?

Kai pulled out my desk chair and sunk into the seat, leaning his elbows on his knees.

"I was angry with you," he told me. "At first, I was so angry when I thought you'd outed us. But I wasn't vengeful. I was never going to do something like this."

He stopped and stared off, and for a moment, it was like he'd gone somewhere else.

"Things changed," he said in a low, dark tone.

I narrowed my eyes, immediately drawn in by the faraway look in his eyes.

What had changed while he was away?

"I never knew people could be that ugly," he told me. "I'll die before I ever go back there."

I sat frozen, wanting to ask him what he was talking about, but I knew I shouldn't care. He was referring to prison, I was sure, and I knew it must've been hard. Hard enough to turn him from angry to vengeful.

I looked over at his tired eyes, once bright with life, and I didn't want him to stop talking. Michael never told me anything—never opened up—and I was interested.

"Are you okay?" I asked.

But he didn't answer, and I saw him drift farther and farther away.

Standing up, I walked over to him and knelt down in front of him.

"Kai?" I asked, trying to meet his eyes. "Are you okay?"

He blinked, and I hated how broken he looked. "No," he whispered.

I couldn't even get him to look at me. What the hell happened to him?

He hesitated, as if thinking, and then continued. "Damon lost what little heart he had," he explained. "People, problems . . . they barely scratch the surface with him anymore. He doesn't care about anything." He ran a hand through his black hair, fisting it. "Will finds ways to cope with alcohol and other things, and as for me . . . I don't want to be around anyone other than the guys. Not even my family. They won't understand."

"Understand what?"

His chest shook with a bitter laugh. "I wish I knew, Rika. I just can't let anyone in. I haven't touched a woman in three years."

Three years? But he'd been out for months. No one in that entire time?

"Michael paid off guards to keep us safe, but he couldn't shield us from everything," Kai went on. "He watched as Will deteriorated, and I withdrew more and more. He was helpless to do anything, and he felt so guilty. Guilty, because he thought he'd incited you. Guilty, because he was free." He took a deep breath and kept going. "He came up with the plan. Something to keep us hot and angry. Something to keep us fighting. And before we knew it, it consumed our every waking moment in there."

And then he looked up, meeting my eyes. "I'm so sorry."

I let out a slow breath, seeing it in his eyes. *I know.*

Reaching out, he grazed his fingers down the side of my face, pushing my hair out of the way. "I haven't been able to talk to any-one," he admitted. "Why does it have to be the one person I hated only just this morning?"

I couldn't help it. I gave a small smile and caught his hand on my face in both of mine and held it.

Kai used to be larger than life. Like Michael, only a straight arrow. Kai was the good one.

But now there was darkness there, too. His fight with me might be over, but there was still something brewing inside.

The light spilling across the floor from the hallway disappeared, and Kai and I turned our heads to see a figure in shadow filling the doorway.

"I told you to go to sleep."

Michael.

I dropped Kai's hands and stood, the corners of my lips turning up. "No, you told me to go to bed. And maybe I was just about to."

I threw a pointed look, hoping he got my insinuation.

"Do you two ever stop?" Kai chuckled, standing up.

Michael remained silent as Kai gave me one last look before turning and walking for the door. He waited for his friend to move and then walked through, disappearing around the corner.

Michael turned back to me, filling the doorway with darkness again, and my stomach flipped and then tightened.

I hadn't realized it, but I'd been relaxed with Kai here. Now I wasn't again.

Michael hadn't changed from before. He still wore jeans and no shirt, and I wondered where the girl was who had her hands all over him downstairs.

"Come here," he told me.

And I did.

I walked over—going to him, just like he asked—and then I smirked as I grabbed the handle to the door and swung it closed.

He shoved out his hand, stopping it, like I'd known he probably would.

"I wouldn't have let anything happen to you," he stated. "I knew it the second you walked through the door tonight. I swear."

"I don't care," I replied in a flat tone. "I don't want you in here."

And then I tried to push the door closed, but he planted a hand on it, stopping me. Forcing it open, he walked through and slammed it shut behind him before pulling me in and swinging us around, so my back was against the door.

"I stopped them." His breath fell over my face. "I chose you over my friends."

"Yeah, it looked like it downstairs," I said sarcastically, referring to the girl in his lap earlier. "I'm tired of your games, Michael, and I'm tired of you. Get out."

"What did he say to you?" he demanded, ignoring my order.

Kai? Was he bent out of shape because Kai had sought me out?

"More than he probably says to you," I answered.

He breathed out a bitter laugh, and for the first time it looked like he was at a loss for words.

"Sick of my games, huh? You've learned to play them pretty well."

"I'm not playing your games. You were wrong." I crossed my arms over my chest. "You want to know what I've learned? I don't win by playing *your* games. I win by making you play *mine*."

His eyes pierced me, darkening as his breathing grew shallow. He was pissed.

I laughed, suddenly feeling ten feet high. "Look at yourself," I joked, elation filling my veins. "You're actually breaking a sweat trying to keep up with me, aren't you?"

He bared his teeth and grabbed the backs of my thighs, hauling me up and slamming me against the door again. My heart jumped in my chest—the rush of fear filling my body—as the wind was knocked out of me.

And I couldn't help it. I locked my ankles behind his back, holding him between my thighs.

"Goddamn," he whispered against my lips. "I want you."

"You're not the only one."

"Kai?" he gauged. "Don't look to him, Rika."

"Why not?"

He darted out, catching my bottom lip between his teeth, the heat of his mouth sending shivers down my spine.

"Because you get everything you need from me," he argued, his hot tongue flicking my upper lip. "And you'd only be doing it to fade me out, anyway, and that will never happen."

He dived in, taking my mouth, and I groaned, my head feeling dizzy. I met his powerful lips as I tilted my head to the right to deepen the kiss. His tongue brushed mine, and I could feel a fire building low in my belly.

I broke the kiss and tilted my head back, so he could trail kisses down my neck. "That sounds really good, actually," I said, groaning at the feel of his lips over my scar. "A new man. A new mouth."

His fist tightened in my hair, and his teeth brushed over my skin, warning me. "If you ever let that happen, I will make you sorry."

And then he came in again, sucking and nibbling my skin as I gasped and dug my nails into his shoulders.

"Oh, God," I moaned, grinding on him. "Oh, Kai. Yes."

I felt his angry breath exhale across my skin, and his hand squeezed my ass painfully through my thin pajama shorts. His nibbling turned to biting, and his kisses became so hard they stung.

I pulled his hair, forcing his head back as I grazed my tongue along his bottom lip. "Trevor," I whispered. "Touch me, Trevor."

He growled and shoved away from me, backing up. I dropped to my feet and breathed hard, holding his glare.

"Fuck this," he barked, and then he reached out and yanked me away from the door, pulling it open. I watched as he charged out of the room, and I couldn't help but smile as he ran away.

I immediately followed.

"Does this mean you're tapping out?" I inquired with fake concern.

"No," he bit out, storming down the hallway, the muscles in his back flexing. "Game change. New players. There are plenty of other girls here, Rika."

"And there are lots of guys here, too," I threw back, following him down the stairs.

He stopped in the foyer and turned around to look at me, a dare in his eyes. "Is that so?" And then he smiled and twisted his head around, speaking to the crowd. "Listen up!" he shouted to all the guests hanging out. "Rika Fane is Horsemen property. Any guy lays a hand on her has to deal with us!" And then he turned back to me, lowering his voice with a smirk. "Good luck."

I clenched my teeth together. *Dammit.*

Play his game. Play my game. It ultimately didn't matter when he had more people on his team.

Fuck.

He turned around, knowing he'd won, and walked toward the kitchen, leaving me standing in the middle of the foyer, surrounded by people eyeing me and thinking God knows what.

Horsemen property? Christ.

But then his words came back to me, and I paused. *Any guy lays a hand on her . . .*

I fought to hold back my grin.

Walking into the sitting room, I scanned the area and then moved into the kitchen, finally spotting Alex at the island fixing herself a drink. She wore a tight black dress held up by a strap on one shoulder, bare on the other.

I approached her, and she immediately looked up. "Hey. Can

you believe Will flew me here in his dad's helicopter for this?" she said, setting down one bottle and picking up another. "Like I'm going to find a lot of business with the high school set. I mean I'm controversial, but not a pedophile."

I snorted.

Not everyone here was in high school, and Alex certainly wasn't much older than them. But yes, I could guess she was used to more sophisticated men.

I took a deep breath before I lost my nerve.

"How much do you charge?" I asked.

She set down the vodka and pinched her eyebrows together. "For what exactly?"

"For women."

CHAPTER 24

MICHAEL

Present

Plenty of other women here. Yeah, that was a fucking bluff if I'd ever heard one. I couldn't keep my eyes off her, and I'd either have to swallow my pride and actually be nice to get into her bed tonight, or . . .

Or I'd have to pick another fight.

Either way, she'd have my number. She'd know I couldn't stay away and that she was the only girl I wanted. How the fuck had that happened?

I stood outside on the patio with a few old friends—some locals who worked in town and some high school friends who never made it out of Thunder Bay—but I wasn't listening to anything they were saying. I stayed rooted, my arms crossed over my chest, as I watched her through the windows talking to Alex at the kitchen island.

I couldn't believe she'd called me Kai. And then fucking Trevor? She was doing it on purpose, but why would she challenge me?

She wanted me. Why not just give in?

But no, the more I tried to get her to melt for me and forget all the bullshit we'd gone through tonight, the more she opened her smartass mouth to feed me her disdain. I couldn't bend her anymore. She was laughing at me.

What if I'd completely corrupted her? What if she'd begun to like playing games too much, and the lust to play—and to win—overpowered her need for me?

What if her heart had hardened so much that she closed herself off in order to survive?

What if I was the one who had to bend?

Unease weighed on my shoulders, and I let out a breath. *I need her.*

I want her.

At least tonight I was safe. I'd won this round. No guy was going to come near her, so she'd eventually just go to bed in defeat.

She had no cards left to play.

I watched as she and Alex walked around the island, "Goodbye Agony" by Black Veil Brides playing through the house, but then Rika stopped, looked up, and met my eyes through the glass. Leaving Alex standing in the middle of the kitchen, Rika opened the door and walked up to me, leaning in.

"You said no *guys*, right?" she asked, sounding mischievous. "Just making sure."

One corner of her lips curled, and she turned, walking back inside. I watched as Alex shot me a smug, devious smile and took Rika's hand, leading her out of the kitchen.

What the . . . ?

I inched to the side, following them through the foyer with my eyes and seeing Rika cast one more glance behind her before they disappeared up the stairs.

No guys. Meaning . . . ?

Charging for the door, I swung it open and bolted through the kitchen.

"Hey, where you going?" Kai grabbed my arm, stopping me. "We've got to talk about Damon."

"Tomorrow." I pulled away, dismissing him, and made my way through the foyer and up the stairs.

I couldn't think about Damon right now. He was injured, and he wasn't doing anything tonight.

Walking down the dimly lit hallway, I approached Rika's bedroom, noticing that the door was open. The entire upstairs was quiet, the echoes of the music downstairs like a faraway hum.

But when I stepped into her doorway, I found the room empty. The lights were off, as they had been the last time I'd been up here, and her bed was still made.

I looked back down the hallway, narrowing my eyes. Where the hell was she?

Throwing open doors, I searched my parents' room, my brother's room, the guest bedrooms . . . But when I got to my room, I noticed a flicker of light coming from underneath the door.

Reaching out a slow hand, I turned the knob and pushed it open.

And my heart skipped a beat.

"Shit," I barely whispered under my breath.

Alex sat on the edge of the bed, and Rika stood between her legs, both girls with their hands on each other. Alex held Rika's hips, staring up her and looking entirely too interested.

And Rika . . .

My fucking stomach was floating up into my throat, and I inched into the room, closing the door behind me.

Rika put one knee on the bed at Alex's side, leaning her hips into Alex's chest and threading her fingers into her hair, caressing Alex's neck and shoulders.

Alex inched up Rika's gray tank top, leaving soft kisses across her belly and darting out the tip of her tongue to taste Rika's skin.

My cock rushed with blood and heat, swelling painfully.

She was going to win this round.

"What are you doing?" I was already sweating. *Jesus.*

Rika blinked her eyes up at me, gentle and calm. "Game

change. New players," she repeated my words. "You're not needed. Sorry."

And then she let out a moan, arching her body into Alex's mouth and letting her head fall back.

I grunted, resisting the urge to adjust myself. Goddamn her. What the hell did she think she was doing?

Was she really willing to go this far to challenge me?

"You're in my bed," I pointed out, trying to look unaffected.

Rika grinned down at Alex, who was still kissing her stomach, both of them practically ignoring me. "Your bed is bigger," she answered. "You don't mind, do you?"

I steeled my jaw, seeing her hands trail down Alex's chest and grasp at her dress, pulling it up and off her body.

But I barely noticed, because I couldn't take my eyes off Rika. She still wore her thin pink pajama shorts, looking so sexy and innocent with her glowing skin and hair. I swallowed the dryness in my throat, not sure if she was bluffing, trying to get me to react, or if she really did want this. Both possibilities, though, would have her coming out on top. She'd know she was smarter and stronger.

Alex's hands ran up and down Rika's legs, and she started pulling down her shorts, nibbling the skin over Rika's hip bone.

"Ah," Rika groaned, her eyes closed. "Michael . . ."

I lost my breath, shaking my head, my heart in a thousand knots.

She was winning. I was playing her game, and I was fucking losing. God, I wanted her so goddamn much.

But this wasn't over.

I circled the bed and grabbed Alex by the arm, yanking her up.

"Leave," I ordered.

"What?" she blurted out, her eyes desperate. "Are you kidding me?"

I guessed she was getting turned on and probably hoped I'd let it continue and enjoy the show.

But I shoved her away, not caring how disappointed she was. Will, Kai, and dozens of other guys—and girls—were out there. Let her take her pick.

Alex snatched up her dress, huffing as she walked out and slamming the door behind her. When I turned back, Rika stood next to the bed, a slight smirk on her face. "Your move."

I breathed out a laugh, towering over her as I hardened my tone. "Did you like that?" I asked. "How far were you willing to go with her?"

She licked her lips. "Maybe farther," she admitted. "Or maybe I knew I wouldn't have to go far at all. Maybe I know you better than you think I do."

Reaching up, I trailed a finger across her jaw. "Do you?"

She held my eyes, her chest rising and falling faster, and I could tell she wanted to lean into my hand. She wanted me to say sweet things and to give in to her, and she wanted my heart. That's why she was pushing me.

But I wanted to play.

"The thing is . . ." I stated, narrowing my eyes on her. "We have a problem. You weren't invited into my bed, and you came in here without permission."

Taking her hand, I pulled her across the room, feeling her stumble behind me as I forced her toward the door.

"Michael!" she cried out, seeing me open it. "What are you doing?"

I dragged her to the opposite side of the empty hallway, two doors down, and hauled her into a bedroom, throwing her forward and closing the door behind me.

"Now, that's a bed you're more familiar with." I gestured to my brother's bed. "Get in it."

She faced me, fisting her hands at her sides and breathing hard, all composure lost. She shook her head, her eyes glistening with tears.

Why was I doing this? I could've told her how much I wanted her, how much I needed her, and how, after nearly a week, I could still taste her. She could be underneath me in my bed right now, and I could be inside of her, listening to her pant and getting lost in the sheets and the feel of her the rest of the night.

"Michael," she begged, her voice brittle. "Why are you doing this? After today and everything you put me through? Why are you trying to hurt me more?"

"Are you tapping out?"

Her face cracked, and she dropped her head, her body shaking with sobs. "You're sick, Michael. You're sick."

I ground my teeth together, approaching her. "When I found out last year that you were dating Trevor, I hated it. I hated you, but I hated that even more. I wanted to come in here and see you in *his* bed and how you would've looked—"

"Why?" she cut in.

I stared into her eyes, knowing that I barely understood the answer to that question myself. Ever since I was little, I remember being angry. Angry that my father tried to mold me into someone I wasn't. Angry that he took her out of my arms. Angry that she and Trevor were always pushed together. Angry that I had to leave for college and leave her alone with my family.

And then I was angry that she'd betrayed me. Or so I thought.

But for some reason, the anger didn't break me. It made me my own person, someone who was defiant and knew their own mind. I stood up to my father, I made my own decisions, and I was invincible. And I became very good at finding my amusement in other ways.

When we were growing up, every time she walked into a room and looked at me, wanting me to look back so badly, I felt powerful when I refused to indulge her. When I left the room as if she hadn't been there at all.

I loved that I dominated her pretty little head more than my brother ever could.

And indulging in a little self-torture, like picturing her in here with him, kept me hot and on edge. I liked that, because I liked who I was. It made me strong. Would giving in to her change me?

"I like to hurt myself," I told her. "I need this. Now, take off your clothes and get in his bed."

"Michael," she breathed out, trying to argue.

But I just stood there like a wall, unbending.

Her chest rose and fell hard, but she calmed her features and squared her shoulders, looking back up at me.

Her mouth twisted in anger, but her eyes turned bold as she tore off her clothes and pulled down her panties, stepping out of them and walking to the bed.

My heart started to beat faster, and I folded my arms over my chest, trying to stay hard.

She pulled back the covers, her long blond hair flowing down her back, and climbed in. She lay down, pulling the forest-green sheet up to her waist and leaving her breasts uncovered.

Resting a hand behind her head, she looked at me, her big eyes taunting me as her other hand rested on her bare stomach. She looked so fucking soft and warm and perfect.

He'd seen her like this. He'd lain next to her like this, and regret racked through me, not because of the picture before me, but because it should never have been him. I could've had her—her first time, everything—and I let her go three years ago.

If it weren't for me, she would never have turned to him.

What the hell was the matter with me? Was all the power I felt pretending like she didn't exist *greater* than how fucking good she felt when I had her in my arms?

No. Not even close.

She cocked her head, her eyes pooling with tears. "I'm in his bed," she pointed out. "You're not going to do anything about it this time? I can moan his name or . . . maybe tell you about the four times in our months together that I let him have me, and how I tried so hard not to picture it being you."

The blue of her eyes glistened and shook as tears started to spill down her temples into her hair.

"Maybe you'd like more of a visual instead?" she asked.

She sat up, pulling the pillow down and swinging her leg over it, straddling it.

Rolling her hips, she began to ride the pillow like it was Trevor underneath her, tilting her head back and moaning.

Her beautiful round ass ground into the fabric, her back arching as she picked up pace, while her hair swayed against her back.

Pain shot through my chest, and my fists clenched.

"Rika," I murmured, feeling like I'd lost her.

But then she groaned and whispered, "Michael."

And I narrowed my eyes, inching up the bed to see her face.

Her eyes were closed, and she let out a hard breath, a small smile crossing her face as she rode the pillow. "Michael."

She picked up pace, grinding harder and faster, her tight stomach waving in and out, and her full breasts swaying with her movements.

She grunted as her dry-fucking grew more rigorous, and her face tightened in pain as she rode harder and harder. "Oh, God. Oh, fuck."

And Trevor was gone. He wasn't in the room anymore.

She was mine.

I unfastened my belt and dropped my jeans to the floor, kneeling behind her on the bed.

I lost track of what the score was, whose move it was, or what game we were even playing anymore.

We want what we want.

I wrapped a hand around the front of her neck and pulled her against me. Her head fell back on my shoulder, and my cock stood straight up, brushing against her ass.

"What are you doing to me?" I asked, not really expecting an answer.

She was tearing me up, and I wasn't sure I cared. I just wanted to burn.

Dipping a hand down to her pussy, I slid two fingers inside her and pumped them in and out, bringing out her wetness and rubbing it over her clit.

She moaned, turning her head toward me as she reached around with her hand and held the back of my neck.

"I'm not tough, Michael," she whispered. "Not really. I can play, and I can let you fuck me in your brother's bed or on your father's desk and use me as an object to get back at them, but in the end—" She paused and then continued. "In the end I'm still here, Michael. I'm still here. It's still just you and me."

She breathed hard against my skin, and I dropped my head, caving. I wrapped both of my arms around her and held her warm body tight as I buried my face in her neck. I couldn't ever let her go.

"Just you and me," she repeated.

"Promise me," I demanded against the silky skin of her neck.

But *promise me* what? What did I want from her?

Promise you'll never leave me? Promise you belong to me? Promise you're mine?

I raised my head, turning her lips toward me and kissing her deep and fast, her taste sending a rush of pleasure to my cock.

I pulled away, breathing against her lips. "Promise you'll never say no to me. Promise you'll never keep yourself from me."

She grabbed my bottom lip between her teeth, sucking and kissing. "I'll never say no," she answered, but then added with a smile in her voice, "As long as you keep me screaming yes."

I groaned, pushing her down on her hands and knees and grabbing her hips, yanking them back as her legs willingly spread for me.

"Only as long as you need me, then, huh?" I said playfully, taking my cock in my hand and gliding the tip up and down her warm pussy. "Only as long as you need this?"

Finding her wet heat, I pushed the head inside, forcing it into her tight body, and then pulled it back out, seeing her shake.

"Michael," she moaned, looking over her shoulder.

And I slid the head back in, her pussy wrapping around me so hot that I just wanted to plunge inside of her. "You'll never say no to me. You know it."

And then I pulled back out, hearing her whine in frustration.

"Michael!" She slammed a fist into the comforter and then shot up, spinning around and pushing me back onto the bed.

My spine hit the footboard, keeping me halfway upright, and my heart throbbed in my chest, seeing her crawl on top of me like a little animal, completely out of control.

She straddled my waist, and I grabbed her hips, smiling and gloating as she dug her nails into my shoulder with one hand and positioned my cock underneath her with the other.

She sunk her body down on me, and I slid inside of her, squeezing her ass in my hands as I pulled her forward to catch her nipple in my mouth. I darted out my tongue, flicking the pebbled flesh and wanting to take a bite out of her. She tasted so fucking good.

She rolled her hips, clutching the footboard behind me in one hand and my shoulder in the other as she let her head fall back, moaning and grinding and fucking.

"That's it." I gripped her ass, pulling her into me again and again. "That's it, baby. This is what you were built for. Me."

I grunted, my cock so fucking hard for her. Taking one of her tits in my hand, I held it to my mouth, playing with her nipple again, licking and biting as she ground faster and faster, fucking me so good.

"Ah, ah," she cried out.

And then she dived down, plastering her chest to my body and kissing me, the feel of her breath against my mouth covering my skin with heat.

God, I was addicted.

"Don't look to anyone else to give you this," I growled in a whisper, kissing her again.

"Michael," she panted softly. "I never wanted anyone else. Don't you see that?"

She pulled back, sitting upright, and I watched her close her eyes and her glowing skin move in front of me as her breasts bounced with her movements. Her hair fell over her shoulders and down her back, revealing her scar, and I reached up, running my thumb down its length.

"So beautiful," I whispered.

She gasped, moving faster and faster. "Oh, God," she whimpered.

And I felt my cock rush with heat, and I tensed up, squeezing my eyes shut. "Christ," I groaned. "Baby, you better slow down or be ready to come."

"I'm coming," she breathed out. "I'm coming."

And then she pumped harder and faster, a light layer of sweat on her neck, and then she locked up, stilling as she dug her nails into my shoulders.

"Oh, God!" she cried out, jerking into me again and again.

And I grunted, pumping my hips up into her and spilling inside of her as my abs tightened and every muscle in my body strained and burned.

She collapsed on top of me, burying her lips in my neck, and for several seconds it was just us breathing. The rise and fall of my chest with hers, and I never wanted to move from this spot.

Rika. *Little Monster.*

"I don't forgive you for what you've done to me," she whispered, her voice still shaking from the orgasm. "But you're right. I don't think I can say no to you."

I closed my eyes, threading a hand through her hair and holding her close.

I don't think I can say no to you, either.

I rub my hands up and down my face, groaning with the weight on my eyes and the ache in my head.

"Shit," I grumble, turning my head slowly and seeing that I'm in the media room.

"Did we finish that whole bottle?" I hear Kai ask.

I tilt my head back, spotting him on the other couch with his face buried in his hands. I glance at the table in front of him, seeing an empty bottle of Johnnie Walker.

Peeling myself off the sofa, I sit up, my stomach rolling and a bitter taste in my mouth.

"Goddamn," he says, pulling out his phone. "She must be pretty damn sweet to get you to drink like that."

"Fuck you," I growl under my breath.

I hear him give a weak laugh as I try to steady myself. The room is spinning, and I blow out a breath, feeling bile rise in my throat as last night comes flooding back.

The warehouse. Rika.

I had her in my arms. Finally. Why did I fuck it up?

But then I hear Kai's ragged breath, and I look up to see him staring wide-eyed at his phone.

"Michael," he says, looking scared. "Get your fuckin' phone out, man."

I reach over to my hoodie, which I tore off last night, and dig into the pocket, pulling out my cell. Swiping the screen, I see a list of notifications, messages, and tweets a mile long.

What the hell? My heart starts pounding, and I start clicking, catching words like "cop," "statutory rape," and "Horsemen."

What?

My mouth goes dry as I see images of Kai, Will, and Damon, and I don't know what the fuck is happening. Why are these pictures online?

"The phone," *Kai breathes out, looking up at me like the wind has been knocked out of him.*

I click on the videos, my stomach dropping when I see Kai and Will with the cop, him hanging on by a thread as they hit him again and again. When I get to Damon's video, the girl's face is as clear as day, and I scan the comments, seeing words like "rapist" and "jail," as well as other girls claiming he'd done the same thing to them.

It's everywhere. Facebook, YouTube, Twitter . . . there's even a news article going on about us as if we're a gang. A fucking gang?

"What the fuck happened?" *I yell.* "How did this shit get online?"

"I don't know!" *Kai bursts out, breathing a mile a minute.* "Will . . ."

We both think the same thing. He has the phone, but he wouldn't do this! To us or himself.

Ignoring my notifications, I dial him to see where the phone is. He doesn't answer, but when I glance back at my screen, I see missed texts from Damon.

We're so fucked! *the first one says.*

And then another one a few minutes later. Rika has the phone! She had Will's sweatshirt last night!

I shake my head, meeting Kai's eyes, knowing he got the same texts. No. She wouldn't do that. She would never hurt me.

Throwing down my phone, I charge out of the room, hearing loud knocks on the front door as I rush through the house.

Excited voices fill the downstairs, and I feel like the walls are getting closer and closer, and I can't turn anywhere.

Coming up outside the kitchen, I stop, hearing Trevor's voice.

"So those are the guys you want to be around?" he snarls. "Rapists and criminals?"

I know he's talking to Rika, but I don't hear her say anything. The vein in my neck throbs, and I hear feet storming through the house. I don't have to look to know it's the cops. They might be looking for me, but they are definitely looking for Kai.

"Michael's nothing, and if you want to be around him so much, you'll end up just like his friends," Trevor goes on.

"I have no interest in being around him," Rika replies, a bite to her voice. "And his friends got what they deserved."

My lungs empty, and I step into the doorway, glaring at her back. Trevor looks up at me, and Rika spins around, hurt and sorrow in her bloodshot eyes. She can barely look at me.

And then my gaze drops to her hand, spotting Will's black hoodie with the tear in the sleeve from the fight with Miles last night.

Clenching my teeth so hard my jaw aches, I back away, holding her eyes. Kai is shouting down the hall, the cops having found him, no doubt, and I stare at her, rage wrapping around every inch of my body like steel armor.

This is my fault.

I'll never be able to make this right.

They'll suffer because I trusted her.

Opening my eyes, I throw the sheets off, sweat covering my chest and neck.

The memory of that day was like a sickness I couldn't shake. Seeing Kai in handcuffs, my friends splashed all over the local news, and knowing that none of it would've happened if I hadn't brought her with us the night before.

That Sunday, they would've gone back to school and carried on, building their lives and looking forward to the next time we could all wreak a little havoc together. Nothing would've ended.

If only I hadn't brought her with us.

I turned my head, seeing her fast asleep next to me, and my arms hummed with the need to hold her. Her lashes were dark against her alabaster skin, and there was the smallest little space between her lips as she breathed in and out calmly.

Shifting onto my side and propping myself up on my elbow, I ran a light hand down her face, tracing the scar on her neck and continuing down her body.

I leaned in and kissed her hair, breathing her in.

Nothing was her fault.

She was one of us—she was ours—and not only did I have a mountain of shit to do to make this right, but I almost feared that nothing would be enough. I didn't know exactly what I wanted from her, but I knew I didn't want to lose her.

And she'd grown very good at knowing her own mind.

Leaving her to sleep, I showered and dressed in black pants and a white dress shirt, knowing I'd have to take care of some business today.

The house was a disaster, and since my parents were out of town, our housekeepers and cook were on vacation, as well. I called in a temp crew, and by the time I got everyone left over from the party the hell out of my house, the workers were already there, getting started on the main rooms first, as well as cooking breakfast.

I called the facility where Rika's mother was and informed them that Christiane Fane's daughter would be in contact with her mother, and then I called a lawyer—not the family lawyer, someone who wasn't paid by my father—to discuss Rika's estate. I knew she didn't trust me with it—why should she?—but I didn't want it reverting back to my father, either. We'd have to try to contest the will.

I got all of her money transferred back into her accounts, which was easy enough, since the guys had bluffed last night at Hunter-Bailey. We hadn't quite gotten the shares doled out yet, so I still had access to everything and was able to put it all back and reactivate her credit cards with no problem.

After a couple of hours, I sat at the dining room table, a breakfast spread sitting out, Kai quiet and Will drifting in hungover. He looked a mess and immediately demanded to know what was next.

He wanted to go after Trevor.

"I can't clean up one mess and then jump right into another," I gritted out. My plate was already too full.

"Yeah, that was your fault," he threw back. "And Damon's, for giving you bad information. We followed like we always do." He looked to Kai for backup. "But I'm doing it my way now. I would like you with me. If not, I'll survive."

He tossed back some aspirin, chasing it with an entire bottle of water.

Yeah, it was my fault. We'd hurt Rika when it should've been Trevor, but I needed a breath first.

I pushed my plate away, sitting back in my seat and looking up to find her standing in the doorway.

I locked eyes with her, my heart skipping a beat. She looked absolutely beautiful. As if she hadn't been through hell last night.

She'd showered, put on some makeup, and straightened her hair, and she was dressed in tight jeans, a white shirt, and a little red jacket with black shoes.

Was she leaving?

"Rika." Kai stood up, looking contrite. "Would you like something to eat?"

I narrowed my eyes on him.

But she ignored him and met my eyes again. "My mother," she demanded.

I nodded, picking up a card off the table and holding it up for her. "Her counselor's number. You're on her list of contacts now. Call whenever you like."

She walked over and took the card, looking down at it.

And I could tell that whatever happened between us in Trevor's room last night was over for now. She was clearheaded and back to business.

Before she got a chance to say anything else, Will shoved a plate into her hands. "Here."

He reached over, grabbing a serving spoon full of scrambled eggs, and began loading Rika's plate.

She stared, dumbfounded, and I turned my head away, trying not to laugh.

"Now I'm sick of talking," Will continued, standing up and dishing her fruit and potatoes, as well. "No more plans. No more waiting. No more getting everything in place and all our ducks in a fucking row. Let's do this." And then he stopped with tongs in his hand and looked at her. "You like sausage?"

Without waiting for her to answer, he just shrugged and put two links on her plate.

She stared at him like he'd just pissed in the sink.

"We know where he is, and I don't want to kill him," Will gritted out, sitting down, "but I'm sure as shit going to change his life forever. Just like he did to us. Are you in or not?"

I let out a breath, hooding my eyes. Rika continued to stand there for a moment, but then she turned and walked down the table, setting her plate down.

"He is my brother, okay?" I argued, facing Will.

I didn't know what my feelings were about Trevor, but he was my mother's son—and my father's, of course—and hurting him would hurt them. I couldn't decide this today.

But Will kept arguing. "Don't give me that shit. He can't stand you, and you hate him just as much. The only reason you're holding back is because of her."

And he jerked his head at Rika.

She gripped the back of the chair, still not sitting. "I'm not involved," she replied calmly. "I'm going back to the city today, and I want nothing to do with any of this."

"But you are involved," Will retorted. "You're the whole reason for all of this. If you hadn't been with us that night, Trevor would never have shown up. Now, don't get me wrong. I don't blame you. And now that I know you're one of the good guys, I can admit that I actually really like you. But you're Trevor's motive, and you're in Michael's head. He needs to stay focused, and you're the reason he's not right now."

"I am focused," I bit out.

"Great!" he said, smiling. "Then when do we leave for Annapolis?"

I ran my hands over my eyes, ready to punch him in the fucking face.

Rika pulled away from the table, disengaging herself. "I'm going to go call my mother."

She turned and walked out of the room, and I darted my gaze to Kai, seeing him rise and follow her.

I moved to get up, too, but Will grabbed my arm, stopping me. "Your season starts soon," he pointed out. "This needs to happen now."

I sat back down and glared at him. "You listen, and you listen good," I warned. "Trevor doesn't even know that we know. He's not going anywhere. Damon is the threat right now. We have no idea where he is, and he's pissed off. I'm not stalling. I'm getting organized."

And I shoved my chair back, storming out of the dining room, through the foyer, and up the stairs.

But before I made my way to Rika's room, I stopped, seeing Kai at the second-floor window, peering down into the driveway.

"What are you doing?" I asked.

Walking up to stand next to him, I followed his gaze outside and spotted Rika on the phone, tossing her purse into the back seat of her car. Alex, who I'd forgotten was here, sat in the passenger seat.

"Goddammit."

Damon was out there somewhere, and I didn't trust him. She couldn't just leave.

"Aren't you going to stop her?" Kai challenged, sounding amused.

"I'm . . ." I shook my head, leaning on the window frame. "I'm not sure I can."

I heard him breathe out a laugh. "You finally met your match, huh?"

She stood outside her car, still on the phone, probably with her mother. The smile on her lips reminded me of a younger Rika. A gentler, happier one.

Before I'd gotten ahold of her.

"I don't know what to do with her," I said in a low voice.

She was in my body, in my head, and . . .

I looked down at her, my heart aching at the way she pushed her hair behind her ear.

And she was creeping into other places, too.

"You really think you need to prove anything to her?" Kai asked. "You think she hasn't been in love with you just the way you are her entire life?"

I continued staring out the window, not wanting this conversation with him.

"That's what scares you, isn't it?" Kai prodded.

"It doesn't scare me."

"I hope not," he said, staring down at her. "Because you've corrupted her nice and good. She's a force now, and it won't be long before she's brave enough to demand what she wants. If you don't give it to her, she'll find someone else who will."

I turned my head, peering over at him. "I don't need your warnings. I don't lose."

"That wasn't a warning," he shot back, not taking his eyes off her. "That was a threat." And then he looked at me as he turned to leave. "Watch your back, brother."

CHAPTER 25

ERIKA

Present

I dropped my head back, letting the tip of my blade fall to the ground as I tried to catch my breath.

I hated fencing alone.

I hated being stuck alone.

It had been five days since I drove back from Thunder Bay, Michael and the guys following close behind, and if I wasn't in class, then I was in my apartment.

Per Michael's orders.

And if I strayed—to the bookstore or the grocery store—he'd be calling or texting, wondering where I was. I think he had Mr. Patterson and Richard alerting him when I didn't walk in the front door at a certain time every day, and I was about done with it.

Alex had invited me for coffee with her friends tomorrow, and I was going to go.

Now that I knew my mother was safe, and actually sounding hopeful and more energetic, judging from the tone of her voice on the phone, I wanted to keep moving forward. My accounts were back to normal, and several contractors were assessing our house in Thunder Bay, getting ready to make bids on the restoration.

Whatever Michael and his friends were planning for Trevor and Damon, I didn't care. I didn't want any part of it.

Sick Puppies' "You're Going Down" played on my laptop in the kitchen, and I stood at the island, chugging a bottle of water, the light layer of sweat on my back cooling my skin.

I'd spent twenty minutes in front of a floor-length mirror, checking my footwork and parrying with a tennis ball before finishing with thirty minutes of sequences.

Fencing wasn't something I competed at, but it was something I endeavored to perfect. My father had wanted me to study it, and even though I could've quit at any time, I refused. It would've been closing a door. Leaving him behind in a way.

I just wished I had someone to practice with—a club or a program at a gym or something. It was dull training on my own, which was why I'd barely done any workouts since moving to Meridian City.

My phone started ringing, and I set down my water bottle, staring at Michael's name on the screen.

Hitting *Ignore*, I turned off my phone and pushed it away.

Every time he called or texted, it was demands, orders, and updates about where I was, what I was doing, and if I'd talked to anyone today. He never asked me how I was or said anything nice.

Until he finally showed up, late and worked up from his basketball practice, wanting in my bed.

He'd walk in, lock the door, and start stripping off my clothes, and everything I told myself to strengthen my resolve when he wasn't here went out the fucking window.

I'd wrap my legs around his waist and let him carry me to my room.

He was winning, and here I was again, playing *his* game.

I made my way to the refrigerator to get another bottle of water, but three quick knocks hit the front door, and I halted, the hair on the back of my neck standing up.

It's okay. If it was Damon—or Trevor—the door was locked, and no one could get in.

Walking slowly toward the door, I tightened my fist around the handle of my foil and leaned in, peering through the peephole.

Nothing but black. The lapels of his jacket, a shirt, and then there was a sliver of smooth, tanned neck. I couldn't see his face, six foot four as he was, but I'd know Michael anywhere.

"Who is it?" I asked playfully.

"Who do you think?" he snapped. "Open the damn door."

I shook my head, laughing to myself. Any opportunity to aggravate him was a small victory.

Opening the door a few inches, I stood there, fixing him with a defiant stare.

"A little early, aren't you?" I challenged. "You usually like your ass around ten."

He hooded his eyes, not the least bit amused. "Let me in."

But I shook my head, keeping him at bay. "No, I don't think so. I'm not interested tonight."

"Not interested?" He scowled. "What the hell does that mean?"

"It means you can't keep me locked up to be at your service whenever you're in the mood."

He narrowed his eyes. "Is that what you think I'm doing?" He pushed open the door and walked in, forcing me to back away. "You think I'm hiding you?"

He took another step toward me, but I immediately raised my pathetic sword between us, stopping him. Its flat tip pressed into his torso while the hilt nearly pressed into mine, keeping forty-three inches between us.

He let out a bitter laugh, looking down at my weapon. "My games are more fun."

But I wasn't playing. "You took Alex out," I reminded him. "My first night at Delcour, she was in a dress, you were in a suit, and you both had just gotten back here from wherever you were at. You haven't taken me anywhere."

He swiped the sword away and walked into me, backing me up

against a wall. Leaning his hand above my head, he dipped down, holding my eyes.

"So what do you want?" he sneered. "Flowers? A nice, polite dinner in a pretty dress, and a nice, polite fuck in a hotel room? Then I'll see you to your door at the end of the night? Come on, Rika. You're disappointing me. That isn't us."

"Us?" I argued. "There is no 'us.' You have no idea what makes me happy, and you don't care."

"Really?" He nodded with a sarcastic lift to his eyebrows. "So sneaking into Hunter-Bailey for their open bouting event tonight wouldn't make you happy? Because that's what I was coming to get you for."

My eyes rounded, and my mouth fell open.

"But if you'd rather dinner and a movie, hey." He shrugged. "I can go buy some boring fucking flowers, too."

I broke out in a wide smile, squealing as I jumped up and wrapped my arms around him.

He tried to stay stiff and aggravated, but I could see the smile trying to break out.

"You suck," I teased.

"So do you," he retorted, wrapping his arms around my waist. "Don't tell me how to treat you, okay? I know exactly what you like."

And then he pulled away, giving me a light slap on the ass. "Now, go shower and change. You stink."

I couldn't stop grinning as I spun around and dashed into the bathroom.

Stand up straight," Michael scolded, tossing his keys to the valet. I followed him to Hunter-Bailey's stairs, immediately squaring my shoulders and clutching my forest-green duffel over my shoulder.

"Are you sure this is going to be okay?" I asked, facing him.

He reached behind my head and grabbed the black hood of the oversize sweatshirt he'd put on me, pulling it over my hair.

"Who's going to stop us?" he shot back.

I twisted my lips to the side as he tucked my long hair inside the hood.

Who's going to stop us? Would I ever learn to retort with that when I had doubts? No, because I was a worrier.

"Well, what if they find out I'm a woman?" I pressed, my skin tingling as his hands grazed my face.

"Then smile and own it," he replied. "The only way we find out what we're capable of is by getting into a little trouble."

I cocked an eyebrow. "Sometimes getting into trouble can get you into *a lot* of trouble. Just ask Kai and Will."

He looked at me like I was an idiot. "Are you planning to beat up any cops or sleep with underage girls?"

I rolled my eyes.

"Come on." He took my hand, pulling me up the stairs.

Opening the door, he entered, letting me follow, and I kept my head down, hearing glasses clink and boisterous laughter coming from the dining room.

The pungent scent of cigars drifted out, assaulting my nostrils, so I inhaled short, shallow breaths.

Michael laid a hand on my back, guiding me toward the stairs.

"Mr. Crist?" a male voice called, and we stopped.

My heart jumped in my chest, but I didn't turn around.

"Policy requires that everyone check in, sir," the man said. It must've been one of the attendants.

"This is William Grayson the third," Michael answered, his voice calm and confident.

I could feel the man's eyes on my back.

After a few moments, he cleared his throat and answered, "Of course, sir."

Relief swept over me, but I knew he knew. How could he not? If he knew Will at all, he would know I was several inches shorter and eighty pounds of muscle too small.

But he wouldn't challenge a member. If Michael said I was Will, then I was Will.

"Come on." Michael nudged my back, sending me up the staircase.

I tightened my grasp on my bag and jogged up the stairs, hearing footfalls above me and chatter coming from the rooms we passed as he led me down the hall.

"Follow close," he told me over his shoulder. "Don't look up."

I kept my eyes down and my head bowed, simply watching the backs of his shoes as I shadowed him down the hallway. We walked through a door and across another room.

It was the gym. I could tell by the glossed wooden floors, the sound of speed bags being hit, and the squeaks of tennis shoes. Following Michael's order, I didn't look up, simply walking as quickly as possible to the locker room door as he opened it, rushing me in.

He led me past the steam room, the sauna, and the spas, their water vapor winding up out of the pools like a witch's brew, then led me past the lockers and the few male voices I could hear lurking about in the vast room. Curving to the right, we stepped into a row of frosted glass doors. Michael grabbed the handle of one and pushed me inside, stepping in behind me and closing the door.

Looking up, I spun around, seeing that it was a shower. The rainfall head sat directly above me on the ceiling, and a built-in soap dish on the wall held three large bottles with pumps—shampoo, conditioner, and body wash.

Michael took my bag and opened it, pulling out my pants, jacket, gloves, socks, and shoes.

Tossing the bag down, he dropped to a knee and started unfastening my pants.

I laughed under my breath, grabbing at his hands. "I can do it," I protested.

"But I want to," he said, sounding playful and making my heart flutter.

I heaved a sigh and stood up straight, letting him take off my shoes and socks before pulling down my jeans and slipping them over my feet. I stripped off my sweatshirt and T-shirt together, dropping them to the floor.

I crossed my arms over my chest, waiting for him to get out my white fencing pants and dress me, but instead, his eyes locked on mine as he slid his fingertips up my legs.

His lips quirked, and heat spread into his hazel eyes.

Curling his fingers under the hem of my panties, he pulled them down my legs, and I simply watched, trying to stay calm despite the butterflies in my belly.

I loved it when he watched me.

His rudeness and coarse attitude made the rare times he was soft so captivating that I wanted to slap myself. He was a sadist, and my little heart just had to go pitter-patter the second his yanks, grabs, and pulls turned into gentle caresses and his frowns, scowls, and snarls turned into whispers.

I fell, and I never even tried to stop myself.

Lust and logic sat on my shoulders like the modern-day angel and devil, one telling me to trust my heart and the other telling me that I would never be able to trust his.

Michael slid his hands up my thighs, and I stood there, completely naked for him, as his hot eyes drank me in and his fingers kneaded my skin.

"Don't even think about it," I scolded. "I want to fence."

He broke out in a smile, knowing he was caught. "You're so beautiful," he said, sliding his hands up my ass and holding my hips as he looked up at me.

I couldn't believe it. Michael Crist was on his knees, telling me I was beautiful.

I pushed his hands, heaving a sigh. "Just get me dressed."

I wasn't sure why he wanted me completely naked—no bra or panties—but arguing would tell him I was nervous, and screw that.

If he wanted me naked under my gear, it wasn't anything I couldn't handle.

He helped me get into my socks and then my pants. I slipped into my jacket, which zipped up the front, and then twisted my hair into a bun on the top of my head and wrapped a rubber band around it, securing it before sliding on my white gloves.

We got my shoes and mask on, making sure any stray hairs were tucked in.

"Let's go," Michael stood up and turned for the door, grabbing my hand.

But I yanked it out, smiling even though he couldn't see my face under the mask. "Do you normally hold Will's hand?"

He paused as if realizing what he'd done. "Good point."

He opened the shower door, and I followed him out, past the lockers, spas, and steam room and sauna again. Just as we were heading for the door leading back into the gym, Kai walked through, entering the locker room with a bag over his shoulder.

"Hey, what are you doing?" he asked, stopping in front of Michael.

Michael shook his head, blowing him off, but then Kai's eyes flashed to me and instantly narrowed.

Without hesitation, he reached out and lifted the mask up, seeing my lips twist to hide my smile.

"Nice." He laughed, dropping my mask back down. "Well, this should be fun."

Shaking his head in amusement, he walked around us into the locker room, and Michael stepped forward, opening the door to the gym.

Leading me through the maze of treadmills and weight machines and the large boxing ring and supply of punching bags, he entered another room, a little darker, with a large wooden floor and a few fencers already sparring and lunging. Cushioned brown leather chairs sat around the floor, while some men enjoyed the bouting while drinking and talking.

Michael led me to the wall where a plethora of épées, foils, and sabers were displayed and gestured for me to choose one. Glancing back at the men on the floor, I noticed most were using foils.

My heart started racing, hearing the clang of swords in the background, and I reached out, taking a foil with a pistol grip.

"Hey, are you up for sparring?" a man's voice said at my back, and I whipped around, my heart jumping into my throat.

"Uh . . ." I looked to Michael.

But he just smirked and leaned in. "Have fun," he whispered in my ear and walked off.

What? I straightened, suddenly nervous and feeling alone.

"Collins," the guy said, holding out his hand.

He had light red hair, balding on top, with a shiny, pale face. He offered a wide, close-lipped smile, and I noticed he had a mask secured under one arm and a foil in his hand.

"Uh," I stammered and then shot out my hand. "I'm Erik." And then I lowered my voice, repeating for extra measure, "Erik."

He grabbed my hand, damn near pulling my arm out of its socket as he shook it. "Well, come on, kid," he urged, turning around and putting on his mask.

Kid? I wasn't sure if it was my voice or my smaller frame, but at least he didn't think I was a girl.

We stepped onto the sparring floor, and I glanced around, finding Michael sitting in a chair at a table to my right. A waiter brought a drink, and he looked up at me as he took a sip.

The rough threads of my fencing suit rubbed against my skin, and I started breathing harder, feeling the seam in the pants graze my clit.

I held back a groan, a drop of sweat gliding down my back.

"I don't think I know you, do I?" the guy, Collins, asked.

I whipped my head back around, assuming the en garde position. "We going to fence or what?" I bit out, holding up my foil.

He chuckled and got into position, as well. "Okay."

I immediately advanced, using the footwork I'd been taught and had practiced for years as I challenged him, taking the offensive. I parried, moving my foil in small circles and forcing him to defend as I pushed farther and farther. His arms were longer, as were his legs, so I moved fast, trying to be bold.

Trying to be the little dog with a big bark.

I circled and played, and just when I thought he was caught up with trying to keep up, I lunged and darted out my sword, sticking it into his chest.

"Whoa!" he exclaimed. "Nice."

The thin blade bent, and I pulled back, breathing out, "Thanks."

I backed up, setting us in position again, and continued to advance or retreat as we bouted, him getting more comfortable and more aggressive.

He continued to challenge me, and I retreated, backing up as he advanced. But then I surprised him when I shot out and scored, stabbing him in the stomach.

"Dammit!" he growled.

And I stood up tall, tense that I might have pissed him off.

He pulled off his mask, his hair wet with sweat as he laughed, and I relaxed.

"Nice job, kid," he granted, breathing hard. "Now I need a drink."

I nodded, smiling as I let him walk off the floor. My mouth was also parched, but I wasn't ready to take off my mask to get a drink yet.

I turned my head right, realizing I'd forgotten Michael was even watching. He swirled his amber drink as he stared at me with heat in his eyes, and I couldn't get my breathing to calm down. At that moment, every inch of my skin was aware of him.

I was damp with sweat, and the clothes stuck to my body. Every little hair was sensitive, and I wanted his mouth everywhere.

"Care for a match?" a man asked.

I twisted my head, seeing another guy with tousled black hair and dark eyes.

I nodded, not saying anything.

Positioning my feet, careful of the other fencers around us, I began sparring with him, but I was no longer thinking about fencing.

Michael. Michael, Michael. Always on my mind. Always inside of me.

I could feel his eyes on me now, and all I wanted was to strip out of these clothes and feel his skin on mine.

Forever.

What was I going to do?

"Hey, hey, hey . . . ease up," the guy demanded. "I'm trying to enjoy myself here."

I slowed my advance, breathing hard. "Sorry."

I scored two times and he once, but I could barely concentrate anymore. Michael was watching, and now, instead of sparring and scoring, I wanted something else. The sweat on my bare skin under the clothes made the fabric chafe, and the threads rubbing my clit made me wet. I could feel my pulse between my legs throbbing, and I turned my head quickly to see Michael's jaw flex and his chest rising and falling faster.

The corner of his mouth lifted smugly; he knew I was getting worked up.

But then I grunted, feeling the flat tip of a sword digging into my stomach.

"Ugh," I growled, backing away. "Dammit!"

The guy laughed at me, and I scowled at Michael, seeing him smile to himself.

My skin was so hot, and frustration nipped at every nerve on my body. The suit and mask felt like a pile of blankets on top of me, weighing me down so much that I was suffocating, and I wanted to rip everything off just to breathe.

I clenched my fists, seeing the challenge in Michael's eyes. *Oh, no. It's my way this time.*

"Good match," I ground out to the guy, and then I walked away, leaving the floor.

"Hey!" I heard the guy exclaim.

But I didn't turn around.

Tossing my sword at Michael, I saw him catch it before passing his table and walking out of the room, knowing he'd follow.

I made my way through the gym and into the locker room, turning my head and seeing him come up behind me with fire in his eyes. He didn't have the sword, so he must've left it at the table.

Twisting back around, I headed for the showers again, knowing we'd have privacy in the separate stalls, but he grabbed me by the hips, stopping me instead. Swinging open the door to the steam room, he forced me inside, and I glanced around quickly, making sure it was empty.

Steam hung in the air of the huge beige-tiled room, several areas difficult to see with all the water in the air. The rectangular area was scaffolded like a movie theater, with four levels of seating and plenty of room to lie out.

But it was empty. The door didn't lock, but we were alone for the moment.

I spun around and grabbed the bottom of my mask, tearing it off my head and letting it fall to the floor.

"Games, games, games . . ." I scolded, unzipping my jacket. "You're driving me crazy."

He grabbed me, pulling the white fencing jacket down my arms and coming down on my lips hard. The jacket fell to the floor, and I gripped his shoulders as he pulled me up and into him, covering my mouth with his taste and heat. His tongue slid in, flicking mine as he moved strong and powerful, devouring me.

"I like you crazy," he gasped, pulling back an inch. "And I like you wet. How are you feeling down here?" He pushed his hand down the front of my pants, having no problem finding how slick I was. "Yeah. These pants rubbed against you good, huh? I knew they would."

I shot back up, meeting him full force as we continued to kiss, bite, and play. I worked the rubber band out of my hair, finally freeing it and letting the long tendrils fall down my back.

His needy hands covered my skin, damp with sweat, and then slid down my pants, cupping my ass and pulling me into him.

The thick ridge of his cock nudged my clit, and I groaned, it felt so good.

"Somebody could come in," I whispered against his neck as I pushed his black jacket down his arms. "We should go to the shower."

"No," he growled low, ripping open his shirt, the buttons flying. "I want to see you sweat."

I glanced nervously at the frosted door, knowing someone could enter at any second, but my pussy was throbbing, my nipples were so hard from brushing against his clothes, and I didn't care about anything except having him inside me.

Within seconds, my pants, shoes, and socks were gone, and Michael had shed his shirt before picking me up and wrapping my legs around him.

He stood there, in the center of the room, gripping my ass and kissing my neck, my jaw, and then my lips. I could feel my hair sticking to my back, and the air in the room grew thick, every inch of my skin coming alive as I tilted my head back.

"Rika," he whispered against my neck. "I need you. I need you every day, every hour, every minute . . ."

I brought my head back up, hugging him close and wishing time would stand still.

He was everything.

My entire life, I only felt completely alive when he was close, and while I knew nothing would ever be easy with him, I also knew nothing would ever be good without him, either.

Dipping my head into his neck and closing my eyes, I whispered, "I love you, Michael."

He remained still, his hold on me not changing, but it felt like he'd stopped breathing.

Tears sprang to my eyes when he didn't say anything, and I held him tight. *Please don't push me away.*

I wasn't sorry I'd said it. I'd owned it, and there was no other choice. But I couldn't face his silence. Or the truth that what was in his heart might not be what was in mine.

But I wasn't sorry.

"Rika . . ." he said, sounding like he was searching for words.

But I shook my head, dropping my legs and forcing him to let me down. "Don't say anything," I told him, not meeting his eyes. "I don't expect you to."

His hands stayed on my hips, and I knew he was staring at me.

"Tell her you love her," a deep voice echoed. "Jesus Christ."

I shot my head up, Michael doing the same as we scanned the billows of steam and finally made out a pair of legs on the top level swinging over the edge as he sat up.

"Is it that fucking hard?" Kai set his feet on the tile of the next level and leaned down on his elbows, staring at Michael. "You're so tortured. Had it real tough, haven't you, Michael?"

I sucked in a breath and dived down, picking up Michael's black shirt and covering myself.

Oh, my God. He'd been here the whole time? What the hell?

"A beautiful girl looks at you like you're God her entire life," Kai continued, shifting something small and red from one hand to the other over and over again, "and you're never going to get anything better, because there is nothing better, and you still can't say it? Do you know how lucky you are?"

Michael stood silent, his eyes narrowed on Kai. He wasn't going to argue with him. He never would. Giving Kai's accusation any attention would give it credibility.

Kai dropped his eyes, still spilling the small red items from hand to hand and looking solemn.

Do you know how lucky you are? Had it real tough, haven't you?

"What are those?" I asked, tightening the shirt around my chest.

"Shells," he answered.

Shells? I peered more closely at them, seeing the gold ends and tattered heads, scrappy and blown out.

Shells. Shotgun shells.

And they'd been fired. My heart started thumping.

"Why do you have them?" Michael demanded.

But Kai just shrugged. "Doesn't matter."

"Why do you have them?" I demanded, stepping in.

I knew Kai was struggling, but why the hell did he have shotgun shells?

"They're from the last time my grandfather took me shooting clay pigeons," he explained, no emotion in his voice. "I was thirteen. It was the last time I remember being a kid."

He stood up and walked down the levels, a white towel wrapped around his waist and his black hair slicked back.

"Sorry I didn't make myself known sooner," he said, approaching us. "I guess I . . ."

He trailed off as if thinking better of what he was about to say.

"You guess you what?" I asked.

He shot a glance at Michael before averting his eyes, admitting, "I guess I wanted to see if it would turn me on."

Heat spread up my face, and I remembered what he'd said about not touching a woman in three years.

Had it really been that long?

He moved to walk around us, but I instantly stepped in front of him, not sure why.

He was so fucking lost and guarded, and if he was going to talk, I didn't want him to stop until . . .

Until he felt good again.

"Did it?" I asked, barely audible. "Did it turn you on?"

His eyes shifted, and I saw him swallow like he wasn't sure what to say. Maybe he was afraid of Michael. Maybe he was afraid of me.

I didn't know why I did it, but I slipped off Michael's shirt and let it fall to floor, feeling Michael tense next to me.

Kai kept his head level but his eyes were on the floor, staring at the shirt.

Every hair on my neck stood up, and I worried about what Michael would say or do or if he'd hate me, but something made me push forward.

I inched closer to Kai, the steam sitting like a cloth on my skin as he refused to look up.

"Why won't you look at me?" I asked softly.

He breathed out a small laugh, looking nervous. "Because you're the first woman I've said shit to since I got out, and I'm afraid . . ." His chest rose and fell faster. "I'm afraid I'll want to touch you."

I turned my head slowly, looking at Michael. Droplets sat on his chest, and his piercing eyes watched me as if waiting for what I was going to do next.

I faced Kai again, trying to catch his eyes. "Look at me."

But he just shook his head and tried to veer around me. "I should get out of here."

I put a hand up, touching his chest and stopping him. "I don't want you to leave."

His chest rose and fell under my palm, and his whole body was rigid as he continued to avoid my eyes.

I didn't know what I was doing or how far this was going to go, but I knew Michael wouldn't hold me back.

And I wasn't so sure I wanted him to.

"Why are you doing this?" Kai finally raised his eyes, looking down at me.

"Because it feels right," I told him. "Do you feel comfortable with me?"

He glanced at Michael, who had inched closer to us, and then turned his eyes back on me. "Yeah."

But he didn't say anything else, and I wondered what he wouldn't talk about. Where was the old Kai?

He looked so alone all the time, and tears lodged in my throat, because we'd all been changed forever. Michael had hated because he couldn't take being helpless. Kai had suffered because his limits had been pushed, I'd gathered. And I had struggled to find out who I was and where I belonged for so long.

We'd all been so alone and so lost, wandering aimlessly, because none of us could admit that—not only were we not alone, but we couldn't be happy alone. I needed Michael, Kai needed his friends, and Michael needed . . .

I wasn't sure what he needed. But I knew he felt. He felt a lot, and I wanted that from him, and I wanted Kai to release everything that was holding him back, and I wanted the three of us to vent the pain and frustration, because it had been bottled up inside of us for so damn long.

I reached out and wrapped my arms around Kai's neck.

Burying my face in his neck, I held back the tears pooling in my eyes as I pressed my body into his and hung on to him like I was the one who needed him.

"Touch me," I whispered. "Please."

I heard his heavy breathing, and the pulse in his neck throbbed against my lips. His skin smelled like the salt from the spas, and the wet heat of his body melted to mine as he slowly relaxed.

He swallowed, and then I felt his hands rest on my hips. He stayed still for a few moments, catching his breath, but then I felt his fingers spread out over my back, his fingertips digging into my skin, growing stronger and more urgent.

His touch lowered, his hands running down my ass, and I started to follow suit. My hands came down over his shoulders, gliding down his chest, feeling the smooth skin of his collarbone and the ridges of his abs and slim waist.

"Does this hurt?" he asked.

I brought my head up to look at him, but he wasn't looking at me. He was looking at Michael.

I twisted my head, seeing Michael's mouth open a little, taking in quick, shallow breaths.

"Yeah," he said in a low voice, his eyes meeting mine.

"But you like it," I stated, feeling one of Kai's hands trail up my belly between us. "You like the sting. It turns you on."

Taking Kai's hand, I hung on to him with one arm around his neck and pressed my forehead to his as I brought his hand up and put it on my bare breast.

He immediately exhaled a hard breath and started slowly kneading the skin, my nipple tightening and tingling under his touch.

I closed my eyes, the pleasure seeping into my muscles and making them float. "That feels so good," I told him.

And then I opened my eyes, feeling a chest at my back.

Michael took hold of my hair, and my head jerked back as he wound the strands around his fist. He then pulled, forcing my neck to turn and my eyes up to him.

"You're fucking perfect," he said, and then reached around in front of me, sliding his hand between my legs.

His mouth came down on mine, Kai dived into my neck, and I moaned in surprise, the sound getting lost in Michael's throat.

Oh, my God. My knees nearly buckled, and I couldn't help arching my back, doing everything to meet Michael's mouth, kissing him and feeling the sensation of his tongue, while my breasts pressed into Kai's naked chest. Pleasure, like a cyclone, swept through my belly and down between my legs as he devoured my neck.

It was too much. Their lips sucking on me, tasting me, greedy and going back for more and more, and their hands groping and taking. I raised one arm, circling Michael's neck behind me while my other hand clasped the back of Kai's neck in front of me.

Michael slid his fingers inside of me, and I could feel how wet I was when he brought them back out. My head might be in a cloud and running on instinct right now, but my body definitely knew what it liked.

Michael's tongue dived into my mouth, making me groan as the pulse between my legs got faster and harder. Kai took one of my breasts in his hand and dipped his head down, covering my nipple with his mouth.

"Oh, God," I groaned, stilling as Michael continued to flick his tongue over my lips.

With the heat of Kai's mouth and the play of Michael's, I was ready to explode. Every muscle in my pussy tightened, and I looked up at Michael, begging, "I need to come."

He pawed my ass, kissing and nibbling my lips softly. "You hear that, Kai?" he asked but still looked at me. "She wants to come."

I felt Kai's breathy laugh against my skin as he switched from one breast to the other. He darted out his tongue, licking the pebbled flesh before sucking the whole thing into his mouth and dragging it out with his teeth.

Then he stood up, pressing his body into my front as Michael locked me in from behind.

"You need to come?" Kai taunted, nibbling my jaw and chin.

And then he went for my ear, whispering a low growl, "I can handle that, baby. I'm going to lick you so good."

I moaned, my stomach shaking with butterflies. I watched Kai drop to a knee and stared wide-eyed as he whipped off his towel.

Jesus. His erection and the size of his cock, full and hard, had my body on fire.

"Open her for me," he told Michael.

Michael reached down, took my leg under the knee, and lifted it, spreading it to the side and opening me for Kai. All I could do was dig my nails into his neck behind me and close my eyes as his friend covered my clit with his lips, sucking it into his mouth hard and making my legs go weak.

He was going at me like he was starved, gliding his tongue along, swirling it around my clit, and making me so hot and ready.

"You like my friend sucking on you?" Michael taunted in my ear, groping my tits with both hands. "Yeah, I think you fucking love his mouth on your pussy."

I let out a groan, my back arching and my tits jutting out as Kai's tongue slid inside me, moving and licking. I pressed my pussy into him more and more, trying to keep him in that exact spot.

Heat filled my womb, my entrance throbbed, and I started moaning and gasping as I rolled my hips, chasing the orgasm that was coming.

"Yes, yes," I cried softly.

I felt Michael's hand lower to my ass behind me and slip between my legs, rubbing one of his fingers up and down my length.

He stopped at the tight entrance, the one Kai wasn't eating out, and I blinked, a moment of alarm settling in.

My mouth went dry as he pressed there, and I sucked in a breath as he fit the tip of his finger inside me and just stayed there, not forcing it further.

"Come on," Michael urged, leaving soft kisses on my cheek. "Show me how much you like my friend eating your pussy."

"Yes," I whimpered, feeling my clit hum with need. "Kai, fuck, you feel so good."

I rolled my hips, gritting my teeth together as the orgasm got closer and closer.

Come on. Come on. Come on.

"Ah. Oh, God!" I cried out, fisting Kai's hair, grinding and jerking as the orgasm spilled over me, filling me with pleasure that racked through every nerve and over every inch of skin.

Michael's finger pumped behind me, but it didn't hurt. Not at all.

I ground my ass into him, as well, feeling the need build there as both of my entrances filled with longing, lust, and then satisfaction.

My heart pumped like crazy, and I relaxed into Michael's chest, feeling weak.

"Kai," he choked out behind me.

And I looked down to see Kai pull back, his eyes closing for a split second as if he'd enjoyed that just as much as I did.

He brought up a hand, easily catching the condom that Michael tossed him.

"I need you," Michael breathed out against my hair, sounding desperate.

I felt him take off his pants and drop everything to the floor, while Kai stood up and ripped open the condom with his teeth, sliding it on the hard length of his cock.

He grabbed my wrist and pulled me into him, picking me up by the backs of my thighs and lifting me up. I wrapped my legs around his waist, holding on to his shoulders as I stared into his dark eyes.

"Thank you, Rika," he said, sincerity clear in his eyes.

And then he kissed my lips as he positioned his cock at my entrance and worked the head in, going nice and slow as he slid inside.

I groaned, feeling him enter me as he grabbed my ass, holding me tight on him.

"Do you want me, Rika?" he asked, our stomachs and chests molding together.

"Yeah." I nodded, knowing what he needed to hear.

Did I want him?

I wanted *this*. I wanted him and me and Michael and making something good out of the last three years, and I wanted him to know he wasn't alone.

He was loved, and he had people he could count on.

But I wasn't in love with him. My heart was always Michael's. But I was his friend, and I wanted this.

Michael came up behind me, and I felt his dick on my back.

"So fucking hot," he said as he held my hips and kissed my shoulder. "Drop one leg for me, but hold on to Kai."

My heart skipped a beat, but I obeyed, knowing he needed me at a certain height to make this work.

Keeping one leg around Kai, with him still inside me, I dropped my right leg, lowering a bit. Kai held me tight, the cords of the muscles in his arms flexing as he kept me up.

Michael rubbed his cock against my tight entrance, my body already nice and wet from the steam and from Kai. I was so relaxed from my orgasm, and I was too exhausted to be too afraid.

I'd never done this before. Two guys—or this—but I knew it was going to happen.

"Hurry up," Kai told Michael. "I have to start moving. This feels too good."

Michael's dick pressed into me, and I sucked in a breath, holding it.

"Relax, babe," Michael pawed my behind. "I promise, you're going to love this."

I let out a breath, forcing my muscles to uncurl and remain still as Michael pressed harder and harder.

I winced at the burn as he pushed the head through and sucked in a breath. "I don't think—"

"Shhh," Michael soothed in my ear as he reached around to play with my clit. "Your ass is so fucking tight. You think I'm going to let you stop this after I've had a taste?"

And then he fisted my hair, pulling my head back. "Huh?" He bit my cheek, taunting me. "No one can hear you scream, Rika. We're both going to fuck you, and you're going to love every second of it. No one's coming to help you."

My heart jumped, and I gasped, feeling my clit throb harder with the fear. "Yes."

Goddamn him.

The fear. The fucking fright got me hot, and he knew exactly what to say to get my body needy again.

Slowly—so slowly—he sunk deeper and deeper inside me, and I was so turned on as Kai dived into my neck, sucking and kissing my skin. He pulled out and thrust into me, and I moved with the motion, backing up into Michael's cock. I felt the groan in his chest as he came down on my mouth.

They went slow, finding a rhythm and moving in and out of me at the same time, and I circled an arm around Michael's neck again, pulling Kai closer with my other hand.

I was stretched and filled and my entire body tingled with the friction of skin and sweat and my hair sticking to my neck.

"Harder," I groaned, sucking in air through my teeth as I arched my back for Michael and dug my nails into the back of Kai's neck.

They moved faster, and it fucking stung where Michael was entering me, but it felt so good, too. Like my orgasm was coming from ten different places, all leading to one spot where they'd come together and explode.

"Jesus," Michael gasped, his hands squeezing my hips as I backed up into his thrusts, taking everything he was giving me.

"God, Rika," Kai growled, one hand under my thigh at his waist and the other on my breast.

He dipped his head again, taking it in his mouth, and I pushed up against him, begging for it.

Tipping my head, I hovered my lips against Michael's. "Are you going to blame me for this in the morning?"

"And if I do?"

I breathed hard, Kai's and Michael's thrusts growing more powerful. "Then I'll leave," I told him, "and I won't come back until you chase me down."

His lips quirked in a smile, and he wrapped his arm around my neck, whispering in my ear, "I wanted this as much as you. I wanted to see how much this would hurt me."

"Does it hurt at all?"

He stopped breathing, looking pained. "I want to kill him."

And I smiled. "Good."

He dived down, capturing my mouth, and I had to force myself to stay upright, because he was kissing me so hard that I could feel it down to my toes.

And then he pulled away, dropping his head back and thrusting his dick inside me, caught up in the pleasure. I turned around, taking Kai's lips next, moaning into his mouth as his tongue caressed mine and my pussy started to build with pressure deep inside.

Kai held me by the back of my head, forehead to forehead, our hot breaths mixing together. "Rika," he panted. "Jesus, you feel so good. I can't believe I went without this for so long."

Sweat made his body shine, and I sucked his bottom lip between my teeth. "You're so deep. Make me come again, Kai."

He tightened his fist in my hair. "You don't even have to ask, baby."

He started thrusting harder, and I hooked my arm around Michael's neck again, feeling them both fill me up, going deep and hitting me so good inside.

I bit my bottom lip, squeezing my eyes shut as my blood rushed and my pussy pulsed and throbbed around his cock.

But it was Michael who made it spread throughout my body. His dick slammed into my ass, his skin on mine, and my entire belly and thighs burned until I'd gotten into a rhythm and was fucking them both back.

"Oh, God," I moaned. "Harder, harder!"

"Come on, baby," Michael urged me on.

"What the hell's going on in here?" I heard from behind us, and it momentarily registered that someone had walked in.

But I was on another planet. I didn't care.

"Get the fuck out of here!" Michael shouted.

"Goddamn!" Kai dropped his head back, fucking me harder, and I knew he was close.

No one even spared the intruder a glance, but I heard the door close, so I knew he was gone.

"Yes," I gasped. "Yes!"

The orgasm crested and then exploded, down my thighs, up my back, and all over inside. I stilled, letting it ride out, as they kept entering me again and again, the sensation making my eyes roll into the back of my head.

Michael.

Holy shit. I would never worry again when he wanted to go in that way. That was the best orgasm I'd ever had.

Michael thrust into me a few more times and then dug his fingers into my hips, stinging the skin, as he came.

"Fuck," he choked out, gasping for breath and sinking his weight onto me as he dropped his forehead to my shoulder. "Jesus."

But then Kai pulled me away, and I winced at the burn of Michael leaving my body. He laid me down on the tile bench, lifted up my knee, spreading my legs, and thrust his cock inside me, entering me again.

I arched my back, moaning.

He lay down on top of me, plastering his body to mine and wrapping an arm around the top of my head as he covered my mouth with his.

He fucked hard and fast like he was possessed, and I couldn't even look up to see where Michael was, because Kai had taken me over.

I felt his moan in my mouth as he thrust harder and harder and then jerked, his whole body tensing and his skin burning up as he came, filling the room with a loud groan.

I held his back, continuing to kiss his still lips as he tried to catch his breath.

"Holy shit," he panted. "That was better than anything I remember."

After a few moments, he slowly pushed himself up, sliding out of me, and sat back.

"Are you okay?" He looked at me with concern.

I closed my legs and turned my head, seeing Michael sitting in a tiled seat off to the right, leaning his elbows on his knees, watching us.

I nodded.

Bending up my legs, I gazed up at the smoky ceiling, feeling warm, blissfully exhausted, and satisfied.

Kai got up and disposed of the condom in the trash right outside the door and grabbed his towel off the floor, wrapping it around him as he came to sit next to me.

We all just sat there for a few minutes, letting our hearts calm down.

My body was floating like a balloon, and I felt my cheeks warm again, thinking about what had just happened. My heart pumped, and there were still butterflies in my stomach.

What would people think if they saw us now?

Alex would be proud. She'd want in.

Trevor would call me a whore.

My mother would have a drink, and Mrs. Crist would blow it off like she'd just walked in on a pillow fight.

But a calm washed over me when I realized that the only opinion I cared about was the one that never made me feel shame. The one that always pushed me to take what I wanted, and the one that only ever asked that I never quit on him.

Never tap out.

With anyone else—at any other time—I might be scared that our relationship was in danger, or that he would feel threatened by Kai, but Michael knew where my heart was. He didn't doubt me.

He doubted himself.

Kai finally stood up, turning around to stand over me. His eyes were heated, and a smile danced across his face. He looked young again.

"Aren't you worried?" he said, glancing to Michael. "I could try to take her from you."

"You could try," Michael shot back.

And Kai smiled, leaning down and kissing my lips softly.

"Your dick's working now," Michael warned behind him. "Go find someone else."

I heard Kai snort and his mouth shake on mine as he laughed. Pulling his lips away, he looked down at me with calm and a new confidence. "I have no words," he said. "Just thank you."

He turned and walked through the frosted door and into the locker room.

Michael and I sat in silence for a few moments, and I heard voices outside, suddenly remembering that we'd been caught before. Someone might've gone to get security.

Sitting up, I swung my legs over the bench and stood, my legs shaking and my body aching from what we'd just done. I could feel Michael's eyes on me as I walked to my clothes on the floor.

"You know," I started, slipping on my pants. "I don't remember a time when I didn't love you."

I didn't look at him but kept going, slipping on my jacket and grabbing my shoes and socks, sitting down on the bench to put them on.

"When you look at me," I continued, "when you touch me, when you're inside me, I'm completely in love with my life, Michael. I never want to be anywhere else."

I finished pulling on my socks and shoes, bending down to tie them.

When I was done, I sat up straight and looked at him. "Will you ever feel that for me?" I asked. "Will you ever need me or fear losing me?"

Kai had made me feel good. He'd needed me. Been grateful for me.

Michael held my eyes, nothing but a dead calm in his depths, and I couldn't tell what was happening inside of him.

"Will you ever let yourself be vulnerable?" I pressed.

And when he just sat there, not answering, I finally got up and walked toward the door.

"I'll meet you outside."

CHAPTER 26

ERIKA

Present

W e should study tonight," Alex said as we walked down the sidewalk, having just left class. "I've got this great technique where I let myself eat a Skittle every time I get the right answer."

I let out a weak laugh, shaking my head at her. "But they're essay questions."

"Shit," she grumbled. "That's worth at least a snack-size bag per question, then."

She turned left, and I followed her inside a small outdoor café area, watching her plop her bag down on the ground next to a table full of women.

"Hey, Alex," a redhead chirped, looking up as the other girls finished laughing about whatever it was they'd been talking about.

"Hey, everyone," Alex greeted, pulling out a chair. "This is Rika." And then she turned to me. "Rika, this is Angel, Becks, and Danielle. We lived in the dorms together last year." She leaned in farther, mumbling under her breath as we both sat down. "They think I have a rich married lover who supports me, so hush and just feel special that I trust you with shit, okay?"

She shot me a warning glare, and I snorted, sitting down in the seat.

"Hey, everyone," I said, looking around at them.

They smiled, and the conversation picked up again, moving from boyfriends to midterms, and I sat quietly, trying to relax and take in the late afternoon energy around me.

The taxi whistles, the car horns, the conversation going on at the tables around me . . .

But slowly, all the noises began to fade. The girls' conversation became a distant echo, and heat spread up my neck just like it did every time I sat still today, and I could feel them all over again.

Their bodies. The steam room. The sweat.

And I closed my eyes, feeling the little aches I had from what we'd done. My limbs were sore, and I could still taste them in my mouth.

I couldn't believe that had happened.

Michael.

Last night I swallowed shame and pushed boundaries, and I didn't know if it was to test the trust, to test his love, or just to see the emotions that the experience would unfold between us, but I came out of it knowing one thing: that nothing could stop us.

If he loved me, we would be invincible.

Nothing had happened between Kai and me, not really. It was between Michael and me, and Kai had helped.

He'd helped me see that Michael wasn't ready. Not yet. He needed the back-and-forth—the games—too much to give in to me.

My phone buzzed in my pocket, and I fished it out, seeing Michael's name on the screen.

I ignored the call, sliding my phone into my bag. That was six times today already, as well as six voicemails and a few texts.

I knew what he wanted, but if he wasn't giving me his heart, then I wouldn't listen to him give me orders.

"Is that Michael?" Alex piped up, sliding me one of the waters the server had set down.

I nodded slightly and leaned back, resting my forearms on the wrought iron chair.

"Is everything okay?"

I shook my head, hooding my eyes. I had no idea how to talk about him.

"No, everything's not okay," a deep male voice said behind me, and I stilled.

The other girls at the table stopped talking and looked up, and Alex twisted her head around to see who it was.

I closed my eyes in frustration and then looked over my shoulder, seeing Kai and Will standing behind me, a black Jag parked at the curb.

"Michael's been trying to get ahold of you," Kai informed me, coming to stand between my chair and Alex's. "When he couldn't reach you, he sent us to look for you."

"And I would've answered the phone if I wanted to talk," I retorted.

"He thinks it would be best if you went home to wait for him," Kai suggested, but I knew it was an order. "He's concerned it's not safe."

"Noted," I replied. "Thank you."

And I picked up my glass of water, dismissing him.

He grabbed it out of my hand, and I hissed as the icy-cold liquid spilled on my fingers. He flung the contents on the little potted tree behind him and tossed the glass onto the table with a clatter.

He leaned down, eyeing the girls at the table, who watched wide-eyed and still.

"Excuse us, ladies," he bit out, and then growled in my ear, his scent bringing memories of last night flooding in. "He's worried about you, Rika."

"Then he needs to say that," I snapped back. "Not send his dogs to fetch me."

He shot up, and I yelped as he yanked my chair back and grabbed me by the upper arm, pulling me up. Pushing me toward Will, he picked up my bag and threw it at me.

I caught it, but I threw my hands out again, flinging it right back in his face.

"Get in the car," he ordered, holding my bag in one hand, "or you're going over my shoulder."

"Rika, you okay?" Alex stood up.

But Kai turned around, his body towering over her. "Sit down, and don't interfere."

She dropped into her seat, and for the first time since I'd known her, she looked scared.

"Let's go," Will pulled my arm, but I yanked it away, storming for the car.

Kai followed, and we all got in, slamming doors as Will pulled away from the curb.

I ground my teeth together, Kai's tall frame next to me in the back seat filling the small space, and his glare scorching the left side of my face.

He reached over and grabbed me, and I pushed at his chest as he hauled me over onto his lap.

What the hell was he doing? Did he think last night meant he could handle me anytime he wanted now?

"While you're busy pouting," he said, his breath falling across my face as he held the back of my head in one hand and squeezed my jaw in the other, "let me paint a picture in your head that apparently isn't clear enough."

I jerked, trying to hit him and twist my head out of his hold, but his grip was too tight.

"Think about the last time you let Trevor inside of you," he spoke in a hard voice, biting out every word. "Think about how he smelled, how his sweat and lips felt all over your body, how hard he rode your pretty little ass, and how much he fucking loved it . . ."

I growled and fought, trying to pull away.

"You want to know what was going on in his head?" Kai taunted. "Hmm?"

I breathed hard, anger like lava all over my skin.

"Stupid. Fucking. Bitch," he answered, speaking as Trevor. "She's so goddamn clueless, the brainless twit doesn't even know it was me that night in the mask. On top of her, touching her, and here I am, still getting the goodies. What a brainless twat."

He released me, and I shot over to the other side of the car again, breathing hard, with fire raging through my blood.

Fucking Trevor.

The last time we slept together he must've really enjoyed the sight of me bent over for his pleasure. Powering me over and taking me for an idiot.

I ran a frustrated hand along the top of my hair, feeling my back cool with sweat.

"I hope you're good and mad now," Kai continued, "because that's exactly how mad Michael is. Trevor fooled us all, and you should know by now that the only dangers we can fight are the ones we can see coming. And right now, we're blind." His voice filled the entire car, and I refused to look at him. "Trevor is unpredictable and unreadable, and Damon has one emotion. Hate."

I stared out the window as we pulled onto Delcour's street. He was right. There was possible danger, and I was being childish.

But they were treating me like a child, too.

"Is it so difficult to understand that Michael wants his girl safe?" Kai asked, his tone gentler.

"Maybe," I admitted, turning my head to look at him. "But maybe you guys could talk to me like a person instead of manhandling me? Is that possible?"

Kai's eyes softened, and his gaze lingered on me. I held my breath, a moment passing, I think, where we were both remembering last night.

The car was suddenly too small.

Will pulled up in front of Delcour, and I hopped out, grabbing my bag.

"I'm going to check her apartment," I heard Kai tell Will. "You go park."

I slammed the car door, giving the doorman a quick smile as he opened the building's door for me. Kai followed as I walked to the elevator and pressed the button.

"You don't have to come up," I insisted. "I'm quite capable of locking myself in."

He exhaled a quiet laugh. "It won't be too long. Michael will come by later to keep you company, I'm sure."

I stepped into the elevator as soon as the doors opened, pressing twenty-one. I knew Michael was at practice, which was why he'd sent the guys after me, but I wasn't sure I'd let him in the door later.

What was worse than him coddling me was him sending his friends to do it, as well.

Once in my apartment, Kai walked ahead, searching all the rooms and checking the rear exit and balcony doors.

"Everything looks fine," he said, strolling back across the living room and checking the locks on the front door.

"Of course it does," I replied. "Trevor's in Annapolis, and Damon is probably drunk and buried under an endless supply of teenage hookers in New York City."

He grinned, holding the door open and standing on the threshold.

But then his eyes came to rest on me, looking thoughtful, before slowly falling down my body. His gaze lingered long and intense, and I froze, feeling the heat on my thighs and down my legs.

He looked back up at me. "I could stay with you if you want," he offered, his voice deep and husky.

I tilted my lips in a half smile, approaching him. "And what would we do?"

A sexy smirk adorned his beautiful face. "Maybe order food," he hinted and then cast a longing glance down my body again, "or have something to drink?"

I came up and held the door. "Or maybe . . . you're testing me. Seeing if I'll invite you in behind Michael's back."

"Why would I test you?"

"Because you love Michael more than me," I shot back.

He dropped his eyes, smiling. "Maybe," he answered, reaching out and brushing his thumb across my chin. "Or maybe I liked it. Maybe I'd like to see what it's like having you to myself this time."

I cocked an eyebrow, giving him a knowing look.

He dropped his hand and broke out in a quiet laugh. "Sorry. I had to make sure."

I stared at him patiently, knowing exactly what he was doing.

Kai had nothing to worry about. I loved Michael, and I would leave him before I ever betrayed him. I knew Kai was testing my loyalty to protect his friend, but it would never be necessary. While I didn't regret last night, it wouldn't happen again. We were friends.

Kai backed out of the doorway, leaving, but before I could shut it, he turned. "It's not just Michael, you know?" He peered over at me. "Will and I were worried about you, too. You're one of us. It would be hard to . . ."

And then he dropped his eyes as if searching for the right words. "We feel close to you," he admitted, gazing up at me again. "We don't want to see you hurt, okay?"

It warmed me to hear him say that, but I couldn't help but retort, "If I'm one of you, then why is it I'm the one being cut out of the plans and guarded?"

"Because he loves *you* more than us," Kai answered, flipping damn near close to my own words back at me.

I wanted to believe that. I'd waited for longer than he knew to hear it.

Closing the door, I locked it and soaked in the peace and quiet. My phone was buzzing again, and I checked it, seeing that it was Alex, probably calling to check up on me.

But unless it was my mother, I wasn't interested in talking to anyone.

I stood at the island, thinking about the assignments I had to get started on, the reading that was due in a few days, and the fact that I hadn't checked my social media in over a week.

But all of a sudden I was exhausted.

Kicking off my shoes and socks, I walked into my bedroom, dropped my phone on the nightstand, and collapsed on my bed, my body immediately melting into the soft, cool comforter and my eyes falling closed.

M ichael?"
I popped my head up off the pillow and twisted it around, blinking my eyes open.

I thought I heard something.

The room was dark and silent, and I peered out the door, into the hallway, seeing it completely dark, as well.

I noticed the light blinking on my phone, and I turned over, my back crashing to the bed again, knowing that's what must've woken me up.

"Shit." I rubbed my hands up and down my face, trying to wake up.

Turning my head, I glanced at the clock, letting out a frustrated sigh. Six hours. It was just after eleven.

I couldn't believe I'd slept that long.

Picking up my phone, I saw several texts from Michael, the last one saying,

You better open the fucking door when I get there.

I hadn't read his texts all day, but I guessed there was a progression of anger that was probably justified, since I'd failed to answer any of them.

Tossing my phone on the bed, I sat up and climbed off, padding my bare feet out into the hallway and toward the kitchen to make something to eat.

I'd skipped dinner, and I was starving.

But then I noticed something out of the corner of my eye, and I swung around, my heart leaping into my throat as I saw the back door sitting wide open and the light from the stairwell pouring in.

A dark form, dressed in a black hoodie with the hood drawn, stood in the doorway, staring at me through a white mask. The same mask that the guys wore when they'd lured me to the Crist house.

I breathed hard, my hands shaking at the rush of danger crawling on my skin.

But then I stopped and glued my teeth together, anger tensing my muscles.

Michael.

"What?" I demanded. "You need your midnight snack?"

Him and his goddamn games. This wasn't the time, and I wasn't in the mood for kink tonight.

"Just get out of here, Michael."

But then he raised his hand, digging the point of a massive butcher knife into the wall of my hallway. My heart picked up pace again as I stared wide-eyed, watching him stalk toward me, the steel blade scraping as it dragged along the wall.

I expelled every inch of breath I had and backed away. "Damon," I choked out.

And at that moment, he dropped his hand and broke out in a run, charging me. I screamed and spun around, racing for the front door.

I slammed into the wood, immediately grabbing for the locks, but it was no use. He crashed into my back, wrapping a hand around the front of my neck and digging the tip of the blade under my chin.

The sting made me cry out. "Damon!" I dug my nails into the door. "Don't do this!"

He squeezed my throat, and then the hand with the knife came down over my mouth, a cloth covering my lips, suffocating me.

"Who's going to stop me?" he whispered in my ear.

And then everything went black.

CHAPTER 27

ERIKA

Present

Floating.

My head was swaying, and for a moment it felt like it was lifting off my body and drifting up into the air. A seed of pain sat in the side of my head but quickly bloomed, spreading and searing across my skull as I grunted.

"What the hell?" I blinked my eyes open, putting my hand to the sore spot above my temple and hissing, "Shit."

I checked my hand, not seeing any blood, but the spot was definitely tender.

Damon. I stilled, remembering that he'd been in my apartment.

"Oh, my God," I breathed out, fumbling as I sat up and the room came into focus.

Where was I?

Planting my hands on the soft fabric under me, I quickly looked around, noticing the beige and wood furniture and fixtures, the glass doors leading to a wooden deck, the paintings and gold sconces on the walls, the carpets, and the impersonal but very familiar feel of the room.

And then I felt the hum underneath me. The hum of engines below.

Pithom. We were on the Crist boat.

I'd only been on it a handful of times growing up—parties and day excursions down the coast—but I knew it well.

"I'm glad you're okay," I heard behind me, and I jerked my head around.

Damon stood on the other side of the couch from where I was lying, leaning a shoulder on the wall with his arms crossed over his chest and his black eyes fixed on me.

"I was starting to worry," he said in an eerily calm tone.

He was dressed in black pants and a white button-down that was loosely tucked in and open at the collar. His black hair looked tousled like he'd just woken up, but his eyes proved the contrary. They were fully zoned in on me, alert and ready. He didn't look at all like he'd just been stabbed and bloody a week ago.

"I never really thought about it before, but watching you sleep—here and in your apartment . . ." He dropped his eyes for a moment, looking serious. "You're very beautiful. Long blond hair, full lips . . . You have this innocent calm about you."

I stared, my heart racing, feeling sick. He'd watched me sleep in my apartment? God, how long had he been there before I'd woken up?

I shifted my eyes, stealing glances around the room again. I needed to get something in my hands. I wished I had the Damascus blade.

"Yeah, so clean and perfect," he mused, pushing off the wall and walking around the couch. "Just like he wants you."

I narrowed my eyes, slowly standing up and backing away as he approached. "Who?" I asked, my voice shaking.

Who wanted me clean and perfect?

My head throbbed, and I felt dizzy, but I held out my hands, trying to keep him away.

"Only you're not so clean anymore, are you?" he gloated, ignoring my question. "Michael got his hands on you, and you're only good for one thing now."

"What are you talking about?" I stumbled backward, my fists curling as fear coiled in my gut.

"Don't worry, he'll get some fun out of you." Damon inched toward me, a sick smile in his eyes. "But he'd never marry his brother's whore."

Marry . . . what?

And then Damon's eyes flashed, and I swung around, seeing Trevor standing right behind me.

He stood tall and imposing, dressed in jeans and a navy blue polo. His blond hair was still cut close to the scalp, military-style, and his blue eyes pierced me, looking smug.

I shook my head. "Trevor?"

And I only had a second before his hand came down and whipped across my face. I stepped back, trying not to fall as my head jerked to the side and fire blazed across my cheek like a million needle pricks under my skin. Tears sprang to my eyes, and I held my face as the pain in my head exploded and everything became blurry.

Damon grabbed me and spun me around, throwing me over his shoulder.

"No!" I cried, pushing at his back and squirming. I coughed, feeling the bile in my stomach rise into my throat as he carried me off down a dark passageway.

"Damon!" I choked, feeling the heaves rumbling through my stomach. "Damon, please."

He carried me through a doorway, and I grabbed hold of the frame, stopping him as I kicked and struggled. "Let me go, you sick piece of shit!" I screamed, because I was sick of being afraid. "You're nothing! You hear me? You're nothing but garbage, and I hope you die!"

He yanked hard, and I lost my grip, my arms shooting with pain from being nearly pulled out of their sockets.

I flew through the air, my breath catching in my throat as I landed on a bed. I immediately shot up to a sitting position, but he came down right on me again. Grabbing my wrists, he pulled me up on the bed and planted his knee in my chest, holding me in place.

"Damon!" I barked, but my lungs emptied with his weight on my chest, and I couldn't take in anything but short breaths.

"Don't talk," he growled.

I thrashed and pushed my body up off the bed, choking and coughing as I tried to suck in air and get him off me.

"Fuck you!" I tried to yell, but it came out strained.

He pulled rope out of his pocket and wrapped the itchy material around my wrists.

"No!" I tried to yank my hands away, to swing at him or throw him off or anything, but he just held me tighter.

I tried sucking in a breath, despite the weight on my chest, but it was ragged. He tied me up, securing my hands to the headboard.

Looking around quickly, I noticed an entire wall of windows behind Damon, showing a vast blackness outside and stars in the night sky. There was nothing on the bedside tables I could use as a weapon, but if I could get free, there was no doubt something in one of the drawers or in the bathroom.

"Where are we?" I demanded, my skin burning under the knots he tied.

"Two miles off the coast of Thunder Bay."

I slowed, staring up at him. We were out at sea? Why?

I thought maybe we were docked in the marina, where the yacht was usually kept, but there could only be one reason to take it out.

There wouldn't be any help out here.

"Michael . . ." I said quietly, not sure what I was asking.

"He'll be here soon," Damon said, sounding like he was saying, *It'll all be over soon.*

A shiver ran up my spine, and I sucked in a welcome breath as he took his knee off my chest.

But the freedom from his weight didn't last. He came down on me again, forcing my thighs apart as he nestled his waist between my jean-clad legs. Every muscle in my body tensed as he propped himself up with both arms, staring down at me.

"Now that I have you to myself," he taunted, his gaze turning heated.

I jerked, pulling at the restraints and letting out a growl. Tears spilled down the sides of my head into my hair, and I heaved breath after breath, trying to yank my arms free.

"Such a fighter," he commended. "I knew you were going to be a lot of fun."

I pressed my bare feet into the mattress, squirming and trying to arch my body off the bed, but he only laughed, pressing his hardening cock between my legs.

I cringed, turning my head away and trying to sink into the pillow to get away from him.

"Keep doing that," he begged. "It feels so good, Rika."

And then he lowered his mouth to my cheek. "Come on," he breathed out, his tongue flicking my jaw. "You know it's going to happen. I think you're afraid you'll like it."

I shook my head and turned to meet his eyes, glaring at him. "You won't do this. I know you."

"You don't." His voice turned threatening.

But I pressed forward. "You're mean and you're sleazy, but you're not evil," I gritted out. "I thought you and Kai—or Trevor— were going to hurt me that night, even for just a while. I didn't know if it was a joke or if you were for real, but I didn't feel safe. I was scared out of my mind."

He watched me, hovering his mouth over mine.

"But you didn't let him," I shot out. "You didn't let him hurt me. It was a joke for you, but once you realized Trevor was carrying it further than you'd planned, you stopped him. You're not bad."

His tongue flicked my chin, and I squeezed my eyes shut, my

chest shaking with sobs as he trailed it down my neck and to my breast, over my blouse.

"You're not bad," I said, pulling against the restraints and feeling his tongue circle my nipple through the fabric. "You're not bad."

"No, I'm not," he said, hovering over my breast. "I'm nothing. I'm a piece of shit. I'm garbage."

And then he pushed up, climbing off the bed and looking down at me, his eyes now ice-cold. "And I'm going to be your nightmare, Erika Fane."

He turned around and walked to one of the chairs to my left and sat down, looking disturbingly calm.

There was a shield over his eyes now, and I forced the hard lump down my throat, fearing he was done talking.

He sat. And waited.

"So what?" I argued. "Trevor's in charge of you now? Did you learn how to be somebody's bitch in prison?"

He smirked, leaning back in the chair with his forearm resting on the table to his right.

"If you do this," I bit out, "you'll lose them forever."

"Who?"

"The guys," I clarified. "They're your family, and they'll never forgive you for this."

He shook his head, looking away. "It's too late anyway. Things will never be the same now."

He stared off, a look of solemn resolution crossing his face, as if nothing was ending.

It was already over, and Damon was already lost.

"Do you know why we took you out there that night?" Damon asked. "Normally, I don't care who Michael fucks unless I like the look of her and want my turn, but you were different. I knew it that night. He wanted more from you than just pussy."

I tensed my arms and pulled at the rope, the coarse threads digging into my skin. "Why did that bother you so much?"

"Because when it comes to women, there is nothing more than just pussy," he snapped. "You were going to come between us. Change us and ruin what we had."

The creases in his forehead dug in deeper, and he glared at me. I didn't understand what he was talking about. How would I come between them?

"When I ran into Trevor," he continued, "we thought we'd mess with you. Scare you off. I'd get what I wanted, you away from Michael and the rest of us, and dickless little Trevor, who was always jealous of his older brother, would get you back on a leash."

He licked his lips and continued. "Will was easy. He was three sheets to the wind, and even sober, that fucker can't add two plus two, so once we got Kai's mask on Trevor, the rest fell into place."

"But when we got to the clearing," I cut in, "you realized Trevor had a plan you didn't know about. You wanted to scare me, freak me out, maybe fuck me in a moment of weakness if I let you, so I'd feel too ashamed to ever face Michael again, but you didn't want to hurt me." And I took a deep breath, finishing, "And you don't want to hurt me now."

He absently picked at something on the table, shaking his head. "That's where you're wrong," he said, meeting my eyes. "I do want to hurt you. I want to fucking kill you, and then I'm going to kill Trevor."

"Trevor?"

He nodded. "Oh, he'll get what's coming to him. Now that I know he stole the phone, oh yes. You'll be just because I'm fucking angry, and I've got nothing to lose. I already lost everything, because just like a woman does, you fucked everything up. You came between brothers."

I didn't come between them. I never made Michael choose, and I never wanted to ruin what they had.

I wanted to be a part of it. I was curious, and I wanted to have some fun, but I never wanted to change them or stop them or . . .

And then I paused, dropping my eyes as I remembered the gazebo. The way I'd protested when I didn't agree with what Will was doing. The way I'd walked off when Michael told me to stay. The way I'd looked down on what they were doing.

Maybe Damon was right.

I didn't regret backing out of that prank. It was shitty and stupid and wrong, but while Michael may have stayed by his friends' side that night, maybe there would've come a time when he didn't.

Maybe, eventually, after more pranks and more nights of careless decisions they'd make that I'd want no part of . . . maybe there would eventually be a night when Michael would choose me over them.

I'd done nothing wrong, of course. This wasn't my fault, and I knew that.

But now, seeing it through Damon's eyes—him knowing I'd eventually get into Michael's head and knowing that none of this—none of this—would have happened if I hadn't gone with them that night, maybe I needed to acknowledge that I was, at least, part of this. Like Will had said . . . I was already involved.

"We were all hurt by what happened," I said, locking eyes on him. "I'm not the one to punish."

He remained still and quiet for a moment.

"Maybe," he finally answered. "Maybe you're just a victim like the rest of us."

Something crossed his face, a weariness bubbling under the anger and hate he tried so hard to keep on like a mask. There was something playing behind his eyes, a scene or a memory, but I couldn't figure it out.

"It doesn't really matter anymore," he said in a quiet voice.

But before I got a chance to ask him what he meant, a shadow fell across the floor, and I twisted my head right to see Trevor standing in the doorway.

"Are you two bonding?"

His voice sounded so smooth and light, as if he hadn't just hit me.

I narrowed my eyes, noticing that he looked thinner.

Annapolis.

Wait, he wasn't supposed to be here. He couldn't just leave the academy whenever he wanted. Had Damon gone to him after the blowup at Michael's parents' house? He had to have.

Trevor had loose ends to clear up, and he had to fear Michael would come after him. He was beating him to the punch.

Damon rose from his chair and left the room, and I tensed, realizing he was leaving me with Trevor. For some reason, I felt in more danger.

"He'd never help you," Trevor stated, stepping into the room. "He hates women."

He approached, and I wrapped the slack of the rope around my fist and inched up the bed, away from him. My hand hit the mirror of the headboard, and I stopped, tapping it with my nail.

Glass.

"Did you know that he was twelve when his mother started fucking him?"

My heart skipped a beat, and I turned my eyes on Trevor, horror racking through me.

What?

"And when he was fifteen," Trevor continued, "he beat the shit out of her and threatened to kill her if she ever came back. I overheard my father talking to his a few years ago."

My bottom lip quivered, and I didn't know if he was telling the truth, but why would he lie?

It would explain why Damon hated women, I guess.

"His father swept it under the rug and never talked about it again. The guys were all he had, and you took that from him."

"*You* took that from him," I growled, tightening every muscle as he sat down on the bed.

Trevor's hand trailed up my leg, and I kicked, shoving him off, but he only smiled and gripped my thigh harder, making me cry out.

I couldn't believe I ever let him touch me.

Last year, I'd given in to the years of pressure of being pushed together for dances, parties, and pictures, and I stopped fighting the constant assumptions that we were together and finally just let it happen. Trevor gave me stability, he wanted me, and I was too stupid to believe I deserved better. But most of all, he was a distraction from Michael. I thought he would make me move on and forget.

It didn't take long for me to realize that Trevor gave me nothing. In one night, Michael had showed me that I wasn't weak. That I was beautiful, wanted, and strong, and even though that night was short-lived, I knew what I felt for Trevor didn't even compare to everything that Michael was for me.

Trevor only claimed me as a prize. He didn't see me.

"How can you do this?" I demanded. "What do you want?"

"I want to see you both lose," he retorted. "I'm done being in Michael's shadow, and I'm done watching you pant after him." He raised his eyes, looking at me. "I want to see you both hurt."

I ground my teeth together, jerking at the rope again and again. "Let me go."

His hand slipped under my shirt, and I tried to twist away, his touch making my skin crawl.

"As for Damon? He just wants everyone to hurt," he pointed out. "He and I make a great pair."

"Why would he cover for you?" I demanded. "He knew it was you in that mask that night. Why would he let me think it was Kai?"

Trevor shrugged, watching his hand slide over my stomach. "You'd already been kicked to the trash by Michael. It served our purpose if you didn't think you had a friend out of them left. Plus," he said with a smile, "he doesn't give a shit about you. After he and the rest of them thought you outed them, I think he got off on the idea that the only real threat to you was right under your nose."

Meaning Trevor. Always there. Just one room away. Lurking, waiting . . .

"But you knew they thought I took the phone and uploaded the videos. You had to know they'd come after me."

"Which wouldn't have been a problem if you hadn't decided to leave Brown," he shot back. "I could've kept Damon at bay, and he could've kept the rest of them waiting." He sighed and then continued. "But you left my protection, and maybe I just decided to let it play out. If they hurt you—if Michael hurt you—before they realized their mistake in blaming the wrong person, then maybe you'd give up on him once and for all."

And then he got up on his hands and knees and crawled over me, hovering his face over mine. "Maybe you'd finally knock him off that pedestal you always put him on and see him for what he really is."

"Which is what?" I bit out.

"Lesser than me."

And then he popped his head up, as if hearing something. He shot off the bed and walked around the room, gazing out the windows.

"The only mistake I made," he commented, peering out into the night, "was quoting my father that night in the forest. Otherwise you may never have figured it out."

My body shook with fear, and I tilted my head back, squirming as I pulled against the ropes again.

"So what's your plan now?" I demanded. "What could you hope to accomplish by this? Michael has everything that belongs to me—the house, the deeds, everything—and you'll never get me back. I'd rather die than let you near me again."

"You think I want you back?" He turned, folding his arms over his chest. "My brother's whore?"

He chuckled to himself and walked over to me.

"Oh, no," he replied, looking smug. "I can do so much better than you. And as for Michael having everything, that's easy. The dead don't own property."

The dead? Did he mean . . . ?

If Michael was dead, everything would revert to Mr. Crist. And if Trevor no longer wanted me to get at what was mine, then, for him to get everything, I would *also* have to be . . .

Michael.

I jerked at the ropes, trying to pull my wrists free. "Fuck you!" I cried out, feeling the burn of my tears fall across the spot on my cheek where he'd hit me. My wrists stung from the layer of skin I'd probably worn away, but I growled, thrashing and pulling at them harder and harder.

"Listen," Trevor chirped. "Do you hear that?"

I didn't stop, but I heard it. It was a high-pitched motor, and it was getting louder.

Nearer.

A speedboat.

I stilled. *No.*

"He's coming," Trevor said, excitement in his eyes.

And then he held up his wrist, checking his watch. "It's midnight, baby," he announced and then leaned down, close to my face. "By twelve-oh-five, you both will be on your way to the bottom of the ocean."

CHAPTER 28

MICHAEL

Present

F aster," I shouted, the speedboat bouncing over the water as I spotted the yacht ahead.

The lights in the hull glowed purple on the black water, making the large white vessel look like a star out in the night.

"It's at top speed," Will threw back, his face twisted in worry. "Relax. He left that note for a reason. He wants us to find her."

"That doesn't mean he's not hurting her," I gritted out. "Hurry!"

Gusts of wind hit us as we raced over the water. Kai and I had to hold the dash and windshield to keep steady as the small black speedboat gained on *Pithom*.

Fucking Trevor.

When I'd gotten to Rika's apartment, she hadn't answered the door, so I used my key and barged in, finding the whole damn place dark and empty, with nothing but a note lying on the floor.

One word. *Pithom.*

I flew out of the apartment and called the harbormaster as I sped out of the city. He confirmed that *Pithom* was in Thunder Bay today and Trevor had, indeed, had a small crew take it out this afternoon. I then called Will and Kai, telling them to meet me at the docks, where Kai's family kept a speedboat. My family's speedboat was probably with Trevor—and Damon, who was no doubt in on this, too.

I love you, Michael.

My chest shook, and I ran my hand through my hair. "Rika," I murmured to myself. "Please be all right."

The yacht got bigger as we got closer, and Will slowed the engine, circling the craft all the way around to the stern, where we slowed to a crawl. I immediately jumped out, while Kai secured a line.

I spotted my family's red speedboat on the port side and turned to Will. "You stay here," I told him. "Keep an eye on the speedboats and blare the fog horn if you see anything."

I didn't want Trevor or Damon trying to take off with her.

He nodded, reaching into the compartment near the steering wheel and pulling out the horn.

I looked at Kai, gesturing up. "Top deck," I ordered. "And keep your eyes open. They know we're coming."

Kai took the stairs to my right while I walked across the deck, past the pool, and into the salon. I didn't blink, forcing myself to go slowly even though every muscle in my body wanted to charge ahead, looking for her.

A Glock was tucked into my black pants, loaded with all ten rounds, but I kept it hidden under my T-shirt. Chances were they'd see me before I saw them, and I wanted the element of surprise.

I darted my glare to the white camera in the ceiling, the small ball rolling and zooming in.

He knew I was here and exactly where I was.

Treading lightly and keeping my eyes open, I crept across the room and into the dimly lit passageway. There were two cabins on the left and one on the right. She could be anywhere, and I hoped Kai, who was one deck above, had found her already.

I took a step to the left, grabbing the door handle, but a whimper stopped me in my tracks, and I listened.

A grunt followed, and I turned toward my parents' cabin and threw open the door.

Rika lay on my parents' bed, struggling with the rope tied to her wrists. She jerked her head toward the door, noticing me, and sucked in a breath, her face cracking.

"Michael," she cried softly. "No, you shouldn't have come."

I charged over and grabbed the rope, seeing the broken glass. "Goddammit, what did they do to you?"

Her hands were tied above her head, bleeding, and her hair was damp with sweat. Little pools of blood sat in the creases of her hands, and she held a shard of glass in her fist.

"I needed to cut the rope." Her voice shook, and I noticed that the glass in the headboard was shattered. She'd broken it trying to escape.

I took the shard out of her hand and sawed the remainder of the rope. "I'll get you out of here. I'm so sorry, baby."

A horn blared outside, and I shot my head up, my veins firing. "Son of a bitch."

Something was wrong.

I severed the rope, tossing the shard on the bed, and pulled her up, the binding still wrapped around her wrists.

"Come here." I took her hands and turned them palm up.

But she pulled them away. "I'm okay," she insisted. "We have to get out of here. They wanted you to find me. They could be anywhere."

My arms ached with the need to hold her, but I held back. We couldn't waste time. Will needed us, and she was fine.

I turned around but held her wrist, keeping her close behind me as I walked through the door, looking left and right to make sure it was clear.

"Damon's with Trevor," she whispered.

"I figured."

"He's the one who took me from my apartment."

I shook my head, trying to keep the anger at bay. Rika's hands were shredded because she was saving herself. Not waiting for me.

I'd always wanted that for her, hadn't I? To fight for herself?

But all I felt was rage now. They'd taken her from me, and they could've taken her forever.

I might never have found her.

"Come on," I urged, pulling her through the salon again, toward the sliding glass doors and the stern.

But as soon as we stepped on deck, I spotted Kai on the ground, and I straightened, bracing myself. He was breathing heavily, with blood coming out of his nose and mouth. Damon stood over him, glaring at me, and I shot my eyes to the speedboat behind him.

It was empty. Where the fuck was Will?

I inched out into the still air, pushing Rika behind me. *Shit.*

Kai and Rika were hurt, Will was missing, and I had no idea how the hell I was going to get us out of this.

Then I saw Trevor. He stood next to the side of the yacht, amusement in his eyes as he stared at me.

He crooked a finger, urging us over.

Rika tried to inch around me, but I tightened my grip on her arm, keeping her there. Leveling my gaze on my brother, I stepped over to the side and peered over.

"Will." I lost my breath.

He was in the water, his head barely staying above the surface. I spotted a line of rope coming out of the water near him and followed as it trailed up the side of the boat, over the edge, and onto the deck. The end was tethered to two cinder blocks at Trevor's feet, and there were also two more sets of blocks with ropes secured to them.

Jesus.

"He's got my hands tied behind my back, man!" Will shouted.

Which meant he couldn't untie the other end of the rope, most likely secured around one of his feet or both.

Will bounced in the water, trying to stay afloat with his legs, but he was struggling.

I lurched for Trevor.

But he pulled his hand out, holding up a pistol, and I stopped, glaring at him.

"What the fuck?" I yelled.

"Did you know that the average depth of the Atlantic Ocean is ten thousand nine hundred fifty-five feet?" he asked calmly, ignoring my anger. "It's dark. Cold. And when something goes down there, it's not coming back up."

And then he glanced at Will in the water before turning his eyes back on me. "You would never find him."

I shot my gaze to Kai. He rested on his hands and knees, trying to stabilize himself, and I could see blood streaming down the side of his face.

"Are you okay?" I rushed out.

"I'm fine," he bit out, but I could tell he was shaky.

"I should've done her before you got here," Trevor went on, gesturing to Rika behind me. "But really, what fun is it if you can't watch, right?"

"What the fuck are you doing, Trevor?" I asked as I slowly reached behind me and tapped my back, signaling to Rika.

She slid her hand up the inside of my shirt and pulled the gun out, slipping it into my hand behind my thigh.

"I don't know," Trevor answered, fake confusion on his face. "But I'm certainly enjoying myself."

What the hell was the matter with him? He hated me. I knew that. But Will? Kai? Rika? He couldn't get away with this. Had he lost his fucking mind?

"Go ahead," he challenged, pointing the gun at me. "Rush me. You'd take a bullet, but you'd still take me down."

I shook my head and turned my eyes on Damon. "Don't do

this," I implored. "Will and Kai have never hurt you. Rika's never hurt you."

"But hurting them will hurt you," Damon retorted, planting his foot on Kai's back and shoving him back to the ground.

Kai grunted, squeezing his eyes shut. From the way he grabbed his side I could guess he had a few broken ribs.

"You've never suffered," Damon snarled. "You've never had to lose, and this will change your life forever. You should never have chosen her over us."

"You're a fucking coward!" Kai shouted at him.

Damon just scowled in return and then looked up at me again, an ocean separating us. I didn't even recognize him anymore.

"Tell me you'll let her go," he demanded. "Tell me everything can go back to the way it was in high school."

I steeled my spine, squeezing Rika's arm behind me.

"She has no place with us, and you give her too much power over you," he continued. "Tell me she's nothing. Tell me you'd choose us over her. Or better yet . . ." He paused, a glint in his eyes. "Tell me you'd trade Rika for Will and Kai."

My throat tightened, and my heart hammered in my chest.

"Choose," Trevor pressed. "Rika can take Will's place, and the four of you can be like none of this ever happened."

I heard her breathing behind me, shallow and fast, and I knew she was scared.

I could feel her everywhere. On my skin, in my chest, in my hands . . .

The sweetness of her lips as she panted against my mouth in the steam room . . .

I love you, Michael.

"Will and Kai will be fine," Damon assured me. "But you have to sacrifice her."

Sacrifice her. I can't . . .

I swallowed the lump in my throat.

She was everywhere. Always everywhere. Years and years, and there was no shaking her. Every time I closed my eyes she was there.

It feels like you.

Sixteen and looking at me like I was God.

You're in everything.

The moment I knew that heart of hers was mine, and I couldn't wait to be inside of her.

Yes, it turns me on.

Seeing her go over that edge and trust me to jump with her as I felt her from the inside for the first time and she came apart in my arms. God . . .

I dropped my eyes to Kai, seeing my friend, and I could hear Will calling us from the water, begging, and what the fuck was I supposed to do?

But Trevor didn't wait for an answer.

He reached down and hauled up the blocks, sitting them on the edge of the yacht.

"No!" I shouted, letting go of Rika and holding out my hand. "Stop! Just . . . just wait!"

He tilted the blocks back and forth, toying with me.

"Stop!" I growled. "Just . . ." I ground my teeth together, my head swimming. "Fuck you!"

If I shot one of them, he would still have time to dump the blocks, and Damon could make short work of Kai before I even had a chance. I might be able to get Rika out of here, but I wouldn't be able to save them.

"Why are you doing this?" I bared my teeth, seething. "Why?"

"For this!" Trevor finally growled, showing his anger. "For this, right here. To see you exactly like this. You're so fucking desperate, it's priceless."

He took his hands off the blocks, leaving them to sit on the ledge, teetering and threatening to fall with the slightest vibration.

"I could say it was all the attention laid on you for your basketball career," he explained, "the way you always finished things I could never even start, or the way Rika always loved you, not once ever looking at me the way she did you."

He hung the gun at his side and glared past me to Rika, who had stepped up next to me.

"But really?" He gazed at her. "I think it's because the great Michael Crist is so fucking helpless right now, and I want to see the look in her eyes when she knows it's about to end and that you can't help her."

I breathed in and out, my lungs getting smaller and smaller.

"Don't worry," Trevor soothed. "You'll join her soon."

And then Trevor shot out his hand and pushed the blocks off the ledge. I growled, raging as I rushed forward, swinging out my arm and firing the gun three times, hitting him.

But I didn't see where.

I threw the gun down and leapt up to the ledge, diving off just as Will's head disappeared under the surface.

I crashed through the water, my body immediately submerging and going cold with the rush of the icy black October sea.

I opened my eyes, seeing Will just ahead of me, sinking fast and struggling against his ropes. I kicked and pushed my way through the water, reaching out and grabbing him by the shirt.

But when I tried to pull him up, kicking and fighting my way to the surface, the purple light overhead was only disappearing.

We were sinking.

I dived back down, keeping hold of his clothes as my lungs stretched, growing desperate for air. Reaching his foot, I worked the knot, the fucking weight of the blocks making it hard to get the rope to thread back out.

Will twisted and fought, keeping his eyes on the surface, and I yanked and jerked at the rope, trying to get him free.

But the water was only getting blacker. The lights from the yacht were all but gone, and Rika and Kai were up there alone.

I growled, the sound muffled in the water as I pulled and thrashed. *Fuck!*

I couldn't let him go. *Please.*

Not again.

Squeezing the rope between my chilled fingers, I worked and pried, tearing my skin until . . .

It gave way. The rope dislodged, and I quickly unraveled it, pulling it apart and letting the blocks and rope sink away into the black depths. I kept hold of Will and pulled him to the surface as he kicked.

We broke through the water, sucking in air, and I darted my gaze up, seeing Kai with his hands around Damon's neck. He pressed him against the edge of the yacht and then pulled his fist back and punched him.

Rika.

"Go over there!" I shouted at Will, gesturing to the speedboat.

"What about my hands?" His body was shaking from the water.

"I have to get to Rika." And I swam for the yacht again.

But then something crashed into the water on my right, and I looked up to see a rope draping down the side of the boat.

What the . . . ?

Two blocks came spilling over the edge then, sinking into the ocean, and I jerked my head up, seeing Trevor hunched over and heaving. But there was a twisted smile on his face.

"Fuck!" I bellowed. I dived down, shooting my arms out in front of me and pushing the water back, struggling through the icy sea as I fought and kicked.

Rika.

I darted my eyes everywhere, looking for her hands, her white T-shirt, her hair, but . . .

I swam down, down, down, as fast as I could, looking from side to side and not wasting a second.

But as the moments passed and I didn't see her, fear thundered in my chest. I was going to lose my fucking mind.

Where the hell was she?

Pressure built in my lungs, and my eyes blurred. I heaved, needing air, and bellowing into the water, I shot back up for the surface and sucked in a hard breath as I came through.

"Rika!" I raged, spinning in a circle to see if she came up. "Rika!" Nothing.

I shot my head up, seeing Kai hanging over the edge, breathing hard and looking exhausted.

"Kai, get in here!" I yelled. "I can't find her!"

He looked up, narrowing his eyes in worry. I couldn't see Damon or Trevor, but I didn't fucking care anymore. Will was still tied up, and Rika was . . .

I dived back down, hearing the distant sound of Kai entering the water seconds later, and we descended, pushing through the water and into the black.

So far.

It was so far down.

She was down there already, getting farther and farther away from me, and I would never find her.

Ever.

Please, baby. Where are you?

And then my heart stopped, seeing a flash of white.

Rika was rising faster and faster, her arms pushing her up and her legs kicking as she came into view, getting closer every second.

Kai and I grabbed hold of her arms and pulled her up. We broke through the surface of the water, and she coughed and gasped, trying to take breaths. I held her up, touching her face.

"Rika," I breathed out, my heart aching like I had a knife

lodged in it. "Are you okay? How did . . . ?" I trailed off, feeling my stomach coil at how close I'd come to losing her.

She nodded and started to shake, her face cracking as she started to cry. "He hit me after you shot him," she choked out. "It knocked me out long enough for him to tie me up. By the time I came to, he was forcing me over the edge."

I pulled her along, swimming back to the yacht. We climbed up onto the deck, Kai holding her as I pulled her up.

"How did you get free?" I asked.

"The shard." She opened her fist, shivering. "I pocketed it after you tossed it on the bed."

I pulled her into me, wrapping my arms around her and squeezed her so hard, my body shook.

"Where's Damon?" I asked Kai, seeing him pull Will up and untie his hands.

But it was Will who answered. "He took off in *Pithom*'s speed-boat while you guys were under."

I just closed my eyes and squeezed Rika in my arms.

Kai and Will climbed the steps to the main level, and I pulled her along. She needed a hot shower, a warm bed, and me.

We walked across the deck, and I spotted Trevor lying at the edge of the pool, bleeding and struggling to get up.

He could barely lift his head.

I didn't know how many shots he'd caught out of the three I'd fired, but the blood spilled over the deck and he was breathing heavily.

"Michael," he said, sounding out of breath as he held his hand against the wound on his chest. "Take the boat into port. I'm bleeding."

Kai and Will stood near, watching him, while I held Rika in my arms, anger and hatred boiling inside of me.

None of us made a move to help.

He'd nearly killed her. Tried to kill Will and Kai and threatened to kill me.

"Michael," he pleaded. "I'm your brother."

I stood there, not seeing a brother. I saw blocks go over the edge. I saw Rika dumped like she was garbage and Will sent to the bottom like he was nothing.

I could've lost them. I could've lost her.

Forever.

Where was my brother then?

Something fell behind my eyes, and I didn't blink. I might not have been able to choose between Rika's life and the lives of my friends, but I had no trouble choosing between them and my brother.

Raising my foot, I planted my shoe on his shoulder and shoved.

He grunted and grappled for my leg, fear rounding his eyes before he rolled and fell into the water, his arms flailing as he sunk lower and lower. He tried to struggle. Tried to grab at the water like it was a wall he could climb.

But only his eyes broke the surface as he drifted to the bottom, peering up at us and seeing his hope only feet away, not coming for him.

"Michael." Rika looked at me, breathing hard. "You . . . please. You'll have to live with this forever."

But I just turned my gaze back to Trevor, keeping my feet planted where they were.

I knew she didn't want me to do it. I knew she worried I'd regret it, and I'd suffer consequences. I knew, no matter what, that Trevor was my brother, and he'd been a part of both of our lives.

I watched as he struggled and tried to take in breaths, his body too weak from the blood loss to save himself and swim back up.

And when he stopped moving, going still in the water, I closed my eyes and let my fists slowly uncurl.

"You would never have been safe," I told her.

She buried her face in my chest, and I held her as her body shook with silent sobs.

I turned my eyes on Kai. "Get the boat into port, okay?"

He nodded, holding his side. "Just take care of her. We got this."

I took Rika's hand and pulled her through the salon and back down the passageway again, taking her into the cabin designated for me when I was on the yacht.

I ran my hand through my hair, slicking back the wet strands and feeling like my heart was about to jump out of my chest.

I almost lost her.

Squeezing her hand, I headed straight into the bathroom, turned on the shower, and started throwing open cabinets, not sure what I was looking for.

"Here." I went to her, rubbing my hands up and down her arms. "You're freezing. Get out of these clothes." And then I turned around, checking the shower temperature. "I'll run it hotter, okay?"

"Michael," she said gently, trying to stop me.

But I pushed forward, feeling my stomach roll. "We've got towels here for when you get out." I gestured to a cupboard. "Unless you want a bath instead. I can run one. Maybe soaking would be better."

"Michael."

"I just . . ." I rubbed a hand down my face, trying to find my words. "I'll just try to find you some clothes. My mom probably has things here that you can wear, so—"

"Michael," she said louder, reaching up to take my face in her hands.

But I tore myself away, leaning back on the sink and bowing my head, feeling pain everywhere.

Was this what she wanted? For me to be vulnerable and feel the fear I felt tonight?

Is this what she felt for me?

"I thought you were gone," I said, barely audible. "The water was so black, and I couldn't find you. I thought I'd never get to you."

She came up to me, taking my face again.

And I looked up into her blue eyes, knowing that would always haunt me. What if she had never come back up? What would I have done?

I slid a hand around the back of her neck and wrapped my other arm around her waist, taking her lips in mine and kissing her so deep the heat of her mouth filled my entire body.

I could kiss her forever.

Touching my forehead to hers, I ran my thumb across her face, caressing it. "I love you, Rika."

I've always loved you.

She broke out in a smile, tears streaming down her face as she circled her arms around my neck and pulled me in close. I squeezed her tight, burying my face in her hair, never wanting to let her go.

After all the years and all the times when I should've known, it took her nearly getting killed for me to realize what she meant to me. For me to realize how ingrained in every moment of my life she was and how she'd always been there, right in front of me.

Her, riding her bike around my driveway when she was five. Her, learning to swim in my pool. Her, running around and doing cartwheels in my backyard.

Her, biting her nails when I entered the room.

Her, sitting next to my mother at every basketball game in high school.

Her, refusing to even look in my direction when I hung out with a girl.

And me, barely able to hold back the smile at the little looks she stole and how nervous she was when I was close.

She was always there, and it was always us.

Trevor made me want to resent it, but it was seeing her with Kai last night that made me feel it. Nothing could shake us. She was mine, and I was hers, and it would never break.

I inhaled a deep breath, finally feeling my stomach unknot. "Did they hurt you in any other way?" I asked.

She pulled back, shaking her head. "No."

"Damon's still out there."

"Damon's gone," she stated, so sure.

She took the hem of my wet shirt and pulled it up over my head.

"How are we going to tell your parents about this?" she said, worry written all over her face. "About Trevor?"

"I'll handle it," I told her, pulling her shirt off, as well. "I don't want you to worry about anything."

And I scooped her up, wrapping her legs around me and sitting on the sink edge, just holding her close.

She hovered her lips over mine, sinking her body into me like she was about to melt. "You really love me?"

I closed my eyes, breathing her in. "I love you so much," I whispered, tightening my hold on her. "This is where I live."

CHAPTER 29

ERIKA

Present

Walking into the Crist home, I gave Edward a small smile as he took my coat and then helped my mother with hers.

She looked so beautiful.

It had been three weeks since she'd returned from the facility in California, and although every day was like a ticking time bomb, I grew more and more relaxed as the days passed that she wouldn't relapse.

Her A-line black dress hugged her body, which no longer looked so frail, and the color in her cheeks made her seem ten years younger. She was looking more and more like the mother from my childhood every day.

I wore an ivory-colored dress that fell to the tops of my knees, and my mother had politely mentioned that it might be too tight for Thanksgiving dinner. I didn't hesitate to let her know that Michael liked looking at my body, and I liked him looking, so there.

She blushed, and I laughed.

"Rika," I heard Mrs. Crist call.

I looked up to see Michael's mother strolling through the foyer, decked out and looking elegant as usual.

"Darling, you look wonderful." She embraced me, giving me a quick peck on the cheek.

Then she turned to my mom. "Christiane," she said, hugging her. "Please come and stay with me. Since your house won't be ready until next summer, I don't see any reason why you shouldn't be here."

My mother pulled back and smiled. "I would love to, but right now, I'm enjoying the city so much."

No one except Michael, Kai, Will, and me knew the real cause of the fire, and since the restoration on our house here had slowed down due to the falling temperatures, I'd brought my mother to Meridian City with me. I'd offered her the spare room in my apartment, but she wanted to give Michael and me our privacy, opting for a hotel instead.

I'd stayed with her there for a couple of weeks—to make sure she was okay—but I slowly relaxed when she started spending her time at the gym, getting her health back, and volunteering at a shelter to keep busy and meet some new people. She was eating well, sleeping even better, and surprisingly, in no hurry to return to Thunder Bay.

Eventually, though, I gave her some space and took myself back to Delcour. Much to Michael's relief.

Not that he didn't want me around her, but he still got antsy about my safety. He said it had to do with Damon's unknown whereabouts, but I knew it was something else.

Since the night on the yacht over a month ago, he'd woken up in the middle of the night a few times sweating and breathing hard. He'd had nightmares about the water. About me being pulled down and him grabbing for my hand just like he had that night.

Only in his nightmares he didn't find me. I was lost.

"Mrs. Crist, I can't believe how busy you've been." I said, looking around, amazed at the newly redecorated sitting room and all of the holiday décor splashed around the house. Garlands and wreaths hung from the walls and stairs, and I looked up, seeing Michael appear at the top of the stairs. He descended in his pressed black suit with the smallest smile curling his lips. His eyes zoned in on me, and I inhaled a deep breath, feeling my stomach flip like always.

"Well," Mrs. Crist said, sounding sad, "I needed to stay busy."

I tore my eyes away from Michael and met his mother's glossy eyes, which welled with tears.

Guilt washed over me. "I'm so sorry."

Trevor was dangerous, more so than Damon because Trevor hid it so well, but I couldn't imagine losing a child. Even one like that.

I hoped I never had to feel what she did.

But she just shook her head at me, sniffling. "Please don't say that. Who my son was wasn't your fault, and you're both safe," she said and then looked to Michael. "I wouldn't trade that."

Michael stared down at her, a look of regret crossing his face.

Other than me, I was pretty sure his mother was the only woman he loved. And while his first instinct had been to protect me, his second had been to protect her. After Trevor had drowned, Will tried to talk Michael into dumping him into the ocean on the way back, so Michael wouldn't have to deal with telling his parents that he'd killed his brother.

Michael wouldn't even listen. He couldn't leave his mother's son out there. At the very least, he had to bring a body back to her, and he knew he couldn't look at her day in and day out and lie to her.

So after we'd brought the yacht into port, we'd called the police and told them everything. How Trevor took me, lured Michael and his friends there, and nearly killed Will and me.

It was devastating, and while Mrs. Crist was thankful we were okay, she would hurt for a long time.

Mr. Crist, on the other hand, seemed more disappointed than grief-stricken. He only had one son now, and instead of the contempt with which he usually treated Michael, he began getting very involved in his life, wasting no time in shifting the hopes he had for Trevor onto Michael.

Good thing for Michael he had plenty of practice standing up to his father.

My mother and Mrs. Crist walked toward the kitchen, and Michael's father approached, carrying a drink in his hand with a cigar between his fingers.

"I want to sit down today. We've got things to discuss."

He spoke to Michael but glanced to me, his indication clear. Since I wouldn't be marrying Trevor, his plans now included Michael.

"Things to discuss," Michael mused, taking my hand. "You mean my future and Rika's money? Because it's too late. I broke the trust. Everything is in her name now."

"You did what?" his father growled.

I grinned, letting Michael lead me away. "I'd love to sit down and discuss my future next time you're in town," I told Mr. Crist, letting him know I was the one in charge of my family's business now.

There were several pieces of real estate he and my father co-owned, so I had no choice but to work with him, but I wasn't a pawn for men to marry and govern. Now he knew.

Michael and I walked into the dining room, seeing Will and Kai standing around the table, talking with drinks in hand while their parents and several others congregated in small groups around the room.

Servers flitted in and out, carrying trays of hors d'oeuvres and refilling champagne glasses.

Kai met us halfway, closely followed by Will.

"I found Damon," Kai told Michael right away.

"Where is he?" I asked.

"St. Petersburg."

"Russia?" Michael said, a stunned look on his face. "What the fuck?"

Kai continued. "His parole officer came looking for him.

Damon missed his check-in with him, and after tracking his passport, they found him there," he explained. "It makes sense. That's where his father's people are from, so he's on friendly ground. They're not going to go after him, of course, but we can."

I shook my head. "Just leave him alone."

Michael turned his eyes on me, looking down. "I'm not waiting for him to just show up back here, Rika. He's dangerous."

"He won't come back," I stated. "He won't want to fail a third time. Just leave him alone, and let's move on."

Kai and Michael studied me for a few moments, and I hoped they understood what I wasn't saying.

There had been too much pain. Too many years and too much wasted time. We all needed to start living again.

Damon wouldn't try to hurt me again. Another attempt after two failures would make him look pathetic. He was gone.

And since we'd found the phone from Devil's Night right where I suspected—in Trevor's cabin on board *Pithom*—and destroyed it, there was absolutely nothing holding us back anymore. It was time to start having some fun.

"So what do we do now?" Will asked.

The corner of Michael's lips lifted. "What we're good at, I guess. Wreaking a little fucking havoc."

And then he jerked his chin, gesturing to the two female servers behind Kai and Will.

The guys turned around, seeing two college-age girls dressed in black pencil skirts, white blouses, and black vests. They tried to hide their smiles, eyeing them as they lit candles and checked the table settings.

"Delay dinner for us?" Michael asked.

Kai turned back around, his chest shaking with a quiet laugh. "How long do you need?" he asked, backing away with mischief in his eyes.

"An hour."

Kai and Will turned around with shitty-ass grins on their faces as they followed the girls and disappeared into the kitchen.

I narrowed my eyes up at Michael, confused.

"Come on." He tugged at my hand. "I want to show you something."

And then he pulled me along, out of the dining room.

I stepped out of the car, the leaves rustling under my heels as I pulled my ivory-colored coat tight around me and slammed the car door.

The day was clear, not a cloud in the sky as I breathed out steam and looked up, seeing the scaffolding, tarps, and small yellow bulldozers sitting around the old cathedral.

"What's going on?" I asked.

It wasn't being torn down, was it?

"I'm having it restored," he answered, taking my hand and leading me inside the front doors.

I walked in, my gaze immediately shooting everywhere as I took in all the work the crew had already done.

The broken and trashed pews in the balcony were now all torn out, and all of the garbage and piles of debris around the floor were completely gone. The sanctuary and old altar had been removed, and there was now a proper door hung at the entrance of the catacombs. Tarps hung over exposed areas in the roof and walls, and a new cement foundation had been laid, clean and solid.

To the right and left, scaffolding went all the way up to the roof, and I also noticed wood framing, as if a second floor were being added.

There were no workers here, probably because it was Thanksgiving.

"Restored?" I repeated, still confused. "As what? As a church, a historical site . . . ?"

He opened his mouth, taking in a deep breath as if he were a little apprehensive. "As a . . . house," he finally answered.

"A house? I don't understand."

He breathed out a laugh and approached me. "I should've talked to you about it, but I . . ." He looked around. "I really wanted this, and I was hoping you'd want to live here."

I froze.

"With me," he added.

Live here? With him?

I mean, yeah, I was already practically living in his penthouse in the city with him right now, but I still had my apartment, and this was a house. A whole different level.

I loved the idea of turning it into a home. As strange as it might be to other people, it was where some of my favorite memories with Michael occurred. I loved it here.

But . . . would this be just his place, and I'd live here? Or would it be ours? Could he send me packing anytime he wanted?

Or did a house mean something more?

"So what does this mean exactly?" I inched out, my heart drumming faster.

He kept his eyes on mine and walked up to me slowly, moving forward and pushing me back. I gasped, hitting a stone column.

With amusement in his eyes, he leaned in, whispering, "Turn around."

I hesitated, wondering what he was up to, but . . .

I never backed away from a challenge.

Turning around slowly, I let him take my hands and plant them on the column in front of me. Then he snaked a hand around my waist and covered my back with his chest, nuzzling my neck with his lips. I wasn't cold anymore.

"It means that I want to keep playing," he said, his voice deep and filled with heat. "It means that until the house is done and we're ready to settle back here, my apartment is your apartment, my bed is yours, and my eyes are only on you."

He kissed my neck, his hot lips sending shivers across my body.

"It means that I'm going to do my best to piss you off every chance I get, because there's nothing hotter than you when you're mad." I could hear the grin in his voice.

He dipped his hand down to the inside of my thigh. "And then I'm going to do my best to remind you of how nice I am, so you can't stop thinking about me when we're not together."

I sucked in a breath, feeling his fingers inch up my thigh, already making me throb.

"It means that you're going to finish school, but I respectfully request that, when you come home, you do me before your homework," he continued, brushing his thumb over my clit through my panties. "And it means that you're going to have to constantly look over your shoulder for what I have up my sleeve next, because I'll always be coming for you."

And then his other fist came up, and I watched wide-eyed as he uncurled his fingers and a glint of sparkle appeared in front of me. I stopped breathing as he slid the ring on my left hand and continued to whisper in my ear. "And you're going to want every second of it, because I know what you like, Rika, and I can't live without you."

I shook, my eyes pooling with tears as he wrapped both arms around me and held on for dear life.

"I love you," he breathed out in my neck.

Oh, my God. I pulled my hand down, holding it with my right, as I looked at the ring.

A flood of heat hit my chest, and I stopped breathing. *I know this ring.*

It was a platinum band with an array of diamonds, looking almost like a snowflake. One stone sat in the middle, surrounded by ten more, with yet another circle of about twenty diamonds on the outside.

"This is one of the rings I took on Devil's Night," I said, my voice shaking as I looked up at him. "I thought you had returned everything."

"I did." He nodded. "But this one I bought."

"Why?"

Why would he buy a ring for someone he hated? It would have been after the videos exploded online, so it didn't make any sense.

He tightened his arms around me. "I don't know. Maybe I couldn't let a piece of that night go." And then he leaned in, whispering in my ear, "Or maybe somewhere down deep I always knew this day would come."

I smiled, tears streaming down my face. It was perfect. The ring, the house, even the proposal.

He'd promised to piss me off, but he also promised to be good to me and always come for me.

But I had to wonder . . . would we really be able to do this? Keep up the games? The excitement? The passion?

"People don't live like we do, Michael." I turned my head to look at him again. "They go to movies. They cuddle in front of fires . . ."

"I'll fuck you in front of a fire," he retorted, spinning me around and smirking as I laughed.

But then he came in and leaned his lips into my forehead, speaking quietly. "Other people don't matter to us, Rika. We don't let their rules contain us. What we can and can't do is irrelevant. Who's going to stop us?"

I wrapped my arms around his neck, elation sweeping over me as I tilted my head back, staring up at the high ceiling.

"What?" he asked.

I inhaled a deep breath, my veins charged with excitement.

"Our house," I mused. "I can't believe this is ours." And then I met his eyes. "I love you."

He grabbed my face and kissed me, his warmth spreading down my body. "I love you, too," he told me. "So is that a yes, then?"

I nodded. "Yes." But then I popped my eyes wide and pulled away. "The catacombs!" I blurted out. "They're not filling them in, are they?"

He laughed. "No. They'll stay accessible."

I dropped my arms and walked toward the door, slipping off my coat and hanging it over the scaffolding.

"Hey, what are you doing?" he asked.

I spun around, cocking my head coyly. "You forgot to get on one knee."

He snorted. "Well, it's a little too late, Rika. I already proposed."

"You can still get on your knees." And I crooked a finger, turning back around.

"Well, the contractor said he might stop by today to do some more assessments," he warned.

But I only grinned and shot him a challenge over my shoulder as I opened the door. "Are you tapping out?"

He shook his head, his mischievous eyes telling me everything I needed to know as he walked toward me.

He was always game.

And thanks to his tutelage, now so was I.

He'd corrupted me.

EPILOGUE

MICHAEL

The smell of lilies and rain drifted into my nose, and I chased it, burying my face in the pillow.

Rika.

Sleep weighed heavy on my eyes, and I put out a hand, smoothing it over the sheets and searching for her next to me in bed.

But she wasn't there.

I blinked, forcing my eyes open. Alarm set in as I turned over and propped myself up on one elbow, quickly twisting my head around to look for her.

And I immediately found her.

I relaxed, a grin lifting my lips as I watched her in the shower, the one that sat in my bedroom as a feature in my Delcour apartment.

Our apartment.

Within a month after everything had happened at the yacht, I moved her in. She slept here every night anyway, and since Will wanted to be close, we gave her apartment to him.

Kai, on the other hand, opted for distance. He bought an old Victorian on the other side of the city, and I wasn't sure why. He could've had any apartment he wanted here, and I didn't see the value in the black monstrosity he'd purchased that should've been condemned.

But for some reason, he wanted to be on his own.

Rika ran a loofah down her arms, soaping up her body, and I turned on my side, propping my head up on my hand as I watched her.

She must've sensed me, because she turned her head, smiling at me over her shoulder.

She placed her foot on the edge of the tub and bent over, running the loofah down her leg slowly and playfully, knowing what she was doing to me with her fake, innocent little smiles.

The rainfall shower fell over her body, but her hair wasn't wet, since she had it tied up in a loose bun. And despite my growing erection under the sheets and the smell of her body wash filling the room, I stayed put, just watching her.

The reward for my patience would come soon enough.

Sometimes, I just had to watch her. I had to keep my eyes on her, because it was still so hard to believe that she was real. That she was here and mine.

I'd asked myself a thousand times how we got here. How we found each other and made it here.

She would say that it was Devil's Night.

Without the events of that night, I wouldn't have challenged her. She wouldn't have learned how to be strong and fight back or how to own who she was and save herself.

We wouldn't have been locked palm to palm, trying to push the other one down, and we wouldn't have made each other the people we were now. *Everything happens for a reason*, she would say.

She would say that I built her. That I created a monster, and that somewhere during the blood, tears, struggle, and pain, we realized that it was love. That all sparks lead to a flame.

But what she failed to remember was . . . our story started long before that night.

I stand outside my new G-Class, leaning back against it with my arms folded over my chest. I have shit to do and places to be, and I don't have time for this.

Turning over my palm, I look down at my phone and the text from my mom again. Stuck in the city, and Edward is busy. Pick up Rika from soccer practice, please? 8 p.m.

I roll my eyes and check the time on the phone. Eight fourteen. Where the hell is she?

Kai, Will, and Damon are already at the party, and I'm late, because why? Oh, yeah. I guess being sixteen and finally getting my fucking license means playing chauffeur to thirteen-year-olds whose mothers can't get off their drunken asses to pick them up.

Rika walks out of the soccer complex, still dressed in her red-and-white uniform and shin guards, and stops, seeing me standing there.

Her eyes are red as if she's been crying, and I can tell by the way she stiffens that she's uncomfortable.

She's scared of me.

I hold back my smile. I kind of like how she's always aware of me even if I would never admit it out loud.

"Why are you picking me up?" she asks softly, her hair pulled back in a ponytail with flyaways floating around her face.

"Believe me," I shoot out sarcastically, "I've got better things to do. Get in."

And I turn around to open my door and climb in the car.

I start the engine, shifting it into gear as if I'm not going to wait for her, and I see her walk hurriedly around the front and open the passenger door, climbing in.

She puts on her seat belt and stares at her lap, remaining silent.

She looks upset, but I don't think it has anything to do with me.

"Why are you crying?" I demand, trying to act like I don't care if she answers me or not.

Her chin shakes, and she puts her hand to her neck, touching the fresh scar from the accident that killed her father only a couple of months ago. "The girls were making fun of my scar," she says quietly.

And then she turns her eyes on me, looking hurt. "Is it really that ugly?"

I look at it, feeling anger. I could get those girls to shut up.

But I push down my emotions and shrug, acting like her feelings don't matter.

"It's big," I answer, pulling out of the parking lot.

She turns back around, her shoulders slumping in sadness as she drops her head.

So fucking broken.

I mean, yeah, she lost her dad recently, and her mom is caught up in her own misery and selfishness, but every time I see Rika, she looks like a feather that will blow away with the slightest breeze.

Get over it already. Crying's not going to help.

She continues to sit quietly, so small next to me, since I'm nearly six feet now. And while Rika isn't short, she looks like something that has melted and is about to disappear altogether.

I shake my head, checking my phone again for the time. Damn, I'm late.

But then I hear a horn blow, and I pop my eyes up, seeing taillights race for me. "Shit!" I bellow, slamming on the brakes and jerking the steering wheel to the side.

Rika sucks in a breath and grabs the door as I spot a car stopped in the middle of the country road and another one swerving ahead of it and then speeding off. I come to a screeching halt off to the side, both of our bodies pushing against our seat belts with the sudden stop.

"Jesus," I bark, seeing a woman kneeling in the street. "What the hell?"

The taillights of the other car grow smaller and smaller in the distance, and I look over my shoulder, not seeing any other cars coming.

Opening the door, I step out of the car, hearing Rika do the same behind me.

I walk over to the middle of the road, and as I get closer, I see what the woman is hovering over.

"I can't believe that asshole just drove off," she fumes, turning around to look at me.

A dog, barely alive, lies in the road, whimpering as it struggles for short, shallow breaths. There's blood spilling out of its stomach, and I can see some of its insides.

It's just a little guy, some kind of spaniel, and my stomach rolls, hearing its strangled breathing.

It's suffocating.

The prick that sped off must've hit it.

"Shouldn't the kid go sit in the car?" the woman asks, looking at Rika next to me.

But I don't spare Rika a glance. Why did everyone try to coddle her? My mother, my father, Trevor . . . it only weakened her.

The lady's kids sat in her car, calling for her, and I looked down at the dog, hearing it whimper and seeing it jerk as it struggled.

"You can go ahead and go," I tell her, gesturing to her kids in the car. "I'll see if I can find an open vet."

She peers up at me, looking half-uncertain and half-thankful. "Are you sure?" she asks, shooting her children a glance.

I nod. "Yeah, get your kids out of here."

She stands up, gives the little dog a sad look, her eyes watering, and then turns and gets in the car. "Thank you," she calls.

I wait for her to leave and turn to Rika. "Go sit in the car."

"I don't want to."

I narrow my eyes on her and snap, "Now."

Her tear-filled eyes look up at me desperately, but she eventually spins around and rushes for my car.

Kneeling down, I put my hand on top of the little dog's head, feeling his soft fur between my fingers, and stroke him gently.

His paws shake as he fights for breath, and the gargled sound in his throat is making my eyes blur and my heart pump painfully.

"It's okay," I say quietly, a tear spilling down my face.

Helpless. I hate being helpless.

Closing my eyes, I stroke his head and then slowly trail my hand down.

Down the back of its head, down the back of its neck . . .

And then I curl my fingers around its throat and squeeze as tight as I can.

It jerks, its body shaking just barely as it musters the last of its energy to fight.

But there's barely anything left.

My body burns, every muscle tight, and I steel my jaw, trying to hold out for one more second.

Just one more second.

I squeeze my eyes shut, tears caught in my throat.

The dog spasms, and then . . . finally . . . he goes limp, the life drained out of him.

I let out a shaky breath and pull my hand away.

Fuck.

Acid bile fills my throat, and the pangs of nausea hit the back of my mouth. I heave, but I force deep breaths in and out, pushing it back down.

I slide my hands under the dog and lift him up, ready to carry him to the car, but as soon as I turn around, I stop. Rika is standing a few feet behind me, and I know she saw everything.

She looks at me like I betrayed her.

I avert my eyes, hardening myself, and walk around her, putting the dog in the back of the G-Class.

Who the fuck is she to judge me? I did what I had to do.

I grab a towel from my duffel, having just gotten done with basketball practice before picking up Rika, and lay the dog on it. Taking out another towel, I wipe up the small amount of blood on my hands and then lay that on top of him, as well, shutting the back hatch.

Climbing back in the car, I start the engine as Rika opens up the passenger door and plops down, not saying a word to me.

I speed off, gripping the steering wheel, and her silence is as loud as my father's insults and berating.

I did what was right. Screw you. I don't fucking care what you think.

I breathe hard, getting angrier by the second.

"You think that the vet who put your cat to sleep a year ago is any better?" I charge, shooting her glares as I watch the road. "Huh?"

Her lips tighten, and I can see the tears pooling again. "You did it with your hands," she cries, turning to me and yelling. "You killed him yourself, and I could never have done that!"

"And that's why you'll always be weak," I throw back. "You know why most people in the world are unhappy, Rika? Because they don't have the courage to do the one thing that will change their lives. That animal was in misery, and you were in misery watching it. Now he's not suffering anymore."

"I'm not weak," she argues, but her chin trembles anyway. "And what you did didn't make me happy. It didn't make me feel any better."

I smile nastily. "You think I'm bad? You think less of me? Well, guess what? I don't give a fuck what you think! You're a thirteen-year-old piece of baggage my family has to look after who's going to turn into nothing but an eighteen-year-old copy of your drunk mother!"

Her eyes flood, and she looks about ready to break.

"Only you probably won't be able to land a rich husband with that scar," I growl.

She sucks in a breath, looking stunned. Her face cracks, and her body racks with sobs. She grabs the door handle and begins yanking and pulling it, trying to get out of the car.

"Rika!" I yell.

I'm going sixty fucking miles an hour!

I dart my hand over, grabbing her wrists and swerving the car off to the side, screeching to a halt.

She fumbles, unlocking the door, and jumps out, running away into the trees.

I put the car in park and set the parking brake, pushing open the door and jumping out.

"Get back in the car!" I yell, slamming the door shut.

She swings around. "No!"

I run after her. "Where the hell do you think you're going? I got shit to do! I don't have time for this!"

"I'm going to see my dad," she calls over her shoulder. "I'll walk home."

"Like hell you will. Get in the damn car and stop pissing me off."

"Leave me alone!"

I stop, fuming. The cemetery is right over the hill, but it's pitch black outside.

I shake my head, backing away. "Fine!" I bark. "Go visit your dad, then!"

Spinning around, I storm for my car and climb in, leaving her out there.

I hesitate for a moment. It's dark. And she's alone.

Fuck it. If she wants to be a brat, then it isn't my fault.

I put it into gear and speed down the road, heading straight to my house.

Leaving the car running, I hop out and walk to the garden shed, digging out a shovel and going back to my car.

My ears turn cold from the October chill, but the rest of my body is still on fire from the fight.

She looked at me just like my father always did. As if everything I do is wrong.

I bottle up what's inside me—the anger and this need I can't explain. Something inside of me wants to self-destruct, wants to make messes, and wants to do the things others won't do.

I don't want to hurt people, but the more time that passes, the more it feels like I'm trying to crawl out of my head.

I want chaos.

And I'm tired of being powerless. I'm tired of him keeping me down.

I tried to do the hard thing today. The thing no one else would do but had to be done.

And she'd looked at me just like him. Like there was something wrong with me.

Tossing the shovel in the car, I race down the driveway and make my way to the only place I can think of.

St. Killian's.

Pulling up outside the old cathedral, I keep the headlights on and walk around to the side, starting to dig the hole. The dog hadn't had a collar, and it can't stay exposed long enough for me to find its owner, so I have to bury it.

And this is the one place I like, so it makes sense to do it here.

After digging the hole about two feet deep, I return to my car and open the back door, hearing notifications from my cell phone up on the front seat.

The guys are probably wondering where the hell I am.

I was supposed to go home and collect our stock of toilet paper, spray paint, and nails for some Devil's Night pranks. The same boring shit we always do before we go get drunk at the warehouse.

I cradle the dog in my arms, leaving him wrapped in the towels, and carry him to the hole, kneeling down and gently placing him in.

The blood has soaked through the towel, and my hand is stained red. I wipe it off on my jeans and then take the shovel again, filling in the hole.

When I'm done, I stand there, leaning on the long wooden handle of the shovel as I stare at the mound of fresh dirt.

You're weak.

Nothing.

Stop pissing me off.

I'd said the same things to her that my father says to me. How could I do that?

She isn't weak. She's a kid.

I'm angry at my father, and I'm angry that she pulls at me as much as she does. Ever since we were little.

And I'm angry that I grew up so pissed off about everything. There's not much that makes me feel good.

But I shouldn't have hurt her. How could I have said those things? I wasn't him.

I let out a breath, seeing the steam expel from my mouth. It's freezing out here, and the chill finally seeps into my bones, reminding me that I left her. Alone. In the dark. In the cold.

I charge up to the car, throwing the shovel in the back and grabbing my phone, checking the time.

An hour.

I left her an hour ago.

Climbing in, I start the car and put it in reverse, backing up and turning around. Slamming into first, I peel out of the clearing, down the old dirt road, seeing the cathedral disappear in the darkness in my rearview mirror.

I speed down the highway and through the community gate, turning into Grove Park Lane and racing to the end, where St. Peter's Cemetery sits.

Rika dived into the woods, coming into the cemetery through the back, but I just drive in, knowing right where to go.

Her father's headstone sits not far from my family's tomb. He could've afforded something that grandiose, too, but Schrader Fane wasn't a pretentious asshole like the men in my family. A simple marker was enough and all he deemed appropriate, according to his will.

I drive down the dark, narrow lane, nothing but trees and a sea of gray, black, and white stones to my left and right.

Stopping at the top of a small hill, I park and turn off the car, already spotting what I think is a pair of legs lying on the grass a ways down.

Jesus.

Racing down the grass in between headstones, I see Rika lying over her father's grave, curled up and tucking her hands into her chest.

I stop and gaze down at her sleeping, for a moment seeing that baby from so long ago.

Kneeling down on one knee, I slide my hands underneath her body and lift her up, so small and light.

She squirms in my arms. "Michael?" she says.

"Shhh," I soothe. "I've got you."

"I don't want to go home," she protests, reaching up to hook a hand over my shoulder with her eyes still closed.

"Neither do I."

I spot a stone bench a few yards back up the hill and carry her, guilt racking through me over how cold her skin is.

I shouldn't have left her.

Sitting down on the bench, I keep her in my lap as she lays her head against my chest, and I hold her close, trying to warm her or do anything to make her feel better.

"I shouldn't have said those things to you," I admit in a raspy voice. "Your scar isn't ugly."

She slides her arms around my waist and presses close, shivering. "You never apologize," she states. "To anybody."

"I'm not apologizing," I shoot back, kind of joking.

I am apologizing, actually. I feel bad, but I have a hard time ever admitting I did anything wrong. Probably because my father never fails to let me know anyway.

But she's right. I never apologize. People take the shit I dole out, but not her. She ran away from me. In the dark. Into a cemetery.

"You got a lot of guts," I tell her. "I don't. I'm just a coward who picks on kids."

"That's not true," she replies, and I can tell there's a smile in there somewhere.

But she doesn't see what I see. She's not in my head. I'm a coward, and I'm mean, and I feel so fucking aggravated all the time.

I tighten my hold on her, trying to keep her warm. "Can I tell you something, kid?" I ask, a lump swelling in my throat. "I'm always afraid. I do what he tells me to do. I stand and speak, or I stay silent, and I never say no to anything he wants. I never stand up for myself."

I told her she was weak. But it was me. I'm weak. I hate who I am. Everything gets in my head, and I have no control.

"People don't see me, Rika," I confide. "I only exist as a reflection of him."

She tilts her head up a little, her eyes still closed.

"That's not true," she mumbles sleepily. "You're always the first person I notice in a room."

My eyebrows pinch together in sadness, and I turn my head away, afraid she can hear my heavy breathing.

"Do you remember when your mom made you and your friends take Trevor and me hiking with you last summer?" she asks. "You let us do everything. You let us get close to the edge of the cliff. Climb boulders. You let Trevor swear . . ." Her fingers curl into my back, clutching my T-shirt. "But you wouldn't let us go too far. You said we needed to save our energy for the return trip. That's how you are."

"What do you mean?"

She inhales a deep breath and then exhales. "Well, it's like you're saving your energy for something. Holding back," she says, nestling into me and getting comfortable. "But it doesn't make any sense. Life is one-way, and there is no return trip. What are you waiting for?"

My chest shakes for a moment, and I stare down at her, her words hitting me like a truck.

What am I waiting for?

The rules, the restraints, the expectations, and what is considered acceptable are things that hold me back, but they are all things of other people's design. Other people's restraints. Other people's rules and expectations.

And they are all an illusion. They only exist when I let them.

She's absolutely right.

What is my father going to do to me, and do I care?

I want that.

You can't have it.

Well, what happens if I take it anyway?

I want to do that.

You can't.

Who's going to stop me?

Jesus, she's right. What the fuck am I waiting for? What can he do?

I want a little havoc, a little trouble, a little fun, a chance to go where my heart takes me . . . Who the hell's going to stop me?

Every tense muscle in my body begins to slowly relax, and the knots in my stomach start to uncoil. My skin buzzes, and I feel my insides flip, forcing me to hold back a smile.

And I inhale a deep, cool breath, filling my lungs with air that tastes like water in a desert.

Yes.

Keeping her in my arms, I stand up, holding her tight as I carry her back to the car.

I don't bother taking her home. I don't want her to be alone.

I carry her inside my house, the foyer dark since it's almost ten. My father is no doubt in the city for the night, and my mother is probably on her way to bed. But as I climb the stairs, I pass her in the hallway, Rika passed out in my arms.

"Is she okay?" My mom rushes up to us, already dressed in a nightgown with a book in her hand.

"She's fine," I reply, stepping into my room.

Walking over to my bed, I lay her down on top of the comforter and pull the blanket kept at the bottom over her.

"Why don't you put her in a guest room?" my mother suggests.

But I shake my head. "I'll sleep in one tonight. Let her have my room. She needs to feel safe."

And then I look at my mother. "She should have her own room here, though."

She sleeps over a lot since her father's death, and given her mother's behavior, I don't see that changing anytime soon.

Let her have a space here that feels like a home.

My mom nods. "That's a good idea."

I walk past my mother, grabbing a clean pair of jeans and a T-shirt out of my closet. "Poor thing." My mother strokes her hair. "So fragile."

"No, she isn't," I correct. "Don't coddle her."

I snatch my black hoodie off the chair by the door and head into the bathroom to change, since the dog's blood is all over my jeans.

After I'm in fresh clothes, I dial Kai, hearing loud music and lots of voices in the background.

"Do you still have those masks we used for paintball last weekend?" I ask, stuffing my wallet in my new jeans and running my fingers through my hair.

"Yeah, they're in the trunk of my car," he answers.

"Good. Get the guys and meet me at Sticks."

"What are we going to do?"

"Whatever we want," I reply.

And then I hang up, walk back into my bedroom, and take one last look at Rika as she sleeps on my bed.

The corners of my mouth lift, and I can't wait for tonight.

She corrupted me.

CORRUPT BONUS
VALENTINE'S DAY SCENE

This scene takes place a few months after
the final chapter of *Corrupt*.

RIKA

Swimming pools creeped me out.

It never used to be like that—and if I weren't alone, it wouldn't be so nerve-racking—but I hated being by myself in a pool now. Or probably in any body of water.

Which is exactly why I forced myself to use Delcour's indoor pool at least twice a week. Ever since *Pithom* and Trevor and the cinder block tied to my ankle, I . . .

I ground my teeth together, blowing out a hard breath as I slammed my hand across the water, sending a small wave crashing against the side of the pool.

Damon could go fuck himself.

And wherever he was I hoped he was in a lot of pain.

I was constantly walking around with one eye trained over my shoulder, and all the happiness I'd felt the past several months was only ever overshadowed by a tinge of black cloud that would pop up here and there to remind me that I wasn't safe. Not completely.

He was still out there, and I hated it.

And . . . I didn't.

While I tried to deny the fact that he rented a space in my head, there was a part of me that understood more and more that the threat of him might be a good thing. He kept me on my toes, and I was grateful for that.

Damon or no Damon, I shouldn't get too comfortable. I shouldn't relax. I should always keep in mind that the rug could be swiped out from under me at any time, and while I could lean on Michael, Kai, and Will . . . my survival, my success, and my life were ultimately in my own hands. I had to know how to take care of myself.

I hadn't realized that last October when Michael and the guys came after me, and I hadn't been prepared, but now I understood.

Don't be lazy. Don't be quiet. I'm in charge. I set the pace.

Thank you, Damon.

Walking through the water, I climbed the steps out of the pool, wringing out my hair as I dripped all the way to my towel.

Grabbing my cell phone, I checked the time, seeing that it was after six. Michael would be home soon.

I dried off quickly and slipped on some shorts before swinging the towel over my shoulder. Grabbing my phone and water bottle, I jetted out of the pool room in my bare feet and into the elevator, holding up my card key to scan for the penthouse.

As the elevator ascended, my stomach dropped a little, and I couldn't help but smile as the butterflies took off. Michael had left town for a game, and I hadn't seen him in three days. I didn't care that today was Valentine's Day or about the opera tickets he got for tonight, or even if we went out at all. I just wanted him.

I hated him being gone, but I loved him coming home. It was a conundrum.

The doors opened, and I stepped inside our apartment, immediately hearing music cranked up to an ear-splitting level. It echoed down the hallway from the apartment, and I stopped, every hair on my arms standing up in sudden awareness.

Music? I hadn't left music on.

But then I noticed the song. "Bodies" by Drowning Pool.

I let out a sigh and rolled my eyes. Of course.

Will.

Michael never took his key away, so he'd show up at any time and raid the refrigerator or we'd find him in the middle of the night using the court.

Walking into the apartment, I spotted him sitting on the couch, slouched back in his crisp black suit and holding a sandwich in one hand and spinning a basketball on the finger of the other.

The music screamed. "Let the bodies hit the floor! Let the bodies hit the floor! Let the bodies hit the floor!"

Yeah, yeah.

Dropping my stuff on the counter, I grabbed the remote and turned off the music. How could he listen to that song *all* the time?

He dropped his basketball, finally noticing me. "Oh, hey," he greeted and then took a bite of sandwich.

His green eyes were always so big and puppy-dog-looking that I couldn't help but melt a little. Despite his behavior. It aggravated me that he always just showed up—I could just be getting out of the shower, after all—but he always gave the impression of a child who just drew you the worst picture but did it with the biggest heart.

See, Mom? Did I do good?

I gave him a half smile and made my way over to him, nudging his feet off the coffee table. "Michael's not here."

"Yeah, I know."

"So why are you?"

He took another bite of sandwich and set the rest down on the sofa before sitting up and grabbing the towel off my shoulder to wipe off his mouth.

I scowled, about to scold him if he didn't get his food off our furniture.

But he stood up, swallowed his bite, and smiled down at me, only a couple of inches from my face. "I'm picking you up," he announced. "I'm under strict orders to bring you to Michael and Kai, so go get ready."

I stayed rooted, staring up at him, confused. Picking me up?

Michael *and* Kai? What?

It was Valentine's Day. Michael and I had plans.

"I don't understand," I argued.

But he just smirked and swung the towel around my neck and pulled me in, playing. "Didn't Michael warn you?" he taunted in his smooth voice. "You're everyone's valentine tonight, baby."

I cocked an eyebrow and swatted his hands away.

He walked off, chuckling. "Get cleaned up, Little Monster."

So should I be scared?" I asked, sitting in the back of Michael's G-Class, slipping on my stockings as Will drove.

Shower, hair, makeup, and squeezing into my evening gown took nearly an hour, so Will had rushed me out the door before I was even fully dressed.

"You don't get scared," he retorted. "You get excited."

I smiled to myself. "Touché."

He wouldn't tell me where we were going, but from what I could see out the window, we were off to the other side of town. To Kai's side of town.

Maybe we were finally going to be able to see inside his house? Probably not, but the prospect had me intrigued.

I slipped on my heels and fluffed the long black gown down over my legs as I inched up and double-checked my hair and makeup in his rearview mirror.

I'd put in some loose curls and pinned back the top half, leaving my shoulders exposed in the halter-style bodice. The opera was much fancier than our usual outings, and I'd really enjoyed shopping for the dress, with its array of beads and jewels, the sexy cut, and the way it moved when I walked.

Will met my eyes in the mirror. "You look great, by the way."

"Thanks. So do you."

He turned his eyes away, breathing out a small laugh as if that was the farthest thing from the truth.

And I knew. While Will always looked healthy and happy, I knew how he looked on the outside wasn't even close to what he felt on the inside.

"How are you?" I looked down, trying to avoid his eyes and not be too invasive as I went through my small clutch purse to make sure I had everything.

He grabbed a cigarette and stuck it in his mouth, lighting it as he spoke. "Fuckin' awesome. Did you see my pictures from Mardi Gras on Facebook? I could be that drunk every day."

He inhaled and blew out a cloud of smoke. I leaned forward and plucked the cigarette out of his fingers, flinging it out the window. "You are that drunk every day," I shot back.

He caught me in the rearview mirror, shooting me a winning smile like it was all fun and games.

But the people who smile the most are also covering up the most. And I knew . . .

All the times he sneaked into Michael's and my apartment to hang out, all the partying, all the nights with girls he didn't even know, trying to avoid ever being alone; Will was not okay.

I leaned forward again and hooked my arms over his seat, sitting my chin down on the leather as I peered at him through the mirror.

He sighed, continuing down the street. "Stop looking at me like that," he quietly scolded. "I'm only twenty-three. I'm fine, and I'll find something to do with my life. Don't worry."

I grinned, sliding my hands around his neck and locking them in front of him.

He glanced at me through the mirror and pinched his eyebrows together, looking confused. "What?"

"Well, I have an idea," I teased.

"Oh, you do, do ya?" he challenged. "Well, stand back, every-one. The blonde's brain is working."

I scowled playfully. "Ass."

His chest shook under my hands, and I watched as he turned on the windshield wipers, the sprinkles of rain when we got in the car turning heavier now.

"So what's this idea?" he mused. "You want me to go to college? Or maybe put myself in my dad's and my grandfather's hands and see what office they can hide me in for the next ten years? Or maybe"—he grabbed another cigarette, sticking it in his mouth—"I should strap on a backpack and go off to explore the world. I always wanted to be Indiana Jones."

I snatched the cigarette again, snapping it in half and dumping it in the cup holder. "Yeah, I can see that." I indulged him. "You'd work that whip like a champ."

He shook his head, laughing it off.

Wrapping my arms around his neck again, I snuggled in close, peering at him through the mirror. "But actually, I was thinking something different." I dropped my voice, staring at him as he stared at the road. "I was thinking . . . you could rebuild the gazebo."

I watched him closely, seeing his face still and his smile slowly fall away. He didn't say a word as he continued to stare at the road in front of him.

Okay, maybe that was going too far, bringing up the past.

Maybe I'd finally found Will's trigger and pushed the wrong button.

But no.

No.

I flexed my jaw, narrowing my eyes on him.

He needed to be pushed. Michael and Kai covered for him, never making him stand up and deal, figuring he'd handle his shit when he was ready, but I refused to enable him. I'd done it for my mother, and I wasn't following their lead on this one.

"Well, what do you think?" I pressed.

But he remained silent.

All I could hear was the rain kicking up under the tires outside as the bustle of the city fell away and we entered what I liked to call "the dark zone." It was the East District, an area of Meridian City that was once vibrant and busy, but now it was just . . . well, dark.

And abandoned. Kai had purchased a huge turn-of-the-century house over here, and while I knew he had his work cut out for him renovating it after years of neglect, I was suspicious as to why that was a good enough reason to keep us away. Were we going there now?

"She wouldn't see it anyway, Rika," Will finally spoke up. "I hear she hasn't been home since high school."

I looked back up, seeing him in the mirror.

The gazebo. She. Emory Scott.

"So it's only worth doing something good if people are around to see it?" I prodded.

I looked at his face, the lost, forlorn look he seemed to always have when he didn't think anyone was watching, and I let out a sigh, dropping a trail of cookies for him.

"And she doesn't need to see it," I teased, leaning in to whisper in his ear. "She just needs to hear about it."

He broke out in a huge grin, turning down a dark alley as the rain made the street shimmer under the streetlights.

"You're almost as good a talker as me."

I leaned back and peered out my window as he shut off the car. "Almost," I mumbled, suddenly forgetting our conversation.

Chills spread down my arms as I gazed up at the old black building. There were no lights on, no cars around, no sign of life . . . Where the hell were we? Where were Michael and Kai?

Will opened his door, the sound of rain rushing in and making me immediately rub my hands up and down my arms to warm myself.

"Hang on, I've got an umbrella," he said, reaching over to the passenger's seat.

Popping it open, he dived out into the rain, the drops pummeling the umbrella as he hurriedly closed his door and swung mine open. I stepped out, hunching over as he closed my door and we both hustled to the small awning hanging over a narrow black door on the side of the building.

"What is this place?" I asked as Will opened the door.

I went in first, while he closed the umbrella and shook it out.

"It used to be apartments," he shouted over the rain before dropping the umbrella on the floor and closing the door, "around the turn of the century, I think. Then someone bought it, knocked down all of the walls, and turned it into an art gallery in the sixties." He gazed around the dark space lazily. "Now it's abandoned."

I couldn't see much with the lights off, but there was a small amount of light coming in through the windows, and I spotted a stove, a makeshift island, and some counters. I guessed whenever they renovated it from apartments, they decided to keep one of the kitchens.

"Are you going to tell me what's going on now? Where's Michael?"

I was starting to grow aggravated that Michael's first stop back in the city wasn't me.

But Will simply turned to me, held out his arm, and gestured for me to go ahead. Looking to where he was directing, I stared down a long black hallway, hesitating a moment.

I couldn't tell where the dark abyss ended, but I straightened my back despite the flutters hitting my stomach.

Michael, Michael, Michael. And here I was, thinking the games would get boring after a while.

Shaking my head, slightly amused, I went first, slowly walking down the long hallway and passing a few doors on both sides with a narrow staircase on my right. The air was chilled, and I wished I'd worn a coat or a cover-up.

Coming to the end, I stepped over a threshold and into a larger room. I immediately spun around, taking in the rafters crisscrossing through the air high above and the windows lining the walls all the way up to the ceiling, proving that, yes, at one time there must have been apartments here.

Everything was dark and old. The wooden floor creaked under my steps, and the steel beams around the room were the only things breaking up the massive space.

This would be perfect as a dance studio.

Off to the sides of the room sat more doorways, and I also spotted a few hallways with more staircases.

"I love places like this," I mused to Will. "Lots of nooks and crannies to explore."

I turned to look at him, but then my smile fell.

He wasn't there.

Where the hell . . . ?

"Will?" I twisted around, trying to search the room in the near darkness.

My breathing picked up pace. Goddammit . . .

The rain tapped against the windows, the sound surrounding me like I was in a tunnel, and I shot my head up, hearing the wind howl in the rafters above.

I swallowed the lump in my throat. "Will?" I shouted.

"So do you like it?" a smooth voice asked.

I whipped around, searching the space behind me. No one was there.

But a flash of movement caught my eye above, and I looked up, seeing a dark figure standing still on the second level as he leaned against the railing.

"Kai?"

"It's important that you like it," he went on. "You'll be here a lot."

His hand—the only part of him to catch the light—moved across the railing, and I knew he was walking.

"Turn on the lights," I demanded.

"Can't," he replied. "Power went out. So what do you think?"

I squinted, trying to see him, but even more, trying to understand what the hell was going on.

"What do I think about the space?" I asked. "Well, I guess it depends on what it's used for."

"A lot of good things could go down in a place like this." A husky whisper hit my ear, and I jumped as long arms wrapped around me, pulling me in.

"Michael," I gasped out, smiling in relief as his warmth and smell fell over me. "What are you guys doing? Someone turn on a flashlight. This isn't funny."

"Feeling a little déjà vu?" he teased against my neck. "I know you like it."

I turned my face to him, brushing my lips against his. "Turn on a light and tell me what all this is about," I whispered, "or I'm going to go pick up Alex and she can be my valentine tonight.

"Now, what are you all up to?"

"We're saying we love you," he replied, turning me around in his arms and holding me close. "And we have something for you."

"Oh?"

"You promised me forever," he reminded me. "Are you still sure about that? You're in this for the long haul?"

I narrowed my eyes on him, wondering what this was about. "You don't have to ask that any more than I need to answer it," I maintained. "There is no choice. Now, what is going on? What is this place?"

"It's ours," Will answered, strolling up to us and handing me a flashlight.

I took it and looked at Michael, confused. Ours?

But it was Kai's voice that came next. "You were looking for a fencing club when you first came to the city," he explained, coming down the stairs and strolling over to us, "so we thought, why not start your own?"

I just let the flashlight sit in my hand as Kai, Will, and Michael surrounded me.

"A fencing club?"

"You don't like it?" Michael asked.

"No, I do . . ." I looked up again, now seeing more than just a big, empty space. "But . . ."

"But?" Michael pressed.

"But I have school," I continued. "And I have Fane and my mother's house to manage, and we're overseeing the reconstruction of St. Killian's, and I don't have any experience teaching fencing—"

"Have you ever heard of kendo?" Kai spoke up, stepping closer.

I finally caught him in the light and took in his black suit, the way the crisp white shirt and black tie sat against the smooth olive skin of his neck. His hair was perfectly styled, not that it wasn't always. Kai rarely had a wrinkle on his clothes or a hair out of place.

I called him anal to his face. Alex called him a serial killer behind his back.

"Kendo," I repeated. "Japanese fencing?"

He nodded. "My father taught it to me. As well as jujitsu and aikido. I could teach you."

Teach me? But what did that have to do with—

And then realization hit, and I froze.

Why were they all here? Why would Kai offer to teach me martial arts, and why would he offer now?

I held out my hand to Michael. "Let me see the deed."

"Why?"

But I snapped my fingers, losing patience.

He reached into his breast pocket and took out a fold of papers, placing them in my hand.

I quickly opened them up and turned on my flashlight, scanning the papers. I spotted all the guys' names . . . and then I spotted mine.

This wasn't a present just for me.

I looked up at them. "We all own this building."

Michael hooded his sexy eyes. "Of course. 'We all go. That's the rules.'"

And then he smirked, knowing I would remember the words he'd said on Devil's Night more than three years ago.

"So it's not just me starting a business, it's all of us."

They watched me, and I turned in a circle, full understanding dawning of what the plan was. "A dojo—with fencing," I said to myself, trying to see how this was going to work.

Michael had no interest in fencing. Or martial arts. He got plenty of exercise with basketball.

But Kai would be here a lot, taking a vested interest in the business, and Will would be here, the other guys probably trying to keep him busy.

But I still didn't get it. Michael and Kai were already overloaded with projects, so why would they take on this, as well?

And then I realized something else.

I turned back around, cocking my head as I handed the papers back to Michael. "So . . ." I started. "This place, the dilapidated office building you bought a few weeks ago . . ." I ran down the list and then looked to Kai. "Your little hideaway a few blocks away that you're renovating, and then the lots on Darcy Street Will was scoping out yesterday . . ." I looked around, meeting all of their eyes. "Why are you buying up the East District?"

This wasn't just about giving me a place to fence. This was something else.

Michael quirked a smile, while Kai stood next to him, his arms crossed over his chest. "The Horsemen are building their empire, Rika," he answered. "Will you join us?"

"We have an opening," Will teased as he walked past me, nudging me with his shoulder.

I hooded my eyes, trying not to laugh. Oh, for crying out loud.

"I was going to save this for tomorrow when we had more time to discuss it," Michael said, taking out another set of papers, "but you may as well see it now."

I took the papers and opened them up, scanning the documents. Again, all of our names were on them, and while the legal jargon was difficult to understand, my heart started to pound harder anyway.

"Graymor Cristane?" I questioned, looking up at them.

Michael just stared at me, waiting.

These documents were the establishment of a partnership between Kai, Will, Michael . . . and me. Everything was here. Who would manage what. The division of any profits. How decisions would be made, and even the details of the bank accounts that had already been set up to keep everything separate from our personal accounts.

Jesus. They were really doing this? Graymor Cristane was us. Parts of our last names to name the partnership.

I drew in a long breath, not realizing I'd stopped breathing as I continued to study the papers. "Your fathers won't like this," I warned.

Michael's father, especially. They had built their own legacies and would expect their sons to continue their work.

"We're counting on it," Michael replied. "So what do you think, Little Monster? You wanna have some fun?"

I heard Will laugh and I glanced up, seeing the three of them looking amused like they just couldn't wait to jump from one fire to the next.

Acknowledgments

First, to the readers—so many of you have been there, sharing your excitement and showing your support, day in and day out, and I am so grateful for your continued trust. Thank you. I know my adventures aren't always easy, but I love them, and I'm glad so many others do, too.

To my family—my husband and daughter put up with my crazy schedule, my candy wrappers, and my spacing off every time I think of a conversation, plot twist, or scene that just jumped into my head at the dinner table. You both really do put up with a lot, so thank you for loving me anyway.

To Jane Dystel, my agent at Dystel & Goderich Literary Management—there is absolutely no way I could ever give you up, so you're stuck with me.

To the House of PenDragon—you're my happy place. Well, you and Pinterest. Thanks for being the support system I need and always being positive.

To Vibeke Courtney—my indie editor who goes over every move I make with a fine-tooth comb. Thank you for teaching me how to write and laying it down straight.

To Ing Cruz at As the Pages Turn book blog—you support out of the goodness of your heart, and I can't repay you enough. Thank you for the release blitzes, blog tours, and being by my side since the beginning.

To Milasy Mugnolo—who reads, always giving me that vote of confidence I need, and makes sure I have at least one person to talk to at a signing.

To Lisa Pantano Kane—you challenge me with the hard questions.

To Lee Tenaglia—who makes such great art for the stories and whose Pinterest boards are my crack! Thank you. Really, you need to go into business. We should talk.

To all of the bloggers—there are too many to name, but I know who you are. I see the posts and the tags, and all the hard work you do. You spend your free time reading, reviewing, and promoting, and you do it for free. You are the life's blood of the book world, and who knows what we would do without you. Thank you for your tireless efforts. You do it out of passion, which makes it all the more incredible.

To Samantha Young, who shocked me with a tweet about reading *Falling Away* when I didn't even know she knew who I was.

To Jay Crownover, who came up to me at a signing, introduced herself, and said she loved my books. (I just stared at her.)

To Abbi Glines, who gave her readers a list of books she'd read and loved, and one of them was mine.

To Tabatha Vargo and Komal Petersen, who were the first authors to message me after my first release to tell me how much they loved *Bully*.

To Tijan, Vi Keeland, and Helena Hunting for being there when I need you.

To Eden Butler and N. Michaels, who are ready to read my books at the drop of a hat and give feedback.

To Natasha Preston, who backs me up.

To Amy Harmon for her encouragement and support.

And to B.B. Reid for reading, sharing the ladies with me, and giving me a Calibre tutorial at twelve thirty in the morning.

It's validating to be recognized by your peers. Positivity is contagious, so thank you to my fellow authors for spreading the love.

To every author and aspiring author—thank you for the stories you've shared, many of which have made me a happy reader in search of a wonderful escape and a better writer, trying to live up to your standard. Write and create, and don't ever stop. Your voice is important, and as long as it comes from your heart, it is right and good.

Copyright © Penelope Douglas

Penelope Douglas is a *New York Times*, *USA Today*, and *Wall Street Journal* bestselling author. Their books have been translated into twenty languages and include the Fall Away series, the Hellbent series, the Devil's Night series, and the stand-alones *Misconduct*, *Punk 57*, *Birthday Girl*, *Credence*, and *Tryst Six Venom*.

VISIT PENELOPE DOUGLAS ONLINE

PenDouglas.com

PenelopeDouglasAuthor

PenDouglas

Penelope.Douglas

Ready to find
your next great read?

Let us help.

Visit prh.com/nextread

Penguin
Random
House